When the Butterflies Dance

Letters to Layton
Book Two

Kim Williams

Thank you for reading my story
Kim

When the Butterflies Dance

Copyright © 2018 Kim Williams

ALL RIGHTS RESERVED

Front cover by Kim Williams
Cover design consultant: Allen Oliver
Cover photo: Doug Frazier Photography
Interior layout by Jeff M. Miller | FiveJsDesign.com

ISBN-13: 978-1987565850
ISBN-10: 1987565851

For Lindsay, Paul, Jake, and Sarah. You make my heart glad.

In memory of my mom, Shirley, who would have fallen in love with her first great grandchild, Judson.

When the Butterflies Dance

Outside, the crepe myrtles blew in the breeze and a single butterfly…

Part One
1920

Chapter 1

March 1920 | Layton, Texas

If my husband were dead, would the pain of our separation be more bearable? Katherine pulled the gold band over her knuckle and slid it off her left ring finger, then stared at her hands. How had he ever held them and thought them beautiful? She shook the thought from her mind.

She reached inside the open dresser drawer and pulled out the bundle of objects she kept tied together. Today she was moving them out of her sight. Her fingers gently tugged on the bow, and the satin ribbon loosened. Katherine thumbed through the bundle.

There lay her mother's handkerchief—the one Katherine had carried on her wedding day in 1918. She'd been a blushing eighteen-year-old marrying Ben, a widower ten years her senior.

She ran her finger around the lid of a round, silver tin that contained lavender lotion. She'd gone months without smoothing it into her skin—four to be exact, since the day she'd insisted Ben leave and never return. He had called lavender the aroma of their marriage. Katherine couldn't discern if she still loved the scent or had come to hate it. A bit of both she presumed.

She moved the tin to the dresser, but her eyes stayed captivated by the bundle and what now lay on top. His letters.

She touched the ones he'd written as her friend after their first encounter, although they both had known from the moment he'd walked into her house as a stranger, that they belonged to each other. Between working railroad routes, her brother Joe had simply brought home a fellow railman to stay at the plain, rural house her grandparents had owned where the two siblings and their younger sister, Lena, now lived alone. The stranger became a friend who returned to visit, then came to be the man she had loved.

A folded telegram fell to the ground. Katherine leaned over and picked it up. He'd proposed on a visit, and the telegram announced his intended arrival back into town for their upcoming marriage. He'd only proposed once he knew that she could love his son Sammy. Sweet Sammy, crippled and deaf. She'd realized she could. She still did. But she had also been responsible for the boy's accidental death last spring, after mothering him less than a year. She stuffed the telegram back into the stack.

Katherine touched the velvet heart on the front of a card tucked among the letters. Opening the card, she read the printed message from a lover to his Valentine, but it was the handwritten message that had melted her heart that day a year ago. He'd written it for her.

An essence fluttered by then returned to flit before me.
A dancing flower against the sky.
A hush. A glance. A sigh.
Light upon me, Butterfly.
Kiss me with your russet wings.
Rest in my winter. I'll dance in your spring.
I love you, my Butterfly.

Ben

She placed the card back in the stack. Behind it lay the letters he'd written her begging for her forgiveness and pleading to return home with just a word from her. She pulled out the most recent one and read it.

Flaydada, Texas
March 10, 1920

Dear Wife, my Butterfly,

Darling, why on earth can I not come back to you? I have done everything on earth I know to do. Oh, how my heart aches to come back to you. Katherine, I love you and would do anything on earth for you. I plead to you to let me return. I would give my life for you, darling Butterfly. I wonder if you do not have the love for me that I have for you. Love that is strong enough to forgive my weakness and sin. If you cannot bear to live with me in Layton among the people who know us, would you come to me instead?

I am leaving Flaydada next week and can arrange a stop at home in Layton to pick you up. If you want to live with me, you can do so. Neither of us will be satisfied living apart from one another. You know this in your heart. Our souls are knit, and we belong together. Don't you know that I have been punished for my wrong? I've lost so much. I'm so alone.

I feel I am at my road's end. Must I live my life apart from the woman I love? If I continue to hear no word from you, then I will love you from wherever I am, and you cannot stop me.

May the God you trust take care of you and our sweet baby. So many times He has taken what was precious to me. How can I trust a God who does that? Yet, I am forced to depend on Him to watch after you for me. My soul wars with the truth I've heard of God and the truth I've lived from God.

You know that I want to be a loving father to our child. To abandon my family is like death, yet it is forced upon me by the very one I love.

I ask again—was our child born and is it living? Do I have another son or a precious daughter? How can you keep my child from me? Tell my baby that Papa loves it. Please go to Sammy's grave and tell my boy that his Papa misses him and loves him.

With all the shattered pieces of my heart, I love you, Katherine. I need you. I want you. I beg your forgiveness. I am a living body without a life.

I am, as ever, your husband.

Ben

Katherine stuffed the letter back into its envelope. No tears fell down her cheeks. Perhaps tears didn't accompany numbness.

She rubbed her finger over the last letter in the stack. It was the only one she'd written after he left home at her insistence, but it was never sent. Katherine didn't need to unseal it, for she knew exactly what it said.

Ben, Come home.

Katherine

She straightened the stack of letters and arranged the items again in a neat bundle. The ring became a part of the satin bow once she'd slipped ribbon through the gold band. Perhaps today would be the day she would stop loving Ben—unlike every day before it since he'd left. Perhaps removing the ring from her finger would remove the longing from her heart. Perhaps. She picked up the bundle and carried it to his trunk and hid it under clothes and other items he'd left behind.

Lena would be angry that she had removed the band, but at thirteen, her sister still believed in happily ever after. Mrs. Justice, Abigail Forder, and Amy Carlson, dear friends, would be saddened by her action, but none of them had needed to send their husbands away for kissing another woman—the town seductress—only weeks from his first wedding anniversary and the expected birth of his child.

It had been one kiss, in a moment of anguish, he'd said, and it had destroyed every future moment of Katherine's marriage. Only days after the birth of her first child, any notion she had of asking him to return had faded. Despite what Ben and others had shared to the contrary, she imagined that had the kissing couple not been caught by Joe, Ben may have moved beyond the touch to her lips and possibly created another human being with that woman. He'd cheapened the physical intimacy of their marriage, and the hurt took deep roots inside her.

A whimper caught her attention. Nearby, her four-month-old lay in the cradle. Closing the trunk lid, Katherine moved to the little wooden bed and leaned over it to pick up her child.

She'd sent Ben away from home, but his presence still lingered. Time had proven that except for the russet hair, every facial feature on their little girl resembled Ben. She had his chin, his nose, his eyes, his smile.

"There, there now, sweet baby. Momma will take care of you, my little Clara."

Chapter 2

April 1920 | St. Louis, Missouri

The moment Ben stepped from the Union Station building and onto Market Street, he wanted to cover his ears. St. Louis roared. He was tired from his journey and needed a bath. His suitcase was heavy in his grip. Ben placed the luggage piece beside him, then pulled off his hat to brush back his hair and wipe his brow. A heavy breeze brought little relief from the heat. From his viewpoint he could see that streets were crowded and chaotic as automobiles, pedestrians, bicycles, and streetcars shared the space. Few autos had made their way through his home in Layton, Texas—usually only one at a time along a dirt road. Could he adjust to working in such a large, noisy city? He had no choice. St. Louis was where he could make the most money working for the Cottonline Railroad.

He had thought Pine Bluff, Flaydada, and Commerce to be big towns when he worked there. What did he expect? St. Louis had surpassed being a town and was a thriving city, mocking the new Prohibition law that shut down one of the city's most lucrative industries. Or so he'd read in the newspapers.

He ached to be in Layton hearing nature and glancing at the crepe myrtles. He longed to lie next to Katherine in their bed and inhale her lavender scent. How soft his newborn would feel nestled in the crook of his arm. The infant's squeaks and grunts a pleasure to hear. In contrast to his current hustle and bustle, Ben wanted the peace of sitting near Sammy's grave. He missed his son's animated smile.

A streetcar heading to the corner intersection caught his eye. He placed his hat atop his sweaty head, grabbed the luggage strap, leaving the spires, red roof, and windows of the brick station behind him. He reached the corner just as the car slowed to a halt, guided by the overhead wire. He made eye contact with the uniformed driver.

"Will this streetcar get me near Chamber Street?"

"About eight blocks south of here takes you to the east end of it."

"Well, I don't really know if I need the east or west end, but I'll take my chances." Ben hefted his bag over the steps, then pulled his body up by the handrail and dropped a coin in the slot.

"Looking for a residence or a factory?" The driver was thin and serious looking but offered a smile. Ben thought his double breasted uniform jacket seemed too large for his frame.

"6710 Chamber Street. A residence."

"It's your lucky day. That's on the east end. Pick your seat."

A woman with two young children began to board behind him. Ben saw the oldest child, a boy, who looked about four, let loose of the woman's grip as he exclaimed, "Momma, my postcard blew away!" He stepped down to chase after it. The young mother turned quickly to retrieve her son and lost her balance.

"I gotcha'!" Ben steadied the woman just as her son started running down the sidewalk. "Alexander! Stop!" With panic on her face, the woman caught Ben's eye and pushed her infant toward him. Ben instinctively released his luggage to hold the baby. The infant, clothed in a pink dress and wearing a small bow in her hair, began to cry while Ben stood in the aisle patting her back, still uncertain as to how he came to be holding an infant on a streetcar in St. Louis.

Within a moment, the mother and her son were back on the streetcar. Ben noticed her face was beet red, whether from heat, fear, or embarrassment, he couldn't tell. She reached to take her infant from him.

"Thank you. I suppose I owe you an apology." Ben was moved with compassion wondering if the reality of what she'd done with her infant must have hit her. "You're a stranger, and I shoved my baby at you. You must think me a careless mother. And thank you for helping me."

"I would want someone to help my wife and children the same way." He swallowed the lump in his throat as his left thumb rubbed the gold band on his ring finger.

"My husband will be grateful and a bit upset with our son." She turned the boy toward a seat and settled him in. "And with me too, I suppose. He's a cop, so he's always warning me of dangers."

Grasping his suitcase, Ben walked to the middle of the car and glanced at the mother as she was seating her family on the third row, "He sounds like a good man." He sat down and put his suitcase in his lap. The woman smiled, and life returned to its previous state. Ben—alone, in a big city, able to assist a young mother with two children, but miles and a mistake from doing so with his own.

Fifteen minutes later, the streetcar slowed to a stop at a curb. "Mister, this is Chamber Street where you get off."

Ben rose and exited, giving a slight nod to the young mother and the two children, who were now sound asleep.

"Walk two blocks that direction, and you should find your house." The driver pointed as he spoke just as the streetcar began to roll again.

"Obliged!" Ben hollered.

The weary traveler took in his surroundings. Rows of two level brick homes mimicking each other lined both sides of the street. A sidewalk ran in front of the houses. Every twenty-five feet or so a shorter sidewalk jutted from the main one and led to the cement steps of a house. A small porch, adorned with metal numbers announcing the address, welcomed the residents and guests who came to the front door. The unvaried, symmetrical layout created a patchwork look. The houses seemed new, and Ben wondered if Katherine would enjoy such order and close living quarters for a new home or would she feel like a trapped butterfly?

Ben saw the house he was looking for and walked up to the front door. Before he knocked, he straightened his tie, tucked his shirt, and once again adjusted his hat. Someone pulled open the door. A teenage boy stood before him muttering "What can I do for you?"

"Hello. I'm looking for Mrs. Martin. I'm the new renter."

Before the boy could speak again, a very short woman with gray streaks in her black hair, cleared her throat. "I'm Mrs. Martin. This is my son, Eddie. You must be Ben Williams."

She motioned for the boy to move along, then extended a pudgy hand toward Ben. "Come in."

Ben took the hand that felt wide and thick and shook it. "Yessum, I'm Ben. Good to meet you." With his free hand, he pulled a slip of paper from his front shirt pocket. "Here's my paperwork."

The landlady released his hand and after a quick glance at the paper, she moved from the doorway for Ben to enter. He grabbed his suitcase and followed her inside.

The house smelled clean, like pine, and appeared orderly. He looked to his left. Lamps lit the front room where a large sofa and two chairs boxed in a fireplace. A compact, maple desk sat in the back corner. A radio sat atop a small table with tall legs. A rocker sat next to it. A set of stairs stood directly in front of Ben. Ben smiled at the contraption sitting on a small table beside the stairs. *A telephone!* The smell of roast wafted in the air. Ben eyed a kitchen through a doorway in the front room.

"I'll show you to your room and the shared bathroom. You can unpack, clean yourself up, rest a mite. Make yourself comfortable. Dinner is at six sharp." Ben followed Mrs. Martin as she walked up the stairs and led him to a room at the end of the hallway. One side of his mouth curled up. Her words were monotone as though she had tired of speaking them long before his arrival as a boarder. He followed her through the doorway feeling as though he didn't belong in this room, this house, or this city. He set the suitcase at his feet.

Mrs. Martin cleared her throat. "This is where you'll be staying. I wash the sheets every Friday. I expect them stripped and sitting outside your door before eight every Friday morning. Make your bed daily. No clothes left on the floor or bed." Mrs. Martin took a step back into the hallway. "And as I mentioned in our correspondence, no female visitors allowed in here." Her righteous indignation didn't sound directed at him personally, but toward the whole of humanity. However, guilt washed over him. The thought of being with a woman other than his wife pained him.

"Thank you, Mrs. Martin. This is a mighty fine room."

She excused herself and closed the door behind her. Ben stood still and absorbed the silence. The quietness evolved into loneliness and rolled through him causing his knees to buckle. Heartsick and tired, he got his balance, then made his way to the bed that gave way when he sat upon it. He surveyed the room.

Wooden floors, a bed with a metal frame, a small round table with a lamp, a closet with a door, and a chair next to a small dresser graced his living quarters. His Katherine would enjoy the colors. Deep green, velvet cushions on the chairs. A pale green and yellow quilt over the sheets and mattress. Floral curtains on the window above the bed. He stood and made his way to the chair beside the dresser and slid his hand over the velvet. He sighed. Yes, his russet-haired wife—his Butterfly—would envy such a fine piece. He sighed. No place would be home, but this room was welcoming and would suffice a lonely railman.

Ben's minimal wardrobe fit in the two drawers of the dresser, save his suit, which he hung in the closet. He lined his two pair of shoes on the closet floor then noticed a mousetrap in the far-right corner. He chuckled. *City mice.* He placed his personal papers, rabbit's foot, Katherine's hair clip, and other treasures in the bedside table. Settled in, he lay across the bed. The clock read three-thirty in the afternoon. He closed his eyes and let sleep settle in. Perhaps his dreams would place him with the ones he loved.

The sound of an auto beeping startled Ben awake. He pulled up the shade on the window and opened the curtains to discover that evening was settling in. He'd slept longer than he intended. Remorse and despair lingered in him from dreams of begging Katherine to forgive him. Grabbing his kit, he made his way down the hall and entered the bathroom, happy not to encounter other residents. His breath caught—no boarding house he'd ever been in graced a bathroom with this much square footage. For the moment, he'd shave and make himself presentable. Tomorrow he'd soak in the ceramic tub.

Dinnertime came, and Ben quickly learned the routine of the group. Mrs. Martin seemed relaxed, but in charge, as she sat at the head of the table that had six chairs around it. His designated seat was the second on the left from the hostess. Her awkward teenage son sat down at the other end, after he pulled out the chair between Ben and Mrs. Martin. The chair was soon filled by a lanky, quiet woman with dingy blonde hair cut to her shoulders. She wore a brown tweed skirt and a yellow blouse. She'd come rushing in just as everyone had started to be seated blaming the traffic for her tardiness. Ben learned at the meal that she was a secretary to the manager of the Barton Metal Factory.

Seated across from Ben was a tall man who looked to be in his early twenties. Grease lined his fingernails and sat in the creases of his knuckles. His blond hair was wet. His wrinkled, but apparently clean shirt made Ben suspect he'd come from a hard day's labor and bathed hastily after Ben left the bathroom. He seemed both captivated and intimidated by the secretary, directing looks at her with his large green eyes, then turning quickly when she seemed to notice. Ben later learned that the young man worked as a low-level employee in the same factory where she held her secretarial job. The sixth chair was vacant. "That chair belongs to my brother whenever he stops in to do repairs or yard work," Mrs. Martin explained.

After dinner, Ben sat politely in the front room with the others and made small talk. Yes, this was his first time in St. Louis. Yes, his home was Texas. No, he'd never spent time in Dallas, other than passing through on a train. Yes, he followed baseball. No, he didn't need to know where the closest Baptist, Methodist, Presbyterian, or Catholic Church was. Yes, he was still a moral man just the same, Yes, he was married. *No, he didn't want to talk about it.* If they'd excuse him, then, yes, he needed to let his family know he'd arrived safely. No, his family didn't have a telephone he could call. Relieved to be freed from the conversation, he bid the varied group goodnight and headed to his room. Tomorrow he would report to the train yard, which he learned was a mile walking distance when he'd contacted Mrs. Martin about boarding here, but tonight he would write to his wife, who had not replied to any letters he'd written her since she asked him to leave home. He sensed she was miles from forgiving him.

April 15th, 1920
St. Louis, Missouri

My Dear Katherine,

If you read my last letter, then you know I have left Flaydada, and I know you did not want me to return home, for you never acknowledged me. I do not want to write of my despair in this letter. I simply wish to talk with my wife.

I am in St. Louis, hundreds of miles from all that I hold dear. I came here for better pay and a hope to leave the rails and work as a yard manager. The pay is much better in that job. I have set up an account and will wire money to it every time I am paid. If you or the baby have any needs or wants, wire me at this address. I will wire money back to you.

My baby…Katherine, I beg you to tell me about my baby. Write me words to tell if our child is alive and well and if he or she looks like my russet Butterfly. My wife, I will not seek a divorce. Please do not either. I want to return to you. I miss you. I grieve alone for Sammy. I long to meet my new baby. How much agony must I bear? Please forgive yourself over Sammy's death. It was never your fault. I wonder if you did that, maybe you could also forgive me. My Katherine, must we both live in so much pain?

I have gone into the dark depths of despair anyway. I must begin again.

I am living in a five-bedroom residential home with two other renters. The owner is a widow with a teenaged son. Katherine, it has running water and electricity and a telephone. I wish you could see it. I wonder though, if you would like to live on a street with houses very close together. I would much rather live in Layton. But, if you wish to have a new home in a big, noisy city, you and the baby can come here, and I will find a home for us. I would live anywhere with you, my darling wife.

I rode a streetcar today from the train station. You should see how large that train station is. It makes the Forder mansion seem like a dollhouse. A young mother with a son about Sammy's size and a baby girl were three seats ahead of me. I thought of my family. Then, I chuckled at the difference between the streetcar and good ol' Gitter pulling our cart.

I am weary, so I will close for now. My dearest wife, we will never be happy apart. Do not live in anger. I beg you to forgive me. Kiss my child for me. And if it's not asking too much, take care of our Sammy's grave.

I love you dearly, my Butterfly, and I remain as ever, your husband.

Ben

I reside at 6710 Chamber Street St. Louis, Missouri. You can wire me at this same address.

Ben kissed the letter and sealed it in an envelope. He would leave it for the postman tomorrow. His eyes were heavy, so he undressed and slid beneath the covers, propping up a pillow to lean against. Before he would allow sleep to come, he had one more letter to write. He'd waited too long already to contact his dear pastor friend. He picked up the writing tablet he'd placed on the bedside able.

April 15th, 1920
St. Louis, Missouri

Dear Wendell,

I hope you do not mind receiving a letter from me. We parted as friends and I trust we still are. I left my job in Commerce within days of being there and took a job on the rails in Flaydada. Commerce only reminded me of my past pain and melded it with my present. I left Flaydada, and I am now in St. Louis, hoping to make more income for my family. I've not stepped foot in a church since I sat in your service the last time. In fact, I refused to hear where the local churches were this evening when I was talking with the other renters in the place I live. I have not opened my Bible, although I carry mine with me still.

Is there hope for me, Wendell? I still deserve to bear the consequences of kissing a woman who was not my wife, but I do not think I can bear the burden of it any more. I don't know if Katherine will ever forgive me or if I can ever forgive myself. But can God?

Wendell, I must ask you something else too. Can you tell me about my baby? Is it alive? Did we have a girl or a boy? I long to know my child's name. I have given up hope that Katherine will tell me anything about our child.

I have set up a bank account here for Katherine and the baby and have told her to wire me at my address should she and my child have needs and wants. She is proud and hurt, so I worry that she will not take money from me. Perhaps I could work with you to move my money to an account at the bank in Layton so that maybe you and Carl, a good friend to both of us, could help her when I am on the rails. Wendell, please, don't let my family suffer when I have means to help them.

I've asked a lot of you in this letter. I remain grateful for your compassion, honesty, and friendship. I hope to hear from you. Give my regards to your wife and to Carl Justice too.

Your friend,
Ben Williams

6710 Chamber Street
St. Louis, Missouri

Setting the letter aside on the table, Ben adjusted his bedding and lay his head on the unfamiliar pillow in the unfamiliar bed in this unfamiliar place, despairingly far from the people he loved. The loneliness and heaviness of his situation bore down on him. He sat up and opened the bedside table drawer and pulled out his Bible. He looked in the table of contents and found where the book Psalms began. Thumbing through the pages, he came to chapter twenty-three—the only familiar location in the entire book. Perhaps it was time to give the Bible a chance. He read the chapter twice, then closed the book and set it on the table. He pulled the lamp string and the room became dark. Ben turned his face into the pillow and wept himself to sleep.

Chapter 3

April 1920 | Layton, Texas

A slam at the front door caused Katherine to jerk as she stood tying her hair into a bun. The scents of coffee and biscuits drifted under her doorway, hinting that Lena had already risen and started breakfast. She must have let the door close abruptly. Clara began to cry in her cradle. Sticking the last pin into her hair, Katherine moved to her child.

"Good morning, sweet angel. Did the door scare my baby?"

She lifted Clara. Goodness. Doubled diapers hadn't kept her child dry. She'd be boiling the cradle blanket and these diapers today. Thankfully, she'd pulled the clean ones off the clothesline yesterday afternoon. Katherine changed Clara, who at this point was wailing, and carried her to the rocker, then sat down to nourish her child. She enjoyed these moments alone with Clara, staring into her daughter's eyes and listening to her gentle purr as she fed. However, the heart can have a mind of its own, and this morning Katherine's did. Uninvited longings clothed as images pranced before her mind's eye, disrupting the contentment she'd been savoring.

Ben bent at the rocker and ran his calloused hand over Clara's soft, russet curls as she lay nestled against Katherine. "Good morning, my tiny Butterfly." Their child smiled at the timber of his voice. He stood, then leaned into his wife. That same calloused hand slipped around her neck and pulled her face toward him. "Good morning, my lovely Butterfly." His kiss warmed her. The feel of it lingering behind as he pulled back and stood to his full height. She sensed his presence filling the room. He was in the air she breathed. He was all she needed. All she wanted. Her heart tore in two. Had his kiss been warm against the vixen's lips? He the rescuer. Her the damsel in distress.

Katherine's eyes shut against that image, and a prayer slipped through her lips.

"God, help me. I can't forgive Ben's failure. And I especially can't forgive my own in causing his son's death."

Clara wiggled, and Katherine used the motion to draw her mind back to her child. Nestling her close, she hummed "Rock-a-bye Baby," and fixed her gaze on the child who resembled her Papa.

Her thoughts were interrupted by a clanging sound coming from the kitchen. Had Lena dropped a pan? Once again, Clara whined at the disturbance and stopped eating. Katherine adjusted her clothing, then made her way to the bedroom door and opened it with her infant in tow.

"Joe?"

Her brother stood behind Lena at the stove, awkwardly close to their sister with his hand resting on her shoulder. She watched him jump back as she called his name. Joe looked her in the eye. Lena startled as well but turned her head away from Katherine.

"It's Saturday. I wasn't expecting you home until Monday afternoon."

"I got here about fifteen minutes ago."

"So that was you who slammed the door, I suppose. Why are you home early?"

"I'll tell ya over breakfast."

Joe began walking into his room, then halted his steps and looked back at Lena.

"I was telling Lena how good breakfast smelled, ain't that right, little sister?"

Katherine darted her eyes over to Lena. The lanky young teen continued to stare at the stove.

"Right, Joe. Whatever you say."

Katherine darted her eyes back to Joe. He wore a smirk on his face as he left the kitchen.

Katherine moved toward Lena and hoped their voices were muffled by Clara's crying.

"Is Joe drunk or is he just being pesky?"

"Neither. He smells and was making me feel sick. I told him so."

Katherine chuckled, despite feeling wary over the flush of Lena' s cheeks as she spoke.

"Lena, how about taking Clara while I finish breakfast. Maybe you can settle her down."

The suggestion prompted a smile from Lena who stepped away from the stove with arms extended.

"Is she dry?" Lena giggled.

"At the moment."

"Ca'mere sweetie." Lena took the child and began to bounce up and down with her.

"Did you drop a pan? I heard a loud clang."

"Oh, that. Joe startled me when he slammed the door, then I was jittery, and it scared me again when he came in the kitchen."

Katherine shrugged her shoulders then cracked six eggs into the iron skillet and began to stir. A sense of dread came over her as she wondered what news Joe had about his early arrival. Had he been drunk on the job and gotten fired by the railroad? Katherine had news of her own to share. Would Joe's words put a damper on what she had to say? She slid the eggs onto three plates, then pulled the biscuits from the oven and added two to each plate. The other six she piled onto a separate plate then covered them with a clean cloth.

"Joe, breakfast is ready."

A shuffle through the doorway announced her brother. Lena handed Clara to Katherine, poured the coffee, then the ladies joined Joe at the table. He began eating before Lena or Katherine had even begun to say a blessing.

"Well, if you ladies are done with your religious stuff, I got news to share."

Clara cooed and gurgled. Lena seemed to have a special, calming way with the child.

"I'm all ears," Katherine said just after she took a sip of coffee.

"Well, you know I just made that high chair for my friend, the manager of Gibsons Store in Greenville?"

"Yes."

Lena offered silence.

"Well, he ordered five more from me to sell."

"Hum."

"Said he'd take a table and chairs and sell them too, if I ever had the time to make 'em."

"That sounds great Joe, but how will you ever have time for that?"

"Well, I'm no longer an employee of the railroad."

Lena offered a gasp. Katherine did the same.

"I gave notice two days ago. I'm officially self-employed."

"You mean broke," Lena offered.

"I got some money set aside, little sister. I'll use it to buy enough lumber for the high chairs, then use that money for more wood. I done put in for a permit to run a business."

Katherine cleared her throat. She certainly hoped Joe ran a better business than their father had. He'd gambled away his earnings on just about every piece of furniture he made and sold.

"Joe, you got a talent for building furniture, I can't deny that. But, where you gonna build? We can't put our poor mule, Gitter, out in the field. He needs our shed."

"I'm going to the sawmill today and picking up some wood to build a smaller shed for my workshop."

"Joe, you got enough money to help pay the bills and buy food in the meantime? And don't you dare plan to spend all your furniture earnings on liquor."

Katherine watched Lena's eyes widen while she hurled words at Joe. Her sister was feisty, and Katherine adored that about her.

Joe ran his hand through his hair making his look edgy. Katherine had always thought his eyes to be beady.

"Look, Lena, you just think about your books and fairy tales and mind your own business. But, as it is, I got the money. So quit worryin' that head of yours."

"The day you cook your own biscuits and wash your own filthy clothes is the day I mind my own business."

Katherine chuckled.

"Joe, you're gonna be home a lot more. I can't put up with your drunkenness all day long. Lena is right about your money. You need to sober up and stay away from whatever still you've been visiting."

"Katherine, rest assured my still is far from here."

"Then wherever it is, stay there and sleep it off before you come home. Better yet, get your problem under control. You're a drunk, Joe."

"Too bad I'm not a saint like your Ben Williams was."

"Shut up, Joe. I've had enough of your mouth this morning." Lena's voice was slightly below yelling.

Joe chose to remain silent.

Katherine took a deep breath then exhaled.

"Speaking of jobs, I've got some news."

"I'm all ears." Lena mimicked her sister's earlier remark.

"Lena, remember you told me about Mr. Justice needing someone to keep his ledgers? You said he talked about it one Saturday when you were working the diner."

A grin spread across Lena's face.

"Yes…"

"Well, I'm good at math and thought I'd talk to him about it."

Katherine patted Clara's back.

"I start working for Carl Justice on Monday."

Lena jumped up from the table and clapped her hands.

"You're gonna be one of those fancy career women."

Katherine shoulders shook with laughter.

"No. I reckon I'll walk to work in my old boots, wearing the same two or three dresses I wear working here at home."

She took the last bite of a biscuit.

"I'll still do my mending and sewing. But, here me now. I ain't ever going back to those cotton fields if I can help it."

Lena hugged her sister. "I'm so proud of you."

"Well, thank you. I'll work in the back of the store and try to do it when you're home from school to help with Clara."

She looked at Joe.

"Well? Do you have an opinion?"

"I reckon I can't deny you're good with numbers."

Joe made a loud slurp with his coffee and stood from the table.

"Maybe I'll make Clara a high chair when she's a bit older."

Katherine and Lena looked at one another and shrugged their shoulders.

"That'd be good, Joe. Thank you."

Katherine rolled her eyes behind Joe's back when he made his way to the door.

"I'll be driving the auto to the sawmill today."

Sawmill.

Would she ever hear the word and not think of Ben? He'd enjoyed his job there, and she'd relished seeing him so happy.

Katherine lay Clara on a blanket lying in the corner of the kitchen then helped Lena clear the table.

"You're right, Lena. Joe stinks."

The two of them bent over with laughter until Lena began to wheeze. When her sister caught her breath, she winked at Katherine.

"A bookkeeper. I'm right proud of you."

A bookkeeper—would Ben be proud of her?

Of course, she'd chosen not to know the day she sent him away.

Chapter 4

July 1920 | St. Louis, Missouri

"Fried chicken." Ben recognized the pleasing aroma that hit him as he walked down the stairs from his bedroom. With the work week behind him, he looked forward to the weekend and some time away from the railroad.

He sat in his usual place at the dining room table. His stomach growled as he waited for the entire household to be seated for the blessing. Henry was the last to arrive.

"Henry, will you offer our blessing?" Ben held back a chuckle. Mrs. Martin's question amused him since Henry had been asked to pray at every meal that Ben had eaten with the group. The moment the blessing concluded, "Miss Tweed," as he'd dubbed the office assistant, Dorothy, cleared her throat. "I need everyone's attention."

Ben rolled his eyes at her demand.

"My boss has given me two tickets to the baseball game tomorrow. He had to leave town suddenly and left these with me. They are…" Ben, his interest piqued, watched her pull the tickets from a pocket in her skirt, "third row, first base seats."

"Nifty!" Eddie exclaimed, with a frog-like teenage voice. "Who's goin' with ya?"

"Oh, I'm not going. I have plans already to shop with my friend Stella." She cleared her throat. "So, I'm offering them up."

Ben glanced at the young factory worker, Henry, who caught his eyes. "Don't look at me. I gotta work tomorrow." The young man shrugged his shoulders.

Ben allowed a smile to spread across his face. The feeling was still unpracticed and unfamiliar to his lips since the time he'd left Layton, but it felt good to him. "Well, I can take Eddie if he wants to go." A yelp escaped the gawky boy. "Of course, that's up to Mrs. Martin," Ben added.

"Who are they playin' against?" Eddie rubbed his palms together.

"Hum." Miss Tweed looked at the tickets. "The Pirates."

A memory of Sammy's dog Pirate flashed through Ben's mind.

"Nifty!" Eddie blew out a whistle. "I'm a big baseball fan."

Henry groaned. "That's a game I'd quit my job to see."

Miss Tweed clicked her tongue, and Henry rolled his eyes at her. "It's a joke."

"Then, Eddie, I suppose you're going to the baseball game tomorrow." Mrs. Martin's smile was that of a mother. "Thank you, Dorothy. And Ben."

Ben mimicked Eddie by rubbing his palms together then whistling. "Glad to do it."

Henry laughed. Ben had come to enjoy having the young man around the boarding house. He was good-spirited, respectful, and Ben suspected, a bit lonely like himself. His demeanor reminded Ben of his friend, Pastor Wendell Carlson.

Miss Tweed handed the tickets to Ben who in turn handed them to Eddie who in turn reverently set them beside his plate.

Ben stirred from his nightmare in a daze with arms flailing against the large black birds that swarmed him and pecked at his head and face. "Ahhh!" The sound of his own voice startled him fully awake. His eyes adjusted to the light, and the familiar surroundings of his stand-in bedroom focused into view.

Ben gulped in a full breath before relaxing his arms. He ran his fingers through the spikes in his rumpled hair, then smirked at himself. The birds chirping outside his window had slipped into his sleep and made his subconscious conjure up a nightmare. "Blast it, sparrows!" He'd borrowed the annoying phrase from Katherine. It was one of her favorite expressions when she was flustered. Ben sat up in bed and raised the white shade on the window. *Safe inside.* "Morning, sparrows. You're noisy, but harmless." He tapped on the window, and the unpretentious brown birds flew away.

His mild trauma behind him, Ben wrinkled his forehead to recall what day it was. *Saturday*. "The St. Louis Cardinals!" Ben shot out of bed, slipped on his wrinkled pants, grabbed his kit, opened the bedroom door, and dashed down the hall to the bathroom. Today he would be going to Sportsman Park to attend his first baseball game.

The cool tile floor of the bathroom felt good to his feet. The upper window was open enough for a breeze to flow in. He leaned down and placed the rubber stopper over the drain hole of the small tub, turned the handles connected to the water tank, and let the water run deep enough to soak in, then slipped inside. Steam began to fill the bathroom. There wasn't a day he sat in this ceramic tub that his mind didn't wander back to home. The luxury of this tub paled in comparison to a bath in the metal tub sitting in the middle of his and Katherine's bedroom, where his body was soaked, and his soul was soothed.

"Katherine, I guarantee you I'd treat you right and take care of you, if only you'd give me another chance." He whispered the words, wishing they would float through the open window, then be carried by the sparrows to the front porch of his home. He pulled the plug, and the water began to gurgle and swirl down the drain hole. Ben slipped his designated towel around him, wiped the steam from the medicine cabinet mirror and proceeded to shave. A knock on the door startled him and caused him to nick his chin.

"Mr. Williams, you in there?"

"Yep, Eddie."

"What time we leaving today?"

"We'll leave at noon, so be ready."

"We riding the streetcar?"

"Yep, now dry up and let me shave."

"No need to get in a lather!" Eddie's comeback at Ben made them both laugh.

Startled at the sound of his own amused voice, Ben thought of Sammy and Lena. Those two could always make him laugh. *How could a soul as sorrowful as mine have the audacity to laugh?*

His bath and breakfast behind him, Ben positioned himself on the front porch steps. He opened his Bible to read. His hands became sweaty when he read that God was close to those with a broken heart or those who had a crushed spirit. *Crushed?* Ben swallowed, and tears welled up in his eyes because he knew that was exactly how he felt. The burden of his unfaithful kiss to another woman was crushing him, yet according to what he'd just read, God was nearby, ready to remove the burden. He knew this was called forgiveness. He'd asked Wendell in his letter if God could forgive him. Perhaps God Himself was answering him through this passage of the Bible.

The screen door squeaked, pulling Ben's attention away from his thoughts.

"Didn't mean to disturb you."

"You didn't, Henry. I just wanted some fresh air. I'm about to write home."

He noticed the young man's eyes glance at his Bible. "I gotta hoof it. I'm late."

"Headed to the factory?"

"Yep."

Ben moved his legs, and Henry strode down the steps, then gave Ben a quick nod of his head. "Enjoy the game."

"Ever been to a baseball game?"

"Nah."

"Well, me neither. I'll enjoy it for both of us."

Henry chuckled. "That'd be swell. You can tell me all about it later." The young man strode down the sidewalk toward the factory.

Ben put his Bible aside despite the twinge of guilt nagging at him for not returning to his earlier thoughts. He picked up the small tablet of writing paper sitting next to him on, then took the pencil from his pocket, where his fingers lingered for a moment rubbing the fur of the rabbit's foot that had belonged to Sammy. He set out to put his heart into words.

July 3, 1920
St. Louis, Missouri

My Dearest Katherine,

I've lived without you now for almost eight months. No, I haven't lived. I've breathed. The way we are living is not worth living to me. I know I will never be satisfied living without you. I don't think you are satisfied either. Sometimes I would rather be dead and in the grave than to exist without you. I don't say that to scare you. I say it because being separated in life from you and my baby is worse than being separated in death. I know this to be true, because I have had a wife and a son taken from me in death.

I want to take care of you as long as I have breath in my body. If you can show me a man that has never done wrong, Katherine, then I will show you a gold house. I admit again, my shame and sorrow over that kiss, and beg your forgiveness. I ask you to let me come home.

I cannot write you idle conversation today, for my heart is aching too much. I miss you, Katherine. I miss my baby. Please tell me about my baby. Please promise me that you will let me help you with your needs. Surely the baby must need more clothes because it is growing. Surely you must need something for the house or yourself. I cannot think to bear what my mind assumes, that you are working the fields because your needs are so great. I love you, Darling, my Butterfly, my Katherine. I love our baby. I always will.

I am as ever, your husband,
Ben

Drained, rather than comforted, by what he had written, Ben folded the letter and placed it in the envelope he'd previously stamped and addressed. He'd leave it in the house mailbox for the postal service to pick up. He stood, his legs stiff from their position, and stuffed the pencil into his dress shirt pocket. The screen door creaked behind him as he stepped into the house, where he noticed Mrs. Martin coming from the kitchen.

"Oh, Ben, your sandwiches are ready. I was just about to call you and Eddie for your early lunch."

"Thanks, I'll be right back down. Need to put some things in my room."

"I hope you feel hungry so soon after breakfast."

I feel empty. I feel hollow.

"Count on it, Mrs. Martin."

She smiled a mother's smile, one of satisfaction for fulfilling her role.

North Grand Avenue was filled with autos and pedestrians as St. Louis fans made their way to Sportsman Park. Men were dressed in suits and hats; women wore heels and adorned themselves with feminine hats and jewelry. Ben's heart was discordant. Despite the despair that had erupted when he wrote to Katherine, he found himself pleasantly mesmerized by his surroundings and the entire baseball game experience.

He and Eddie sauntered around the exterior of the ballpark and found the entrance noted on their tickets. A Cracker Jack stand had been set up near the ballpark, and he had purchased two boxes of the caramel popcorn for he and Eddie. Finding their row and excusing themselves as they passed in front of fans already seated, they settled in. Ben and Eddie turned toward one another and smiled, communicating without a word—the seats were so close they both felt part of the action.

St. Louis had beat the Pittsburgh Pirates in the first two games of the series. Pittsburgh hadn't scored in the top of the first, so when the Cardinals came to bat, Ben leaned up in his seat feeling the adrenaline run through him.

"I'm feeling good about another win today, Eddie. How 'bout you?"

"Ab-so-lute-ly!"

With one on base and two outs, the clean-up hitter Rogers Hornsby came to bat. When the right fielder scored a run, Eddie cupped his mouth and yelled "attaboy!" At the same time, Ben elbowed Eddie, and just as he did, a pang ran through him. *I'd like to be sitting here with Sammy.* He could count on grief to show up whenever it chose to do so.

Ben had spent days at a time on trains. He'd spent hours sitting in a boarding house parlor where he'd lived or stayed. He'd spent moment after moment sitting on a front porch with Katherine. Yet, he'd never sat through nine innings of a baseball game. When the final out was made, the Cardinals walked away with a loss, but Ben walked away with a victory of sorts. He'd managed to take pleasure in an activity, despite the curveballs grief kept throwing at him pitch after pitch. The Cracker Jack prize, a dog charm, reminded him of their pet Pirate. The smell of popcorn reminded him of Lena. The couple sitting shoulder to shoulder one row down made him miss his wife. The laughter of Eddie made him miss his son. The multitude of people made him miss the one person he'd most like to meet—his infant child.

Tired and hot, the two baseball fans arrived back home. Ben had no sooner crossed the threshold and begun heading to the kitchen for a cold drink when Eddie hollered out for his mother and began blurting out the details and highlights of the day. The normally demure woman rounded a corner laughing at her son's joy, then Ben saw her turn toward him and nod her head. "A letter came for you today. It's by the telephone."

Ben's heart skipped a beat. Perhaps today would be the day he'd read Katherine's words asking him to come home. He snatched the thick letter from the small wooden table that held the telephone then made his way to his room, taking two stairs at a time. His words whisked behind his shoulder as he spoke without making eye contact. "I'll be down for supper, Mrs. Martin."

Closing the bedroom door behind him, Ben dropped his coat jacket that was draped across his arm. He threw his hat on the bed, then yanked off his tie and let it land on the floor. It was then that he noticed the handwriting on the letter. It was not the small, precise lettering his wife belonging to Katherine. He ran his pointer finger under the seal of the envelope, careful in his anxious state not to rip it or the enclosed letter. Slipping out the lined paper, unfolding it, and then looking at the last page, Ben felt his heart jump when he read the signature. *Wendell Carlson*. Disappointment and anticipation collided, forcing a deep breath from him. Standing in the middle of his bedroom, he began to read. His curiosity forbid him to sit.

June 20th, 1920
Layton, Texas

Dear Ben,

My friend, how good it was to receive your letter. I felt such relief. Indeed, your letter was an answer to my prayers, asking God to keep you safe and well. Ben, I know you must be anxious to know my response to your inquiries but read slowly and take in what I write to you as though we were sitting at the pond fishing and talking. I miss your companionship.

I admit I was surprised to know that you are in St. Louis, so very far from our humble town. I cannot imagine the sights that you are seeing, my friend, although none of them are the inside of a church. I laughed as I wrote that, knowing you are doing the same. I am grateful you have your Bible with you, but you need to read it. As to your question about is there hope for you, the answer is yes. Ben, you are not expected to carry the burden of your wrong actions, disappointments, and mistakes. That burden is the very reason Jesus died. He took it on Himself. We may live with sin's consequences, but not with its burdens.

I think of the father that you were to Sammy. You lifted him in your arms and drew him to you, carrying him because he could not walk on his own. God is like that. He desires to help us spiritually because we fall on our own. He draws us with love. I am certain Sammy did not always obey or honor you, but you loved him and carried him anyway. God wants to do that for you, Ben. Crippled by your sin, he wants to pick you up. He draws you with the Cross of Jesus. Freedom from the burden comes from confessing your need and accepting the gift of forgiveness. My prayer is that you accept the gift and let yourself be forgiven and loved in your imperfections. Experience God's grace.

As to your request to open an account here for your money, that took some time to arrange without you being around. It will require trust on your part and a risk on the behalf of your friends. As a pastor, I was not comfortable to handle another's money. My motives could be questioned. Carl Justice and I turned to Mason Forder for help, and he was more than willing to give it. I trust you are not angry by this choice. He has great respect for you and does not hold any grudge toward the incident between you and his niece. He considers himself a friend and wishes amends could be made between you and Katherine. His wife has spoken to Katherine on your behalf.

Ben hung his head, feeling humbled by the grace Mason Forder, his former boss, was extending toward him.

Mason set up a joint account for he, Carl, and yourself through his bank in Dallas. He preferred the larger bank over the local one. You will wire your money to Carl. He will keep some on hand for Katherine's immediate needs. Mason will deposit any leftover balance in a savings account where it will draw interest. Either man will be able to access the savings any time. If you agree to this arrangement, I have enclosed a document Mason's lawyer prepared that explains the arrangements. Mason covered the legal fees to draw up this document. If you agree, you must sign and date it and designate how much you want Carl to keep on hand. The document includes a statement that either party can end the arrangement at any time and savings money will be wired back to you. Carl will keep a running total of expenses Katherine encounters through him or any transfers of cash he gives to her.

My friend, as to your inquiry about your child, I struggled to do what is right, since Katherine should be the one to share the news with you. My wife and I prayed and talked about the matter, for it puts us both in an awkward situation. If I have made the wrong choice, then God will have to help me, but I am at peace at the time I write this letter.

Ben, you have a daughter. Her name is Clara.

Ben collapsed to the floor as a moan escaped his soul, slicing his heart on its way out. "A girl. I have a baby girl. Clara. Oh, my baby, Clara." The words were hardly above a whisper to his own ears. His body rocked back and forth. His vision blurred, and he felt hot tears escape his eyes, while his lips spread in a smile. With awe, he rolled the name around on his tongue, savoring its sound. "Clara. Clara. Clara." His body felt conflicted by the extremes of emotions it produced. His pain and his joy joined hands as he wept. Embarrassingly.

Unaware of how much time he'd spent in his emotional state, Ben startled at the knock on his bedroom door. "Mr. Williams? Ben? Are you alright?" *Mrs. Martin*. "We were all concerned at the supper table when we heard your wailing." Ben wiped his nose on his sleeve and sat up from where he'd lain on the floor. "I'm alright. News from a friend. I wish I was home."

The words had come out sickly and weak. Silence followed them until he heard a weak clearing of Mrs. Martin's throat. "I'll fix a plate of food for you." Ben heard the rustle of clothing followed by the rhythmic thud of her feet upon each stair as they carried her body back to the others. He wiped his eyes and smoothed out the letter he had crushed in his hands and resumed his reading.

She was born about five days after you left Layton that Monday. Her hair is the color of Katherine's hair. Babies look the same to me, but I reckon I can see your features on her face, my friend. Her smile is just like yours. She has a light brown mark on her cheek. My Amy calls it an angel kiss. She is healthy. Katherine is well. My heart is heavy thinking of you taking in this news alone. Amy and I have prayed about this moment from the time I decided to write you.

Ben, take to heart all my words in this letter. I want to hear from you again.

I remain, as ever, your friend,
Wendell Carlson.

Ben lay down with his back to the wooden floor and clutched the letter to his chest with arms that ached to hold his Clara.

He would not be down for supper. Instead, he remained in his room and fed his soul with all the words his friend had written.

Chapter 5

JULY 4TH, 1920 | ST. LOUIS, MISSOURI

Every head turned and stared at him, and an uncomfortable silence barged in on the conversations he'd overheard while walking down the stairs. Ben knew he should expect no less from his fellow house companions. How often did a grown man weep loudly in his bedroom behind a closed door, refuse supper, and stay holed up until every member of the household had made their way to the breakfast table the next morning? Then again how often did a man hear from a friend that his wife had given birth to his baby girl and named her Clara. Not often, he presumed.

Ben felt his cheeks heat up, then cleared his throat. He had to put everyone at ease. "Morning. Pardon me for being late to breakfast and for missing supper last night, Mrs. Martin." He seated himself, and the chair made a screeching sound as he pulled up to the table. *Or was that my nerves?* Other than himself, the other residents were clothed in dresses and suits for Sunday church. He glanced at the lady of the house and saw that she was about to speak. Ben wanted to keep control of the moment, so eyeing Mrs. Martin, then glancing around the table, he smiled a closed-lip smile and felt his forehead wrinkle. "I received a letter yesterday with news I should have only heard at home, in person, surrounded by the people I love."

Soft gasps mingled with Ben's words in the breakfast-scented air as he continued his explanation. "Although I think highly of you all, I can't say I love you like I love my wife." Soft laughter replaced the gasps.

"Ben, I hope your family is well," Mrs. Martin spoke up, and Ben suspected she felt it her right and duty to speak for the group.

"They are. No harm has come to any of my family. Quite the opposite, actually."

His mind flashed back to the bedroom he shared with Katherine and to the cradle he'd fingered before he left in shame. He imagined his russet-haired newborn asleep in it and her mother nestled beside him on their bed. The longing made a chill run down his spine that jerked him back to the conversation. Should he bear a part of himself to these folks? Should he risk the curiosity for more that his explanation of the news might conjure up? Some decisions must be reasoned and pondered, because so much is at risk; some require a moment's notice because so much is at risk. His longing to speak his good news was demanding and strong. He chose.

"I have a new baby daughter. Clara." Mrs. Martin and Dorothy both sighed, and Henry blew out a whistle.

"I should have been there," Ben whispered, but it was drowned out by the congratulations, which he breathed in like a person breaking through deep, dark water and gasping for air.

The conversation would meander to another topic briefly, only to return to him until mealtime wound down. To his relief everyone must have assumed Clara had been born just days before the letter arrived. The relief was short lived when he realized their lack of inquisitiveness could indicate suspicion that everything was not good in his life. No one asked why he wasn't telegrammed. No one asked if his family would move here. Miss Tweed had cleared her throat, then asked if he had other children. Some decisions require a moment's notice because so much is at risk. Once again, he chose. To explain Sammy would risk his sane state of mind. He simply told her no.

"Is everyone still planning to attend the Fourth of July Parade this afternoon?" Mrs. Martin asked the question just as she rose from her chair and began to clear her plate.

"Yes" sounded through the room as the group left the table.

As was his custom when he was in town on Sunday, Ben remained behind while the others attended church. He settled himself on the couch in the front room and opened his Bible that he now read every day. Perhaps one day he'd go to church. Perhaps.

Reading about forgiveness, Ben clearly realized that his need for it hadn't begun with his impure kiss outside of marriage. Years before that, he had embraced a grudge against God. It had been somewhat neglected when his focus turned to the marriage he had ruined, but it was still alive, vying for his attention.

A lousy father who beat him, a young wife snatched by death, a son crippled and deaf—these were matters that had hardened Ben's heart and formed a grudge. Pastor Wendell Carlson had told him once while they fished as friends that he didn't understand his own need to be forgiven. *Debt.* He'd called it a debt God was willing to pay through Jesus. Ben had come to realize his debt the moment he fell morally, but only now did he understand that his sin was foremost against God.

Burdened, Ben stood and walked into the kitchen hoping to shake the heaviness that lingered where moments earlier longings to share his good news had lingered. Standing at the kitchen sink, he reached for an apple and knife, then sliced off bites until he'd eaten the entire fruit. The burden had not subsided.

He turned and rested his back torso against the counter. His need for forgiveness was because he was unworthy of purifying himself and unable to carry his burdens. He'd chided Katherine for not forgiving herself after Sammy's accidental death, yet he held his own collection of guilt tightly in his fist and depended on his good attitude to mask the despair. He needed to release his grudge against God.

In a motion driven by repentance, Ben made a fist and then released it. He turned again and lowered his head. Leaning over the sink in the kitchen of a St. Louis boarding house, alone, ashamed, and assured, Ben gave up his burden. "Forgive me, God. I've sinned against you. I accept forgiveness and salvation through Jesus."

The words were plain, but the relief was profound. Deep within him where his soul blended into eternity, he felt cleansed. He thought of Wendell, who preached of God's grace. He understood now. He thought of Katherine and how he loved her even in her imperfections. God felt that way about him. He thought of Sammy and how he loved carrying him because he had been unable to carry himself. Ben chuckled. His eternal situation had changed instantly, and although his earthly one had not, he sensed that his mode of bearing it had transformed.

He stood silent and still for a moment or many moments, he wasn't quite sure, taking in the gift he had just received. Ben didn't know what to do next, so he picked up the knife beside him and wiped it clean with the dish rag. A sound caught him by surprise when a familiar habit roused itself. He was humming.

The commotion of the front door opening and folks chattering interrupted his humming, and he sat down the knife. Ben turned to greet the residents just as the scent of Henry's after shave lotion assaulted his nose. The young man stood in the kitchen doorway.

"Henry, you bathe in that spicy lotion today?" He walked forward and playfully punched him in the arm then noticed the twenty-something man blush.

"Too much? I put it on right before I left the house this morning."

"If it's those Baptist women you're wanting to attract with that lotion, subtle is better. Don't want them gagging and coughing as they pass by you on their way to Sunday School class." Ben feigned a gag and a cough, then patted Henry on the back. "It's a good smell, big timer, but tone it down some."

Ben noticed Henry nod his head in understanding just as he tried to slip past the young man to enter the front room. He was held in place by Henry's grip to his forearm.

"Was that you humming?"

Ben laughed out loud. "I reckon it was."

Henry's brows wrinkled as he looked Ben in the eyes. "You only hum when you're alone?"

Warmth radiated through Ben. "I only hum when I'm happy."

"Happy? But just last night, you wailed like a dying animal. I don't..."

"I know it don't make sense. We'll talk about it later."

"I hold you to it."

Dusk settled in as Ben stepped onto the streetcar and took a seat behind Mrs. Martin. They had waited in line more than an hour for a ride, and the group was tired. The parade had been loud and crowded as people crammed along Olive Street for a good view. Ben had never experienced so many people standing shoulder to shoulder, waving at folks they recognized in the parade or somewhere along the crowd. Parents had children hoisted on their shoulders, giving them a good view of what was happening, but also blocking the view of the people standing behind them. He knew this firsthand, but he would have proudly sat Sammy upon his shoulders had he been able to.

Ben sat down next to a window and closed his eyes while weary parade watchers continued to fill the seats. Thoughts of the people he lived with filled his mind. Since April, he'd only come to know bits and pieces about each of them and they about him. He smiled to himself. The residents of 6710 Chamber Street were an odd collection of people no matter how he grouped them in his mind. The two women, Mrs. Martin and Dorothy—why he didn't even know her last name—were iconic women of the times. Mrs. Martin was the traditional homemaker, and Dorothy was the emerging independent woman. Although Mrs. Martin ran a boarding house, it was her brother who handled the business side of it. The males—Henry, Eddie, and himself—were stair-stepped in age, and Ben enjoyed the company of them both. But unlike meeting Lena, Katherine, and even Pastor Wendell and Carl Justice, whom he came to know intimately, his knowledge of the two of them was limited to generalities. A common interest in baseball was the thread that ran through their conversations.

Despite generalities, the three boarders had come to know one another's habits. Dorothy laid claim to the common bathroom first in the mornings, yet she was always the last to arrive at the breakfast table. She spent her Saturday's with friends away from the house and would return with packages and shopping bags. She considered herself an expert on Hollywood. Henry had proven to be helpful around the house, offering to make simple repairs for Mrs. Martin. He had noticed that Henry would make his way to the kitchen from time to time on Saturdays when he was home and reluctantly, Mrs. Martin would allow him to help prepare the food. As for himself, Ben felt that he remained mysterious to the fellow boarders, but he felt respected, as though his opinion mattered. He knew he could draw the group together in conversation. However, his presence was the lesser among them since he was gone for days at a time with the railroad. Ben smiled to himself realizing there was no sense of family lingering among the group, just comfortable familiarity.

The sound of the streetcar bell caused him to stir, and Ben leaned forward to tap Mrs. Martin on the shoulder.

"The parade was a good idea."

"Worth the weariness, I suppose." The lady smiled, then elbowed her son who snoozed beside her. "Eddie, you're snoring." The teenager shook his head, then went right back to his nap. His mouth hung wide open.

Ben chuckled at the sight, then addressed Mrs. Martin. "I want to ask you a favor."

"A favor?" Mrs. Martin turned awkwardly to face him more directly.

"I'm heading out for work again in two days, and I'll be on the railroad for a week. I marked it on the house calendar in the kitchen."

"Yes, I noticed."

"If I left you some money, could you buy my baby girl a Teddy Bear at Woolworth tomorrow? I know you usually do your shopping on Mondays. Oh, and a little dress—maybe for a one year old."

"The teddy bear is no problem, but you sure you don't want Dorothy to pick out the dress? She shops in the finer stores." She nodded to indicate Dorothy sitting three rows ahead of her.

He patted the woman's shoulder. "Mrs. Martin, I'd be happy with whatever you pick out. I'll mail the package on Tuesday before I leave on my route. Thank you."

"You're welcome." Ben saw her eyes glisten with tears that had formed. "Makes me happy to do this for you."

Ben sat back in his seat just as the streetcar took a curve. His left shoulder bumped against Henry who sat beside him, looking down.

"I was in love once." Ben clinched his teeth to keep his mouth from gaping open with surprise at the young man's confession. Not that he didn't think Henry could have been in love, he just never expected a raw statement out of the blue spoken on a public streetcar.

"I was eighteen; she was seventeen. We grew up in the same community. Even got engaged."

"But you didn't marry?"

"Nah. She fell in love with someone else. A newcomer. 'Bout a month before the wedding. I reckon she agreed to marry me because people around us expected it. My reason for marrying was love. How foolish is that?"

"That's not foolish at all."

"Felt foolish at the time. When I was a kid, my family was well off. My mother was sick, and my Pa did whatever he could to get her medical treatment, mostly a live-in nurse, but I realized when I got older that it came at a high price. He pretty much spent his last dime on housekeepers and personal medical staff, trying to keep her out of hospitals and institutions. My fiancée despaired over our future, worried she'd live poor and wondering if I'd get sick too someday. When another prospect came into town, I reckon his shiny pocket change and robust build appealed to her." Henry looked over at Ben and raised his eyebrows.

"I'm sorry." Ben wanted to ask about his mother, but that was Henry's story to tell.

"So was I. Still am sometimes. I pray about it a lot. I was judged for what I didn't have. But, I reckon I don't want to be alone, so I bathe in after shave hoping to find me a girl." Henry's laugh lightened the mood.

"You interested in Miss Tweed, uh, Dorothy?'"

Henry laughed again.

"Miss Tweed. Nah. I thought about it, had a crush for a bit, but she's not my type—all business-like in that tweed."

Henry turned in his seat and rested his right shoulder against the back, leaned toward him, then continued talking.

"One day at the factory, my shift supervisor needed some documents taken to the factory manager's office. My boss is a big man, not wanting to walk the stairs any more than he must, so he sends me on the errand. I washed the grease from my hands, ran my fingers through my hair, and headed up to the fourth floor and stood at Dorothy's desk. 'How can I help you, sir?' That's what she said. Not a smile. Not a hint that we'd eaten pancakes at the same table that mornin'. I handed her the document."

When Henry chuckled at himself, Ben couldn't suppress his own smile, seeing how the young man seemed amused with his own recollection. Henry took no breath between his chuckle and the continuing narrative.

"I reckon I was put out by her treatment, so I asked her if she had ever visited the lower factory floors where the work is done. She said she hadn't. 'Well, you might learn somethin' about the business, Dorothy, if you see us folks hard at work.' I walked off."

Ben laughed. "She mention anything at supper that night?"

"Nah, but when our eyes caught, I nodded, gave her a slight smile, then asked her to pass the gravy. I reckon life went back to normal for us. I was judged again for what I didn't have—this time it was a job requiring a suit and tie." Henry laughed. "But it weren't 'til later that my crush went away. I think it was when I first saw her in the awful brown tweed suit."

Ben slapped his own knee as he laughed at Henry's comment. The young man turned and faced forward again.

"St. Louis your home, Henry?"

"Nah, I'm more of a country boy than you might think. I grew up in Stillwater, Oklahoma. Worked a sawmill before I moved."

"Me too, back home. What brought you here?"

"Came here for a job because I didn't want to stay around my fiancée My cousin used to work at Barton. That's how I landed the job. He's since moved to Jefferson City."

"I'm a rural man myself." He blew out a short whistle. "Tried to imagine my family here, but just can't see it."

Ben felt a bit uncomfortable when the young man turned to him with a serious face. All hint of the previous humor had vanished.

"You got a sad story, don't you?"

The streetcar made a stop and afforded Ben a pause before needing to reply. He could feel his brow wrinkle and express his confusion. Had his face hinted at his own broken heart as he'd listened to Henry's story?

"I do. But, it's not over, and I'm longing for it to have a happy ending."

"I hope you get it."

Ben took in the young man beside him. Perhaps he'd been misjudging his maturity.

"How'd you know?"

"I see myself in you. Loneliness. Sadness." Ben shook his head slowly in acknowledgment, then made another choice about bearing his heart.

"Grab a coffee with me on the front porch after supper, if Mrs. Martin doesn't protest. I'll tell you a bit of my story."

"Including the part about the humming?" Henry eyebrows were raised.

"Especially that part."

Ben laid his head back against the seat. Perhaps with Henry familiarity would begin to edge its way to something more meaningful. Tonight, he'd bear a bit of his soul in conversation with Henry. Then, he'd lay his soul bear in writing.

Once supper was behind them, Ben and Henry each took a cup of hot coffee and settled on the front porch steps. Ben took a sip and shuttered. The coffee tasted bitter, and in addition, his full stomach had suddenly become nervous over the thought of sharing his personal story outside the circle of people he held close to his heart. Ben rubbed his hands on the warm mug and cleared his throat. He rested his right ankle on his left thigh and allowed his story to seep out from his soul.

"I was married once before to a pretty lady named Addie. She was the cook at the boarding house where I moved in. Petite little thing. Yellow hair. Freckles. We had a crippled, deaf son named Sammy."

He noticed Henry's eyebrows rise, but the young man remained silent.

"Addie died. I reckon having Sammy alone sounds like a burden, but it weren't. He made me happy. I hated leaving him to work the railroad, but a middle-aged couple took care of him when I had to be gone. Thing is, I felt happy about Sammy, but I felt angry with God. He'd already made me grow up with a drunk father who beat me and my mother."

"That's sad."

"I got comfortable with that grudge until I met Katherine—my wife. She's young and beautiful. Katherine loved my Sammy like he was her own child, and he loved her back. We had another child on the way. Anyway, Katherine had a strong faith that made my heart starting pondering on God. Then tragedy struck me again. My boy was bit by a rattler twice in the leg, and he died."

Ben noticed that Henry threaded his hands resting his arms on his knee. The young man slumped and stared at the ground.

"Katherine blamed herself 'cause she was there when it happened. I didn't blame her, but tension caused a distance between us. Then one night, I was caught kissing a woman who wasn't my wife."

He let the hot tears roll down his cheeks. Henry remained silent and expressionless.

"The compromise took only seconds, but I've lived with the consequences every second since then. Katherine insisted I leave and hasn't forgiven me. Last evening I found out in a letter from a friend that our child is a little girl. Clara."

He saw Henry look up. Their eyes were locked. "It's a good name." A pause lingered between them. "I'm sorry for your story."

"Thank you, Henry. I hadn't shared it with anyone."

"You got brothers and sisters, Ben?"

"Nah. I reckon Pa beat up my Mama's insides, so she couldn't have more kids. Then one day, I beat him back."

"How old were ya?"

"I's twelve. I walked into the house and found my Mama lyin' in a heap on the kitchen floor. My Pa was standing over her kickin' her ribs and yellin' about how useless she was. Something stirred in me, and I walked up and shoved him away from her. He fell, and I kicked his gut no telling how many times. He finally got himself back on his feet and aimed his fist at my face, but before it hit me, I punched his gut. He fell again and passed out. Then I tended to my Mama like I had many times before and counted the years until my Pa died."

"That was the first time, but not the only time?"

"Nah. After that, I came at him every time he tried to beat either one of us. Sometimes I won. Sometimes he did. Now that I'm right with God, I can't say I'm proud of what I did, but I can say I think it was the right thing to do."

Ben set his empty coffee cup on the porch and swatted at the bugs flying around. Henry shifted his feet.

"I reckon I understand a bit of what you're saying about your boyhood, Ben. My mother's sickness made her unpredictable."

"I assume by what you said that she was bad sick."

"I reckon so. More like long sick—all my life, to tell you the truth."

Silence.

"She shifts in and out of moods. Me and my Pa call it darkness and light. I reckon that sounds made up."

"No. I believe you. Sounds hard and, well, sad."

"She got so bad that he sent me to live with my aunt and uncle. It's their son who got me my job here."

Henry looked away from Ben then spoke.

"I worry that there's a darkness lurking inside me like her—not an evil, but a despair."

He turned once again toward Ben.

"I reckon I could hold a grudge against God about her, but I chose not to. I'm not saying I'm some kind of saint. I struggle with all that's happened in my life."

Before Ben could respond, Henry pointed at him. "What's the rest of your story?"

Ben shared the story of the forgiveness he'd sought in the kitchen that morning. Evening had become night when he finished, stood, and came eye level with Henry who was now leaning against the porch post. He'd come to respect and appreciate the young man as a believer and as someone who understood the throbbing pain of being torn from the woman you love.

Just as Ben opened the screen door to step inside for the night, Henry cleared his throat.

"There's something I got on my mind."

"Speak up."

"I'm mighty tired of working at the factory. Reckon I could get on at the railroad? I'd like to give the rails a try."

"You won't know 'til you ask."

Ben saw the young man grin. "I suppose you're right."

Weary, but wide awake, Ben made his way to his bedroom and pulled a well-worn writing tablet from a drawer. His harmonica rested in the drawer and caught his eye. He pulled it out and played a few bars of the Irish ballad Katherine grew to love the night before their wedding. Setting the harmonica back in the drawer, Ben realized he'd kept it silent since before he walked out the door at Layton.

His mind returned to the tablet and letters, and he made himself comfortable on the bed. In two days he'd leave for a long route on the rails, and he wanted his mail posted before his departure. He had much to say to Wendell, his beautiful Katherine, and his baby Clara.

Gratitude, love, and vulnerability made his emotions raw. Adrenaline made his hands tremble as he took up the pencil and formed the first word.

Chapter 6

July 1920 | St. Louis, Missouri

Thunder roared outside, and rain pelted his bedroom window as Ben latched his leather bag and left it sitting on the quilted bedspread. Along with a couple of changes of clothes, the bag contained a few precious possessions that always traveled with him—Sammy's rabbit foot, the butterfly clip he had bought for Katherine, his harmonica, and documents. He fingered the letters from Wendell, deciding to pack them or not, then tossed them back into the drawer. He would add his Bible to the bag before he left. Ben placed his dirty linens outside his door since he would be gone for ten days on a run that went more than five hundred miles to Sherman, Texas—a little over fifty miles from Layton. He reckoned it may as well be five thousand miles considering how distant Katherine's heart was to him.

Ben sighed. As a railroad fireman, he was paid by the mile, and a long route meant a great provision for her cold heart and their little girl. He couldn't give his presence, but he could give his time and provision.

Today was his first day to awaken forgiven by the God he was now eager to know. Grabbing his Bible, he positioned himself in his chair and began to read where he had left off, but his mind was busy throwing accusations at him, making sure he remembered his unfaithfulness to his wife and the losses he had suffered in his lifetime. *God may forgive, but I can't forget.*

His memories had clothed themselves in their well-worn emotions—anger, guilt, regret. Ben had literally shaken his head side to side to loosen the thoughts when he sensed a whisper he could not explain. "I've forgiven you. Forgive yourself. Today." *Today?* A realization hit Ben. In his humanity, he may have to forgive himself time and again, unlike God who could forgive and not struggle with recall. Today he didn't have to live with guilt. He could move forward. Today.

Closing his Bible, Ben bowed his head, certain that was expected of anyone who was praying. The words he wanted to pronounce became trapped somewhere between his soul and his tongue. *Katherine said in her first letter to me that she talked to God just like she talked to a friend.* "God, you mind if I talk with you like I'm sitting beside Wendell at the fishing pond?" He reckoned God didn't mind.

A man's longings can twist up his insides, but as Ben prayed for Katherine, Clara, Lena, and his friends, the knot in his soul seemed to untwist and smooth itself out. For the first time he could recall, Ben sensed the love and guidance of a father—a Heavenly Father. He sat and inhaled the comfort, filling his soul with breath.

The smell of pancakes and coffee made its way into Ben's bedroom causing his stomach to growl. After stuffing his Bible into his leather bag, he slid the strap across his shoulder, tugged his rail cap onto his head, grabbed some money, the letters he'd written last night, and the package for Clara, then headed downstairs for breakfast. Mrs. Martin stood at the stove and flipped a pancake. On the counter next to her, a plate was piled high with the soft, warm food. The thoughtful landlady has risen earlier than usual to feed Ben before he headed to the train yard.

"Mornin' Mrs. Martin. Thank you for gettin' up early."

"Can't send a man to work without a full belly." She turned and smiled at him. "Coffee just finished brewing. Pour yourself a cup. You can sit at the small table here in the kitchen and eat."

Ben patted her on the shoulder, then freed himself of his belongings and cap. He picked up a white coffee cup from the counter and poured the hot, black liquid into it. Taking a sip, he almost spewed the liquid on the counter. Mrs. Martin didn't make a good cup, but he'd learned to tolerate the taste. However, he hadn't expected to scorch his tongue. Perhaps the coffee had usually sat and cooled a bit by the time he normally drank it. He swallowed, then ran his teeth over his tongue, trying to stop the discomfort. Great. He'd have no working taste buds the next few days. He hated having a scorched tongue.

Mrs. Martin placed a plate in front of him and offered butter and syrup. To his surprise, she sat across from him holding her own cup of coffee. He was about to warn her that the liquid was hot when he saw her take a sip and swallow it without any grimacing sign of pain. He cut a chunk of butter and smeared it on his pancakes, drenched them with syrup, cut off a bite, and just as he was about to fill his mouth with the delicious food, he remembered to pray. He smiled at himself. This blessing was the first one he'd initiated on his own. He wasn't praying simply because his family or fellow boarders insisted on it. Mrs. Martin must have noticed, because she was staring at him when he opened his eyes. Ben smiled at her, then explained.

"I'll have to tell you a story when I get back in town. But, you might need to know that I won't be cleaning up after Sunday breakfast anymore. Gotta get to the Baptist church." He tapped the table with his fingers in validation of his words.

"Sounds like a story I want to hear." Mrs. Martin set her coffee cup on the table and folded her hands together next to it. She tilted her head slightly before addressing him. "Somethin's changed with you. Ever since you got that last letter from home." Ben smiled as she mimicked him and tapped her fingers on the table. "And, I like it, Mr. Williams."

Ben slid a last bite into his mouth, then muttered before swallowing. "Yessum." He gulped down the bite. "I been released of a burden." With that, he slid his chair away from the table and stood. "Oh, here is the package for the postman. I addressed it." He reached over and took the box from his belongings and handed it to her. "Thanks again for helping with this."

"Happy to do it."

He hoisted the shoulder strap of his leather bag on his shoulder, pulled on his cap, and headed to the front door. "I'll be back in ten days. Bye now."

Just as he reached for the door knob, he heard a heavy footstep behind him. A step creaked. Ben turned to see Henry, hair sticking up, eyes squinting, and cheeks covered with shave cream. He held a razor in his hand. His voice was raspy. "Safe travels."

Ben smiled up at his new comrade and tipped the bill of his rail cap. "I'll see ya in a few days."

"I'm heading to the train yard and ask to see the master mechanic about being a fireman."

Ben shook his head in agreement. "I reckon they'd start with a lower position like an engine watchman first. Good luck to ya my friend."

He turned the knob and stepped onto the porch. Lifting the lid of the post box, he slipped his three letters inside and muttered "please" under his breath, hoping the words he'd penned of his provision, his love, and his longing to meet Clara would soften Katherine's heart toward him. Perhaps he would return to St. Louis only to leave again and return home to Layton. He ran his teeth over his tongue. The scorch was going to be a nuisance.

Ben grunted. His overalls were getting heavier with rain water. He'd accumulated it when he ran to catch the streetcar, and more so now as he walked through the train yard. His mind was on the letters he'd mailed. He felt confident that Wendell, Carl, and Mason would finalize the bank arrangements. Tonight, while he stayed over with the crew in Texarkana, he'd wire some of his current funds for Katherine to use. He reached the train office and pulled open the thick wooden door and stepped inside. He shook his feet to free some of the water, then wiped his face where the rain had dripped off his cap. His bag was slightly damp.

"Mornin, Leon."

Leon Machette, the engineer, sat in a chair near a wood-burning stove. They'd begun working together on Ben's first route out of St. Louis. Ben smiled. He enjoyed working with the talkative man who shared humorous stories about his family. "Trying to dry off?"

"I reckon, but I'm just gonna get more wet when we walk to the train."

"Ready to head over there?"

"Nope. Sit a spell. They ain't ready for us yet. Something about a loose latch on one of the cars."

Ben sat in a wooden chair, stretched his legs, and pulled his cap over his eyes.

"Wake me when it's time to go."

His mind wandered to the letters he'd written last night.

> *Wendell, when God took my burden, and I took His forgiveness, I realized the value of my own soul. Its worth comes from His unconditional love for me as a Father. Your example of me as Sammy's Papa is what opened my heart toward making God my own Father.*

He'd enclosed the bank documents in the letter to Wendell.

Katherine, the weight of my grudges, self-reliance, and my sin was crushing me. I thought I deserved every bit of awful pain my heart felt. I came to realize the amount of love it took for Jesus to die. And much like I cheapened the physical gift of love you had so sweetly offered, I was also cheapening God's love. I came to understand I was proud. Choosing to embrace the pain in my soul as my self-declared punishment cheapened the real punishment Jesus suffered. Oh, dear Butterfly, don't think I am done regretting what I did to you. It took me only hours to realize that God's forgiveness was final, but I might battle with forgiving myself for a long time. Every moment I live with the consequences of my mistake.

He rubbed his chin, wondering what Katherine would think about the words he'd penned as a man in love.

Oh, how my heart aches to be with you. I love you more and more each day. How strange love is to grow when it is starved. I cannot bear to think of spending more days without my sweet, darling wife. Please tell me to come home. I ache to hold you and kiss you and touch your beautiful hair.

Ben's stomach knotted as he reconsidered his decision to not tell Katherine how he learned of Clara. The letter addressed to his sweet daughter would make it apparent that someone was writing to him, and he reckoned she would assume it was Pastor Carlson.

"Katherine, please read my words to Clara."

"What's that?" Leon spit out his tobacco.

"Oh! Just thinking out loud."

His letter to Clara lingered at the front of his mind.

My Sweet Baby Clara,

I love my little girl. I know now that you are alive and well. How I long to hold your tiny body in my arms and look at you. I yearn for your little fingers to wrap around my big, calloused fingers. Although my eyes have not seen you, I know that you are beautiful with your angel kiss. Forgive me for not being there with you. I pray that one day I will see you and live with you.

Please know that your Papa loves you very much. Your Momma will take good care of you there at home, and I will do all I can for you until I return home to be with my little Butterfly. You are precious to me. I am proud to be your Papa. I long to be with you.

Your Papa, Ben

He jerked when a voice emerged from the back side of the room.

"Crew, report to your posts."

Ben gathered his things and walked beside Leon. Once he arrived at the train, he left his bag with the other railman bags.

As a railroad fireman, Ben was responsible to make sure the coal-fed steam locomotive produced enough heat to power the engine. He crouched down to work through his series of checks before the train departed. After checking the ash box, water valves, and firebox grate, he added enough coal to the tender to make the first stop in Pine Bluff, Arkansas. With all his checks completed, Ben took his seat on the left side of the cab. Leon took the seat to the right. The two of them would spend hours together on this long route.

Time rolled by, and Ben checked his watch. They had left the last water station about a half hour ago and settled in for the next leg of the route. He took his role as the fireman seriously. It was up to him to know the details of the routes and plan how to keep the steam in proportion to the curves and hills of the tracks for proper speed. He also had to know the location of junctions and spurs where a train would be guided by a switch to another track.

"We got a switch about ten miles ahead." Ben bit down on his irritating scorched tongue as he relayed the information.

Leon spat tobacco into a cup. "A'right."

Fifteen minutes later as Leon was, no doubt, embellishing a whopper about his cousin joining the circus, Ben sat up with a jolt. Another train was heading toward them and at a seemingly high rate of speed. Ben realized that a curve in the track had kept it hidden from sight, but now it loomed in the distance with nowhere else to go but directly into his train.

Ben swallowed a lump in his throat. His palms got sweaty as realization set in. The switch operator must have made a mistake and sent that train on the wrong track. "Dear God, help us!"

Instinct told him that neither train would be able to slow enough to avoid disaster. Ben yelled as he yanked on the whistle. At the same moment, he heard Leon curse as he pulled on the throttle to slow the train. His companion screamed with exertion as he tugged. The whistle from the other train sounded to no avail. Ben felt his chest heave in and out as he attempted to keep his panic under control. The screech of metal reverberated in the air, piercing Ben's ears. From the corner of his eye, he saw streaks of orange sparks fly through the air outside the window. On the first day that his soul was prepared for eternity, Ben felt death's grasp. He'd certainly looked death in the eye more than once in his life, yet never had he felt it grip his hand to claim him. He sat on his seat, turning his body away from the firebox, lowered his head into his chest, spread his legs, and grabbed the seat, bracing himself for the impact. "Leon, release the throttle. Brace yourself!"

He longed to live, to meet his daughter, to kiss his wife, and to play and rest and grow old beside them. Despite his efforts, the collision threw his body into the firebox, and he released a piercing scream. Excruciating pain seared his entire right side, and the scent of his own skin burning accosted his nostrils with a charcoal like odor. "Katherine." He released the name in an agonized whisper, just as his body propelled through the air and landed with a thud on the hard ground. Ben screamed as his burnt right side took the brunt of his fall.

Struggling to remain conscious, Ben squinted through the dense, smoke-filled air and noticed mounds of twisted steel and wood where a train car should have been. The sound of a male groaning alerted him to a body lying near his feet. Screaming and shouting reverberated around him. *Hellish.* His scorched tongue licked sweat from his lips. Overcome with pain and the pungent smells of smoke, coal, and burning earth, his stomach revolted, and he choked on its release. Ben sensed a presence and instinctively lifted a trembling hand toward the hovering figure. *Death?*

The screams became distant as he let the blackness overcome him.

Chapter 7

July 1920 | Layton, Texas

Katherine pulled out the three straight pins secured between her lips. "Stand still or I'll never get these seams measured to fit you." She chuckled. "Amy Carlson, you shift and wiggle more than a little child."

Amy Carlson, Pastor Wendell Carlson's wife and her dear friend, stood before her wearing the partially completed maternity dress that Katherine was making for her.

Amy sighed. "I can't seem to help myself. This belly keeps gettin' bigger and bigger, and I just keep getting more uncomfortable." Her friend peered over her belly in an exaggerated motion. "Just look at those ankles."

Katherine twirled her index finger prompting Amy to turn, and when she did, Katherine began pinning the seam after a quick glance at Amy's swollen feet.

"July heat doesn't help much."

"No, Katherine, it doesn't." Amy moved her arm to mimic an elephant trunk.

"Lands sakes, Amy, be still."

"Sorry. I was just trying to show you that I feel like an elephant. Did you feel this way with Clara?

"I sure did."

"Well, as I recall, you were a beautiful pregnant woman."

"And so are you—you petite little thing. Now, let's get you out of this pinned dress, very carefully. Did you bring the buttons you picked out?"

Katherine pulled the dress over Amy's head as her friend answered. For the sake of decency without bulkiness, Amy was covered in one of Katherine's thin gowns for the fitting.

"Uh huh."

Katherine placed the dress carefully across the back of her rocker.

"I'll have this ready by the weekend. Now, head into Lena's room and get your dress back on."

Amy leaned down and rubbed the material

"The color is pretty. Maybe I'll feel pretty wearing this."

"You'll be beautiful. Glance at Clara sleeping on the bed and make sure she is okay. She's a wiggler. I'll get us some sweet tea."

"Yum."

She returned to the front room and found Amy seated in Lena's rocking chair. She handed the glass filled with a dark brown beverage to her friend.

"Whew. It sure is nice to relax a bit before Pastor comes to get you."

She handed her glass to Amy, then carefully folded the pinned dress and set it on top of her sewing basket. The rocking chair squeaked when she sat. Amy handed her the glass of tea.

"Thank you."

Amy took a sip and cleared her throat.

"Too sweet?"

"No, the tea is just fine. Speaking of Clara, I want to tell you something."

Now Katherine cleared her own throat fighting the tightness she felt in it. What would Amy have to say about Clara? If she had questions about being a mother, she'd have said "ask you something," not "tell you something."

"Alright."

"I feel certain you're still hearing from Ben, because Wendell has gotten more than one letter from him. I doubt he'd write Wendell without writing you."

Katherine's stomach soured.

"I've heard from him. He's working in St. Louis. He became a believer. He has money for the baby if we need it."

Her friend turned in the rocker and stared. Katherine shifted away and investigated her tea glass.

"He hasn't heard from you, has he?"

Her eyes welled up. It was useless to try and hold them back.

"No."

"Why?"

"Because I still hurt thinking about him kissing another woman."

"Of course you do. I know I would too. But…"

"You don't have to say it, Amy. I'll say it for you."

Katherine put her tea glass on the floor.

"You were gonna say, 'But you need to stop thinking about it.'"

Katherine huffed.

"No, I wasn't going to say that. I was going to say that you need to release your grudge against him. I'm not sure the hurt will ever go away."

"I deserve the hurt for letting his son die."

"That is ridiculous reasoning. Besides, you didn't *let* his son die. Sammy's death was an accident."

"In my care."

Tea sloshed from Amy's glass as she sat it on the floor.

"I need to stand up. My belly is tight."

Katherine rose then pulled Amy to her feet. Standing face to face with her, she didn't release Amy's hands. They were warm and comforting.

"Listen, Katherine. Your guilt excuse is getting old. You need to forgive yourself for what happened to Sammy. You can grieve his loss but stop carrying the blame. Then you need to forgive Ben and reconcile with him. If you don't, I think I'll sadly watch my friend turn into a bitter, hard woman."

The reprimand was true. "I can't forgive myself."

"With God's help you can. I'll be praying that you will."

Amy freed her hands and sat back down. Katherine stepped to the screen door and stared out.

"Katherine, that's not all I have to say. Ben deserves to know his daughter. He asked Wendell to tell him about his child."

Katherine spun around. "What?"

"We talked and prayed about what to do. Finally, Wendell wrote and told him about Clara, but Ben should have heard it from you.

Katherine slid down to the floor.

"Are you mad at me and Wendell?"

Katherine looked up and nodded her head no.

"I'm ashamed. I'm lonely. I'm hurt. I'm confused."

Before Amy could reply, the sound of a cart rolling onto the front yard came through the screen door. Katherine welcomed the distraction.

"That must be Wendell," Amy noted.

Katherine stood and made her way to Amy. With a gentle tug, Amy was on her feet again, and the ladies embraced one another.

"Only a good friend, like a good sister, would speak to me this way. You tell Pastor I'm not mad. I should've done what he did."

"Me and Wendell care about you."

Footsteps sounded on the porch.

"Afternoon ladies."

"Afternoon, Pastor. Come on in."

The screen door squeaked as Wendell pushed through it. Katherine smiled when he kissed his wife on the cheek before speaking.

"Ready to go, Amy?"

"Yes. Katherine, thank you for sewing for me."

"My pleasure. How about I bring your new dress to church Sunday?"

"I look forward to it."

"Thank you for taking care of my wife, Katherine."

Her guests walked through the door.

"Bye now! See you Sunday."

Avoiding the pins, Katherine folded the dress, placed her pin cushion into her sewing box, and closed the lid. Her left hand rested on the handle of the box. How bare it looked without her wedding band. Strange. She'd only worn the band for a few months of her nineteen years. How could her finger look so naked without it?

Katherine stuffed the sewing box and dress underneath Lena's bed, moved aside a pillow, then lay down next to her sleeping child. The sound of Clara's rhythmic breathing was pleasurable. She wiped sweat from her baby's brow then touched the small birthmark on her cheek—her angel kiss. A painful, familiar truth came to mind again, but this time it took root. There is plenty of guilt to be had by her parents, but Clara is innocent. She doesn't deserve to be punished for the tension between me and her Papa. Katherine pressed her fingers against her temples. She could work on forgiving Ben for Clara's sake. And for her own sake as well.

Katherine knew from his letters that he was a grieving, hurting man. *She* was the reason for some of his grief—the loss of Sammy. Sending Ben away instead of facing the hurt he'd cause her was another reason. After all, hadn't she hurt him too by distancing herself after Sammy's death?

She adjusted the pillows placed around Clara to secure her on the bed, then made her way to the back of the house and opened the door to the storage room. Ben's trunk rested in the back corner. Just as she reached it, a mouse trap snapped. She yelped. Because Joe was away for work, she'd ask Lena to clear the trap. Katherine had never been able to stomach that job without gagging.

Her hand trembled when she raised the trunk lid. She moved articles around until she found the bundle of his letters and other sentimental items. She untied the bow. How smooth the wedding band attached to it felt when she rubbed her finger over it. Careful to keep the stack in order, she pulled out the bottom letter, tied the ribbon back together, then placed the bundle into the trunk.

"Achoo!" Too much dust in the room. She stepped over items hurriedly as she made her way through the door and back to her bed. Katherine slid the letter out of the envelope. Should more be written? No. "Come home," was all Ben needed to read.

"Blast it!" She'd forgotten to look at the St. Louis address on his latest correspondence. She dropped the letter and envelope on the bed and made her way back to the trunk. She repeated the untying ritual and found what she was looking for. *Hurry!* She was anxious, knowing Clara could wake up any moment. If she didn't complete the task now, would she ever muster the courage to try again?

Back at the bed, she wiped sweat from her brow and pushed back the loose, damp tendrils hanging in her eyes. She stared at the original envelope addressed to Commerce, Texas where Ben had fled when she demanded he leave. She hid that envelope in a drawer, pulled out a new one, and blotted her ink pen that rested atop the dresser.

Ben Williams
6710 Chamber Street
St. Louis, Missouri

She placed the yellowed letter inside the envelope and sealed it. Tomorrow she would sneak it to the post office inside the Justice Store when she and Lena made their run for groceries and supplies. "This letter is between me and Ben. Nobody else needs to know I sent it."

Katherine bit her lip. Privately, she'd relish his return. Was she frightened he may not come? Surely Ben would return to them. After all, he'd begged to come home. Thank goodness her letter would remain her secret alone. Louise Justice would not be running the post office tomorrow since she and her husband were out of town visiting her ailing aunt for a couple of weeks. Louise's usual replacement, the extra postman from nearby Evan, would be working the post office in her place.

How long would it take for the letter to arrive in St. Louis? How long would she have to wait for his reply? Should she adorn her finger with the wedding ring? No. She'd wait until he returned. How many days would pass before he stood, once again, in their home. An emotion moved through her. She recognized it as hope, but it would come with the high price of pain and humility. It was a price worth paying. No doubt, Ben was willing to pay it too.

She hid the letter under her pillow just as Clara's wake up cry sounded through the house.

"Momma's coming."

And Papa will be soon.

Chapter 8

July 1920 | Layton, Texas

"Mr. Justice."

"Katherine, I've told you to please call me Carl, even while you're working."

She nodded her agreement and grinned. This man was a father figure in her life, yet he combined fatherhood and friendship in a way that made her feel both comfortable and secure somehow.

"Yes. Carl,' she chuckled. "I'm done with the ledgers for the last week of the month."

She looked down toward her feet as she spoke.

"It seems that the Jacksons owe five dollars and Joe McGinn owes twenty dollars."

She heard him clear his throat.

"Well, I reckon the Jacksons will catch up next month. They've never fallen behind. I know she was sick and needing medical attention. I can afford to wait for their payment. Now, as for Joe…"

She cut him off.

"You should take my pay for his bill. It's two months' worth of pay owed to you. You were generous not to take my pay last month."

He tapped her shoulder.

"Look at me, Katherine."

She did.

"He payed me with a check. But turns out his account wasn't good for it."

"I'm sorry."

"It wasn't your doing."

He took in a breath then blew it out.

"Your brother can no longer do business in this store unless he pays in cash—not with a worthless check and not on an account. But, that is my concern. Not yours."

"Thank you, Carl. I can't rightly take your pay knowing my brother owes you."

"Did you do work for me?"

"Yes."

"Has Lena worked the diner for me?"

"Yes."

"Then both you and your sister will be paid."

"Thank you."

"Now, you got more work to do, right?"

She bit her lip.

"Sure do. I got to close out the vendor ledgers."

With that, she moved to her small desk in the back room of the store.

Katherine had grown accustomed to hearing the bell above the store's door ring when someone opened it. She reckoned she rarely noticed the jingling anymore, but an hour after to talking to Carl, a familiar voice mingled with the sound of the bell drew her attention. She cringed.

"Hello, Carl. Katherine here?"

"Joe, she's working."

Katherine stood from the desk and peeked around the divider curtain in the doorway. There stood her brother with a lady on his arm. She assumed this was Rosa, the woman from nearby Josephine who owned an auto. Joe had been bragging about her for weeks.

"Carl, this here is my girl, Rosa. We're heading to her uncle's house for the weekend."

"Hello, Rosa. Not sure I know you from around here."

The woman's voice seemed to come from her nasal cavity. Her brown hair was cut just above her chin, and it was apparent she'd attempted to manage its tight curls. Despite having never met the woman, Katherine reckoned she wouldn't like her simply because Joe deemed himself a ladies man, and Katherine thought the term "ladies" was certainly a misnomer for the women Joe had favored in the past. She swallowed and stepped through the doorway.

"Joe, hello. Did you need something?"

"Katherine, meet Rosa. Rosa, my oldest sister."

"Hello." Katherine spoke first. Rosa echoed her response.

"Just came to tell you I won't be home this weekend."

"Can't say I'm surprised."

Her brother's face reddened, but not in embarrassment. His steely eyes indicated she'd made him mad.

"Well, me and Rosa got plans. I'm gonna stop by the house and grab a bag."

Carl came from behind the register and addressed Rosa.

"If you'd like to help yourself to a cola, it's on the house. I need to speak to Joe."

The woman smiled, and Katherine noticed her glance at Joe as though needing approval. Her brother's head nodded toward the diner section of the store as he addressed her.

"Go head. Maybe you can meet Louise Justice and my sister Lena. They're prob'ly at the diner counter or the post office."

Katherine interjected. "Louise isn't here today. She's visiting her sick aunt." Before Katherine could explain that Lena was at home today, Rosa cleared her throat and spoke.

"Thank you. I'd enjoy a cola." With that, Rosa strode to the back.

"I reckon, Carl, this is about my account. Well, I'm getting paid from Gibsons Store next Friday. I'll be sure to make my payment."

"Joe, from here on out, you are cash only in this store."

The sharp edge of Joe's silence seemed to cut Katherine's emotions. She realized at that moment she was afraid of her brother's reactions. Would he seek revenge for Carl's decision on her, or worse, her daughter or sister? Although he'd never beat them before, the threat of it seemed to linger as though it were another member of their household.

"I'm a businessman myself, making and selling furniture, so I respect what you got to say. I'll get my account in order. Rosa! We best get going." Joe began to walk toward the back of the store, then turned his face toward Katherine.

"I'll see you Monday morning. Is Lena here at the diner?"

"No, she's at home with Clara."

Katherine observed him make his way to the diner near the post office in the back of the store and take Rosa's hand. Katherine stood near Carl as Joe returned, pushed open the screen and walked himself and Rosa through it. The screen door slammed behind them.

Katherine squinted through the mesh. Was Joe carrying something in his hand? Carl turned to Katherine.

"That young man has become a scoundrel. He looked angry. Will he take out revenge on you ladies—drunk or not drunk? I've seen him in a drunken stupor enough to be concerned."

The care in Carl's words soothed her. His concern would have been greater if he'd known Katherine's thoughts.

"He's never taken revenge on us before but thank you for asking."

An hour later Katherine was walking the mile home from the store, anxious to hold Clara after being separated from her most of the afternoon. July air was humid, and by the time she arrived home, Katherine had determined to take a bath. From opened windows on the front porch, she heard Lena talking to Clara in her bedroom. The smell of chicken and dumplings welcomed her as she walked into the house and took an immediate right, slid open the curtain in the doorway, and walked into Lena's room. A metal bath tub sat on the floor.

"Hello, my little angel."

Katherine walked to the rocker where Lena sat holding Clara and took the child into her embrace.

"How's my little girl been, Lena?"

"She's been perfect. Just woke up. I reckon she'll be ready to eat."

"No doubt. It's time. I see you took a bath. I'm gonna take one." Katherine spoke the words as she sat on the bed to feed Clara.

"Yep."

"Has Joe and his girl come by?"

"His girl? Joe came in for a bit, said he was packing a bag."

"He didn't mention Rosa?"

"No. Came in through the kitchen and left out the front. Said I startled him being here."

"Startled him? He asked me where you were, and I answered that you were here with Clara."

"Well, all I know is he came and stuck his head in this door as I was in the tub. Glad I was facing away from him. Said he heard a noise and it spooked him."

"That makes no sense." She felt her brows wrinkle. What had Joe been thinking? Perhaps he was drunk, and she just hadn't noticed at the store. But neither had Carl for that matter. She was baffled.

Lena stood. "I better finish supper."

"I'll be there to help in a minute."

Lena walked toward Katherine, then bent and touched Clara's head.

"I been thinking, Katherine, that maybe I should start taking my bath in your back bedroom. More privacy with the wooden door than my curtain one."

"That's a good idea."

"Oh, and Joe told me he brought home the mail. Nothing in it, he said, but a farmer's advertisement and the newsletter from his masonic lodge."

"Alright."

Her mind strayed at the mention of mail. *Had Ben received her letter yet?*

Lena moved out of the room with her shoulders appearing slightly slumped.

"Is something bothering you, Lena?"

"Just embarrassed that Joe walked in and saw my back while I was bathing."

"I wonder if he was drunk. I clearly told him you were here."

"He probably had his mind on something and forgot—especially if he had his girl waiting for him outside in the cart."

"You mean in her *auto*."

Lena smiled and moved on. An uneasiness settled over Katherine, but she couldn't put a name to it. She ran a hand over her face and sighed.

This would be a good day for Ben Williams to walk through the front door and return home.

Chapter 9

July-September 1920 | Pine Bluff, Arkansas

"Mr. Williams?" Ben moaned in resistance to the shaking he sensed on his shoulder. His eyes strived to see, but the heavy weight covering them prevented it as Ben fought to find his way out of the darkness. Another shake. "Sir, can you hear me?" The voice was quiet and feminine. *Katherine?*

Ben felt his spirit soar at the thought. *I must see her.* He tried to call to his wife, but his tongue felt thick and dry. With determination, he pushed it through his teeth and used it to part his lips. He concentrated and then began to blink against the weight on his eyes—realizing the heaviness was his own lids. Every part of his body fought the effort to break through the darkness, except his heart. He felt its pounding effort against his chest.

"Mr. Williams, can you wake up?" *I'm coming, Butterfly. Wait for me.* His heart won the battle, and his eyelids opened, then reflexively shut against the brightness. Frustrated, he pulled her name from his dry throat and forced it over his tongue. "Katherine."

"That's good, Mr. Williams, you keep trying to wake up."

Ben pushed out her name again in urgency, forcing his lungs to take a deep breath. "Katherine!" His eyelids opened while he felt a smile form on his lips at the hope of seeing her. His sight betrayed his heart. The woman before him was not his Katherine. Warm tears rolled down his cheeks.

"Good morning, Mr. Williams." Intense pain slammed against him. His body throbbed, but his heart broke.

"Katherine?"

"I'm Nurse Walters. Katherine is not here." A sob escaped him. "Perhaps we can find her later." The tall, thin, middle-aged figure in crisp white leaned over him; he felt her eyes look into his. "Do you know where you are, Sir?" Ben groaned but shook his head side to side. "You are in the Pine Bluff hospital. You've been injured."

The memory came crashing in. The whistle, the screeching of metal, the heat, the pain. Death had not come to him.

Ben wept.

"You were identified by a railroad employee at the crash site as Ben Williams."

"That's me."

He grimaced at the pain on his right side.

"Do you remember the accident?"

"Yes." The awful recollection had brought him back to his senses.

"You've been here for two weeks, Mr. Williams. We've been treating your injuries enough to safely transport you tomorrow to the Cottonline Hospital in Texarkana. The doctor will be here to explain more."

"What's wrong with me?" The words fought their way through a dry, raw throat. He watched the nurse purse her lips as she hesitated. "Please. Tell me."

His eyes followed her gaze around the room, and only then did Ben realize he was surrounded by other patients in a long, narrow white room filled with wall to wall beds. Nurse Walters sat in a chair next to his bed and spoke for his ears only. "You have a severely broken right leg. Most of your ribs are broken. Your insides are bruised, especially your kidney. You have multiple cuts. We've stitched you in several places."

She exhaled slightly, and he felt her warm, peppermint breath. "Your right arm and torso are severely burned." He gasped, then felt her hand pat his as it rested on the side of the bed. "We are grateful you are alive."

He groaned against the physical and emotional pain. She continued. "We've kept you sedated, but we wanted to wake you enough to explain your situation and see how your memory is doing. Soon enough, you'll be back in a deep sleep."

"Does my family know?"

"We contacted the residence the railroad had on record."

Of course. The boarding home would be contacted in St. Louis, but not his wife. It occurred to him that the railroad had his wife's name, but not her Layton address. Despite his foggy thinking, he reckoned Mrs. Martin received a telephone phone call or wire intended for Katherine Williams. How would Mrs. Martin handle that type of matter?

Ben sucked in a deep breath and began to pat around his mattress, regardless of the pain.

"Mr. Williams, what are you doing?" The nurse arose from the chair. "You must stay calm. You're very ill."

"My rabbit's foot. It was my son's treasure."

He heard her chuckle. "I have it in a leather bag. They both survived the crash. It will travel with you."

"A letter. I've got to write my wife." His anxiousness agitated him.

"You can't write."

"You can."

She smiled and patted his hand. "Yes, I can. After the doctor sees you."

"No medicine to make me sleep until I write her."

"Katherine?"

"Yes."

Heavy footsteps echoed on the sterile tile floor. Nurse Walters cleared her throat as the doctor approached.

"Doctor Miller meet our patient, Ben Williams."

The doctor appeared younger than the nurse, despite the wire rimmed glasses he wore. His black hair was neatly parted to one side. His smile appeared to be institutional and practiced.

"Has Nurse Walters explained your condition?"

Before Ben could speak, Nurse Walters interjected. "Yes, but not the extent."

Hearing a cacophony of inflections and medical descriptions, Ben was able to decipher that he had a long recovery ahead of him. Most likely learning how to use his leg again. There would be continued care of his burns to alleviate as much scarring as possible. *Scarring*. The next time he woke up, he should be in a top notch modern facility.

"Mr. Williams, you were on your deathbed. We've sustained you long enough to make the medical train ride to the Cottonline Hospital, but do not think you are out of danger. I trust your affairs are in order." With that haunting, harsh statement, he turned and left the room.

Ben felt his energy diminishing as his pain intensified. His mind was foggy.

"The letter." He breathed heavily against his pain. "Write it for me."

"Quickly!" The nurse took a pad and pencil from the bedside table.

Ben's passion was expressed in mumbled words as he watched the nurse concentrate and scribble.

Dear Wife and Baby,

They are sending me to the hospital in Texarkana. I was in an accident and am barely able to move. I am burned. The doctor said I might die. So, in case of my death, I will have money for you. Should I never see you again, Butterfly, I love you and my precious Baby and will see you in heaven. At least now I know I will go there.

When he saw the nurse lay down the pencil, Ben tried to sit up. Searing pain shot through him and made his head spin.

"Don't stop."

"Mr. Williams, you've said enough. Your body needs rest."

Ben was not ashamed of the hot tears that he felt run down his cheeks. "Please, don't stop. Just a little more."

A slight smile made its way through his pain when he saw the nurse shake her head in apparent sympathetic defeat and pick up the pencil.

"Please forgive and be happy. This could likely be my last letter. The nurse will give you the address. I beg you to come and bring our baby. Please come to me. I will love you as long as I live. If I die, then I will finally be free of my lonely love for you. For I do not think love will follow me to my grave. You are my darling, beautiful russet Butterfly. Tell my baby Clara I love her. I am weary.

So, Goodbye.

Ben

P.S. Cottonline Hospital, Dudley Street, Texarkana, Texas

Now that he had laid his heart out for his girls, Ben was ready to succumb to darkness and mask the pain.

"Medicine, please."

The white figure stood, stuffed the letter into her pocket, and leaned over him to administer medicine.

"We have an address on file."

"No. Layton, Texas. Box 18."

He slipped into the darkness, hoping he wouldn't wake up in Heaven—not today. Wishing he could wake up at home in Layton. Hoping his Katherine would come soon.

Ben knew the ointment kept infection away from his tender, scarred skin, but he hated the feel of it on his arm and torso. For the last several weeks, he had been in and out of consciousness to avoid pain. The ache of burnt flesh was torture. He hated the look of his scorched skin. In his journey between consciousness and sleep, each look at his body was as though it was the first realization of his condition. Over time, so he had been told, Ben had been weaned from his pain killer. His memories had resembled torn, scattered pages from a book, with no sequence or plot.

But, today was different. Today, Ben was fully alert, dependent only on aspirin and ointment to pamper his pain. A petite, freckled face nurse entered the room Ben shared with one other patient. Red, unruly looking curls shot out from her nurse's cap.

"Coreen? That's your name, right?" Ben raised his eyebrows and smiled a toothy smile as he waited her affirmation. With freckles spreading across her face as though a breeze had scattered them, the nurse smiled and shook her head yes. "And your husband works here as an accountant."

Coreen laughed. "You're right, Mr. Williams. Your memory seems to fair well coming from such a fog." She completed wrapping his arm with gauze, then stuck a thermometer in his mouth. "Today's a big day for you. An outing to the back porch for some cool, fresh air."

He loosened his lips from the thermometer and spoke through his teeth, "Dat sounds good." Needing to swallow, he waited impatiently until she removed the thermometer. He worked his throat, then spoke. "What is the date?"

"It's September 20th. See, it's marked on your calendar."

Ben glanced at the calendar, grateful it was marked up, but sad to know his life had been reduced to small boxes crossed off in black ink. He felt his brows wrinkle as despair tried to sink into his heart. He'd been here two months. No word to Wendell. No other word to Katherine.

"Coreen, do you know if I've had a visitor named Katherine? A letter from her? Anything?"

"Well, I haven't known of a visitor. Tell you what, let me check while you are at breakfast."

"Thank you."

He flexed his fingertips open and shut. Yep. They were strong enough to hold a pencil, if only his burnt arm would cooperate. Today, he'd attempt to write a letter.

"Coreen, any paper and pencil around here? I gotta write some letters."

The nurse put her hands on her hip. "I reckon I can find some, but don't count on writing them yourself. I'll write for you."

"Only if I can't manage."

"Shake on it." She extended her hand toward him and wrapped her thick fingers around his in a grasp.

"Mr. Williams, tomorrow your cast comes off. You are going to start working on walking again. But for now, let's get you in this wheelchair and get you to the porch for breakfast."

She clapped her hands in excitement, as though she were personally responsible for this achievement. Ben smiled. For all he knew, she was. Her and the good Lord.

Just as Coreen got Ben seated in the wheelchair, a man in a suit and tie walked into the room. He was tall and boasted a head of white hair and a friendly smile. Ben could smell his aftershave, clean and crisp. Ahhh! The smell was a good change from the scents of antiseptic, rubbing alcohol, and Lysol. No doubt his room was pristine and sanitary. The black and white tile shone. The linens smelled of bleach. The white metal bedside tables had no speck of dust and neither did the metal guest chairs. Bed pans were astonishingly clean.

The stranger wearing a suit smiled.

"Well, this is an answer to prayer. Good to see you awake and out of the bed, Mr. Williams. I'm Reverend Lilley—the chaplain here at the hospital.

I've met you several times, but I suspect, by the wrinkled brow I see, that you don't recollect that."

Ben laughed. "I reckon I don't, but I'm sure glad to meet you. Come by anytime." For the first time in two months, he assumed, Ben thought of his Bible.

"Coreen, did my Bible make it to this fine establishment?"

"Yes, right over there in your table."

"Good." Ben took in the memory of his encounter with God in the kitchen of Mrs. Martin's home. He let it soothe him. Yes, he was coming back to life, despite the physical pain he supposed lay ahead, and he wanted to strengthen his soul while he strengthened his body.

"I mean it, Reverend, I look forward to talking with you."

"I'll be by again tomorrow. Right now, you enjoy your time on the back porch, I assume."

Ben took in the scenes around him as the nurse pushed the wheelchair. He enjoyed the sound of her shoes thudding against the tile floor. He glanced into open doorways as Coreen strolled him down the narrow hallway with pale yellow walls. Patient rooms were situated down the entire corridor. The rooms looked identical with two beds, two metal chairs, and stark white walls. Ben suddenly realized that the bed next to his was empty and made up with tight white sheets. The public areas of the hospital boasted wide corridors that were decorated with rich golds and reds. Large paintings of outdoor scenes in ornate gold frames lined the common areas.

Coreen got Ben settled at a table and faced him toward the back of the hospital grounds and told him she'd return later. Before she left, she set pencil and paper on the table for him and smiled. The area was well kept and gardened, and Ben thought it resembled a city park he had seen along the river in St. Louis. The gold and red hues on the trees testified that it was fall. Ben sucked in the cool air and closed his eyes to take in the sunshine. His last recollection of being outdoors was when he loaded the train months ago.

He thought of Henry and their conversation on the front porch before he left St. Louis. He was grateful his young friend and the others had gotten word of the accident from the railroad. He wondered if Leon and other crewmen had survived the collision. Perhaps he would be able to find out. A nurse set milk, oatmeal, and plain toast in front of him. His stomach reacted with a loud growl. Ben blinked.

"Thank you. Could I have some buttered biscuits and eggs too?"

The nurse's face was expressionless. "No. Your stomach needs bland food."

Ben chuckled as he looked up at her. "Stomach sounds pretty healthy to me."

The nurse turned and walked away. Ben gave thanks for the food, wondering if he had survived on oatmeal and soup for the last two months. He consumed the food in no time. Pushing aside his empty plate and bowl, he reached for the pencil and paper.

At that moment, he looked up, sensing someone approaching his table. Coreen took three more strides and stood beside him. Her mouth was turned down.

"My mail?"

She tilted her head. "I'm afraid there is no letter from a Katherine. All the mail is business mail from the railroad. Administration has to give it to you."

He suppressed his disappointment.

"Any visitors?"

He watched her eyes roam the porch, as though she were looking for someone. *A visitor from thin air*?

"Nurse Coreen?"

"No. I'm sorry Ben."

A lump rose in his throat. Coreen had been kind, and he didn't want her to get the brunt of his disappointment. He mustered up a smile.

"Thank you for checking."

Her own bright smile told him she'd shifted back into her cheerful demeanor or perhaps was attempting to. How much bad news had she delivered to people over time?

"Enjoy your breakfast."

She turned and walked briskly toward the door.

No word from Katherine. No visit from Katherine. Ben wondered if she would have preferred his death. *I've lost her*. Shame far worse than that of an immoral kiss washed over him. This was the shame of ruining lives. He loathed himself, and any sense he'd ever felt of God's forgiveness mocked him. His anger roused and mingled with the shame. *Help me God, to be grateful you spared my life, because right now I am angry. I know you have a reason for me to live. Is it only so I can suffer in anguish?*

He began to write, but not the love letter he had composed in his mind just moments ago when he ate. Instead, he was penning the words of the last letter he would ever mail her. He would surrender to her coldness.

His arm throbbed, and Ben felt perspiration roll down his cheeks while more settled in his armpits. When had the September air become suffocating? Ben tossed the pencil to the table, then folded the letter, placed it in an envelope, and wrote the Layton address that was sealed in his heart. No return address necessary.

Eyeing the remaining blank paper and envelopes Ben blew out a heavy breath. There was no need to write Wendell. He'd risk letting the man think ill of him and believe whatever Katherine told him. He could pastor Katherine without being torn by the brief friendship they'd shared.

"Ben, need help with a letter?"

"No." He tapped the envelope that contained his broken heart. "Thank you, Coreen. I think I'm ready for a nap now."

He watched her eyes grow wide.

"Let's get you back to the room. I'll leave this letter at the front desk before the mail goes out today." He observed her slip it into her uniform pocket.

Coreen lifted him from the chair, assisted his physical needs, checked his temperature, changed his gauze, forced him to take aspirin, then finally let him relax in the bed. She turned to leave just as Reverend Lilley appeared and poked his head into the doorway.

"How's the patient, Coreen, after his adventure on the porch?"

"Although he wouldn't say anything on his ride back, I suspect he's feeling a lot of pain in his arm. He insisted on writing a letter himself." She smiled at Ben. He made no attempt to smile in return.

The reverend entered the room. "I finished my rounds sooner than I thought. May I sit a while?"

Contrary to his mood, Ben replied with a yes.

Coreen made a show of fluffing Ben's pillow. "I'll be back to check on you again before my rounds end. Take it easy, Mr. Williams."

The reverend sat down next to the bed and eased into conversation.

"I'm sorry about your accident."

"Interesting thing is, the day before the accident, I asked God's forgiveness and got salvation."

"Well, that's good to hear."

"The timing rattles me. I keep thinkin' about how close I came to dying and not getting into heaven."

"And now you've got a new start on life—physically and spiritually."

"Yessir, but right now, I'm not sure I want it."

"Something has made you feel that way."

"I made mistakes and hurt the people I love the most. I'm grateful God forgave me. But they didn't, and I've lost them."

"I'm real sorry for that." He leaned forward in the chair and continued speaking.

"If you've got questions about God in all of this, it's better to ask them than bind them inside you. I'll be honored to talk with you anytime."

The truth was, Ben needed someone to listen.

"Thank you. You'll be hearing from me." Ben cleared his throat. "I lost two months of my life, Reverend. Was I the only one here from the collision?"

"You're the last one here. Others have come and gone. There's official papers for you in the business office of the hospital."

"Gone, as in healed?"

"Some. Others died here."

A lump formed in Ben's throat.

"Do you know if Leon Machette was here?"

He watched the reverend sit back in his chair, and Ben suspected he didn't want to hear the answer to his question.

"No. He wasn't here. Leon was pronounced dead at the scene."

Sorrow pressed into Ben.

"I'm sure administration will get papers to you soon since you're alert now. But, I kept a newspaper article about the accident. When you're ready, I'll bring it to you. But not today."

"Why am I alive, Reverend?"

"Only God knows why, but be assured He has a plan and purpose, even if you don't care what it is right now."

"I'm feel almost ashamed to be alive after hurting my family, yet, Leon, who was working right next me, is dead."

"God is sovereign, and sometimes our human minds can't reconcile His doings. That's where our faith comes in. But tell Him your thoughts. He'll listen. He'll also comfort, if you'll let Him."

"I've always relied on my reasoning. I got a lot to learn about faith. I got to learn how to have it when my heart is a mess."

"You learn it a day at a time. Why, sometimes, a moment at a time. And with faith, comes peace."

The reverend stood. "But, right *this* moment, I'm thinking you need to rest." He patted Ben on the shoulder. "I'm gonna enjoy getting to know you, Mr. Williams. I'll see you tomorrow."

"Tomorrow it is. Thank you, Reverend Lilley."

The chaplain had no sooner walked through the doorway than Ben let sleep overtake him until a female voice stirred him back awake. He was cognizant enough to realize it was not his beautiful wife standing over him.

"I'm awake now."

"I'm glad you got a nap in. My shift is almost over, and I need to check your bandages before I go."

Ben rolled over on his left side, giving Coreen access to his burns. He hissed and grimaced as she pulled the bandages away then applied the ointment. He appreciated that Coreen was good to chatter as she worked and soon the task was done.

"Clean bandages feel good. Thanks."

"You're welcome. Did you and the chaplain have a nice talk?"

Ben chuckled. "I like him. He reminds me of a pastor I know from home."

Coreen grinned. "Reverend Lilley is a good man. He's collected all the information he can find about the accident, so he could help the men like you who suffered in it. He's been watching after you the whole time you've been here."

"As have you and the other nurses and doctors. I'm obliged."

"You've been an easy patient, but of course you've been asleep most of the time. Don't you start giving me trouble and ruin my opinion of you."

Coreen laughed then startled as the phone rang. Ben was amused that he'd not noticed the phone before. Coreen answered it.

"Yes." Her brow wrinkled, and she glanced at him. "I think he will feel up to it." Her words caused Ben to wrinkle his brow in response.

"Ben, you have a guest at the main desk. Are you up for a visitor?"

His breath caught.

"Yes!"

The letter? Is it too late to retrieve the letter I wrote Katherine? After all she's here.

Chapter 10

September 1920 | Layton, Texas

"Ben," she placed her hands on his face, "why did you wait so long to come home?"

He took her hands in his, then leaned down and kissed her lips. "I came as soon as I could leave St. Louis."

"Every day I looked for you." She ran her fingers through the hair resting on his neck.

He lifted his daughter to him.

"I'm here now, and we're a family again. I'm home to stay."

She wrapped her arms around his waist and felt his free hand come around her shoulder.

"We'll never be apart again."

Katherine shook her head in abrupt back and forth motions to release the scene playing out in her mind. July had become August and August had merged into September with no word from Ben. She soothed her fears by day with dreams of his return. She wrestled her fears by night with nightmares of his death or his abandonment.

She stood daydreaming with a basket on each side of her. One contained the clothes she was hanging to dry. Ten-month-old Clara sat in the other playing with her stuffed teddy bear. Katherine raised her apron to wipe the sweat that ran down her neck despite the cool September breeze causing loose tendrils of hair to tickle her cheeks. A glance at Clara as she pulled the apron made her smile. She'd never realized how much a mother could love a child. The tenderness of motherhood evoked a longing for her own Momma.

"Blast it." Clothespins spilled onto the ground. She'd forgotten they were in her apron pocket, even though she'd been pulling them from there one at a time. She bent to pick them up but chose instead to lift Clara from the basket. The teddy bear dangled from the child's hand. Clara's sweaty head immediately nestled against Katherine's neck, and she hugged it between her shoulder and cheek. Katherine would stop time for a bit if she could and relish the feel of her child snuggled against her, but the moment passed when Clara shifted and wiggled.

Katherine pressed her lips against the light brown angel kiss on Clara's cheek—the fingerprint of her Creator. The marking was beautiful to Katherine. She stood the toddler in front of her, and Clara instinctively dropped the teddy bear and clasped each hand around her mother's index fingers. Together they walked at Clara's pace toward the crepe myrtle trees.

The chirp of a mockingbird caught Clara's attention and the child plopped on the ground. Katherine pulled her hands free then lifted Clara to her hip and pointed.

"Bird. See the bird."

Katherine jerked as the beep of an auto came from behind her. She turned to see Carl and Louise Justice pulling into her yard with a trail of black Texas swirling behind them. Katherine stood on her toes and waved.

"Hello!"

She scurried over to the auto with Clara bouncing on her hip and stood near Mrs. Justice.

"Afternoon, Katherine." Mrs. Justice raised her hand and squeezed Clara's fingers. "And, hello to my sweet Clara."

The child smiled.

"This is a nice surprise."

"We won't be at the store tomorrow 'cause we're headed to visit our grandson for his birthday."

"I know you're excited."

"Can't wait! Anyway, Carl needed tell you something about the accounts. So, we're driving by on our way out of town."

Carl Justice chuckled and patted his wife's back as he chimed in.

"Won't you please come inside the house?"

The auto was still running.

"Oh, thank you, but no need to." Carl Justice took over for his wife. "I want to tell you that Cleaver Brothers has changed their name to Stapletons. The invoices came in that way with no notice today. I had to make a telephone call to their factory to figure it out."

"Goodness. Thank you for telling me. Who knew that cans of lard could be such trouble."

A grin spread across his face.

Clara began to wail and reach outward as though grasping for something.

"She just realized that she's not holding her teddy bear. Shh! Shh! We'll get teddy in a minute." She patted the child's back.

Carl released a pedal and the car began to roll.

"We gotta keep going so we'll arrive in time for late lunch."

"Bye!"

Louise and Katherine waved at one another.

"Oh! Wait," Louise yelled out, "I brought your mail."

Katherine trotted the few feet to the car, and Louise placed the mail in her hand and winked. The car drove away. Katherine stuffed the mail into her apron pocket then walked over and picked up the teddy bear. Clara calmed.

Intrigued by the wink Louise gave her, Katherine settled on the front porch rocker with Clara in her lap. Her fingers slid into the apron pocket and retrieved the small bundle tied with twine. She loosened the course bow and released the mail. Hidden between two postcards addressed to Joe from friends in Greenville, was a letter addressed to Katherine Williams, postmarked from Texarkana. Her heart raced at the sight of Ben's handwriting. When had he moved to Texarkana? Perhaps that would explain his delayed return. Her letter must have been routed from St. Louis and gotten to him later than she'd anticipated.

Clara squirmed, and Katherine hugged her. "I have a letter from Papa." She pressed Clara's back to her and slipped her arms beneath Clara's shoulders.

Her heart continued to race, and her fingers seemed to fight each other to unseal the envelope. She pulled out the lined paper and slipped the envelope under her thigh to keep it from blowing away. Instinctively she brought the letter to her nose hoping to catch any scent of her husband. Unfolding the pages, she let Ben speak through written words.

September 1920

Katherine,

This is the last letter you will receive from me. I will make no more attempts to restore our marriage or family. I do not plan to file for divorce, but if you do, I will sign the papers. If you decide to file, your attorney can attempt to reach me through the railroad. I will continue to support Clara with the financial arrangements I have previously made. I will also write to her from time to time in hopes that one day she will understand that I do love her. I trust that you will not keep the letters from her when grows old enough for them.

May God be close to you and Clara.

Ben Williams

She crumpled the letter in her hands as sobs racked her body. Rocking back and forth so that the rocker finally butted against the house, she clung to Clara and wailed.

"I'm sorry baby. I'm sorry baby. I'm sorry baby. I sent your Papa away and now it's too late."

Katherine yanked the envelope from beneath her thigh and stood. She pulled open the screen door and somehow managed to close herself and Clara into their room and onto the bed before the dizziness and nausea took over. Katherine leaned over the side of the bed and retched into the bedpan. She stuffed the letter under her pillow just before waves of illness came over her again. Sickness wracked her body until she had nothing left to release. Clara lay kicking and crying beside her on the bed.

When the physical trauma had passed, Katherine pulled her child against her. The child fed while the mother wept. Time apparently had passed as Katherine stirred at the sound of the back door. Lena was home from school.

"Katherine? Where are you?" Lena's voice carried through the walls.

"In here with Clara. I'll be out in a minute."

Katherine sat up and pulled her arm from beneath the sleeping Clara and adjusted her clothes. Her hand grabbed the letter and envelope. She smoothed the lined paper as best she could and placed it back inside the envelope. Rising, she made her way to the storage room and found Ben's trunk. In haste she struggled to open the lid. When she did, she stuffed the letter at the very bottom."

Backtracking, she recalled the full bedpan.

"Lena," she spoke loudly, "I'm going to the outhouse. You listen for Clara."

"I will."

Returning from that chore, she pinned her hair bun back in place, and splashed water from her bowl onto her face. She could hear Lena piddling in the kitchen. Katherine was determined to meet her with every bit of emotional pain tucked deep inside her soul. The death of her marriage was her fault, and she determined that no one would think otherwise, for no one else knew she had asked him back. Let them think she never would. Ben's rejection would be her burden alone to bear.

Be that pride or penance, she knew not.

Chapter 11

September-November 1920 | Cottonline Hospital—
Texarkana, Arkansas

No doubt, one set of footsteps echoing toward Ben's room was masculine and accompanied a deep baritone voice. The steps and voice of the other person were familiar and belonged to Coreen. Ben stilled his heart and suppressed the harebrained hope that the escorted guest was Katherine. No need to worry if the letter he'd written at breakfast, his last letter to his wife, had been mailed.

What man would care to visit him? The reverend had just left. A railroad representative? He dreaded that thought. Wendell? The possibility made him smile. Perhaps Katherine had indeed shared the news of his accident with their Pastor and friend and he'd come to see him. No, for Wendell to travel hundreds of miles from his home and his flock for one injured sheep seemed impractical even to the sheep himself.

His speculation gave way to surprise as the figure stepped through the doorway. Anticipation and Disappointment collided. Excitement stepped over them.

"Henry!" Ben slapped his good arm against the mattress. "Buddy, it's good to see you!" A broad smile spread on the young man's face. His wide stride had him at the bed in two steps with his hand extended toward Ben.

"Good to see you, Ben!" Henry had a firm grasp on him as he vigorously shook Ben's hand, apparently not giving one thought to whether that arm was injured or not. Ben wouldn't have cared if it were injured and throbbing with the handshake. After all, Henry was here to see him.

"I can't believe you're here!"

"And how! I can hardly believe it myself. Quite a story." Ben felt Henry release his hand before he sat down on the white metal chair next to the bed."

"Well," Coreen interjected, "I'll leave you two alone to spill your stories. Nice to meet you, Henry."

"Thank you, ma'am. Mind if I stay a while?"

"Stay as long as you can put up with him." The three of them laughed and the nurse left the room.

"She seems swell." Henry nodded toward the hallway as Coreen strode away.

"I reckon she's a good nurse. I been knocked out most of my time here, though. Don't get all goofy over her. She's married." Ben winked at Henry. The young man was dressed in a suit and smelled like bay rum spice. "You're all dolled up. Did you do that for me or for the nurses you'd see?" Ben chuckled, but he saw Henry blush. "Seriously, you look dapper."

"I been traveling."

"Traveling?"

"That's the story I was talking about, but first," Ben saw Henry's face grow taut, "I got to know how you're doing. The newspaper reports said the wreck was a head-on collision."

"Yeah. I reckon the switch wasn't made. I tell ya, there was no avoiding the collision. I got thrown into the firebox and then onto the ground." He shifted slightly, and the bed creaked. Henry leaned forward in his seat. "Broken leg, burns, cuts, to name a few things. The last couple of months are a blur 'cause I been sedated. Doctor said my insides are about healed, and I start learning to use my leg again tomorrow." He felt a tightening in his chest when Henry shook his head and slowly sighed.

"I hear you're lucky to be alive. That's about all the nurse would tell me."

"So they tell me. Got my soul ready for eternity, just in the nick of time." Ben grinned. "But, I ain't over my surprise at your being here. What's the scoop?" He reached over and patted Henry on the knee. The contact was comforting, but also confirming. His young friend was not the result of a muddled brain.

"Well, you remember I told you I's gonna go check on a rail job. I did. Got hired immediately."

"What job?" Ben felt a knot in his stomach at the thought of Henry being a fireman.

"Now, don't you laugh, but I work passenger trains. I'm a porter." Ben saw Henry's face turn beet red again. The young man had no idea how relieved Ben felt over the fairly safe job.

"That's a swell job. How'd you land it?"

"On account of my looks." Henry's laugh soothed Ben as it swirled around the room and filled the vacuous air.

"You just passing through here?"

"Partly. I'm gonna be here until lunch tomorrow visiting you, then I'm on my way to Commerce, Texas. Gonna be working out of that station." Henry's straight and unusually white teeth shown through his smile.

For a moment in time, Ben forgot about his pains. Grinning, he sat up in the bed. "Commerce!" He grimaced as the pain set in.

"Dandy, huh? Your old town, right?"

"Yeah. So, you're done with St. Louis?"

"Yeah."

"Miss Tweed still there?"

"As busy as ever."

"Where you gonna live in Commerce?"

"I reckon a boarding house."

"Then I reckon you need to look up the Cramers who run the boarding house where I used to live. Fine folks. Kinda like family to me. Of course, I'm ashamed to say they haven't heard from me since I moved to St. Louis."

"I'll get their address or telephone number from you."

"Telephone?" He chuckled. "I suppose they could have one, but all I got is an address."

Although Ben felt at ease with Henry and hadn't enjoyed a person's company this much since he'd spent time with Katherine or Wendell, he'd been holding back his sadness and the effort was wearing him out. His friend wheeled him to the dining hall for lunch. Over a bowl of chicken soup, Ben surrendered to his despair.

"My wife still doesn't want me."

Henry looked up from his plate of fried chicken and stared at him.

"Because you're injured? Or is she still angry?" Henry set his fork on top of his mashed potatoes.

"Yes. Both. Maybe. I don't know."

Henry rubbed his forehead. A moment passed before he spoke.

"Then you're not certain?"

"I had the nurse write her and tell her I could possibly die. Please come, bring the baby, all that." He cleared his throat and blew out a breath. "She never came. She never wrote."

"Oh."

Ben relayed the contents of his recent last letter to Katherine.

Henry shook his head. "Ben, that's sad. You sure you want to give up on her?"

"It is sad. But now, you're here. And, that matters a lot to me."

With lunch behind them, Henry wheeled him out to the porch. Reverend Lilley was seated alone at a table.

"Reverend!"

The man turned in his seat.

"Mr. Williams!"

Henry whistled. "Mr. Williams? You must be mighty important around here, *Ben*."

"Knock it off. Roll me over to his table."

"Yessir."

The reverend stood as Ben and Henry approached. He extended his hand down and gave Ben a gentle handshake.

"Reverend Lilley, I want you to meet my friend Henry. We lived in the same boarding house in St. Louis."

"It's good to meet you, Henry."

"You too. I noticed Ben called you a reverend."

"I'm the hospital chaplain."

"Henry, this morning I was telling Reverend Lilley about my asking forgiveness. He didn't get the whole story though."

"It's a mighty fine story. Ben here needs to tell you sometime, Reverend." Henry shifted his stance as he spoke.

"I'd offer you two men to join me," Reverend Lilley explained, "but I got a staff meeting to attend."

Ben cleared his throat. "Uhm, Reverend, I'd like to read that article now, with Henry here, if you have time to get it for me."

"Alright. I got it in my office. I'll be right back."

As the reverend walked off, the men took two empty seats at the vacated table as Ben explained the letter to Henry.

"He's bringing me an article about the collision. I don't know any details other than what I suspect about the switch. And, uhm, that some of the crew came here. He told my engineer, Leon, who died at the sight. The reverend told me that much when I asked, but he wouldn't tell me anything else."

"Hum. If the article is anything like I read, you may learn more than you want to know right now. Besides, considering what you told me at lunch, you've had enough bad news today."

"Maybe, but I got to know what happened sometime."

"The railroad send you any papers here?"

"Yes, but I haven't seen them yet."

"Did you get your box from Mrs. Martin?"

"Box? No. When Nurse Coreen checked on my mail, she was told I didn't have any personal mail."

Ben ran a hand over his chin.

"Well, all I know is that she decided she better rent out your room after two weeks of your being gone, since she didn't know if when you were coming back or if you were going home to Layton when you healed. "

"Hum." Somehow being uprooted without knowing of it didn't set well with him.

"She boxed up your stuff and sent it to the railroad yard to be mailed to you here."

"You certain of this?"

"Yep. Two weeks after you left. She'd gotten that telegram from the railroad saying you were injured and would be in the hospital here. We'd all been worried, not knowing for sure if you were on that wreck we'd been reading about. Anyway, she had me glance around your room to make sure nothing was overlooked."

"Can't seem to recall what all I left behind. Didn't have much."

"She told me. A suit. Pair of shoes. A few personal articles of clothing. Writing paper. Pencils. A couple of letters. That's what I recall."

"Letters?"

Hope awakened. Had Katherine mailed a letter to that address? No. He recollected now that he'd left the letters from Wendell there. He supposed he'd never see those belongings again. Ben sighed just as he saw Reverend Lilley returning to the table. He handed a folded newspaper to Ben.

"The article is on the first page."

"Thank you."

Ben and Reverend Lilley shook hands.

"Good to meet you, Henry."

"You too, Reverend."

"I'll stop by your room tomorrow afternoon, Ben."

With that, the chaplain turned and walked away.

If Ben had wanted a moment to prepare for the details of the collision he was not afforded it. Unfolding the paper, Ben gasped at the picture of the train wreck on the front page. Laying the paper flat on the table, he ran his fingers over the photograph, trying to determine what part of the train he was looking at, but he couldn't figure it out.

"Have you seen this picture, Henry?"

"No. Our paper just had an article on it."

"It makes me feel sick."

"You sure you want to read this?"

In answer, Ben began reading the article aloud.

"At approximately 2:00 PM on July 5th, a Cottonline locomotive headed to Sherman, Texas and a Southway locomotive traveling to Kansas City collided a mile from the next switch. Investigation revealed that two primary errors made the collision inevitable. The Southway locomotive was ahead of schedule due to traveling a high speed of sixty-five miles per hour when it hit the Cottonline locomotive traveling an acceptable speed of fifty miles per hour. In addition, the tower operator gave a clear signal based on an incorrect entry in the time log. It is reported that the collision was heard almost two miles away. Several local citizens came to the collision sight providing aid and assistance. Railroad cars were hurled sideways creating a mangled heap of splintered wood and twisted metal. Twenty-three people were injured, primarily from being crushed in a sideways car or being thrust from a car in the impact. The injured were taken to the Pine Bluff hospital for treatment. Eight were pronounced dead at the scene. The names of the deceased are listed below. May they rest in peace."

Ben looked at Henry and blew out a long breath before he read the list of victims. Leon Machette was listed fifth, but it was not the only name Ben recognized. His name could have easily been in print, but God had kept him alive. Guilt and Gratitude wrestled inside him, and Ben made a deliberate decision to embrace the gratitude and ignore the guilt. At least at this moment.

"I admit, Henry, this is tough to read. But, I'm glad I did, so I can move on knowing the truth." He folded the paper so the picture was out of sight then set it in an empty chair at the table.

"Level with me. Are you upset and need me to leave?"

"Quit bein' a wet blanket." Ben laughed.

Henry pushed Ben all through the hospital grounds, then back to his room. Supper time seemed to roll around quickly, heedless of the foreboding loneliness ahead for Ben once Henry departed for the night. Swallowing his last bite of baked chicken, Ben looked at the young man across the table from him and felt a tightness in his throat that threatened to send the chicken back up. He forced away the sadness that seemed to be rolling in much like a thunder storm. He refused to waste any of today's companionship on tomorrow's loneliness. The squeak of Henry's chair as he backed away from the table startled Ben. This man, who now felt more like a younger brother, put his hands on Ben's wheelchair, and he felt himself being pulled backward.

"You tired, Ben?"

"A bit. I been sleeping for two months, then here you come and wear out my jaws." Ben laughed at his own sarcasm. "Best day I've had…" He whistled. "Best day in almost a year."

"Better than the day at the St. Louis Cardinals game?"

"Nice as it is, this hospital ain't no Sportsman Park, but the company is better."

Henry didn't reply, and Ben wondered if the young man was embarrassed by the sincere sentiment. He decided to lighten the moment.

"If you can write better than chicken scratching, how about helping me with a letter to the Cramers before I'm tucked in for the night. I'll see if I can talk them in to putting up with you."

"I can write and spell just fine, old man."

The squeak of his wheelchair as Henry rolled him down the tile hallway echoed the melancholy Ben knew was threatening him.

Henry wrote while Ben dictated. He relayed the events of his life since he had left them in Commerce right up to the current day. He suspected they'd be disappointed to know he had never returned home to Layton but hoped the good news of his salvation and the birth of Clara would lend them a slight smile. The irony of Henry's well stated recommendation being written in the young man's own penmanship amused Ben. Henry left for the night, and before turning out his lamp, Ben signed the letter with his own hand.

The darkness that surrounded Ben was more than the absence of daylight. The heaviness returned as he bid this day goodbye. He'd fought off guilt today, but it returned, armed with reinforcements—pity. If guilt over surviving couldn't overtake him, then maybe pity over his physical and emotional challenges could. What strong allies the two emotions made. Staring at the wall, Ben opened up his being and let the physical and emotional pain fill him. He wept—embarrassingly.

The next morning, Coreen escorted Henry back to the room. Ben noticed her pat Henry on the shoulder as she walked out without a word.

"I hear you refused to take breakfast this morning. What's eating you? You sick or somethin'?"

"No appetite."

"Well, Miss Coreen is right. She said you need food, so you can practice walking."

"Think about what you just said. I'm a grown man, and I got to practice walking. And I got to do it without friend or family."

"You goof. I know you're hurting over Katherine and Clara, but be grateful you're breathing!" Henry's eyes seemed to penetrate the patient. "It rattled me yesterday, Ben, to hear how near you were to death. At least alive, you can have some hope for the future. Now, I'm gonna put you in that wheelchair, and we're gonna go eat breakfast in the dining hall. Nurse's orders." Ben saw a tight, forced smile spread across Henry's face. "Lands sake, I'm a growing boy, and I need food!" The smiled reversed itself. Henry leaned over, and Ben felt the young, strong hands clasp his shoulders. "God spared you for a reason, Ben. Don't fret over it. Just get well and figure out what it is."

Ben felt the tension leave his body as appreciation sank in for Henry's concern and wisdom. It had been months since loving concern had been expressed through a spoken word rather than a written word.

They took breakfast on the porch, situated to enjoy the view of the hospital gardens. Henry inhaled his eggs while the patient put up with another bowl of oatmeal. Not long after breakfast, Henry said goodbye, carrying a slip of paper with the Cramer's address and the letter they had written the night before. Although Henry promised to write, Ben knew he would crave flesh and blood visits with those that mattered to him.

Moments later, loneliness paid Ben another visit and stayed until Reverend Lilley made his rounds that afternoon. Ben felt exhausted and sore from his exercises, making him more vulnerable to his emotions.

"Am I disturbing anything, Ben?" The chaplain held a Bible in his hand.

"Just me feeling sorry for myself." Ben sat up, turned gently, and fluffed the pillow behind him.

"Happens to the best of us."

"I think if I were home in Layton, Texas with my family, I would never feel sorry for myself again."

"Tell me about your family and home. I never heard of Layton."

Childhood. Romance. Tragedy. Mistakes. Separation. Letters. Salvation. Hospitalization. Apathy. Ben's story rolled off his tongue while Reverend Lilley listened intently.

"Your feelings are understandable, but don't let them consume you. A broken heart can harden or soften toward God. You're alive for a reason. Let that soften you."

"You're the second person to tell me that today." Ben smiled. "Reckon I ought to listen."

It had been two months since Henry had visited, but not since Ben had heard from him. He sat on the edge of his bed and thumbed through the news of his letters. Henry was settled at the Cramers who sent their love each time he wrote. He was getting assigned to a new route that would bring him through town. Perhaps he could stop by for a visit.

This afternoon, Ben would do his exercises with the nurse. His leg had gotten strong enough for Ben to walk with a cane, but he had come to accept the fact that a limp would accompany him the remainder of his life. His burnt skin was beginning to toughen up, but it was patchy in color. Each time he looked at his arm or torso, he flinched at the deep scars. If she had seen him, would Katherine love him the way he looked now? The question was an exercise of futility. Perhaps she had stopped loving him a year ago when he left Layton.

Nothing seemed to comfort Ben today. The letters he held were just words on paper. The Bible was thin pages filled with tiny print. His prayers were words that wouldn't form thoughts. His heart was a weight inside his body. Today, he missed his Clara, who would be turning one year old. Ben's head throbbed. Resentment toward Katherine pulled at his every fiber, wanting to invade him. He'd not stopped loving her, but the gap between love and hate seemed to be closing, threatening to blend them in his heart.

His leg was stiff from sitting, so Ben pulled himself off the bedside chair. The room was quiet, as he'd only had a roommate for one brief period during his hospital confinement. Ben's emotions fluctuated between wanting to be alone and being lonely when it came to having roommates. He grudgingly grabbed his cane, then hobbled into the hallway. Today, he wanted fresh air, and the outdoor sidewalk around the hospital grounds would suit him fine.

As he made his way around the small exterior garden, Ben's labored breaths displayed themselves as smoky puffs in the cold air. His leg throbbed. He'd pushed himself too far. Glancing around, he saw that he was halfway between a garden bench and the backdoor where he had exited. His body shuttered from the chilly air, seemingly begging to return inside. As he turned to begin his walk back, he saw Reverend Lilley approaching. It was then that Ben felt chagrin over his decision to skip the Sunday chapel service yesterday. He had chosen, instead, to sulk in his room. The minister was within ten feet of him when he called out.

"Ben! Aren't you cold?"

"Yep. Might have misjudged the weather and my strength."

"Best get back inside. I spotted you from my office window." The chaplain moved closer and offered his arm for support. Ben grabbed his tricep and held on, struggling to keep pace.

"Reckon I owe you an apology."

"No, you don't, Ben."

"I skipped the service yesterday."

"I noticed. But that didn't offend me. It concerned me."

"I needed to be there."

"Yes, I reckon I agree with that."

The chaplain stopped and looked Ben in the eyes. "What's on your mind, Ben?"

He turned back and continued to walk, apparently slowing down, because now Ben easily met his stride.

"My daughter is one year old or thereabouts, and I've never met her. It makes me feel painful anger toward my wife." He jeered. "How can I still call her my wife?"

"Because you're still married to her. Because you still love her."

"Right now, I feel like I hate her. How can a man who prays, reads his Bible, and goes to church feel that way toward the woman he loves?"

"Hurt tries to soothe itself, so it lashes out in anger or hate. You got to pray through it."

"Faith is real hard sometimes, Reverend."

"Yes, it is. Faith isn't a feeling. It's a choice."

Ben felt the chaplain stop walking and release his arm from Ben's grasp.

"Ben, why don't you just go home? When you leave here, just travel to Layton and walk up to the front door of your house. Maybe your wife is waiting for you to do that. Maybe she's hoping you love her enough to take that risk."

"No. She doesn't want me."

Reverend Lilley shook his head back and forth, then took hold of Ben's arm once again.

"She's hurt, but that may not mean she doesn't want you deep within her core. I'll be praying she faces that hurt and can move forward. I'll be praying that same thing about you."

The two men made their way back to Ben's room in silence. However, Ben's thoughts weren't silent. They whispered loudly to his heart, telling him that if he did have the courage to go home, he could parent his child. Shamed over that truth, Ben placated himself by putting pencil to paper, knowing that served as a pale shadow of parenting.

November 1920
Texarkana

Dear Clara,

I miss my sweet baby. Though we have never met, you are not a stranger to my heart. I pray that I will not be a stranger to yours, but I worry I will be as you grow and come to understand my absence. I do hope you will come to understand that God is never absent.

I cannot believe that you are one year old. Did Momma and Aunt Lena sing to you? I pray that you are a happy child. Did you get your gifts from me this summer? I hope you enjoy your teddy bear. How I would love to see you in your dress.

Maybe your Momma will tell you that I have been very sick and that is why I have not written you much. I am still in the hospital, but I can walk again.

Your Papa loves you. I hum in my hospital bed sometimes, pretending that I am humming to you.

Please forgive me for not being beside you.

I will always be,
Your Papa

Ben folded the letter and put it in an envelope. The familiar address flowed from his pencil. Lying on his bed, Ben relaxed, and he gave way to the sleep his overworked body needed. Perhaps Katherine would visit him in his dreams.

Chapter 12

December 1920 | Texarkana, Arkansas

Ben sat in the cold, white metal chair staring at his hands. He knew he should be happy. He knew he should be grateful. He was not. He blew out a long breath of air and closed his eyes. The hospital was releasing him—two days before Christmas. This afternoon he would leave the odd comfort of his confines, a displaced man with no home and no person to welcome him.

He glanced at the bed. His travel bag was packed tight with letters, documents, Sammy's rabbit foot, his harmonica, Katherine's butterfly clip, his Bible, and the few personal items he'd obtained during his stay. The railroad planned to make him a switch operator, based out of St. Louis. Other than a fireman, the last job Ben wanted was to operate the switch. He was an imperfect man and didn't want to risk making a mistake that would cause innocent people to suffer like he had—or worse. He often thought about the employee who had neglected to operate the switch the day of his accident. Ben reckoned he carried a heavy burden.

His new work was to begin the evening of December 25th. The line had given him time to travel back to St. Louis and a day to celebrate Christmas—alone. Last Christmas, Ben had been away from his family a little over a month. He had spent the day locked in his room in Flaydada, masking his grim emotions as physical illness, while the few boarding house residents there had dinner and exchanged token gifts. He had dreamt of snuggling his newborn, while his Katherine decorated the tree with ribbons, and the aroma of Lena's baking filled the house. This Christmas would be no better. His plight made his body ache.

Dismay at returning to St. Louis, indeed, at his entire lack of a genuine home, had surfaced each time he thought of telephoning Mrs. Martin to see if she had a room to rent. At last, yesterday he forced himself to make the inquiry, and as he suspected, she had no rooms. The conversation had drained his emotions but ended hospitably. Yes, he was saddened that he would not be returning to home to Layton. No, he didn't know when his family would join him in St. Louis. Yes, he understood she had a business to run and had rented his room. No, he had never received the box of his belongings she'd sent to the railroad office. Yes, he accepted her apology for that. No, it was not her fault. Yes, he could buy another suit and some shoes. Yes, he regretted the loss of the letters that were in the box, but it was all fine. Yes, he knew that Henry had moved away. Thank you, he'd be much obliged to freshen up and have a bite of supper at the boarding house before he left for his first route. And yes, he would contact the deacon at her church whose aunt ran a boarding house only three miles away.

A quiet knock on the hospital room door startled him, and Ben looked up to a welcome sight.

"Reverend Lilley. You here to see me off?" Over the last several weeks, the hospital chaplain had become a companion, a teacher, and a father-like figure. Their kinship resembled what had existed in Layton between Ben and Carl Justice.

"Yes, I am. Where you headed?"

"Supposed to be in St. Louis in two days. Today? I don't know. I reckon a room at a motor lodge."

"St. Louis. I see." Reverend Lilly crossed his arms in front of his chest. Ben was suddenly uncomfortable under the reverend's stare. "Go home, Ben."

"No." Ben's stomach threatened to empty itself.

The reverend rubbed his hand over his jaw. "You want to go back to St. Louis?"

"No."

"Go home."

"No! Reverend, I can't go back where I'm unwanted. I owe her that respect."

"What do you owe your daughter?"

"Provision."

"That's a sorry answer, Ben."

Sadness seemed to overtake the chaplain's face. His eyes moistened. His lips turned down. His forehead wrinkled. Ben despised the thought that he was disappointing someone he admired, not to mention himself. *Again.*

"You going back to being a fireman?"

"No, a switch operator. How ironic is that?"

"Do you want to do that job?"

"No, but I got to work, and that's what the Cottonline offered me."

The reverend waited a moment before responding. "Come home with me. At least until it's time for you to take off."

"Thank you, but, I can't impose on your family for the holidays."

"You won't."

"You certain?"

"Sadly, yes. I live alone."

The revelation shocked Ben, then shamed him. He'd assumed the reverend had a fine helpmate, children, and perhaps grandchildren. He'd never asked.

"I didn't know."

"You didn't ask." The reverend's smile relieved Ben. "My wife passed away eight years ago. Our only son and his wife are missionaries in India. I've never met my six-year-old granddaughter."

"India? That's a far piece from Texarkana. Alright, I'll come. You plan on having cranberries with your Christmas dinner?" Ben stood as he spoke, laughed, and patted the good man on the shoulder.

"I reckon I'll have whatever it is they serve here. You and I will be spreading good cheer to the patients with gifts of fruit for those that can tolerate it and a reading of the Christmas story and carol singing in the chapel." The chaplain mockingly patted Ben's back.

Ben felt his face turn red. "Do I got to sing to patients?"

"How about blowing on that harmonica you're so fond of? You can leave the singing to the nurses and orderlies who volunteered. When you're released, just head to my office."

"Reverend?" Ben searched his mind for words. "Thank you." The overused expression would have to suffice.

Once he had been released, Ben made his way to Reverend Lilley's familiar office. An odd, but pleasant scent always greeted Ben when he stepped into the small square space. He breathed it in, reckoning it was after shave, coffee, books, and a hint of antiseptic. Ben grinned, whatever the mixture, he associated the smell with heaven. He knew Reverend Lilley was an imperfect human being, but in the halls of this hospital where so many suffered, his aura was that of God's messenger.

Light peeked through the edges of the shades drawn over the two large windows facing the garden area of the hospital. A desk lamp sent a glow on the right side of the office where an entire wall was covered in heavily laden bookshelves. The reverend was huddled over a book on his desk, apparently deep in thought. Ben cleared his throat.

"Ah! Ben, I see you been released. Come on in and have a seat in that chair you favor."

Ben moved to the brown velvet chair, whose cushion was worn, no doubt from countless others suffering in soul and body. He set his bag on the floor.

"I feel like a man without a home." *Again.*

The reverend cleared his throat, closed the book he was reading, and Ben felt the kind eyes lock on his brown ones.

"Ben, I spoke to someone on your behalf. Coreen's husband told her there was a slot in the business office for someone to file records, match invoices with order requests, and keep ledgers on the outgoing patient records. She mentioned it to me in passing, but I made an inquiry. If you're interested, the manager is expecting you to come by this afternoon."

Ben leaned forward in the chair and rested his forearms on his thighs. The care humbled him. He focused on the wooden floor.

"I don't know what to say."

"You could say, 'thanks, but no thanks,' I'm gonna go home, face my wife, and try to get back my family."

"I reckon you don't know how it feels to be unwanted."

Ben felt slightly ashamed of his retort when he saw the reverend grimace and bite down on his lip. Had he been rejected by someone he loved? Ben truly had no idea.

"I don't think you're unwanted. But, I do think you're scared."

Ben looked up and faced this father-like figure, who apparently did not *feel* unwanted.

"I'm unforgiven, and, yes that scares me. But I also don't want to make things harder on Katherine than I already have."

"That's another poor excuse, son, for giving up on reconciliation. God can work on her heart and yours too. I think you are wrong to stay away, and I suspect God has told you the same thing."

The reverend came to the front of the desk and leaned against it.

"However, I suspect you don't want to go back to St. Louis either, and I rather like your company, not to mention I want to keep working on that stubbornness of yours—fair warning—so, I hope the job here works out."

Two hours later, Ben found himself sitting in the business office, employed as Sr. Records Clerk for the Cottonline Hospital. The dread of becoming a switch operator slid off his shoulders, down his back, and disappeared.

"Thank you, Mr. Miles. I'll see you here first thing in the morning." The elderly, gray-haired man extended his hand and the two shook hands.

Ben walked out of the business manager's office, turned toward the exit, and spotted Coreen standing at a desk. He walked that direction and stood at the opposite end from her. Before speaking, he nodded to the man seated at the desk. He did not want to come across as impertinent.

"Pardon me, Nurse Coreen, I want to thank you for mentioning the clerk opening to Reverend Lilley. I start the job tomorrow. Mr. Miles isn't even waiting until after Christmas to get me started."

Coreen spread her generous smile. "How wonderful, Ben. I want you to meet my husband, Cyrus."

A tall, slender young man wearing fashionable clothes and spectacles stood from the desk chair and extended his hand to Ben.

"Ben Williams, I presume. It's nice to meet you. My wife has kept me aware of your recovery. Cooperative patients make for more pleasant supper conversation. Not that she revealed anything confidential, mind you. Just an overall appreciation for your hard work as a recovering patient." He smiled, a generous look like that of his wife.

Ben found his disclaimer humorous and very tell-tell of his profession that attended to small details and facts.

"Your wife is an excellent nurse in my opinion."

"I agree. I look forward to working in the same office with you. But," he came around the side of the desk and placed Coreen's hand through his arm, "for now, I better punch that time clock and take my lovely wife out to dinner."

"Thank you. Both."

The next morning, Ben lathered his face, held a cold razor, and stood at the sink in the reverend's small quarters provided by the railroad. He nicked himself. "Blast it!"

Clean shaven and still bleeding, he left the bathroom and made his way to the only other room in the reverend's home. The front room served as a sitting area and small kitchen. Electricity afforded him a small stove and icebox, but the reverend took most of his meals at the hospital. Ben joined him at the kitchen table that sat unevenly. He sipped his coffee in between straightening his tie and making sure the table didn't rock. Today he would begin his job at the hospital.

He supposed he had his record keeping and supervisor experience with Mason Forder at the mill to thank for obtaining his new position. He also had another home address, but the only place he'd call home was where Katherine and Clara lived. The two-room furnished apartment he'd rent next to the reverend's abode would house his belongings, but never his heart.

Christmas Day came, and the agenda was much like the reverend indicated it would be. Ben rubbed his injured arm. Both it and his leg were becoming stiff from carrying fruit, holding his harmonica to his mouth, and walking the hospital halls. He was satisfied that the ache was worth it. Visiting the patients kept his mind away from Layton and focused him on others who were away from their families at Christmas.

"Ben, we have one more room to visit before the chapel service. You holding up alright?"

"You betcha'."

The reverend pushed open the door of Room 125.

"Merry Christmas!" Ben sauntered into the room, then froze in his steps. Before him on the bed, lay a body so disfigured, Ben had to swallow to keep his Christmas dinner in place.

Reverend Lilley spoke up. "Ben, this here's Oliver. He arrived a week ago. He was a fireman too, out of Tyler. The boiler exploded. Fortunately, they were in the yard and injury numbers were low, but those who were near the explosion were burnt something terrible. Oliver, I reckon Ben here can relate to your pain, somewhat."

Ben mumbled, "Somewhat." He cleared his throat. "Enough to know that you are in agony." The young man blinked.

"Pardon me, but I need to give Oliver his next round of medication, Chaplain." The tiny, pale-skinned nurse smiled. Ben had been so taken aback by the sight of Oliver's burnt body that he hadn't noticed the nurse standing nearby. Reverend Lilley smiled back, offered up a prayer, and the two of them left the room and headed toward the Chapel. Ben could only assume that Oliver would not be joining them. His reckoned his body couldn't be moved.

The reverend's words broke into Ben's thoughts.

"His parents live in Louisville. The momma refuses to ride a train or see her son in this condition. The father arrived end of last week but had to travel back yesterday."

"That explains why he is alone today, but how about so many of the others?"

"You know why, if you think on it. Many of them come from families who can't leave their jobs to come be by their side. Some can't afford the travel. There's a lot of lonely people in these halls, Ben."

Three days after Christmas, Ben moved into his own furnished residence. The reverend had been gracious, but Ben knew both men needed privacy. Completely alone in his apartment—no fellow borders, no nurses, no patients, no friends, and no family coming or going from his place—Ben felt himself at odds with the solitude. Would he begin spending his evening hours in thought and silence? His apartment was spacious for one person, intensifying its emptiness. He pulled out his Bible and read aloud where he had left off yesterday, then talked to God as though he were physically sitting in the room. He had to laugh at himself, for surely, he'd sound insane should anyone overhear him. His conversation with God behind him, Ben retrieved a pencil and paper from his bag and wrote a letter he had no intention of mailing.

December 1920
Texarkana, Arkansas

My Dear Wife,

I have been released from the hospital. I walk with a slight limp and need a cane when I tire. My outward scars are healed as best they can. My inside scars won't heal until we are back together. I have taken a job in the business office of the railroad hospital. I am happy to no longer travel from town to town. The pay is the same as my fireman job. I have a small place that you and Clara can share with me. It needs a woman's touch—your touch. We could spend our days together, as a family should be. I could even make room for Lena, if only you will come to me, my darling Butterfly. The apartment has electricity and running water and a small electric stove. I must learn to use it. You and Lena would laugh at my efforts, I am certain.

If you will not come to me, then perhaps I should pick up my things and make my way to your front door, despite your silent protest. But I will not, for you told me to never come back. I must be a coward. I tire of my own pleading.

My darling, what else must I say or do to get you to take me back. Let me live with you. Let me live with my daughter.

I am as ever, your loving husband,
Ben

Ben shook out his arm. By the time he had stopped writing, three letters were piled on his bed—only two would be mailed. Henry would read of his new job. Clara would probably never know of his wish to spend Christmas and New Year's Day with her. Katherine's letter would be bundled with others he'd written her since the day he'd declared to write her no more.

Ben thought he heard the floor creak and looked to see who was walking across it, after all, he was alone. Sadness took heavy steps toward him. He spoke to his emotions who seemed to have breath and body of their own. "Leave." The irony that Sadness could have spoken that same word to him muddled his brain. However, Ben knew that his own choice would force him to welcome in 1921 alone in a town of thousands.

As life would have it, four months later, on an ordinary evening in May, Ben was partaking in a bologna sandwich. He'd stopped at the Cane Grocer on his way home to appease his unsophisticated taste buds and purchased Bologna, Swiss cheese, and Fig Newtons. A heavy knock drew him to his door. After sweeping his teeth with his tongue, he yelled out. "Coming." The room had been so quiet, that hearing his own voice startled him. With a turn of the knob, the lock clicked open and he drew the door toward him revealing his guest. Reverend Lilley stood before him, pale and unkempt making him a familiar stranger. Ben's hands felt clammy, and he instinctively knew the chaplain was there to bear bad news.

"Here, come in. Sit." Ben pulled his friend inside the doorway. "Are you sick?"

"I got a telegram."

"With bad news?"

"My son and his wife died."

The news took away Ben's breath. "I'm sorry. Do you know why?"

"Malaria. Virginia, my granddaughter, was spared somehow. A missionary nurse is traveling home with her, so she can live with her other grandparents."

"Reverend."

"It's Harold. Call me Harold." A cold hand came to rest on Ben's knee.

Grief needed no formalities.

"Harold, are her other grandparents here in Texarkana?"

"Pine Bluff. I'll be moving there. She's all I got left, and I want to know her."

"Of course. Yes, you should move."

Do as I say, not as I do. Ben knew he was a hypocrite.

A month later the wise man moved, and once again, Ben found himself separated from someone he cared about. Reverend Harold Lilley had done what Ben couldn't. He'd picked up his life and gone to be with the little girl he loved and wanted to know.

Part Two
1924

Chapter 13

1924 | Layton, Texas

Butterflies. Their delicate wings always seemed to flit with new life and promise of joy. But Katherine knew. She knew their carefree flight would be short-lived. Despite herself, she was mesmerized by them and the ethereal picture they painted of life. *Was Ben so foolish to still think their promises true?* Five years had trudged by in mindless routine since he had left and then refused her offer to return. Katherine's only joy had come from her daughter.

Seated between her and Lena on the church pew, Clara was resting her head on Katherine's arm. She looked down at the book in her child's lap and smiled. The girl's slender fingers were rubbing the picture on the page—a red, pink, and yellow butterfly, drawn by Lena's hand. Beautiful four-year-old Clara had been captivated by the small creatures from the first time she'd noticed them dance in the sky. The small sketchbook with a brown cover had been a gift from Lena who would draw a butterfly in whatever colors her niece fancied at that moment. It had become a treasure to the child who reverently named it her butterfly book.

With her daughter seated next to her on the hard, wooden pew, Katherine's own two hands were occupied as she fanned herself and wiped the sweat from her forehead. Her mind was occupied too, but not with the sermon. Even though Pastor Carlson and Amy were dear friends, that friendship wasn't enough to keep her focused on his sermon today. Her mind was replaying this morning and yesterday's argument between she and her sister.

The October Saturday afternoon had been unusually warm, causing a headache to tease Katherine. With Lena working at the Justice Store Diner and Joe making a delivery of two rockers to nearby Nelson, she lay down on her bed with a cold cloth to her forehead. The gentle snore coming from Clara's small bedroom assured Katherine that her daughter was napping. After loosening the tight bun in her russet hair, she closed her eyes to rest, but the simple pleasure eluded her.

Katherine shifted on the bed, and her eyes roamed her surroundings. She enjoyed the large room containing her bed, dresser, trunk, two rockers, and a door that separated her space from the rest of the house. Within the area, a twelve-by-twelve side room with a door held a small bed, table, and trunk for Clara. Another small side room with a door had become a storage area. She sighed. One day, Joe should put doors between the rest of the interior rooms in the house. Privacy is a nice thing.

Katherine removed the slightly damp cloth pressed against her forehead and placed it on the bedspread then got up. Her heart beat quickly as she wandered to the closed door of the storage room and grasped the tarnished handle. With a turn and a tug, the door opened. Katherine sneezed. Dust tickled her nose when she inhaled the room's musty scent. Her eye caught a skitter across the floor. A mouse. They seemed to frequent this space. She'd need a trap. Traipsing her way around the items shoved in disarray, she ran her hand along the baby cradle. Next she pushed aside a box marked "trains" and felt her chest tighten. *Sammy*. Katherine knelt in front of a green trunk. Its metal had rusted, and the leather strap handles on each side had been nibbled years before by the mice. She lifted the lid, causing the hinges to squeak. Katherine sighed and covered her cheeks with her hands. She'd become adept at this form of emotional self-torture.

She lifted a man's shirt and brought it to her nose. No hint of Ben lingered; only the musty scent of neglect remained. Reverently she placed the shirt back in the trunk and then rummaged through other articles of clothing until she found what she was looking for—the letters she'd received from him, including the one that had broken her heart—his last letter.

She began to pull a letter from the envelope but was distracted by a sound. Lena! Katherine realized her sister was home early from her shift and entering the kitchen from the back porch. She would only be feet away from the storage room. Katherine didn't want to be discovered pining over Ben. She stuffed the letter back into the envelope and secured it with the others in the bundle. Panicked, she tossed the batch of letters into the trunk where they landed on another stack of envelopes. These were addressed to Clara Williams in the familiar, neat, heavy-handed penmanship that slanted to the right. Although Ben had stopped writing Katherine, he faithfully mailed a letter to Clara on her birthday, at Christmas, and once or twice more a year. Not one of the letters was opened. Katherine could not bear to read the words a Papa had written to the daughter he'd never met.

She slammed the trunk lid shut and caught her finger. "Blast it!" Instinctively she raised the lid to free her finger and noticed a bleeding cut. The trunk lay open.

"Katherine, what was that noise?" She could tell by the plodding steps that a weary Lena had entered the bedroom.

"I saw a mouse in here, and I was startled." Misleading truths.

"Why were you in here?" The lanky eighteen-year-old stood in the doorway with her hands on her hips. Katherine noticed shadows under her eyes and heard a gentle rattle as Lena breathed. Her asthma was acting up.

"Just thought I'd glance around. It's been awhile since we cleaned in here." Misleading others had become easy for Katherine. After all, she misled her daughter every time she asked about her father. She misled folks by denying that she'd ever accept Ben if he returned. The cut on the finger began to sting, and without thinking, Katherine brought her finger to her lip and blew on the cut.

"You're bleeding."

Katherine's stomach knotted when Lena peered past her at the open trunk, her brow wrinkling.

"Were you looking in Ben's trunk?"

Lena's raised eyebrows and slightly open lips appeared more hopeful than accusatory, but she wanted no part of her sister's fairy tale mindset about a reunion with Ben. Lena didn't know that those dreams had been shattered for good. However, Katherine couldn't deny that the trunk lay wide open. Katherine's hands and feet stilled and betrayed her inclination to lie and slam the trunk closed. Lena meandered her way to the trunk and pulled out the stack of unopened letters. Katherine couldn't stop her sister's movement. Maybe in the recesses of her heart, she didn't want to stop Lena from looking in the trunk. Maybe she wanted to talk about him.

Katherine observed Lena bend over the trunk and reverently lift the pile of unopened letters addressed to Clara. Lena knew they existed, but Joe did not. At Katherine's request, Mrs. Justice held Ben's letters at the post office to hand the ladies personally rather than putting them in the mail slot for Joe to see. Always Ben's advocate, Lena took ample opportunities to challenge Katherine on her stance against forgiveness and restoration. Of course, Lena didn't know that Katherine had asked him to return nor that Ben had refused to come. That painful secret was hers alone, and she'd say whatever was necessary to keep it covered.

Lena sounded disappointed and slightly angry when she turned to Katherine and spoke.

"I don't know why you keep reading the old letters he's written you and leave Clara's unopened."

Katherine opened her mouth to speak justification for her thoughts, but Lena kept talking.

"One day you'll have to tell her, Katherine. You're being unreasonable."

"All Clara needs to know is what I've told her—she doesn't have a Papa. That is better than knowing he exists but isn't here."

Justification.

"That's absurd! One day she'll understand that she wouldn't exist without a father. She'll be bitter toward you for keeping him from her. Of course, you know all about bitterness, don't you! So willing to share it with your daughter."

"I'm not bitter." A lie. She *was* bitter.

"You're holding on to his mistake."

No, I'm holding on to his refusal to return.

"You're only twenty-four years old and drying up inside—cold and bitter. No freshness can seep through the wall you've built around yourself. You wear your bitterness like a crown. Your taut hair bun, your pursed lips, your jutted chin. Your guarded spirit."

Her sister's voice lowered to a whisper.

"I miss the way you were with him around."

"Enough, Lena! It's not your business."

"You made it my business when you forbid me to answer Clara's questions about her father. Katherine, not only will she realize the truth one day, but there's a little boy's grave in our yard. She'll discover it. You best be ready to answer questions about that!"

Lena tossed the letters back in to the trunk, slammed the lid, and huffed past her. Her sister's quick motion startled Katherine from where she stood frozen in place. She and Lena spoke only what was necessary between them the rest of the night.

Katherine had awakened this morning when the first hint of light broke through the window. She rose and put on her robe and headed to the kitchen to get the coffee brewing.

"Morning."

Katherine startled at the raspy voice, then her eyes focused on the figure hunched over the kitchen table.

"Lena, you already awake?" Katherine tightened the knot on her robe before pulling the coffee tin from the shelf.

"Been awake. Had a headache. I took some headache powder."

Katherine left the coffee canister on the cabinet and headed to the table. She sat next to Lena, their shoulders touching, then took her sister into an embrace.

"I am sorry about yesterday. I know you care about me and Clara, and I understand why you said what you did."

Lena's arms came around her. "I'm sorry too. You're right. I just want you to be happy, Katherine. And Clara too."

Lena sniffled, and Katherine released the embrace.

"And I love you for feeling that way. Coffee?"

Lena pulled a handkerchief out of the pocket of her robe and wiped her nose.

"Yes."

"Amen." The congregation's response to Pastor Carlson startled Katherine back to the present. The small, familiar crowd began to dismiss and move from the pews. Clara's tug on Katherine's sleeve made her bend her head and face her daughter eye to eye.

"Momma, can I play with Maggie and Mary while you talk to grown-ups?" The child's mouth was spread in a wide grin. Her eyes twinkled with anticipation. Maggie's mother, Amy Carlson, stood by a pew in front of them and nodded her approval to Katherine. Clara handed her book to Katherine who watched as the two little girls joined hands and skipped over to where Mary Forder stood with her parents. Amy and Katherine chuckled as all three girls dodged adult legs in the center aisle, smiled at Pastor Carlson as he stood greeting his congregants filing out, and disappeared through the front doors.

"Katherine and Lena, I have to tell you something." Amy's face turned a shade of pink as she spoke. With Amy's two other little ones demanding her attention, Katherine knew the conversation would be short and sweet.

"Did you two ladies notice the auto parked at the parsonage when you rode in this morning."

"No." Katherine looked to Lena as she spoke. Lena shrugged her shoulders and nodded no.

"Well, my wealthy brother in Dallas bought us an auto!"

Katherine grabbed Amy's arm and squeezed it as she and Lena gasped at the same time.

"He said it's to help Wendell better access his people when he was needed. He's gonna send us money each month to pay for gasoline."

"Are you gonna learn to drive?" Lena clasped her hands together as she asked the question.

"Of course! And, I'll drive the three of us all the way to Greenville to shop in that new dress store called Harrisons."

The three of them giggled.

"You mean, window shop." Katherine chuckled.

"We can try on the store-made dresses and pretend we're gonna buy one," Lena interjected.

"I'd just as soon stay put. Those autos kind of scare me."

She noticed Lena roll her eyes.

"Well, Amy, ignore Katherine. I'm up for an adventure anytime."

Amy's two-year-old began to cry, so Lena and Katherine bid their friend good-bye. After a quick hello to Abigail Forder, the wealthiest woman in the county and the most unlikely friend Katherine had, the sisters headed toward the cart, calling for Clara to join them. With the three of them crammed onto the cart seat, Katherine jerked the reigns and the mule Gitter started toward home.

"Momma, Maggie sits in church and smiles at her Papa the whole time he's hollering about God. I guess she likes looking at her Papa."

"I suppose you're right, Clara."

"I would like a Papa who's a preacher."

Katherine's heart skipped a beat at the same time she felt Lena's imploring stare at her. As Katherine hoped, Clara kept on chatting, leaving no room for a response from her sister.

"Mary Forder's Papa looks real old and so does Mrs. Abigail. You know her brother is a grown up, but he still plays with her sometimes. I would like an old Papa."

Clara sighed. "Aunt Lena, would you want an old or new papa?"

From the corner of her eye, Katherine saw Lena smirk at her and then lean down and smile at Clara. "I suppose I wouldn't care if my papa was young or old."

"Me too," Clara said with a sigh. "Momma, I think children are supposed to have Papas, unless they're in heaven. Where is mine?"

"Clara, don't you worry about having a Papa. You, me, Aunt Lena, and Uncle Joe are a family."

"I don't want an uncle. I want a Papa to take care of me."

Katherine continued to feel Lena's stare, causing a chill to form goosebumps on her arms.

"Me and Aunt Lena take care of you. We love you very much."

"Is my Papa in heaven?"

"No."

Clara whispered, "I want a Papa."

Katherine freed a hand from the reins and pulled Clara to her.

"I know you do sweet girl."

Silence settled between the three of them, interrupted only by the sniffles of a distraught daughter.

Arriving home, Katherine felt tense as she put away the cart. Lena and Clara had gotten off and headed into the house to put lunch on the table. Katherine breathed a sigh of relief that Joe was staying the night with friend forty miles away in Commerce. He was pricing furniture, and no doubt, gambling. Whenever tension between Clara and Katherine arose over "Papa," Joe wore a grin that hinted at his pleasure in Katherine's dilemma.

She found Lena was alone in the kitchen where the heat from the stove and lack of breeze made the air stuffy. Katherine wiped her brow.

"Where's Clara?"

"I told her to change clothes and play instead of helping us in here."

"I suppose playing might help her feel better."

"Katherine, I think you should tell her..."

"Don't say it, Lena. I don't want to argue with you again like we did yesterday."

Her sister hushed.

Katherine lit the gas stove to fry some pork chops and made a mental note to wipe the old grease marks off the walls with soap. Lena placed a pan of biscuits in the oven. Not the best cook, Katherine hoped she didn't burn the meat. Barefoot Clara plodded through the kitchen, wearing some overalls and a yellow shirt, and headed toward the back porch.

"Can I go see my sunflowers, Momma?"

The question was simple. The trepidation that crept through Katherine was not. *Why?* She shrugged her shoulders. *A ridiculous feeling*. She tugged at her ear—an old habit she'd finally surrendered, sneaking back up on her. She'd forced herself to stop the instinctive tug because each time she did, she remembered Ben's reactive grin and the feel of his calloused fingers gently pulling her fingers away from her ear.

She wiped her hands on the dingy dishrag. "Don't be long, Clara. And don't wander over to the trees where the weeds are thick and high." Katherine shifted her attention back to the iron skillet to turn the chops. Lena pulled the plates from the cabinet.

The clock in the front room chimed one time. If Clara didn't return soon, she'd go to the door and call her back in.

As though the yesterday's argument with Lena was a warning, Katherine turned toward the dragging squeak of the back screen door just as Clara returned, clutching a weathered, wooden toy train in her hand. Dried black mud was stuck in its crevices.

Lena gasped and dropped the plate she was holding, and it shattered across the yellowed, scratched linoleum.

"Momma, look what I found by a rock with words on it."

The name escaped before Katherine could hold it back. "Sammy."

Chapter 14

1924 | Layton, Texas

"Who is Sammy?"

Clara's question reverberated in the kitchen as Katherine stood stunned. No words formed into thoughts. Clara seemingly had not noticed the broken plate, for Katherine was uncomfortable under her stare as she obviously awaited an answer. Beside her, Lena moved toward Clara and dropped to her knees in front of the child, reverently reaching for the wooden train.

"Aunt Lena," Clara probed as she instinctively drew the train to her chest, "Is this his toy?"

"Whose?"

"Sammy."

"Yes."

"Who is Sammy?"

"Katherine, tell her."

Anger at Lena rose in Katherine, causing her chest to perspire and her hands to shake. She jerked and pulled herself from her trance. She knew her reply was going to be ridiculous and shallow.

"Clara! You disobeyed me and went into the heavy weeds around the crepe myrtles. You will lose your bed time story because of that."

Something overtook her daughter who was weeks from turning five. Katherine saw her eyes bulge and darken. Whether it was anger, hurt, realization, or determination, she knew not.

Clara pounded her fists on her thighs. "Momma, who is Sammy?" The action was bold and harsh coming from the amiable child.

Lena rose and moved toward Katherine, the broken glass crunching beneath her footsteps. She felt the tips of Lena's toes touch her own. "If you don't answer her, Katherine, then I am going to. It's time."

A gentle weeping floated through the harsh atmosphere. Katherine realized that the instant burst of boldness which had overtaken her daughter must have just as quickly dissolved, leaving Clara to weep like a scared puppy. The large tears rolling down her daughter's cheeks made Katherine's heart pound against her chest.

"I'm scared, Momma. About Sammy. Is he bad?"

Katherine held out her arms and stepped toward Clara, just as the young girl's body slammed into her. She lifted the child in her arms and drew her close.

"Sit here in my lap Clara, and I'll tell you about Sammy."

Katherine lowered herself to the kitchen table bench. She looked up at Lena for reassurance, and her sister nodded yes as she wiped her running nose and sniffled. Katherine watched a tear drip down Lena's chin and absorb into her calico collar before she turned to the stove and relinquished the flame and set the skillet on the back burner. She pulled the biscuits from the oven and they sat neglected on a pan. A body could wait to be fed. It was a heart that needed nourishment right now.

Katherine looked into the eyes of Clara's raised face and rubbed her daughter's hair as she spoke. "Sammy was a little boy whose momma died."

"That's sad, Momma."

"Yes. Sammy was sick. His legs and ears didn't work like they should, so he couldn't walk or hear." She reached and wiped a tear escaping from Clara's eyes, then sucked in a deep breath. "His papa brought him here to live with us. He was four years old."

Four-year-old Sammy. Four-year-old Clara. The living and the dead had collided in time, and Katherine's body felt the impact. Tears rolled down her cheeks. Her chest tightened. Having mothered Clara for the past four years, she realized how short Sammy's life had been.

"Did his papa not want him anymore?"

She rested a finger on her daughter's quivering chin.

"Oh, honey. His papa loved him very, very much. He lived here too." Katherine's mind betrayed her will and nestled into memories. Ben Williams pulling her from the kitchen and into the front room for her first ever dance. He'd smelled so earthy—his natural scent mingling with the spicy hint of aftershave. He'd guided her step by step, giving her a prelude to how he would guide her to love him on their wedding night. Another memory swept in unannounced. Her husband proudly showing her the plans he'd drawn out for the addition to her aged family home; it was to be a personal place for him to dwell with his wife and children inside the walls of the house they shared with her siblings.

Clara's voice brought her back to the real moment. "Sammy's Papa lived at our house?"

"Yes. He worked on the railroad like Uncle Joe used to do."

Katherine felt Clara tense in her arms. "Oh. So he must be like Uncle Joe."

"Not like him at all." The tension she felt in Clara's body and her declaration puzzled Katherine.

"Where did Sammy and his Papa go? I never saw them."

"This is sad for you to hear, Clara. You're so young for such news." Katherine could not hold back a gentle sob. "Sammy died before you were born."

"Oh, Momma. Cause his legs broke?" The child's shoulders shook against Katherine's chest. Katherine looked to Lena who had now sat down beside them. Again, her sister urged her on with a nod.

"He was bit by a rattle snake." Clara's hand brushed against Katherine's chin as the child drew it to her mouth and covered a gasp. "His grave is under the crepe myrtle tree where you found the train—one of his favorite toys."

"Do the words say 'Sammy?'"

"Yes."

Her daughter slid from her lap, holding the train tightly to her chest. She stood facing the back porch.

"I wish Sammy didn't die."

"Me too. I miss him very much."

Lena's voice was soft. "I miss him too. I miss his big 'ol smile."

"So he wasn't sad 'cause he was broken?" The question was directed at Lena, so Katherine kept silent.

"I don't think so. He always seemed happy to me."

In silence, Clara walked to the table and began to roll the train across it. Moments passed. Assuming her daughter's curiosity was satisfied, Katherine blew out a breath and returned to the stove. Much to Katherine's relief, Lena followed her lead and began to work on the biscuits allowing the conversation to subside.

"Where did his papa go?"

Katherine set down the pan she'd just begun to reheat and walked back over to the table and sat down.

"He left after Sammy died and hasn't returned."

"Because he was mad?"

"No, because he was sad."

Clara stopped rolling the train, took it in her hands and began to walk toward the front room.

"I'm gonna sit in the rocker a minute."

Good or bad, Katherine did not try to stop Clara. She'd go to her in a moment. Silence permeated the kitchen. The smell of cooked pork chops combined with the emotion churning in her chest made Katherine nauseous. The absence of sound, save a small child's sniffles drifting in from the front room made her cringe.

"Are you just gonna let her cry, Katherine?" Lena slammed her fist on the counter as she spoke.

"No, I'm going in there."

"You're giving her half the truth. You might as well be lying to her."

You only know half the truth.

"Clara isn't even five years old, Lena! She's not mature enough for the whole truth, even if I were ready to tell her."

She would never be able to tell her daughter the whole secret truth about her Papa.

"She's smart and she's far too old for her age. You're protecting yourself, Katherine. Not her."

Katherine walked away from the kitchen and went to kneel at the rocker where Clara sat. She heard Lena's footsteps behind her.

"Momma?"

The furrowed eyebrows and paleness on Clara's face stunned Katherine, and her hands went clammy. Katherine rose and lifted Clara from the rocker, then sat down and pulled her daughter, still clutching the train, into her lap. Lena knelt at the rocker. Clara looked her Momma in the eyes, causing Katherine to assume that realization had settled into her daughter's mind as though her and Ben's tragic story had been narrated word for word.

"Is Sammy's papa my papa too?"

Lena sobbed. Katherine sighed, then a small groan escaped her. Once again, just like the day Ben walked into her kitchen as a guest, just like the day she met Sammy being carried in his father's arms at the train depot, just like the day she became Katherine Williams, just like the day Sammy died, just like the day a broken Ben walked out the door on her demand, just like the day her precious Clara was born in a veil, and just like the day she'd received his last letter, her life and the lives of those she loved would never be the same.

"Yes."

A death-like chill passed through Katherine.

Clara no longer wept. Instead, she wailed. Katherine held her tightly. Lena reached up and rubbed Clara's head. Moments came and went until the child suddenly pushed Lena's hand away, loosened Katherine's grip, and slid from her mother's lap letting the train drop to the floor.

"I hate him! I hate my Papa!"

"Clara, no, honey…"

"He doesn't want me. 'Cause he would come back home if he liked me."

Katherine shuttered.

Neither lady could react quickly enough to catch Clara as she ran through the kitchen and out the backdoor. The slam jolted Katherine to action. She hurried down the back porch steps and tripped. "Clara! Stop! Wait!" Picking herself up, she took off again, seeing that Clara was running directly to the tree where Sammy was buried. A quick glance told her that Lena was following, but at a slower pace as her breath rattled in her chest.

Katherine dropped to the ground and reached for her daughter who stiffened at her touch. Her crying had turned to snubs that shook her body.

"Clara, come to me."

"I'm with my brother."

Brother. In the span of moments, another family connection had been lost to her daughter.

"It's not safe here. The weeds are high and there could be snakes we don't see."

Clara jumped up with a scream, and Katherine realized the insensitivity of mentioning snakes. She took her daughter into her arms, and Clara grasped her neck to the point of almost cutting off her breath. The snap of a twig let Katherine know that Lena had arrived. Katherine nodded with her head to indicate moving out of the high weeds.

"Is it 'cause I have an angel kiss on my cheek that he don't like me? Uncle Joe says it's ugly."

The remark shook Katherine. *Ugly?* "Honey, your angel kiss is beautiful. It makes you special and lovely."

Katherine felt Clara release her grip and lean back to face her. Tiny hands clasped Katherine's cheeks. The child's eyes lit up as they stared at Katherine's.

"Maybe he really went to heaven and you were scared to tell me. 'Cause people in heaven have to stay there. Right, Momma?"

Katherine found herself at a crossroads between a tainted truth and a bold lie. *Wouldn't a Papa's death be easier to face than a Papa's absence?* The letters Ben had sent to Clara flashed in her mind. She couldn't deny the truth of their existence. He was not dead.

"No."

Sweaty palms pressed against Katherine's cheeks. "Why doesn't he want me?"

"He loves you." If Ben had only sent money, she would view that as simple responsibility. But he sent Clara letters. Although she hadn't read them, she viewed them as evidence of love. She swallowed the ache in her throat. "He wants you." Her tears fell freely. "He just can't live here with us."

"Why?"

"It's a big person reason."

"I hate him."

She felt the little palms pull away from her cheeks. Katherine noticed Clara glance at the ground. The child realized they had moved away from the tall weeds. She began to head back to the grave, but Katherine caught her hand. Clara's silence and cold stare filled the young mother with hurt.

Katherine looked at Lena and felt her eyes pleading with her for help on what to do or say.

"Maybe we could wear some of Joe's work boots and come back here to clear the weeds. Then Clara could visit Sammy."

"Her daughter looked up at her. "Can we do what Aunt Lena said, Momma?"

"Yes. That's a good idea." Katherine smiled.

Resignation toward her married situation and restitution with her daughter would not be simple, even if it came in tiny pieces Katherine put together like a puzzle. "We all could visit him."

"Momma, do you ever feel sad?"

"Yes, Clara. I feel sad sometimes about Sammy and your Papa too."

"If you come here and see Sammy, you might feel happy. I know he's in heaven, but this can be the thinking place about him."

Katherine knelt beside her daughter and scraped Texas dirt from the top of the grave. It was dry in her hands as she let it sift through her fingers. She pulled her daughter to her and kissed her cheek. Katherine's little girl had steadied herself. Although brokenness threatened to diminish her light, Clara's resilience never flickered out.

"You make me happy, Clara. But I promise I'll come visit Sammy."

Katherine, Clara, and Lena stood, and began to make their way back to the kitchen, all three hand in hand.

"Bye, Sammy. We'll come back. Right, Momma?"

"Yes, Clara. We'll come."

A breeze blew through and caught the loose strands of hair around Katherine's face. She glanced over her shoulder and smiled. The crepe myrtles rustled, whispering a welcome back.

Chapter 15

1924 | Texarkana, Texas

Wiping the mirror steamed by hot water, Ben stared at himself. The man looking him in the eyes had aged. His temples were flecked with gray hair, and his eyes were surrounded by wrinkles, proving that loneliness packed more than his thirty-three years into his body. For three years, his life had been caught in a loop of one mundane moment after another. He fought insomnia, he shaved, read the paper, read his Bible, prayed, took a bus to the hospital, did his work, spoke to the burn victims, and returned home, managing to swallow three meals a day. His Sundays afforded him a change in routine as he slipped into worship at the local Baptist church, but he felt out of place socially—living like a reclusive single man, yet he was married with no family to show for it.

He endeavored to find contentment, but it eluded him. Several times, Henry had come through on a stay-over and spent time with Ben, making those days the highlights of his last three years. Having Ben's address for the bank arrangements, Mason had telegrammed sporadically. Each time the telegram shouted the same four words at him. "You belong at home."

With 1924 only four months old, the thought of celebrating holidays and birthdays brought him to the verge of despair. "God, I'm sorry I feel this way. I'm desperate to feel content." But contentment wore no flesh, for all his meaningful relationships dwelt in letters. He had a lifeless, paper marriage, existing on a certificate issued by the state of Texas and the words he penned to Katherine. He had no idea if any words he'd written to Clara had been read. The truth was, his soul was weary. Despite his faithful practice of Bible reading, praying, and church going, he knew there was a part of his heart he tried to hide from God, but Ben was no fool, and he certainly knew that God was not foolish either. That one piece—anger—sucked the life out of all the others. Contentment would never survive the anger. Ignoring his soul's promptings to go home or at least contact Katherine would most likely consume every fiber of his being if he didn't release it.

He slipped his arms into his shirt, buttoned it up, then stuffed his shirttail into his pants. His suit coat was thrown over his chair, just as he'd left it the night before. He grabbed yesterday's mail that he'd tossed onto the chair cushion last night. How weary he'd grown of Farmers Almanacs and other useless mail. He'd been too lonely to open the magazine last night to see what other mail was wrapped inside the banded bundle.

He glanced at his pocket watch. "I'm late."

In haste, he slid the rubber band from the stack, then unfolded the almanac. An envelope fell to the floor. Supposing it to be a letter from Henry, Ben stuffed it in his shirt pocket. He'd read it on the bus, hoping the words would pull him from the black hole his emotions had been pacing around.

Ben sat on the aisle and tried to ignore the body odor from the man sitting next to him. He pulled the envelope from his pocket and gasped. The return address was from Mason Forder in Layton, Texas. *Layton.* Ben ran his hand over the word in longing reverence. A small business card fell into his lap. These were pieces of home to touch and hold. Panic interrupted his moment when he realized a letter from Mason probably bore bad news that shouldn't be expressed in a telegram. Had something happened to Katherine or Clara?

The opening sentence put him at ease.

All is well, so don't be alarmed by my letter. To begin, I will take the liberty to share bits of news you would know if you were here where you belong.

Ben's throat tightened, then line by line he read, letting the words soothe him and pain him simultaneously. He learned that Wendell had become a father for the fourth time. Clara was growing tall and slender like her mother, but her face always resembled Ben. Katherine worked the books for Carl Justice. *Atta girl, Katherine.* Her finances were taken care of. Lena was the crowd favorite during her shifts at the diner. Joe made furniture and skipped town for the weekends whenever he could. *No more railroad for Joe?* Ben should come home.

The bus came to a halt, and the passenger seated next to Ben excused himself and an older woman slipped into the vacant seat. "Morning." Ben took the time to acknowledge her, then turned his eyes back to the last paragraph of the letter. His lonely mind must have misread the words, but a second reading assured him it had not.

"Yes." *The answer to the question is yes.*

"Pardon me?"

"Oh, excuse me. I didn't mean to say that out loud."

"Must be a good letter."

"Yes!"

He read the words one more time, already knowing that life for Ben Williams was on the verge of change.

I have an opening for a manager of the large mill in Commerce. I am willing to talk with you about your skills. You were a dependable office employee for me in Layton years ago. I am inquiring if you would be interested in the job. If so, telephone me. I have enclosed a business card. Ben, what do you say? Are you at least willing to move back to Commerce? If you are not interested in discussing the matter, I can only hope it is because you have finally determined to return to Layton and claim your family.

Ben recalled that Mason Forder was a skilled businessman who wouldn't take matters such as this job lightly. The offer astounded him. Although Ben had always wired his money to Carl, no doubt Mason had connections enough to know that Ben's employer for the last years had been the Cottonline Hospital. Therefore, Mason was likely more aware of Ben's skills, so to speak, than he let on in his letter.

Five years ago, he'd fled Commerce due to memories that haunted him there. Today, Commerce sounded like a shadow of home. Indeed, it would be the closest he'd been to Layton since 1919.

Chapter 16

1924 | Layton, Texas

"Whoa! You knocked the breath out of me!" Lena sucked in a shallow breath. Katherine scurried to Lena, whose wheeze filled the air, and reached down to pull Clara from her sister's stomach. They were covered in dry leaves that Joe had gathered with a rake and forbidden them to disturb. *Good thing he's on an errand.* Perhaps her brother was ignorant to think leaves would be ignored by the three of them as they lingered outside anticipating the seasonal butterfly migration south.

"I'm sorry I jumped on you, Aunt Lena." Clara's apology came between giggles. "I thought you'd catch me."

"Aunt Lena's been playing with us in the cool air too long. We best get her inside and let her suck on a menthol drop and sip coffee." Katherine smiled as Clara reached her hand toward Lena to help pull her from the leaf pile.

"Momma, can we go see Sammy first?"

Katherine saw Lena nod her head yes then turn herself toward the back porch to head inside. She clasped her daughter's hand and let the child lead her to the grave.

Katherine frequently witnessed Clara's emotions bounce back and forth between worship and anger toward the idea of a Papa she didn't know. She would prattle on about how handsome he must be and how much she wanted to show him her toys and butterfly book when he came home someday. In contrast, she would express her anger with words or tears over his not being with them.

Katherine, too, was a contradiction of emotions. Love and anger toward Ben resided in the same heart. She wondered if he walked up to her today, would she hate him or love him?

Mother and daughter knelt by the grave. Clara picked up the train that was carefully cared for these days and told Sammy she wished they could play together. Katherine felt her daughter's tiny, slender fingers, slip into her own, and the two of them rose. The wind blew Clara's hair into her face as she looked up to the sky.

"Momma, it's time for the butterflies to dance, right?"

"Yes, but they may not dance much this year. It's getting late in the season. They usually come before your birthday."

"My birthday is tomorrow. Don't forget!"

"Don't you worry about that. A Momma remembers when her girl turns five." Katherine reached down and pulled Clara to her hip and hugged her tight. *She's getting tall. And looking more and more like her Papa.*

"Do you think Papa remembers I'm turning five?"

"Yes."

"He might come home for my birthday. I bet he has a present for me. He probably thinks I'm special since I'm turning five. Do you think he'll come, Momma?"

Katherine ached as she looked down to Clara staring up at her.

"No, Clara. I don't think your Papa will come home. But I reckon he is thinking about you and is proud you are turning five."

She saw tears gather in her daughter's eyes, then trickle down her cheeks as her face took on an angry look. She picked up Clara and hoisted her on a hip.

"I wish he loved me."

Katherine struggled for words to comfort Clara and determined to speak simple truth over deception.

"I'm sorry he won't be here for your birthday."

Katherine awaited further argument from her daughter, but none came. Momentary silence nestled itself between them until resilient Clara transformed back into the little girl excited to be turning five. Small hands pressed against Katherine's cheeks, and her daughter's toothy grin spread across her face.

"Do *you* have me a present?"

"Hum. I guess you'll have to wait and see." She kissed Clara on the cheek, then tickled her belly. The child wiggled free and skipped toward the house singing, "Happy Birthday to me. Happy Birthday to me…"

Katherine couldn't help but wonder how Clara's small heart had the capacity to hold in such strong, conflicting emotions.

As early afternoon set in, the ladies loaded up the cart and headed to the Justice store. Lena would work the supper shift at the diner, and Katherine had hopes that her package from Commerce had arrived. *Commerce*. Her heart tightened because she would always associate Commerce with Ben. With Clara snuggled between them, Lena guided the cart to the store while Katherine listened to her child debate the flavor of frosting she wanted on the birthday cake Lena had cooked that morning.

The sound of an auto drew Katherine's attention to the store just ahead. Two gasoline pumps stood proudly in front of the building, taking their place in progress amongst the diner and small motor lodge. Layton had hoped to be a main thoroughfare to Dallas, but the road had not yet been declared a state highway like motorist preferred to drive. The town had experienced some growth due to the success of the Forder Sawmill, but it had never reached a population worthy of a main route. Automobiles had become common, but the roads of Layton were still dirt and speckled with carts and wagons. Katherine noticed Mr. Forder's auto parked in front of the store. A wagon loaded with vegetables sat to the left of the front door.

"Pony James is here, delivering his vegetables. His vegetables are my favorite. Oh, and Mr. Forder is here too. There's his auto," Katherine observe aloud.

"I hope Mary's here!" Clara clapped her hands as she spoke.

"I suppose Mr. Forder is working, and Mary is at home playing," Katherine remarked as Lena pulled the cart into the store lot.

The sisters made their way into the store behind Clara who had ran ahead, yanked open the screen, then pushed the wooden door open. Just as Katherine crossed the threshold, Clara's voice sounded in her ears.

"Mr. Forder, where's Mary?"

"Hello, Clara. She's at home." His voice quietened to a loud whisper. "I'm here on boring business."

At this point, Katherine had made her way to the aisle where Mr. Forder stood and could see him squat to Clara's level and pat her shoulder. "What brings you here?"

"Aunt Lena's gotta work. But, guess what. We're getting more butter for my birthday cake frosting."

"Happy Birthday! I bet you're turning five." Clara's head wobbled back and forth enthusiastically. "I'll tell Mary I saw you."

His eyes met Katherine's as he stood up. "Afternoon, Mrs. Katherine. I see the account books are all caught up. Good work. You doing alright?"

Not since this time five years ago.

"Yes. Thank you. Tell Abigail hello for me." He tipped his hat, then headed to the back room, his voice trailing behind him. "I sure will. See you Sunday at church. Can Clara come home with us after church to play with Mary?"

Clara yelped.

"Yes, she can." A warmth came over Katherine as she reflected on what a fine family the Forders were, despite their estranged niece who now lived in Houston with her wealthy husband. Her lips had been the ones Ben kissed. A knot formed in Katherine's stomach. Would she never lose that image she'd painted in her mind?

Katherine shook off the thought then led her daughter to the candy aisle. Clara's cheeks puffed out as she smiled and beheld the sweet treasures. Holding back a laugh, Katherine used her most authoritative voice, "You can pick out one package of Lifesavers. No chocolate since we are having chocolate cake." The child looked at her and nodded her agreement.

Katherine turned to go toward the post office just as a boy rounded the corner of the aisle and acknowledged her with a polite looking expression on his face. He was tall, dark-haired, dressed in overalls, and appeared to be around eleven or twelve years old. He resembled Pony, so he must be a son. She'd never met any of Pony's children since he made deliveries alone. Glancing over her shoulder as she stood at the post office, she saw him engaging with Clara.

Mrs. Justice wasn't working the post office today, and Katherine supposed she was relieved, for she could grab her package from Commerce without conversation and move back to where Clara stood. A new attendant greeted her, and Katherine told him she was expecting a package from Commerce. He quickly located it and handed it to her.

"Ma'am, Mrs. Justice left this envelope for you."

Katherine smiled. "Thank you."

Fumbling with the package she held, Katherine was able to open the envelope and find a smaller envelope inside. It was addressed to Clara Williams in familiar handwriting. Words from a father to his daughter.

Katherine almost lost her footing when the guilt slammed against her. She'd stash the letters with the others. It had been right to ask Ben to come home, but it was wrong to keep his letters from Clara simply because he hadn't returned. The knot tightened in her stomach as she made her way to the aisle where Clara stood. She paused at the conversation she overheard.

"I'm helping my Pa with deliveries today. He's teaching me the job."

"My Papa doesn't do deliveries. I think his work is far away, but one day he might finish it and get to come back home. Maybe even tomorrow since it's my birthday."

Sadness embraced Katherine's ever-present guilt.

"Wallace!"

Katherine looked to see Pony James standing at the other end of the aisle. He noticed her.

"Mrs. Williams, I believe. Good to see you."

"Hello, Mr. James. Hope you brought us some good apples."

"I most certainly did."

The boy had come to stand next to him. "This here's my oldest, Wallace James. He normally stays back and oversees the farm while I deliver, but today he's learning this side of the business." Pony patted his boy on the shoulder.

"Good to meet you, Wallace. You met my Clara?"

"Yessum. I told her happy birthday. I heard her talking about it when y'all came in."

"We best be going about our business, Wallace," Pony James indicated as he pressed a hand on the young boy's shoulder.

Katherine felt Clara clasp her arm as she spoke, "Bye, Wallace."

The man and boy waved and started out the door, talking as they went. Wallace probably spoke more loudly than he realized, because his words reached Katherine's ears. "Pa, she was kissed by an angel, just like baby sister." The statement warmed Katherine.

"He sure is a nice, Momma."

The mother looked at the daughter. "Clara, is your birthday all you talked about?" The child's face became crimson. "I was fussing 'cause I couldn't get a Hershey Bar. He told me I shouldn't fuss like that 'cause I'm almost five."

Katherine chuckled.

"Is that all you talked about?"

"He saw my angel kiss. Momma, he knew what it was."

"I'm glad."

Katherine didn't address what she had overheard Clara say about her Papa. After all, the child had not spoken a lie. She had spoken a wish.

The two of them moved and stood at the diner counter where Lena was busy slicing bread. The aroma made Katherine's stomach growl. Only one customer sat at the counter. Katherine eyed the man for a moment trying to decipher who he was. The bits of egg and toast crumbs on his plate told what he had eaten recently. It dawned on her that the man was Mr. Yost, who had replaced Ben at the sawmill office. Once again, the knot in her stomach tightened when he noticed her.

"Mornin' ma'am. Mrs. Williams, right?"

"Yes, and my daughter, Clara. Good morning."

The man smiled at Clara then pulled a wrapped piece of Mary Jane candy from his overall pocket.

"For your little girl."

Katherine felt Clara lean her head against her elbow—a sure sign that she was feeling shy. Katherine reached and took the candy, then handed it to Clara.

"Thank you."

"Thank you, sir," Clara echoed.

The man turned his attention to the coffee cup sitting next to the plate and took a sip.

"Well, Lena, we're heading back home."

"Bye, Aunt Lena."

"Bye, Clara. Bye Katherine."

"Joe assured me he'd be home from visiting his friends in time to see you back to the house." Katherine raised her eyebrows at Lena.

"He's not too dependable."

Carl Justice slipped behind the counter and was grabbing a muffin.

"I'll make sure Lena arrives safely back at the house if Joe doesn't show." He paused. "or if he shows up drunk."

"Thank you, Carl." Katherine grabbed butter from the nearby cooler, then headed to the register with her package and purchases.

"Momma, what's that box you have?"

Katherine winked at Clara.

"You'll have to wait and find out later."

"I think it's my present." Clara clapped her hands and skipped ahead.

Carl was back at the cash register. "I hear someone has a birthday tomorrow." He looked at Clara as he spoke, then glanced at Katherine before handing Clara a book. Katherine saw Clara's eyes widen and a big smile spread over her chin. "It's *Aesop's Fables*. Your Momma or Aunt Lena can read it to you. Mrs. Justice thought you might like the drawings in the book."

Daughter and mother hugged their dear friend, paid him, then headed out the door. Katherine knew that Carl and Louise Justice were saddened that the marriage had never reconciled and that Clara was not united with her Papa. Indeed, they had mentioned it regularly. I wonder who they fault most? Ben or me?

Just as Clara settled in the cart seat asking to hold the package, a wagon pulled onto the gravel lot. Gabriel Hawkins. Katherine hadn't seen the local animal caregiver since his mother's funeral six months ago. Deformed in the face and socially awkward, the man had become a recluse since her death. He appeared in town about twice a month for supplies and mail or when an animal was ailing. The McGinn family had known Gabriel most of his life. He was the same age as Katherine and had always had an attraction to her. He'd felt awkward around her once she married Ben but had overcome it to befriend Sammy in a most unlikely friendship. He had been present the day of Sammy's fatal accident, and since that day, a tension had always existed between him and Katherine.

As the wagon pulled up alongside their cart, Katherine began to speak, but was interrupted by Clara's exclamation. "A doggy!" Katherine's eyes moved to the object beside Gabriel on the seat, and she gasped. She knew that dog. His name was Pirate and had once belonged to Sammy. The puppy had been a gift from Gabriel, but at Katherine's request, Ben had returned Pirate to him after Sammy died.

Looking at Katherine but directing his words to Clara, he uttered, "His name is Pistol." His enunciation of the name was exaggerated, but the nod of his head affirmed to Katherine that indeed, this was Pirate. As socially awkward as Gabriel was, she appreciated that he was able to control the moment. She sensed Clara moving to leave her seat, no doubt to go over and pet the dog. Katherine stopped her gently with a tug on her arm.

"Can I have a dog for my birthday?"

"Nooooo."

Clara grunted.

With her emotions suddenly taking over her nerves, Katherine felt clammy. Five years without Ben or Sammy in Layton, yet their presence seemed to linger everywhere in town.

"Good to see you, Gabe." She tugged at her ear, then grabbed the reins. "We've got a birthday cake to finish, so we best head out. Again, my condolences about your mother." With a click of Katherine's tongue, Gitter began to pull the cart.

"Yes ma'am. Good to see you. And I'm faring well, I suppose." She saw him get down from his seat.

"Good." Katherine moved on, not looking back. Clara's voice rang out a good-bye to the dog.

"Are you excited to finish helping me with your birthday cake?'

"Yessum. But, I wish Uncle Joe was gonna be gone for my birthday."

Katherine glanced at her.

"Clara, why do say that?"

"I dunno."

"Tell me."

"He says I'm in the way when I stay in his shop if you and Lena are both working. I want to start to go to work with y'all instead."

Katherine pulled the reins and stopped the cart.

"Clara, are you afraid of Uncle Joe?"

"No. I just want to be with you and Lena instead."

"Has he hurt you?"

"No."

Katherine got the cart back into motion, feeling unsettled over the conversation. She'd be having a talk with Joe for making her girl feel unwelcomed.

Eight-thirty rolled around. The cake had been frosted, and Clara had licked the spoon. Bath water had been poured into the tub. Katherine was soaping up her daughter when the beep of an automobile horn frightened them both. The sound was familiar, but slightly rare, especially this time of night and so loud. "Stay put, Clara." Katherine went to the front room and looked toward the road. A large gasp escaped her. There sat Joe behind the wheel of an auto with Lena in the passenger seat. Katherine's impulse was to run outside, but she was aware of Clara in the tub. Instead she yelled out the window.

"Whose automobile are you driving?"

"Mine."

Katherine's hands flew first to her mouth and then to her hips. "Joe McGinn, you bought an automobile?"

"Sure did."

Shock and anger tugged back and forth inside her.

"With what?"

"My good looks." He laughed, then beeped the horn. "With money. My hard-earned money and a bank loan."

Anger won the tug-of-war. *His money? A loan!* Katherine felt her body heat with anger. In her mind, what Joe had done was nothing short of robbing his family to pay for his pleasures. Progress came with a price tag, and she didn't think they had the funds to pay the cost. "I gotta check on Clara. Don't you leave, Joe McGinn!" She pulled her upper body back through the window, then remembered Lena and bent back down into the window.

"Lena? Are you alright?"

"Yes."

The strain Katherine heard in her voice indicated otherwise.

Moments later, Katherine returned with Clara by her side. In childlike wonder, her daughter gaped at the contraption. Once Clara had seen and touched the automobile, sat behind the wheel, and beeped the horn, albeit, refusing to be in the car with Joe. Katherine got her into bed, then headed right back outside to confront Joe. She had realized at closer look that the auto wasn't a new one. Joe told her it was a 1913 Ford Touring with a dent on the door, a small tear in the leather, and a scratch on the back. None of this made Katherine feel less angry.

Joe puzzled her. He was a skilled, hard worker who built beautiful furniture and made excellent repairs to homes. He was at his best when he worked. He occasionally attempted kindness toward his sisters and niece, but ruined those with his selfish gambling, money-spending, drinking, and recent mood swings. Over the past couple of years, Joe's vices greatly exceeded his virtues. He had grown jealous of Ben and five years later, still relished in the man's departure. He frequently reminded Katherine of her husband's betrayal.

She turned her attention to Lena, who was trotting from the auto as though she had seen a ghost. Katherine scurried to catch up to her.

"Lena. You look ill, and you're wheezing."

"I guess I'm not used to riding in an automobile. I just need some rest." The tears that Katherine noticed well up in her eyes made her doubt the truth of Lena's explanation. She took her sister's hand while the two of them made their way inside to prepare for bed.

"Lena, you're too quiet."

"I'm tired, Katherine. Stop fretting." Lena snapped, then freed her grasp and walked angrily toward her bedroom. Once again, an uneasiness settled onto Katherine. All was not well with Lena.

Still slightly frustrated over her sister's insincerity, Katherine splashed tepid water over her face then dried it down with a towel and slipped into her worn gown. Releasing her taut bun, she began to brush through her long russet hair. Katherine sighed, knowing she would miss Ben tonight. She always did, lying alone, on the eve of their daughter's birthday.

"Happy Birthday to you!" None of the McGinn clan claimed to be good singers, and the birthday ditty proved them right as their voices screeched out the last notes. Despite unsettled emotions toward Joe, and despite her conversation with Clara yesterday, and despite the tears she'd seen last night in Lena's eyes, Katherine laughed at their rendition of the song.

"Time to cut the cake."

The four of them headed into the kitchen. Her daughter's eyes sparkled, and her face beamed as Katherine sliced a piece.

"The first one goes to the birthday girl."

"That's me!" Clara shouted, causing Katherine to laugh.

They ate their slices then moved to the front room where Clara sat in a rocker, ready to receive the first gift.

The clock chimed one time and the lonely sound threatened Katherine's sane thinking. "One parent," the chime taunted, "One parent." The child had two living parents, yet only one was here to celebrate. Her mind went to the letter she'd hid in the trunk last night. What words had Clara's father written to celebrate his daughter? Katherine felt like an evil mother as she handed Clara her first gift.

Joe had made her a doll bed, and Lena had ordered her *The Night Before Christmas* phonograph record. Clara received them both eagerly. She had no doubt that Lena had held back some of her pay at the diner to afford the present. Lena had winked and told Katherine that Mr. Justice had found the record for her in Greenville at a small music shop. Bending down at Clara's feet that swung from the rocker, Katherine handed Clara the package she had picked up at the store yesterday. It was now donned in yellow paper with a butterfly Lena had sketched on the top of it.

"Don't tear my butterfly," Clara instructed as she held the package toward Katherine, indicating for her to tear away that part of the wrapping, then tiny slim fingers tore at the remaining paper and lifted the lid of the box. The birthday girl squealed when she lifted a child size white coffee cup wrapped in old newsprint. Katherine had ordered Clara a white china play tea set, an exceptional gift bought with the money from her Papa.

At bedtime, Katherine placed the tea set on a small table she had brought to Clara's room. All her gifts were displayed for her to see as she rested her head against her pillow. Katherine listened as Clara said her bedtime prayers, always asking for her Papa to come home and to love her. Always.

After the birthday celebration, Joe had taken the automobile into nearby Josephine to play cards with friends. His absence provided a peaceful stillness to the house and left the sisters to sit alone in the front room reading, but Katherine grew antsy.

"Would you like to listen to a record, Lena?"

"No thanks. I'd rather read."

Katherine shrugged her shoulders, licked her finger, and turned to the next page of her book. The chime of the clock divided the evening into half hour segments. Having grown more weary of the quiet, Katherine closed her book with a thud. She was ready for a game of Gin Rummy. "Lena, how about a game of cards?" Silence met her, causing Katherine to glance at her sister. Lena's brows were wrinkled, despite that fact that she was reading *Pride and Prejudice,* one of her favorite love stories.

"Lena, you still seem troubled, ever since last night."

"I'm just reading."

Katherine ignored the retort.

"You weren't really sick last night from riding in the automobile, but your mood changed in a flash."

Waiting for a reply, Katherine surveyed her sister, realizing at eighteen, Lena was the same age Katherine was when she fell in love with Ben. Lena was once so full of fairy tale dreams. Had Katherine's own marriage destroyed any hope Lena had of living happily ever after? Lena had never shared starry-eyed, secret affections for any young man. The awareness nagged at Katherine.

Lena closed the book and met Katherine's penetrating eyes. Tears began to roll down her sister's cheeks, and Lena's chin quivered. Her hands shook. Prompted by memories that had made her feel strange or uneasy about Lena, an assumption set in, and fear sent a surge through Katherine's body. She fought the urge to retch. Katherine stood from her rocker to sit at Lena's feet. Taking her hands, she whispered the terrible question that had come to mind.

"Did Joe hurt you?" The clock hanging between their two rockers chimed eight times, and a shadow descended into the dimly lit room. A lamp had burnt out.

Lena sobbed. "When you left to get Clara from the house last night, he touched me." Her sister covered her face with her hands and released her next words through whispers. "Man to woman. Cruel. Ugly. He says no man wants me, so he'll just have me himself."

Katherine literally gagged but managed to swallow the rise. Weeping, she drew her sister to her, but Lena resisted with a stiffened body.

"I'm so ashamed, Katherine."

"It's not your fault." The bitter taste rose in her throat again, and her hand flew to her mouth before she forced the gorge down. "How did I not know? Has he touched you before?"

Any remaining remnants of the vibrant young Lena she'd always known seemed to shrivel in front of Katherine's eyes as she grabbed her torso and began to rock back and forth sobbing. Tortuous words fought their way through the wailing.

"Sometimes, here and there over the last few years. He'd run his hand up and down my back. Touched my bottom once or twice as he passed me in the shed. I felt uneasy, but I didn't put the pieces together at first. Then he got bolder. Held me too long in a tight hug and kissed my cheek, whispering a threat into my ear to not pull away. Loosened my braid and stroked my hair when I stood at the stove and cooked, whispering a threat into my ear. You came into the kitchen once right when he was going to tug the ribbon loose. He moved his hand to my shoulder. Came and looked at me when I was bathing, saying he thought I was at work, and that he was looking around because a sound spooked him. Remember? You said Rosa was waiting for him outside in her auto. Anyway, he came toward me, and I covered myself best I could with my towel, but I had to use my arms to fight him off. That's the kind of stuff he did, until last night."

Katherine nodded her head back and forth. Alarmed, she realized that when her sister had insisted years ago that she'd take baths in Katherine's room because it had a door, that she was speaking far more about safety than she was privacy.

Lena took in a breath and released it.

"You and Clara were never in the room, usually not even nearby, when it happened. I reckon he made certain of that."

Lena's eyes looked dark and serious. She sensed blatant fear in her sister.

"He'll hurt me, Katherine, if you talk to him about it. Don't say anything. Never. He promised he won't do it again." Lena's body shook against Katherine.

"Why do you believe him?"

"Because I'm scared not to."

Katherine felt as though the blood had drained from her body. Her lively, sweet Lena had been harmed in their own home, and Katherine had never known.

"Why didn't you tell me? Why, sweet Lena?"

"Like I said, because of shame and fear and because at first I didn't realize what was happening. Last night, though, he touched me like he never had before, and I knew he planned to rape me. Somehow, I fought him off."

"Does Doc need to come by?"

"No! I could never tell a man what Joe did last night. You can't tell either. Besides, I fought him off before he...," Lena swallowed, "it was just his hands inside my clothes and his mouth on mine, so I should be safe, right?"

Katherine could not bring herself to speak the word "yes," so she nodded her head again. Lena may be safe in the way she intended the question, but her sister was far from safe with a predator sharing their home, their genes, and their bloodline. From her place at Lena's knees, Katherine reached up to embrace her sister, but instead crumpled to the floor.

"Clara, are you afraid of Uncle Joe?"

"No, I just want to be with you..."

No. No. No. The word echoed in her ear.

Chapter 17

1924 | Layton, Texas

"Momma?"

Clara's eyes were squinted against the lamp light as Katherine leaned over her child, nestled under the covers of her small bed, hugging her teddy bear. In a panic after Lena's confession, Katherine had pulled her sister by the arm and taken her to the bedroom to gather her clothing and personal items.

"You'll never sleep alone in your room again. You're moving in with me and Clara!" Lena hadn't argued with Katherine. Indeed, she had haphazardly collected personal items into her arms, then clung to Katherine as they walked through Joe's bedroom making their way to the small addition Clara and Katherine shared. Passing through Joe's bedroom, Katherine had cringed. Her anger toward Joe had instantly evolved into contempt. No, it was hatred.

"Is it mornin'?"

"No, sweet girl. Wake up. You're getting in my bed."

"Am I sick?"

"No. I just want you to be with me."

Katherine slid her arms underneath Clara's small body and pulled her daughter against her. Clara whimpered when the teddy bear fell back onto the bed. Unable to lean down with her child in her arms, Katherine sat down on the mattress and grabbed the toy. Clara's slender fingers took it from her and drew it against her neck and cheek.

"Can you bring my tea set? I want to look at it when I'm asleep."

Despite the agony she felt, Katherine grinned at Clara's childlike reasoning. Childhood innocence. Had Clara's been taken from her?

"I'll get it later."

Katherine had taken one step through the doorway of Clara's small bedroom and into her own when her daughter sat up in her arms.

"Aunt Lena! You're sleeping with us too?"

"Yes." Katherine saw Lena give a faint smile to Clara.

"I want the middle."

Katherine patted Clara's back as she eased her to the bed. "You get the middle, Lena gets the right side by the wall, and I get the side closest to the door."

Crawling under the covers next to Clara, Katherine's courage to question her daughter tried to cower. The ugly things of life can seem unreal unless confronted. A lump rose in her throat and blocked her words. Katherine closed her eyes and willed herself to face the truth. Emotions can be reluctant to give into reason.

For the first time in more than five years, Katherine called out to her God. She had gone through the religious motions, even read the Bible, but since the death of Sammy, she'd refused to speak to the Almighty.

"God, help us!"

She felt Clara sit up at the whispered plea.

"Momma? What's wrong?"

Katherine pulled Clara next to her, then reached over her daughter's tiny belly to grasp Lena's hand.

"Sweet girl, Momma needs to ask you a question, and I need you to be a big brave girl when you answer."

"Is it about Papa?"

Katherine grimaced as her mind flashed back to the recent conversation where Clara had learned her Papa was alive—and away. *How much pain can my child bear?*

"No. I want to ask you about Uncle Joe." She felt Clara stiffen beside her then begin to tremble.

"I ask you again, has he hurt you?"

"No." Clara snubbed.

"Has he tried to hurt you or touch you near your underwear?"

Silence. Katherine's chest became heavy, as though she would suffocate.

"No. But he says mean things, like, I'm ugly."

"You are not ugly. He is telling a lie. Does he do more than say mean things?"

"He asks me to sit in his lap or hug his neck when we're in the workshop because he says he loves me even if I'm ugly."

Katherine heard Lena moan. The young mother closed her eyes and released the tears she'd been holding back.

"But, I don't like him. So, I say no. Then he says other mean things."

"Tell me."

"Papa doesn't want me because I am ugly."

Katherine groaned.

"And Uncle Joe says since he loves me and makes me presents, I should let him hug and kiss me. But, Momma, I never did, so he hides my teddy bear and laughs at me and makes me sit real still and watch him work. I can't even go to the outhouse sometimes."

Clara's shoulders were shaking against Katherine. She felt Lena release her hand, then lean over the bed to vomit into the chamber pot.

"Why didn't you tell me?"

"Cause he said he would hurt Aunt Lena." Clara's crying intensified.

Katherine sat up in bed and held her daughter by the shoulders. "Always tell me. No matter what." Their eyes met, then Clara nodded her head yes.

"I love you, Clara."

"I love you, Momma."

Katherine wasn't sure when Lena and Clara finally fell asleep, but Lena's soft purr and Clara's heavy breath let her know she was the only one awake. She'd heard the clock chime midnight, and she expected Joe to be home. At the next half hour, she heard the back door squeak. She listened as his feet dragged across the kitchen linoleum. Rising from bed, she tiptoed to her bedroom door and cracked it open slightly. He had made it to his bedroom and pulled closed the dividing curtain in the doorway.

Fury. It had to be fury that prodded Katherine to open her door and make her way into his bedroom. Joe's back was to her as she shoved the curtain aside and lunged toward him. Flailing her arms against his back, she spoke with seething words.

"Don't you ever touch my daughter!"

Joe swung around and captured her wrists. He smirked. "Katherine, lands sake, you're indecent"

At that moment she realized she had slipped out in her cotton nightgown without her robe. Her hair hung in a loose braid down her back. She wanted to hide.

To her dismay, Joe leaned forward, and his smelly breath filled her nostrils. "And, I ain't interested in what you're showing me. Reckon I can see why Ben went after my Faye."

"You horrible drunk. Is it your friends in the town of Josephine that have a still?"

His grip on her tightened. "Get out."

Katherine jerked her wrists free, then from courage that only a desperate mother might claim, she reached up and slapped Joe in the face.

"Never touch Lena again. Never touch my daughter. Never speak lies to my girl. I'll go to the sheriff."

Joe backed away from her, then she saw his beady blue eyes darken. "Don't threaten me Katherine. You got no one here to protect you. And you ain't brave enough to go to the sheriff."

The thin thread of hope she had always held for Joe during his tender moments as a brother and an uncle broke with a silent snap.

She whimpered. "Why? Why do you do those things to them?"

"Can't rightly say. The feeling just comes upon me."

"You're a wicked man."

"You just now realizin' that?"

"I saw goodness in you at times."

"I reckon my evil wore it out. It don't have much life left in it."

"You betrayed my trust."

"Like your husband?"

Katherine trembled and felt herself grow clammy but allowed her anger to overpower her vulnerability.

"I despise you. Get out of this house and don't you come back!"

"You think you can send me away like you did Ben?" He sneered and laughed. "I ain't goin' nowhere. But, I'll leave your girl alone. She's got some growin' to do anyway. Lena? That depends on my mood."

Katherine raised her arms and began to pummel him. Joe grabbed her wrists again, then pushed her to the floor.

"Get out, Katherine!"

Physically weakened by her emotions, Katherine rose, turned, and headed back to her room. She slipped inside the door, and in the darkness, she saw Lena sit up in the bed, her eyes wide.

"Help me push the rockers in front of the doors."

She watched Lena rise from the bed, then scoot a rocker under the back door knob while Katherine did the same to the door leading into the kitchen.

"He'll hurt me now, Katherine. Why couldn't you leave it alone?"

"Because I'm a momma and Clara shouldn't have to fight for herself."

"We'll live in fear now."

"You would have anyway. Clara already was."

"Ask Ben to come home. We need him."

Katherine stared at her sister, refusing to admit the longing she had to do that very thing again. Refusing to admit that he had turned her down years before.

"We need the sheriff, Lena."

Her sister began to sob. "No! It's our secret. I'm too scared."

"I'm scared too, but not too scared to do something about our brother."

Sleep never came to Katherine. Feeling like a fitful, caged animal, she paced back and forth in her room, unable to reason how to carry on life with a predator sleeping in the next room. By the time dawn broke, no feasible solution had pierced through her intense emotions or jumbled prayers. She found herself sitting on the floor with her back against the wall.

At the sound of Lena whispering her name, Katherine's mind broke free of its trance. She unwrapped the quilt that was around her and stood up from the floor, unable to recall getting in that position.

"Did you sleep?" Lena yawned as she asked the question.

"No. And I'm not sure I ever will again." Katherine rubbed her lower back that was sore from her sitting position. A glance at the mirror made her breath catch. She looked the way she felt—like a crazed woman with mussed hair, wide eyes, and in nightclothes. A flashback of how she stood before Joe without her robe made her feel chagrined.

"It's Sunday. I want to go to church and eat with the Carlson's like we planned, Katherine. I want to escape this nightmare we're living in for a bit."

At the mention of church, a sense of relief swept over Katherine. Perhaps the answer she'd sought all night was with Pastor Wendell. Surely she and Lena could confide in him, and he'd know what to do.

"I think we should tell Pastor about Joe; he would…"

"No!" Lena adamantly resisted the idea. "I can't be humiliated that way."

"Then I'll go to the sheriff. Lena, even together we can't outwit Joe. He's wicked, and I think he's insane too." She hugged her sister.

Lena's sobs and Clara's stirring at their commotion made Katherine hush. *Dear God, what do we do? Please help us.*"

Clara sat up in bed, and Katherine watched emotions play across her daughter's face. Her typical morning smile soon faded, replaced by a wrinkled brow and lip biting. "Momma? It's a secret. What I told you is a secret, ok?"

Katherine walked over to the bed and picked up her daughter, hugging her tightly and petting her russet hair. "I know. Momma will worry for you. You don't have to anymore. Can you let Momma worry for you?"

She felt Clara's head nod up and down.

Katherine kissed her daughter's cheek. "It's Sunday, and we're eating lunch with the Carlsons." The declaration caused Clara to evolve back into a carefree child. Katherine relished seeing her that way. The child carried far too many burdens for a five-year-old.

Tension embraced the ladies as they entered the kitchen to prepare breakfast. Katherine hoped the threatening wolf was dead to the world sleeping off his drunken stupor so they wouldn't have to face him yet. She walked over to begin coffee while Lena and Clara set out to make pancakes. A cough from the next room shattered that hope.

"Katherine, would you bring me some coffee when it's ready?" A knot formed in Katherine's stomach just as Clara gripped her hand and Lena froze in position.

"Come get it yourself, Joe."

"I ain't commanding. I'm asking, for a reason you need to hear."

Katherine refused to reply, and the three ladies worked in silence. However, when the beverage was ready, compelled by curiosity she couldn't resist and knowing she couldn't avoid Joe completely this morning, Katherine poured a cup of coffee, pulled back the curtain, and stood facing the brother she had come to despise. His unmade bed conjured sickening images of the man with his twisted desires. Wearing only his dingy long johns, Joe set down his razor and wiped the remaining shaving cream from his cheeks. The menthol scent turned her stomach. Had she ever looked evil in the face as she did this moment? His eyes roamed over her and she felt the color drain from her face. "I see you're covered this time."

Without a word, she slung the coffee at him and missed. The hot beverage landed near his feet, and the mug hung empty in her hand. Joe looked at the coffee then nodded toward the front room. His sloping shoulders made him look pathetically weak at that moment.

"I got something to say, in private. And this ain't a drunk man talking."

His beady eyes contradicted the weak stature. Defiance rose up in Katherine, and she felt her lips tighten and her hands ball up in fists. Her breathing became rapid, but like an innocent lamb, she followed him into the next room where the grandfather clock chimed seven times.

"You should have minded your own business last night."

"Clara and Lena are my business."

"I reckon they are." He gave a rueful laugh.

"I'll contact the sheriff if you touch them or threaten them again. I got a mind to contact him anyway."

"Katherine, shut-up and listen. I'm back at the railroad. I enjoyed your craziness too much to tell you last night."

He sneered at her. Katherine felt her mouth drop open.

"I'm leaving for Josephine today, then I'll catch the train in Greenville. I'll be gone ten days, then back the night before Thanksgiving."

He lifted a shoulder and smirked. "I miss the traveling."

She felt her face relax and jumped when the coffee mug shattered on the floor. She'd forgotten she was carrying it.

Joe's expression hardened.

"Feel all the relief you want to, but I won't forget your threats."

Katherine reached up and slapped him, bracing herself for his retaliatory slap. Instead, he smiled, shook his head at her as though she were a pathetic being, and walked out the front door. Numbness invaded her. She would have preferred the predictable slap.

Katherine made her way back to the kitchen, shutting her eyes as she scurried through Joe's room. Lena rose from the table where she was eating pancakes and stood before her as Katherine relayed the railroad news. Lena gasped her relief. Clara stopped pouring her syrup long enough to smile. Tension went and hid in the corner. Katherine breathed in the relief—grateful for ten days of God's protection.

Why would God help me after the way I've shunned Him? The answer came as a small whisper to her soul. *Love.*

Chapter 18

1924 | Commerce, Texas

The tightness in his chest nearly choked him. Ben sucked in a deep breath. Could five years absence not dissolve the pain he'd felt the last time he'd entered Commerce on a train, a shamed man departing his pregnant wife in Layton? His hope was that a new job and returning to the Cramer's home where Henry lived would have lessened the sad memory. It hadn't.

Ben exited the train just as the traditional lunch hour became early afternoon. He'd consumed an apple and hoped it carried him until his next meal. Besides, his stomach was in knots. Ben found his luggage waiting for him and handed the luggage clerk his ticket, then eyed the crowd for Mason Forder, wondering if he'd recognize the man after all these years. Of course, he suspected Mason would stand out in a crowd if he came dressed in his business finest. Ben reckoned the question he needed to ask himself was how soon it would take Mason to notice his limp that couldn't be hidden like his scars. He straightened his tie to keep his hands busy. Perhaps he should move closer in to the station.

With that thought, Ben was struck at the view. The original station depot had been built on to, almost doubling its size. A glance to his left showed two buildings since his time here. He squinted. "Brown and Carson Insurance" was painted in dark blue on a large sign attached to the building. He couldn't read the name on the second building further down. Ben closed his eyes as memories seemed to awaken from a long sleep. He and his first wife would wander the city sidewalk as newlyweds. She'd always insist he stop at the one dress shop in town, so she could admire the displays in the window. A gravestone reading "Addie Williams" stepped forward in his mind's eye. He missed Addie sometimes, but he yearned for Katherine constantly. How odd that hurt and bitterness converse with yearning. He shook his head. He and Sammy had loaded a train here and headed to Layton to meet Katherine, then done so again when Ben left to marry her and start a new life.

He hadn't realized until he set foot outside the train that there had been an odd, misguided comfort in being so far from home in Texarkana—as though he weren't quite as weak for not making the trip to Layton and facing his wife. A closer vicinity to Layton was already taunting him to go home. He'd learned the difference between guilt and conviction from God. What he felt now wasn't guilt handed down by humans, but rather an urging pressed upon him by God to try and regain his family. Ben had habitually ignored these nudges.

He startled at the sound of his name. Looking over his shoulder, he knew immediately that Mason Forder was the man coming toward him. Ben's breath hitched. Mason Forder was a piece of home. The impact of his approaching presence made Ben want to drop to his knees and crawl back to Katherine. Instead he lifted a shaking hand and waved, picked up his bags, and moved toward the man.

"Ben!"

"Mr. Forder, good to see you."

Ben stuck out his hand to shake it, but Mason stood motionless with his mouth open. *Did he notice my limp?*

"Mason?" The man's first name accompanied Ben's concern.

Mason closed his mouth and a smile spread across his face, but his eyes looked solemn.

"She looks just like…"

Silence.

Ben raised his eyebrows in question.

"Nothing. Excuse my rudeness."

Mason extended his hand toward Ben, who didn't take it.

"You trying to say that Clara looks just like me?"

Mason blew out a breath and dropped his hand to his side.

"Yes."

"Thank you for sayin' it."

Likewise, Ben extended his hand toward Mason, and he took it. The tight clasp and heavy shaking replaced the thought Ben suspected Mason wanted to express. *Go home.*

"It's mighty good to see you again, Mr. Forder." Ben reached down and grabbed the handle of each bag.

"It's 'Mason' when we're not around employees. And yes, it's good to see you again too. I'm very pleased that you took the job. You need lunch?"

Ben was too anxious to eat.

"No, thank you. Mason, I'm extremely grateful for the offer and your confidence in me."

"I'm very confident." Mason nodded his head then smiled. "I'm glad I was in town today to take you to the mill and introduce you personally."

"I don't know why after all these years you have confidence in me."

"Well, I'm a businessman who recognizes the best fit for a job and goes after it." He turned and was facing Ben directly. "I'm also a caring man who knows when a person needs a push toward something or someone he should go after."

Ben's swallowed despite his mouth going dry. He knew exactly what Mason was trying to push him to go after.

"I'm sure I understand what you mean, Mason."

Ben smiled.

"I'm certain you do. Now, here's my car. Hand me one of those suitcases."

Ben fought to keep his mouth from gaping open as he stared at the blue Rolls Royce Mason loaded with the luggage. He grinned. The finest in St. Louis had nothing on Mason Forder.

"Settled?"

Ben had seated himself. "Yes."

"So, Ben, can I catch you up on family?"

My family? Yes, tell me of every day since I left.

Ben gulped, then deflected.

"Yes, tell me about your family."

Giving no hint that he'd been referring to Katherine and Clara, Mason broke into narration about his own people. Ben heard a sense of deep love and pride in his voice. Mason's son had finished the university and was working directly with his father to one day run the business. Indeed, it was the son who spent more time in Commerce than Mason.

"Our little girl…"

"You have a little girl?" Ben sat up in his seat.

Mason turned with a large grin on his face.

"Mary. In fact, she and Clara are friends. Along with Pastor Carlson's daughter, Maggie."

Ben bounced back against the seat letting the news sink in. The announcement forced him to realize how much time had marched on in his absence. He gathered his composure.

"Does she look like you?" Ben smiled.

"No. She's pretty like her mother." Mason chuckled.

Mason continued to talk, the narrative leading to Pastor Wendell Carlson and his family, the church, and the Justice's. Somewhere during talking, Mason had managed to explain that his niece, Faye, was living in Houston with a family of her own. The sultry vixen had become domesticated. The woman he'd lost his family over had gained one of her own, and the news sliced through his heart.

"Ben, allow me to make clear what I said earlier. When this job came open, I immediately thought about how faithfully you've provided money for your family. So, I hoped that the salary would appeal to you for that reason. I knew if it did, I'd get a good employee, but I'd also get you closer to home."

Ben stared at his hands.

"I appreciate your blunt honesty. I already suspected what you were up to."

"Knowing what you need to do is one thing. Doing it is another."

"You certain you want me for the job?"

"I'm certain." Mason cleared his throat. "Would you be willing to tell me about that limp?"

"Sure." Ben laid out the events of the train accident.

At last, the conversation turned to business as the luxury car rolled through town and then to the outer edge of Commerce where the Forder Sawmill stood like a mountain on the flat Texas land. This mill looked to be about four times the size of the mill Mason owned in Layton where Ben had previously worked. He wanted to rub his hands together at the anticipation of working this large operation, but he kept his composure. Within minutes, he was escorted into the office area, shown around, and introduced to those who needed to meet him.

When Mason excused himself to tend to his own business matters in his on-site office, Ben began to look through files and acquaint himself with the facts and figures he'd need to know for his job. Different from the office at the hospital where multiple staff worked in one large room, Ben would have a small office to himself. A secretary, who resembled nothing of "Miss Tweed" in St. Louis, was situated in the open space between Ben's office and the finance manager's office. She would serve them both.

Mason returned an hour later, and the two of them headed to his auto. Mason planned to drop Ben off at the Cramers before heading to his hotel. He would drive to Layton first thing in the morning. Ben wanted to tell Mason to pick him up on his way out the next day and take him home. Instead, he chose to inflict pain upon himself and said the words he'd swallowed every time they'd risen to his throat today.

"Tell me about them."

Mason exhaled and adjusted his grip on the steering wheel. Then, as though Mason Forder were a storyteller, sentence by sentence Ben's family came to life through his words.

Angel kisses. A butterfly book. Lena at the diner since she'd finished school. Gitter the mule still alive. Katherine doing books for Carl. No more cotton fields. Joe, ever the scoundrel and drunk, making furniture. On and on the news swept over him. Ben felt as though he were drowning in the words, fighting for air.

"Ben, why haven't you come back?"

He closed his eyes as a wave of nausea went through him. His hand perspired. His weak leg ached.

"She doesn't want me."

Mason was quiet for a moment as they reached the Cramer home. He turned off the car, then finally spoke.

"I've *never* heard her say that. I'm certain my wife hasn't either." He scratched his forehead. "I tell you, Ben, I just don't see any hint that she doesn't want you back. And I know for certain that little girl of yours wants a father."

Mason turned to open the door before Ben could reply.

"Meanwhile, I'm glad to have you back on my payroll."

Meanwhile?

Mason had escorted Ben to the porch and was still standing there when Mr. Cramer opened the door. Ben hadn't even had time to knock.

The kind, heavy built man took up the entire doorway as he stood with his thumbs tucked under the straps of his overalls.

"Ben Williams. Welcome back!"

With that said, Mr. Cramer pulled Ben into a bear hug. Ben released his luggage and returned the hug.

"It's so good to see you, Mr. Cramer."

The men stepped back from one another.

"Lands sakes. You've aged a mite, but otherwise, I'd of known you anywhere."

"You reckon?" Ben patted the man's shoulder.

"Mr. Cramer, meet Mason Forder—my boss."

The two men shook hands.

"Happy to meet you, Mr. Forder."

"Same here."

Ben spoke up.

"You look well. How's the arthritis Henry's been writing me about?"

"Giving me fits, but I'm managing. Now you two come on in. Mrs. Cramer fixed her specialty—fried chicken and mashed taters."

Ben looked at Mason, wondering if the man had supper plans already or preferred a quiet evening at his hotel.

"I'd be happy to join you. Thanks."

Mason picked up the piece of luggage he'd set on the porch. Ben grabbed his other piece and motioned for Mason to step inside. Ben followed. Mr. Cramer had vacated the doorway and was calling to his wife.

The scent of cinnamon and furniture polish welcomed Ben inside just as Mrs. Cramer came through the dining room door.

"Would you look at that. Ben Williams is finally standing in my front room again."

A broad smile was spread across her reddened face, whether from the heat of the kitchen or the labored breathing she was doing, Ben couldn't tell. He moved forward and embraced her. His heart was tight. He'd not expected to feel such emotion at the sight of her. This woman had loved and cared for him and his son and had managed to dig out a place in his heart.

He saw from the corner of his eye that Mr. Cramer had tried to slip away with the luggage, but Mason had taken it from him and followed him upstairs.

"Mrs. Cramer, thank you for having me back."

"I'd of kicked out a resident to make space for you if I hadn't had a spare room. Probably Henry."

She laughed so that her shoulders shook. She had to wipe the sweat from her brow and fan herself to get her breath back. Ben laughed along with her.

"Is Henry here?"

"Not yet. He's due to arrive in time for dessert."

"Of course." Ben winked causing another burst of laughter from Mrs. Cramer.

"The place looks nice."

"Upkeep is a bit hard on us now. Henry helps a lot. Which is good, seeing it costs double to feed him."

Another round of laughter. Ben was afraid the woman might pass out if she kept on laughing.

A man entered from the porch and slipped past them.

"Hello, Mrs. Cramer. Supper sure smells good."

"Hello, Arlen. Meet our new resident, Ben Williams."

"Hello there. New to town?"

"Returning to town."

"Ben lived with us before," Mrs. Cramer explained. Ben was relieved she didn't go into details about his prior times at the boarding house.

"Nice to meet you, Arlen. I reckon I'll see you at supper."

"Maybe breakfast. My wife and I are heading to the picture show."

A pain of regret ran through Ben's chest at the comment. He longed to head anywhere with Katherine.

"Enjoy."

The man made his way up the stairs just as Mason and Mr. Cramer were descending them.

"Mrs. Cramer, meet Mason Forder."

"Welcome. I hope you're joining us for supper."

"Thank you. And yes, I love fried chicken. Your husband was kind to invite me already."

Sure enough, just as the residents were clearing their dinner plates, and Mrs. Cramer was serving dessert, Henry walked through the dining room doorway. Ben stood to his feet and headed toward him as Henry teased.

"Mrs. Cramer, you let any kind of riff-raff into your house?"

Ben picked up the pun.

"Only the best sort."

He and Henry hugged while they laughed.

"Sure is good to see you, Ben." Henry's teeth shown with his grin.

"You too."

Ben had teetered between glad and sad all day long. This moment he was glad.

"Come meet Mason Forder."

The man stood to his feet.

"Mason, this here is my friend, Henry Jones. We go all the way back to St. Louis."

"Nice to meet you. Not sure how you've put up with the likes of Ben all this time."

Henry cackled.

"Mercy me. I don't either."

"Henry, you want dessert first or your plate I held for you," Mrs. Cramer interjected.

"Both at the same time."

With that, the company of folks settled back into eating. As supper time wound down, Mason Forder excused himself to return to his hotel. The other residents milled about the house while Henry and Ben helped Mrs. Cramer in the kitchen.

"You boys are spoilin' me."

"That's right," Mr. Cramer, who was toying with a latch on the cupboard, teased. "She'll be bossing me around more than she already does."

Ben and Henry sat up and talked until the clock struck midnight, then Ben made his way to his new room—another place to lay his head and try to call home. In the stillness of that room, Ben felt himself grow ill.

He made his way to the bathroom and retched—not that his stomach couldn't handle the food he'd swallowed, but rather that his heart couldn't handle the emotions he'd consumed.

Chapter 19

1924 | Layton, Texas

Katherine grabbed a clean dishtowel from the counter and wet the end with water from the sink. Giggling, she pulled Clara up to her. "Your face is covered with chocolate!" She bent and kissed her daughter's cheek and ran her hand over her sticky russet hair. Clara sat back down next to her friend. Laughter from young Maggie Carlson filled the balmy, scrumptious smelling air in Amy's kitchen. The playful pair of friends were seated on the door stoop where the breezy air felt cooler and were eating left over pie filling from the bowls their mothers had used. "I pretended my spoon was a fairy wand and touched Clara's head. She's a princess now." Maggie laughed and Clara joined her. Amy Carlson, who was standing over the stove stirring the concoction for a chocolate cream pie, glanced at Katherine apologetically, then chimed in. "Maggie, go put your spoon in the sink. Spoons don't belong in hair." But Katherine didn't mind the childlike behavior. In contrast, her spirit was stirred by the sound of Clara's laughter.

Nine days without the burden of Joe's threats had breathed life back into Clara, Lena, and herself. Knowing how to live with him when he returned distressed Katherine, and her conflicted emotions battled each other. Standing in the kitchen of Amy and Wendell Carlson's home, she felt drawn to tell them the truth and ask for help, but the fear on Lena's face when Katherine had first made the suggestion kept her hesitant. She had a decision to make.

"Amy, I hope you don't mind that Joe won't be coming over for Thanksgiving."

She watched Amy blush. "I know I'm the pastor's wife, but I have to be honest. I am so glad he refused our invitation."

"Me too. 'I refuse to spend my holiday talking religion with the preacher.' Those were his exact words."

"Will he just stay at your house?"

"He'll be with his girl, Rosa."

The loss of Maggie's wand prompted the girls to abandon their post in the doorway, drop their batter bowls in the sink, and head to the children's bedroom for a game of jacks. Amy laughed. "That game will only last until my youngest is up from his nap and crawling on the floor toward the jacks!"

Katherine pulled a pumpkin pie from the oven and replaced it with a chocolate and an apple one. "It's all I can do to manage Clara sometimes, and here you are managing three children."

She saw Amy move her hands in front of her body, indicating, Katherine assumed, that she looked bedraggled, "Wendell's a good father." Her friends face suddenly resembled cranberries. "I'm sorry Katherine. You'd think after five years, I wouldn't allude to fathers and husbands when we talk."

"Amy, I want you to talk about your husband."

"I'd like to talk about yours. If you would only confide in me."

"Obviously, we're not together. That's all there is to know."

"You're my friend. I'm here for you."

"I know." *Tell her. About Lena. About Ben.*

Amy's youngest began to cry. Katherine motioned Amy to go take care of the child. As the mother attended to the little one, Katherine washed up the dirty dishes. The parsonage kitchen was small, but well equipped. Not only had Amy's wealthy brother supported the ministry with a car, he had made sure the parsonage had electricity and running water. He wanted to help make things easier for Amy during the nights when pastor had to be away caring for others. What a contrast in their two siblings. The humble Carlsons always appeared embarrassed by the luxuries, in Katherine's opinion, but the church had voted their approval. A telephone sat in the small front room. Ironically, few of the Layton parishioners had a phone, rendering the one in the parsonage rather useless. With the kitchen clean and the last two pies still baking, Katherine found herself ready to return home. Lena was due in from the diner early evening, and Katherine wanted to have a meal ready for her sister.

Amy returned to the kitchen with her two-year-old son in tow. Katherine went over and kissed his chunky cheek. "I best get on home. Clara!"

"Katherine, let Clara stay and play. I'll bring her home in the auto when Wendell gets here. He's due in an hour. It'll be a treat for her." Amy winked. "It will get me out of the house for a bit."

I'll tell her about Lena when she brings Clara home.

Katherine laughed. "I still can't get used to seeing you drive!"

Amy pretended to flaunt her hair, "I'm a high falutin' city girl."

With the matter settled, Katherine seated herself in the cart and clicked for Gitter to take her home.

With Gitter settled, Katherine walked to the garden and pulled a couple of squash. Tonight she'd be attempting a squash casserole for Lena to enjoy. With a stop at Sammy's grave, a sense of peace came over Katherine that he was no longer a secret. Yes, there was pain in the memory of him, but there was joy in reliving his little life through stories she and Lena now openly told Clara. His trains had become a part of Clara's toy collection. The imprint of Clara's hands had been stitched next to Sammy's on an apron that was a prize possession of "Aunt Lena's" since her thirteenth birthday.

She made her way to the kitchen through the back door. While cutting up onion and squash, Katherine found herself eager to play the phonograph, so she wiped her hands on her apron then made her way to the front room. Moments alone with uninterrupted music and other's preferences on the choice were rare. As she passed through Joe's bedroom, the scent of soap caught her attention, and she glanced at his water bowl. It was empty, but the towel that hung next to it was missing. *Odd.* While pulling a record from its case, Katherine froze at the sound of a groan and labored breathing coming from Lena's bedroom. Although Lena had been sleeping in Katherine's room since Joe's attack, most of her personal possessions remained in her room, and with Joe away, Lena spent her free time in there. Lena's familiar wheeze and another groan sounded. Katherine's skin tightened. She dropped the record into a nearby rocker and made her way to the bedroom doorway.

A scream moved through her body and exited out Katherine's mouth, sounding in every room of the house. "Lena!" Her sister lay crumpled in a heap near the center of the room. One arm was contorted unnaturally behind her back. Her clothing was bloody and torn. Her sister's eyes were hidden behind swollen, bruised lids.

The room spun as blackness threatened to overtake Katherine. She dropped to her knees beside Lena and called her name. A groan escaped her sister. She took hold of Lena's hand that rested against her stomach. "If you can hear me, squeeze my fingers." A weak pressure against her fingers let Katherine know Lena was conscious. "I'm going to the Justice store for help! I'll be back. Keep breathing, Lena!"

Katherine was too afraid to move her sister from the floor, uncertain what may be injured. She stood to her feet, grabbed a blanket off the bed and covered the heartbreaking body of innocent Lena. As she crossed the threshold of the bedroom to open the front door, fear gripped her. Who had done this? Were they lurking somewhere nearby? She backtracked and placed her ear near Lena's mouth. Katherine cleared her throat and steeled herself.

"Lena, did Joe do this?'

The weak, but audible answer caused Katherine's knees to give. "Yes." Lena wheezed out breaths between moans.

Sickening images of Joe and Lena in the scene before her and what might could happen with Clara threatened to collapse her, leaving her emotions to drive her actions. Thus, she found herself fleeing through the front door, down the porch steps, and toward the Justice store on foot, sobbing and screaming desperate pleas for help to the no one's that passed by. Gitter and the cart remained untouched.

Despite her frenzy, Katherine jerked when an auto beeped from behind.

"Katherine! Katherine!"

Someone was shouting her name. Joe? No, the voice was female.

Katherine turned slightly without losing her stride and saw that it was Amy with Clara in the auto. No! Had Clara witnessed the awful sight of Lena beaten and lying on the floor?

"Katherine!"

The auto came close, puttering. Amy moved the brake into gear.

"What's wrong, Katherine?"

Amy's breathing was rapid, and perspiration shown on her brow.

"Did you go in the house, Amy? Did Clara?" Katherine's heart beat rapidly.

"No. I saw you running and beeped for you."

"Momma, what's wrong?"

Clara was crying. The poor child couldn't catch a breath of peace before another wind of agony blew in. Katherine ached for her girl.

"Clara, you ride with Amy to the Justice store. I need to go back to the house."

In an effort to shut out further questions, Katherine walked to the opposite side of the auto and leaned in to hug her daughter. "Do as I say." The two clung to one another tightly.

Katherine released Clara and made her way back to Amy then locked eyes with her. A fresh wave of tears overtook Katherine. Between sobs, she whispered to Amy. "Call Doc. Joe beat up Lena." Amy gasped, and Katherine saw her face blanch. Then with great composure, her friend pumped the brakes and continued driving toward the store.

"Momma! I want Momma!"

Clara's pleas stretched behind the auto along with the black dust from the road. Katherine ran back home, and with sweat dampening her dress, she leaned over her sister and ran her hands over her disheveled hair. In bitter bits, Lena shared what Joe had done to her. Katherine shook with fury, wishing her brother would die. She remained on watch until someone entered the bedroom and placed their hand on her shoulder.

"Katherine."

She looked up at the face of Louise Justice, whose gaping mouth showed the horror she felt at seeing the scene. The stocky mother-figure sat down, ran a hand over Lena's shoulder, then pulled Katherine into her arms and let her weep. A flashback to a similar scene in their kitchen five years ago where Sammy's lifeless body lay made Katherine shutter. Mrs. Justice's mumbled repetitive prayers for God's help joined the chorus of sobs, moans, and labored breath. "Lord, please spare Lena's life."

"Mrs. Justice, where's Clara?" Katherine tugged on her ear, then resorted to petting Lena.

"Amy took her to their house. She'll send Pastor right back here in the auto."

"We need Doc!"

"Carl rang him on the phone. He's on his way. And so is the county sheriff."

"Sheriff?"

"After hearing that Joe did this, Carl rang the sheriff."

Suddenly, Lena's hand was gripping Katherine's as she cried out, "No!"

"Yes." Katherine whispered the command to her frightened sister.

The screen door squeaked, then the doctor appeared in the doorway of the bedroom. Katherine let Mrs. Justice guide her to the side of the room. Soon, Pastor Carlson walked in and acknowledged Katherine verbally, then made his way back to the kitchen where he waited a respectful distance from the injured Lena. He was joined by Carl. Katherine was grateful for their presence and their sensitivity. The doctor was on his knees leaning over Lena.

"She's going to live. I feel a broken rib, but no other internal injuries. I'll be setting her arm." Katherine clasped her hand over her mouth and sniffled, relieved at the doctor's report. "She'll need a good two weeks in bed for recovery." Then, the doctor cleared his throat. "I still need to do a private exam. It's safe to move her to the bed." Katherine sensed Mrs. Justice rise from the bed. "I'll tell the men what Doc said and wait outside for the sheriff." Katherine nodded a thank you, pulled back the bedcovers, and helped the doctor move Lena to her bed. She held her sister's hand and explained what the doctor needed to do.

"Has she told you what happened, Katherine?"

"Joe did it."

Katherine heard the doctor swear under his breath and run his hand over his face. "Is that all she told you?"

"No." Katherine looked at Lena, wondering if she could endure the embarrassment of the details being shared. She felt her sister clasp her hand, so Katherine looked into Lena's eyes. The brave victim nodded a yes. Her sister had understood her dilemma. Katherine wept gently as she told the story.

"She walked home from the diner earlier than expected and was in her room to change clothes. Joe came at her from behind, covered her mouth with his hand and whispered in her ear, 'You'll regret telling Katherine on me.'" Katherine paused. "Doc, you need to know that Joe had touched Lena before." She observed the doctor make a fist and hit it against his own leg.

Katherine continued. "He began to hit her, and at one point he yanked her dress at the collar hard enough to pull off the first few buttons of her dress. He yelled that he would rape her and pushed her to the floor. Perhaps he had one sliver of decency, because instead of defiling her, he kicked her more than once in the tender area instead."

"Thank you, Katherine." The doctor patted her on the shoulder. "Let's proceed." Before he began the exam, Katherine watched the doctor put his hand on Lena's uninjured arm. "I'll take good care of you, Lena."

Evidence showed that Joe had injured her slightly, but he hadn't defiled her, confirming what Lena had shared. Relief set in and nearly made Katherine faint. There was no chance her sister would be birthing their brother's baby. The doctor then set Lena's arm. Her scream reverberated through the household, then Katherine watched the laudanum the doctor administered soothe her sister to sleep.

When the sheriff arrived, Lena was in no condition to talk to him. The doctor confirmed his report, and Katherine shared what she knew from her sister. The obvious conclusion was that Joe had arrived from his railroad route earlier than expected, then drove his auto home from the station in Greenville where he had departed. Joe's auto was not in the yard, but tire tracks in the dirt proved an automobile had come and gone.

Katherine gave a description of the automobile, then told them what she knew about Joe's friends in Josephine, Greenville, and Evan. Remembering the missing towel and scent of soap she'd noticed earlier, Katherine asked Carl to help her search Joe's room. Wendell and the sheriff searched the grounds. Other than the clues already noted and a beaten Lena, there was no other evidence that Joe had stepped foot inside his own home that day. The sheriff would return tomorrow to talk to Lena.

"Katherine," Louise Justice looked at her, "while I make us something to eat, why don't you pack a suitcase for Clara."

"But," tears rolled down's Katherine's cheeks as the truth hit her. Clara could not return home to see Lena in this condition.

"Amy and I will love having her with us until you feel she can come home," Pastor reassured her.

"Where's Amy?" Katherine realized she wasn't here.

"She's at home with Clara and the children." Wendell spoke through a gentle-looking smile.

"Oh. I forgot. Louise told me that." Katherine looked the pastor in the eyes. "Wendell, I was going to tell Amy about Joe. I was going to tell her today when she brought Clara back. Lena didn't want me to tell anyone, but I couldn't hold it in any longer. We need help."

Wendell's voice blended the care of both a pastor and a friend. "We're all your help now."

She began to weep, and Mrs. Justice pulled her into a tight embrace. "Let's take good care of Lena. The men folks will do all they can to handle that no good brother."

Katherine hugged Mrs. Justice in return and sniffled. "I suppose that's best. Let me get Clara a few things."

The forthcoming separation from Clara sucked the last bit of remaining emotion from Katherine. She pilfered numbly through her daughter's clothing and folded pieces into a suitcase. Retrieving the suitcase from the spare room had afforded Katherine a glance at Ben's trunk. An intense desire for his protection had made her knees buckle. Before closing the strap of Clara's suitcase, she placed her teddy bear, her copy of *Aesop's Fables*, and her butterfly book inside.

As she extended the luggage toward Wendell, Katherine stammered, "May I take it to her, Pastor, if you don't mind driving me there and back?"

She saw Wendell glance at Carl Justice. "Louise and I are staying here for a few days. So, Katherine, you go ahead and ride with Wendell, if you're comfortable, and we'll be here when you get back. I'll head to our house for personal belongings tomorrow."

Katherine rode to the Carlson home. Sometimes words comfort; sometimes silence comforts. Wendell was wise at knowing which was needed, and the quiet ride to the parsonage soothed Katherine's troubled soul.

As the auto pulled into the yard, Clara darted outside. "Momma! I'm so scared!"

Katherine scooped her daughter into her arms and pressed their bodies together.

"Momma needs you to stay here until Aunt Lena feels better, then you can come home. We'll miss you so much."

"Is Aunt Lena gonna die, like Sammy?"

"No. She's just real sick." Katherine pulled her daughter away and rubbed her cheek.

"You have fun playing with Maggie. I'll come visit you some, and you'll be home before you can blink an eye!" She kissed her daughter on the cheek.

"Yessum. I'll be good. I'll be brave too."

Amy Carlson walked up to them. "Mrs. Forder called, and tomorrow I'm gonna take you and Maggie over there to play with Mary. Would you like that?"

Clara's nod of approval included a big grin.

"Carl called Mason, to be on the lookout for…"

Katherine nodded her understanding. Joe might travel or hide anywhere in the so-called Forder Empire between Layton and Commerce.

"Don't forget Thanksgiving!" Clara warned.

Katherine glanced up at Amy and shrugged a shoulder. Lena would be too battered to leave the house on Thanksgiving and for Clara to see her quite yet. Carl and Louise Justice would be with their children for the holiday. Katherine and Lena would spend the day holed up at home away from Clara on Thanksgiving Day.

"Clara, Lena is real, real sick. I have to stay and take care of her on Thanksgiving Day too."

"Mrs. Carlson can bring me home."

Katherine kissed Clara's head.

"No, you can't come home. Lena is too sick."

Katherine caught a tear that rolled down her daughter's cheek.

"I'll miss you, sweet girl."

"I'll miss you too, Momma."

Katherine felt relief when Amy took Clara's hand. "You'll be our very special guest." Amy then turned toward the house, and Wendell, who had been waiting beside the auto, moved to start the automobile. With one last hug, Katherine made a quick decision and whispered in Clara's ear, "Clara, you don't have to worry about Uncle Joe anymore. I think he's gonna be gone for a long, long time."

At last, Katherine settled into her own bed next to Lena. Carl had gently carried her from one bedroom to the other. A rocker was once again propped underneath the door knob of the outer door, despite Carl and Louise sleeping in the next room. They had stripped Joe's bed, put on clean sheets, and intended to sleep there, anchored in the center of the home. The household silenced, and sleep came to Katherine.

The clock chimed once, its face without numbers, and the sound brought a smile to Katherine's lips. Time had captured this one hour and ceased to move forward. It was her dwelling place. The masculine hand rubbing her loose hair comforted Katherine as she rocked. "Rest, my Butterfly." A cold rainstorm raged outside the house, but a soft glow from the fireplace offered warmth to Katherine's body. Clara slept peacefully in her Papa's lap as he sat in the rocker next to her. Lena read in the corner, unharmed and happy. Katherine's eyes fluttered open. "I'm glad you came home," she whispered. A handsome face smiled at her. "It's where I belong."

Ben. The longing made Katherine moan, and she stirred from her dream. She licked the salty tears with her tongue, then two words emerged from the depths of her longing.

"Come home."

Dare she ask him again?

Chapter 20

1924 | Layton, Texas

"Yoo hoo!" Katherine sprang from the rocker situated next to the bed where Lena was recovering. Before Carl Justice left to celebrate Thanksgiving with his daughter's family, he had transferred it from the front room because the bedroom rockers still secured the two doors the ladies slept behind. Perhaps the sound of an auto pulling in her yard a moment ago was not her fearful imagination that Joe had returned. The book she was holding fell to the floor.

"Happy Thanksgiving!"

"It's women's voices!"

Katherine blew out a breath of relief just as Lena snickered.

"We're jittery!"

Feeling like a mother more than a sister, Katherine leaned over Lena and pointed her finger.

"We're cautious."

She crept to the bedroom door and hollered through it, refusing to move the protective rocker until she knew who was lurking on the other side.

"Hello?"

"It's Amy and Abigail."

Katherine patted her hand over her heart and sucked in a deep breath. *Good friends.* She glanced at Lena, who was attempting to cover herself with the bedspread.

"Here, let me help."

Cupping her mouth, she yelled, "Just a minute!" Laughter seeped under the doorway.

"No need to yell. We're standing right here," Abigail teased.

Once Katherine was assured Lena was comfortable with company, she wrestled the rocker away and opened the bedroom door. An aroma of turkey and dressing filled the air. Katherine's stomach loudly begged for a bite. The sight of her two friends standing there with smiles on their faces and bowls in their hands breathed life into her suffocating happiness. It was late Thanksgiving afternoon and these women had left their families to stand in this doorway with their arms full of food. Wary not to jostle the contents in the bowls, Katherine leaned in and put an arm around each lady's neck and pulled them toward her.

"I can't believe you're here!"

"Well we can't let you two women go hungry on Thanksgiving Day."

Katherine smelled Abigail's perfume and felt her jaw move as she replied. The women stepped back then walked over to place their bowls on the table. "Mason drove us," Amy explained. Katherine hadn't realized curiosity had wrinkled her brow until she felt her forehead relax. Without a word, they made their way to the bed and each guest clasped one of Lena's hands. Katherine savored the scene of the two women caring for her strong but weakened sister. She wanted to ask about Clara, but this was her sister's moment and Katherine respected that.

Amy suddenly put her hand in her dress pocket. "I have strict orders to show this to you immediately." Katherine covered her mouth with both hands when she saw Amy gently pull Clara's butterfly book out of her pocket. Abigail turned toward Katherine and gave her a gleeful grin. Though older than both Katherine and Amy by fourteen years, Abigail Forder was a close friend full of grace and goodness. Amy continued. "Clara has drawn you a butterfly." Warmth radiated through Katherine. Her little girl had always been the one waiting in anticipation as Lena drew a butterfly to Clara's exact color specifications. Now she imagined her little girl hovering over the book, her tiny tongue protruding slightly from her lips as she concentrated on drawing the butterfly and selecting each color pencil. Amy thumbed through the pages to find the one she wanted. She held the book toward Lena who exclaimed, "It's orange and brown! How precious!" Her sister took the book from Amy and turned it toward Katherine, who was making her way to the bed. Amy's laughter filled the room. "She named it Turkey Butterfly." Katherine joined in the laughter. Her precious daughter was resilient, finding her way out of the sadness that surrounded her to spread joy to Lena.

"How's my little girl doing?"

Amy stood and took Katherine's hand. "You'd be proud of her. She's acting like a five-year-old girl and playing princess all day long."

Abigail stood as well.

"Yes, she called my house her golden castle," Abigail giggled, "and then realized Mary had no intention of giving up her kingdom to either Clara or Maggie. They soon decided they were sisters who shared the golden castle and took turns ruling, with Mary being the one in charge that day."

Lena cleared her throat in an exaggerated manner, getting Katherine's attention. "I'm hungry!"

The statement pleased Katherine. "Yes ma'am, Princess Lena."

Afternoon ushered in evening and the Justice's return. Lena and Katherine bid their lady friends good-bye and sent hugs and kisses to Clara. When Carl didn't leave to escort the women home, Katherine became curious. She hadn't heard Mason's auto pull up in the yard to take them back.

"Is Carl driving them home?" She stood just inside the kitchen next to Louise Justice with the bedroom door wide open. The dear woman gave Katherine a huge smile before she answered.

"You have been hidden inside that bedroom, haven't you!"

"What do you mean?"

"Why, you ladies have been carefully watched over all day."

"Watched over?" Goose bumps tingled her skin.

"The deputy drove by once or twice when we left. Wendell drove by. Mason and Abigail drove by on their way to Pastor's house, and Mason waited outside while you ladies visited. Even Gabriel drove by."

"Gabriel!" Katherine was astonished and puzzled. And hesitant. The last thing she wanted was to be beholding to Gabriel.

"He was at the store that awful day when Lena was beaten and the next day too. He heard about you two being alone on Thanksgiving and insisted on taking a turn to come by when he overheard Carl speaking about a watch. Of course, he doesn't know anything beyond Lena being hurt."

"That's sweet, Katherine." Lena raised her eyebrows at her sister as she chided her. "We have a lot of people to be thankful for."

"Yes. You're right, Lena." Katherine felt chagrined over her initial ingratitude toward Gabriel's concern.

As the day ended, Katherine washed Lena and pulled a clean gown over her head. Before crawling into the bed, Katherine took Lena's hands and prayed with her sister. She could hear Carl and Louise scurrying around in the kitchen, finishing up the quick bite they'd all shared before lying down to end the day. Satisfied that Lena was sound asleep, Katherine let her heavy eyelids close and felt the relaxation move through her body. What felt like only moments later, she bolted upright in the bed.

"Joe!" Lena's voice pierced the air. "No! Don't hurt me."

Breathing rapidly, Katherine's eye sought the intruder. His presence was not there, but the essence of his evil was—in nerve wracking creaks and eerie silence. She shook her head to wake up just as Lena's hands flailed in the air, fighting the phantom assailant.

"Lena!" Katherine grabbed the thrashing arms and held them still.

"Lena! He's not here. Joe is not here. You're having a nightmare."

She felt her sister's arms relax and released them. Katherine slid her body over to Lena and captured her in a hug. Lena began to wail.

"Shh. Shh. You're safe, Lena."

Katherine rocked her sister's torso back and forth, soothing her as she ran her hand up and down the trembling back.

Katherine felt Lena pull away from her.

"I'm sorry for waking you up."

Deep wheezes filled the air.

"Relax. Breathe with me."

Katherine took slow, deliberate breaths until Lena followed suit and her lungs relaxed.

"Here." Katherine wiped Lena's tears with the sheet. "Would you like some water or warm milk?"

"No. In my dream, Joe was yanking me from my bed and laughing at me. Then he threw me on the ground and raised his fist…"

A knock on the door made both Katherine and Lena jump.

"Katherine, it's Louise. You ladies alright?"

"Yessum. Just a bad dream. Thank you."

"Alright then, good night."

Tight arms came around Katherine's neck as Lena hugged her, then cowered back into the covers.

"Good night, Katherine."

"Good night."

Katherine lay still, but her heart raced. Lena's body would mend, but would her spirit and emotions? Katherine hadn't told Lena that every night since the attack, her groans and jerky reactions had awakened her. Katherine would lie still and wait until whatever images or feelings torturing her sister's mind subsided. None of her other stirrings had awakened the household; however, Katherine figured that a full night's rest would elude most all of them until Joe was found.

. . .

The Justice's unselfishly stayed with the sisters for two more weeks following Thanksgiving until the fateful afternoon when the sheriff dropped by with news of Joe. Katherine had just returned from checking the Justice store ledgers and was scrubbing her bedroom floor when a knock came to the front door. Louise was in the kitchen stirring a pot of pinto beans. "I'll see who it is," she said as she passed by the bedroom doorway. Katherine smiled her agreement, and Mrs. Justice's heavy gait sounded through the rooms. Her friend had never been soft spoken, and her greeting reached Katherine's ears. "Come in, Sheriff. I'll get the sisters."

She heard Lena gasp. Katherine's pulse intensified, and she dropped the scrub brush into the bucket, braced her lower back, and stood up. Drying her hands on her apron, she made her way to the bed where Lena lay.

Louise hurried across the room as she spoke. "Katherine, the sheriff is here. He says he has news. Let me help you with Lena." Katherine lifted Lena from the bed, placed her robe around her, and the ladies anchored her on both sides, more for emotional than physical support. They shuffled slowly through the room Joe recently deserted and Louise had recently occupied with her husband.

"Afternoon, Sheriff." Katherine swallowed hard to counter the anxiety she felt.

"Good afternoon, ladies. Miss Lena, I hear you are recovering. I'm glad."

"Yessir, I am." Lena's grip on Katherine's hand was tight.

"You have news?" Katherine inquired.

"Yes, I do."

The two women eased Lena into a rocker and remained standing. Katherine rested a reassuring hand on the victim's shoulder, whose restrained weeping seeped into the crevices of the room. All attention was turned to the sheriff who remained standing in the front room while the smell of cigarettes lingering on his clothing filled the air. Even in the cool autumn weather, perspiration stood on his temples. Louise stood next to Katherine and grasped her arm. Lena moved back and forth in the rocker. The fire crackled.

"Joe was recognized by the police in White Springs. Seems he quickly quit the railroad with no explanation the day after the attack and traveled to White Springs where he sold his car to a local who asked no questions. A deputy recognized the auto's description when he saw it parked outside a cafe. He found the new owner, and the description of the seller verified it had been Joe. A search began. They found Joe working on a rural turkey farm and arrested him. He's been transported to the local county jail to await trial after the new year."

Katherine breathed deeply, feeling the tension release its grip on her nerves. The rocker went silent. Lena stood, and Katherine barely caught her before her knees buckled. Lena spent the rest of the day in bed, silent, solemn, and safe. Katherine never left her side.

The following morning, Carl and Louise prepared to leave for church.

"I hate to leave you with these dirty breakfast dishes, Katherine, but," Louise stood from the table and glanced at her husband who was already standing in the kitchen doorway, "Carl says we best get. We need to stop at the store to check on something before we head to church."

"Katherine, mind if I bring the account ledgers home for you to work on?"

"No, Mr. Justice, I don't mind at all. It will be good to keep them updated. And to have my mind on something else."

Katherine felt Louise's arms come around her for a hug.

"You ready for Clara to come home?"

Katherine's eyes welled with tears, and her heart skipped a beat. She slipped her arms around Louise's waist.

"Yessum. I'm so glad she's riding back home with y'all. I'm making sugar cookies for her while you all are at church. I feel like a child at Christmas."

Louise pulled back, then Katherine felt her palm on her cheek.

"Are you comfortable enough for me and Carl to leave today after bringing Clara by? I know Lena still needs a lot of assistance."

A tenderness filled Katherine. She loved this woman.

"You and Carl have cared far more than I ever imagined. I'm more grateful than I can say."

She kissed Louise on the cheek and took her hand. "We'll be fine. But, before you two leave, Lena and me have a gift for Louise." She pulled her friend into the bedroom where Lena sat in the rocker, robed, and smiling from cheek to cheek. She held a box wrapped in brown paper and decorated with hand drawn flowers. Katherine bounced up and down on her toes as Lena handed the gift to Mrs. Justice and spoke.

"Katherine and I chose this for you. It belonged to our mother."

Both of Louise's hands flew to her mouth before she reached for the gift. Katherine bit her lip and continued to bounce as her friend unwrapped the paper to reveal the present.

"It's beautiful." The vase was white china with gold lacework and a narrow neck boasting a scalloped top. "You're giving me your mother's vase. I'm without words. Why?"

Katherine moved and placed her arm around Louise's shoulders.

"Because you are our friend, but more than that, we love you like a mother, so we give you a piece of our own Momma to try and show you our feelings."

Lena's hand slipped into Katherine's and she felt her pull up from the chair. "Thank you for caring for us." Lena gathered the three of them into a hug. When Katherine sensed her wearing, she released the ladies and motioned Lena to the bed with a gentle touch on her back.

Mrs. Justice was wiping tears from her cheeks. "I love you girls deeply, as though you were my own. I'll treasure this vase."

Katherine linked her arm inside Louise's and begin to lead her toward to the front room. "We best let you go before Carl has a nervous breakdown." The three ladies laughed.

Louise spoke to her husband as they approached him. "The sisters gave me a precious gift." Katherine's heart warmed as Mrs. Justice held the vase for Carl to see. "It belonged to their mother."

His smile seemed to cover his entire face. "That's mighty, mighty nice of you ladies."

"Just one more thing, Carl, if you have a moment." Katherine strode over to him, stood before him, and looked him directly in the eye.

"Thank you for all you do for my family. Lena and me want you to know that our father was not always a kind and responsible man, but we loved him despite that. You are kind and respectable and a good friend, and we love you like a father. We have no token to share with you, but I can give you this from both of us." Katherine stood on her tip toes and kissed him lightly on the cheek. Carl took her hand and squeezed it. "Thank you." He smiled. "We'll bring your sweet girl back home to you." With that, he walked to Louise, and Katherine saw him smile at her then glance at the vase. The two of them opened the door and walked out.

The upcoming trial loomed over the females' new found safety, thus a tainted peace lingered in the household as the Christmas season rolled around. The three of them had just returned from a ride to the Justice store to get Lena out of the house and check the mail. The air had been cold. "Look, Momma, I'm blowing smoke like a dragon!" Clara had been fascinated by the simple act of nature. Rarely did a ride go by with Clara nestled between she and Lena on the cart that Katherine didn't think about Sammy sitting between she and Ben in the same manner.

With Lena and Clara occupied over adding a Christmas butterfly to Clara's book, Katherine moved to her bedroom, then found herself staring at the letter in her hand addressed to Clara Williams. Ritualistically she opened Ben's trunk in the spare room and added the child's letter to the pile of others addressed just like it.

With Clara's letter tucked away, Katherine seated herself on the floor and pulled open the envelopes addressed to her and read every letter Ben had written her—the final one, composed in September of 1920, such a contrast from the one before it in July where he declared his love. *Why didn't you come home, Ben, when I asked you?* No doubt, he finally decided she didn't deserve him.

The laughter of her loved ones drifted from the front room, pulling her toward them. She placed the letters inside the trunk and closed it.

A week later on New Year's Eve, Katherine lay in her bed wide awake, shaken by a dream.

"Shall we welcome the New Year with a dance, Butterfly?" Ben spun her around floating on thin air. Her long tresses billowed behind her. Clara laughed, and Lena hummed. Snow fell from the sky and rested on all their shoulders. The clock struck midnight then vanished into nowhere. Time was no more. She closed her eyes and absorbed the joy. When she opened them again, Ben was pale and fading away. Lena and Clara now hovered in the corner of the room, shivering and horror stricken. Their left sides where their hearts dwelt were burned and maimed. Tears rolled down their blackened cheeks. The clock relentlessly bellowed one chime after another. Katherine gathered her tresses and tied them into a tight, unflattering bun, then set her chin to carry on life despite the pain before her.

It was her sixth New Year as Mrs. Williams to usher in without him. Would Clara and Lena have been safe in his presence if she'd asked him home earlier? Yes, certainly. Would her daughter have known less fear with him here? Yes. No doubt, Clara would have known more love. Would her sister be testifying against their brother in a few weeks? Mostly likely, no. Perhaps he wouldn't have stopped loving and wanting them if she'd only asked earlier. For he must have stopped caring—otherwise he would have come.

She turned to her side and fluffed her pillow. Only God could unravel the strangeness that had become her life. No doubt He was willing.

Was she? Yes.

Chapter 21

1924 | Commerce, Texas

Ben paid for his sundries at the local drug store. Pulling a malted milk ball from the smaller of the two brown bags, he popped it in his mouth. The chocolate sent a sweet flavor to his tongue, and the crunch was a simple pleasure. He swallowed the bite then took a sip of his Dr. Pepper. Nothing like the taste of malted chocolate and cola. He took a left out of the store and headed by foot to the boarding house. Friday was pie night in Mrs. Cramer's dining room, and tonight's selection was lemon. Even with the flavor of chocolate on his tongue, the thought of her lemon meringue pie made his mouth water.

Henry had returned home from his route on the railroad last evening, and the two of them had plans to play cards with the Cramers, Arlen, and Arlen's wife, Betsy. She was a scrawny little woman with large facial features. Ben grinned. The last time they'd all played cards, her bluffing was easy to read through those features.

Ben reached the boarding house and made his way inside. Arlen's wife sat on the couch doing some kind of stitching. Ben greeted her, and she did likewise, never looking up from her work. He took the stairs two at a time, then unloaded his items in his room. He tossed the brown bags into the waste basket, then carried his cola bottle to the kitchen and placed it with the other empty bottles. Mrs. Cramer kept them to return for deposits, despite who had purchased the cola. The money was used to buy the supplies for pies, and the residents happily agreed to the arrangement.

Mrs. Cramer walked through the back door toting a laundry basket filled with towels and linens.

"Here, let me carry that for you." Ben took the basket and set it on the floor by the small kitchen table then sat down. The chair wobbled slightly. Henry would need to take a look at it. Ben had lived alone long enough to know how towels and wash rags should be folded, so he grabbed the first item and got busy. A moment later, Mr. Cramer held open the back door while Henry walked in with a handful of wood for the fireplaces. The cold air slipped in and mingled with the warmth from the oven. Ben hadn't noticed scent of roasting chicken until that moment.

Henry nodded at Ben then continued toward the front room with the wood. His silence was out of character. Mr. Cramer sat down and rubbed his bent fingers.

"He had a letter today. Been somber ever since he read it. I reckon it's his story to tell, even though I got my suspicions—you know his mother isn't well."

"Yessir, I know."

Henry returned, wiping his hands on his denim pants while he made his way to the ice box.

"Howdy." He glanced at Ben as he poured milk into a glass.

"Save that milk for pie. I'm about out."

"Yessum." Henry poured the milk back into the pitcher then sat in the chair next to Ben.

"Got bad news from home. My mother broke her arm. Seems she stumbled when she went out and about in the dark. My father woke up and found her lying on the porch freezing cold."

Mrs. Cramer gasped.

"She's alright now?"

"Yeah. Doctor said it was a miracle she didn't get pneumonia."

"What possessed her go take a walk in the dark?"

Mrs. Cramer's question led Ben to believe she didn't know the type of sickness Henry's mother had.

"Well, when she doesn't feel well, she likes to walk off the pain, she says."

Henry looked toward Ben.

"I know when I was feeling my worst in the hospital, I couldn't think straight just needing relief from pain. When the medicine wore off, I would do about anything to get my mind off it."

Henry smiled.

The telephone rang, and Mr. Cramer stood. "I'll answer it."

"I see," Mrs. Cramer remarked as she moved to Henry and patted his shoulder. "I'll keep prayin' for her."

"Thank you."

Ben heard his name being called from the other room and made his way there.

"The telephone call is for you. It's Mason Forder."

"Thanks."

As he moved to the phone, his mind spun with questions. Telephoning an employee at home seemed out of character for the boss he knew. Ben spoke into the phone. The conversation was brief. Those within earshot would have heard a hello, a sure, and a see you tomorrow.

While Ben was on the telephone, Henry had made his way into the front room and sat in a chair.

"Still got a job?" Henry grinned.

Ben ran his hand through is hair.

"As far as I know. Mason is in town tomorrow and wants to take me to lunch. Said he has some news."

"You're in for a long night wondering what it is, I reckon."

"Yep."

Noon came and through the front window, Ben saw Mason pull up in his Rolls Royce. He wondered what business the man had in town on a Saturday. Surely this appointment was not the only reason the man had driven to town. Ben opened the door and walked toward the car, pulling on his overcoat as he moved.

"Good to see you, Mason."

"Thanks for agreeing to see me. Mind if we keep the meal simple—how about Nathan's Diner?"

"Sounds mighty fine."

In truth, Ben hated to waste a meal from anywhere. His curiosity, and a heavy sense of dread, had killed his appetite. Was a slab of meatloaf at Nathan's Diner to be his "last meal" so to speak, as a Forder employee? Or perhaps Mason had another job he wanted him to take.

A chill moved over him. Surely Mason wasn't bringing news from Layton.

Within the hour, he realized that was exactly what Mason was doing. The words swirled around him like a tornado, leaving anger and guilt in its path of destruction. Ben pushed his question through his dry throat and mouth.

"So, is Lena gonna survive?" *And how is Katherine, and, oh, God help me, please, how is Clara?*

His gorge rose.

"Lena is recovering very well from what my wife tells me. And Joe has been arrested."

"Arrested, you said?"

"Yes."

Ben pictured the small-framed man being handcuffed.

"I'm sorry, Mason, I need to ask before you say anything else. Are Katherine and Clara in danger? Were they harmed?"

"Ben, you're a might late in worrying over your family's safety."

Ben's chin dropped to his chest.

"But, yes, they are safe, and Katherine assured Pastor, us, and the Justice's that both she and Clara were not harmed."

"Was Joe drunk when he did this?"

"I'm not sure. But, evil acts don't always need the cloak of a vice. At its worst, evil is calculated and alert."

Ben nodded in agreement and pushed his plate aside, placing his elbows on the table. He rested his head in his palms.

Thank you, God, that he's locked up.

Mason cleared his throat causing Ben to look up at him.

"The trial will be in January at the County Courthouse, not too far from here."

"Yes, in Collin. When?"

Mason had written the details on a piece of paper that he pulled from his pocket and handed to Ben who read the information.

"Can I be off work to come? I'd slip in and out of the courtroom without Katherine seeing me."

Mason formed a fist and gently pressed it against the table.

"Yes."

Mason's fist pounded the table twice.

"Ben. Go home to your family. Don't wait for the trial. They need you. I don't understand why you can feel good about just attending the trial."

At that comment, Ben couldn't hold back the tears that welled in his eyes.

"Has your wife never wanted to see you again, refusing your pleas to be forgiven and to come home? Would she refuse to see you on your deathbed?"

"No."

Mason laid his napkin across his plate, grunted, then nodded his head back and forth in slow motion. His eyes were closed. Ben couldn't determine if he was admitting agreement to his argument or surrendering all effort to get Ben home. He reckoned it was the latter.

Mason scooted out of the booth and put on his coat then slid his black leather gloves onto his hands. Ben stood as well and slipped into his coat. Tension filled the space between them as they made their way to the cashier.

"Thank you for lunch." The statement resembled an attempted diversion from the matter at hand.

Mason paid, stuck a toothpick between his teeth, and pushed open the diner door. Ben followed, feeling like a child who'd been reprimanded.

"You're welcome." Mason stood in place beside the diner window. "Ben, make sure you ask God what He wants you to do."

Ben nodded silently. Mason had no idea how skilled he had gotten at ignoring God's nudges. They settled into the car, and Mason drove the short piece toward the boarding house. Ben broke the silence.

"Thank you, Mason, for your honesty."

"I can't fathom what you and Katherine have been through, but I also can't fathom that God doesn't want you back home with your family. I can only reckon that He wants it more than you do."

Ben managed to tell Mason good-bye and get to his room unnoticed, despite hearing Henry and Arlen talking in the kitchen. He stretched across his bed and wept.

Could God untangle the knot he'd made of his life?

Chapter 22

1924 | Layton, Texas

"Lena?" Katherine walked out the backdoor and pulled her coat tightly around her. Cold morning wind blew around the corner of the house, stinging her ears. The cold air attacked her feet through thin slippers. When Katherine awoke this morning, Lena had already risen from the bed. Katherine had yawned widely and turned back over for more sleep. A half hour later she awoke again. The air was vacant of the usual morning coffee smell. No clattering of skillets and dishes came from the kitchen. She rose to find her sister, and to Katherine's dismay, there was no sight or sound of Lena inside the house.

The morning was still young with black skies as Katherine made her way to the outhouse, hoping she would find her sister there. "Lena! Are you sick inside there?" Katherine pulled her hand from her coat pocket, remembering that she needed to mend the ripped lining, and banged on the outhouse door.

"Lena! Answer me. Unlock the door."

Katherine wound her cold fingers around the splintery handle and yanked. The motion caused her to fall backward as the unlatched door easily swung open. Lena was not in sight. Katherine cupped her hands around her mouth. The morning was quiet, surely Lena would hear her yelling.

"Lena! Answer me. Lena!"

Perhaps Lena had gone into the shed to see Gitter for some reason. Katherine turned to run toward it but halted and took off to the house instead at the thought of Clara asleep in the bed. She couldn't leave Clara alone to go search for Lena. In jagged motions, she turned again toward the shed. "Blast it!" Yes! She could leave Clara safe within the house long enough to check for Lena. Running toward the structure wonton of repair and leaning slightly to the right, Katherine tripped, giving in to her panic. "What if Lena is hurt and I have to help her. Clara will be alone and get scared." She shook her head against the conflicting emotions. *Think.*

Katherine rose from the cold, hard ground, feeling the pain in her knee. She pulled her right hand from the coat pocket and rubbed the soreness.

Smoky air caused by her heavy breathing surrounded her as she ran to the shed, clear-headed enough to see if Lena was in there.

The door creaked as she pulled it open. "Lena?" Gitter whimpered. A scurry caught Katherine's eye. Rats no doubt. She looked in the corners of the building and under the blankets stacked near Gitter's stall. "Lena?" Convinced her sister was not present, Katherine ran outside and closed the wooden door, suspecting she'd be back in a moment to hitch up Gitter and go searching for her sister.

"Dear God, lead me to Lena." Calmer than earlier, Katherine walked their yard, yelling for her sister. Perhaps Lena had exited out the side door of Katherine's bedroom, but rounding the back corner of the house, a glance at the area near the side door showed no sign of anyone. Next, Katherine made her way to the edge of the yard to see if Lena had gone to sit at Sammy's grave, but there was no hint of human presence. She noted the well-kept mound of dirt *I couldn't bear another loss of someone I love.*

Her nose began to run, and she could sense the coldness in her cheeks. Her toes were numb inside her house slippers as she ran toward the back porch. The screen door to the porch stood wide open just as she'd left it in her panic. She pulled it shut and slipped the lock hook into the latch then yanked open the door to the kitchen. A weak sense of hope spread through her that she and Lena had simply missed each other in passing, but the kitchen was still empty of activity. She walked through the house again. No Lena.

Katherine fought back tears as she pulled her heavy boots from under her bed and drooped onto the mattress to change her shoes, careful to not wake Clara. Had Joe somehow escaped jail, entered their house, and taken her sister? Reason took over. Of course, he hadn't. Katherine bit her lip, there was no reasonable explanation for Lena to have gone missing other than she chose to do so. Such a thought brought literal pain to Katherine's chest, and with that heaviness upon her, she turned to rouse Clara.

Gitter's hoofs clicked on the soil hardened by the cold. With Clara nestled in a quilt and resting against her arm, Katherine guided the cart down the road toward the Justice Store. The five-year-old fully accepted the explanation that they were heading to the store to look for Aunt Lena, who must have walked to work. Another quilt rested in the cart seat next to Clara, a sign of Katherine's hope that Lena would be discovered and in need of warmth. In a moment's decision, Katherine had chosen the direction of the store over the one that led to the church and Pastor Carlson's parsonage.

Halfway to the store, Katherine glanced at the gathering of bare trees to the right where she had shared the news of her pregnancy with Ben.

"Gitter, whoa." She yanked on the reins. At the quick motion, Clara sat up.

"You sit right here, Clara, and don't touch the reins."

Katherine imparted the instructions as she removed a quilt from her own legs and proceeded to jump from the cart and run toward the trees.

"Lena!"

Her sister lay on the ground with her knees pulled to her chest and arms wrapped tightly around her legs.

"Lena!"

Reaching her, Katherine dropped to her knees and ran her hands over Lena's body.

"Are you alive?" Lena's wheezing answered her question.

"Lena look at me. Are you hurt?"

She pulled her sister's arms away from her legs, then took Lena's head in her hands.

"Look at me."

Relief swept over Katherine as Lena relaxed her legs and turned to face her.

"Are you hurt?"

"No."

"Are you sick?"

"No."

Lena began to cry.

"I'm sorry, Katherine."

"We'll talk later. Right now, let's get you home."

Lena said nothing, but she didn't resist when Katherine lifted her into her arms and carried her like a small child toward the cart. By now, the sun brightened the morning skies.

"Momma? Is Aunt Lena dead?"

"No. But she's very sick and tired. We'll take her home."

"Here, Momma." Clara handed her the quilt as she scooted over in the cart seat. "Aunt Lena can sit by you."

Katherine stood Lena on the ground and wrapped her in a quilt, then watched as the trembling young woman pulled herself up and on to the cart seat.

"Did you get sick walking to work, Aunt Lena?" Situating herself back onto the cart, Katherine noted that Clara was rubbing the quilt where Lena' s arm was covered as she asked the question.

"I was feeling bad before I left. I should have stayed home." Lena's wheeze had lightened, but the sound still filled the air around them.

"Me and Momma will take care of you."

"I know."

Katherine felt Lena's head rest against her shoulder.

"Aunt Lena, you need coffee to breath better. Right, Momma?"

"Right."

"Does your stomach hurt?"

"No."

"What hurts?"

Katherine suspected it was Lena's heart that hurt, for there were no indications of other ailments.

"Clara," Katherine smiled at her daughter, "let Aunt Lena ride home quietly so she can catch her breath. And when we get home, she can go to bed, and you can help me make her some coffee."

She watched her daughter nod in agreement, but she saw disagreement in her wrinkled forehead. Clara didn't want to be hushed.

Indeed, the ride home was quiet, save the sound of Lena's labored breathing, that slackened hesitantly moment by moment as they rode. Katherine had spent a large portion of her years riding in this cart. Most trips had been mundane and reeked of hard work and little pleasure. Other rides had traveled to her heart and put down stakes. She recalled her and Joe as young teens, and Lena, a pipsqueak, squeezed between them on the seat, riding to deliver small chairs and pieces of furniture he'd made for the fortunate few in a ten mile spread who could afford a simple luxury. She'd felt proud of Joe, even admired him, for his ability and had been grateful for the extra income his work provided. Sitting now on the weathered cart seat,

Katherine couldn't help but wonder if Joe had already been flirting with his own evil that early on. Had she ever truly known her brother? Katherine swallowed a lump in her throat as her mind wandered to another memory.

A marked day it was when she had met Ben at the train station with his son. He had returned to Layton, so she and Sammy could meet. Although she had awaited their train with a simple foreknowledge that Sammy was not well and whole, the sight of Ben carrying the crippled boy from the train was more than she'd anticipated. The scene lived vividly in her mind. A simple, but life-changing declaration that he was also deaf had left her dumbstruck, while Sammy's wide, beautiful smile had made her awestruck. The three of them had shared colas on the ride to her house, and somewhere along the road, her heart, which was already bonded to the boy's father, attached to him as well.

Katherine blew out a breath. On another journey, she'd risked the life of Gitter as she urged him on to the train depot in a frantic attempt to catch Ben before he left her life for good—the first time. She'd refused his proposal and he was heading back to Commerce with no plans to ever return to Layton. Fear can lead to either inaction or reaction, and Katherine had done both. From fear of not being capable to mother Sammy, she'd said no to spending the rest of her life with the man she loved. On the heels of her refusal, fear of being without him had driven her to forsake all social graces and literally chase after him.

An intimate memory followed, and she felt her warmth saturate her cheeks. Katherine and Ben had ridden toward their honeymoon night in this very cart. He'd lifted her onto the decorated seat—a blushing bride with a new name and a handsome husband seated beside her. The night that had followed had been filled with both patience and passion as the two of them had learned how to love one another.

Their house came into view, and Katherine shook the last memory from her mind. Lena needed tending. Katherine sighed. Tonight would be another marked ride in the cart, and the memory would not be pleasant.

Clara surprised Katherine by not balking on the instructions she'd laid out. The child was carefully scooping coffee into the pot filter as Katherine led Lena into their bedroom. Moments later, with Clara busy drawing Lena a get well picture, Katherine slipped into the room and sat on the bed next to where her sister lay and rubbed her arm.

"Lena, I have to know what happened."

Her sister closed her eyes and Katherine saw a grimace move across her face.

"What's your biggest fear, Katherine?"

The question seemed to be a conversation starter, rather than a diversion.

"We're talking about you."

"Please, just answer me."

"Betrayal. Lena, why did you ask me about my greatest fear?"

"Because I gave in to mine tonight."

Seconds passed and felt like moments.

"I never want to disappoint anyone, but now I've gone and disappointed myself."

"Lena, I don't understand."

"Before Joe was arrested, I was filled with fear that he'd come back for me. Now that he's behind bars, my fear slid over and made room for shame. I couldn't even run away from it as it chased me down the road."

Lena's soft weeping filled the room before she continued her thought.

"I feel so ashamed. If a man ever does consider me for his wife, I'd be a big disappointment to him because I'm kind of marred, and I'm…I'm not sure that I could receive a man's touch."

"Lena, feel anger, feel confusion, feel disgust, but don't feel shame. There is no shame on your part. The shame belongs to Joe. The judgement belongs to Joe."

"Katherine, I know what you're sayin' is the truth, but the shame is like a black hole that I constantly have to walk around and avoid. Tonight I let myself fall into it."

"You don't have to fall in, but if you do, me or someday an honorable man who loves you will help pull you out. Not to mention that God can help you. And if you do fall, He's right there beside you. Inside you."

"I don't want to fall in again, but what if I trip?"

"Grab the hand that will be reaching to pull you out."

"You make that sound so simple."

"It's far from simple."

Chapter 23

January 1925 | Layton, Texas

Her world was small, and she would have been content to keep it that way. Seated in the backseat of the Forder's Rolls Royce, her hand wrapped around Lena's trembling one, Katherine desired nothing more than to return to Layton and know nothing about the world outside of her town's cotton field borders. Regretfully, she found herself staring out the window as the dark Texas earth rolled by her in warped, blurry motion. The sensation made her nauseous if she stared too long. Katherine recalled Ben talking about the extensive Forder Empire when they'd just met in 1918 on the night she fell in love. Her view out the window testified to the truth of his statement and of the wealth Mason and Abigail Forder possessed. The two of them sat in the front seat, kind and caring and unusually normal for the rich friends they were to two common sisters.

The rhythm of the windshield wipers mesmerized Katherine as she turned her focus to their motion. The rain had felt cold as they situated themselves in the auto, and the scent of snow was in the air. She had to admit that the soft leather car seats were comfortable, and oddly, comforting, as though they were attempting to soothe away the pain of today's agenda. Lena's subtle wheezing was evidence that the task ahead of her was stressful. They were halfway through their two hour journey to the county courthouse in Collin. Today, Joe would stand trial for his actions against his sister.

Katherine's mind wondered to Clara. No one outside the family knew about Joe's threatening actions toward her daughter. Clara had been spared physical encounters, and therefore, public enlightenment. With the privacy, came the burden of being her daughter's only source of healing. That concern nagged at Katherine. Surely God would heal a little girl's heart.

Wendell and Amy Carlson agreed to keep both Clara and Mary Forder during the trial period. There would be no traveling home until the ordeal ended. The Forders had arranged a hotel stay near the courthouse since no one knew how long the proceedings might last. Clara's recent separation at Thanksgiving had made this stay with her friends less of an adventure than

Katherine had hoped. The child had wept when Katherine placed her in Amy's car alongside her suitcase and prized possessions.

"Momma, will you come back before the butterflies dance?"

"Yes."

"Is it almost time for the butterflies?"

"No, Clara. They just danced. They migrate, I mean dance, after the hot weather."

"Momma, don't forget to come home."

"Clara, I won't forget, and I'll be home a long, long time before the butterflies dance."

"Promise?"

"There is nowhere I would rather be than at home with you. I will be home as soon as I can and a long time before the butterflies dance."

Katherine leaned over and kissed the face that belonged to Ben Williams. How she loved this child. "Aunt Lena and I will try to call you on the telephone. Won't that be fun!" Her daughter smiled at her, then licked the salty tears from her lips. "Sort'a fun, I guess."

Lena's squeeze on her hand drew Katherine back to the present moment, and the sound of Abigail Forder's voice. "...and so, we'll arrive in time to eat in the hotel dining room if you two can hold out another hour."

Katherine squeezed her sister's hand as a gesture of gratitude for getting her attention. "That will be fine by us."

Abigail turned around and offered a grin at the two sisters, and Katherine returned it.

"Mason, is that a good plan?" Abigail raised her eyebrows at her husband. Katherine noticed Mason Forder pull one of his gloved hands from the steering wheel and squeeze his wife's fingers. "Seeing I'm outnumbered, I suppose whatever you ladies want is a good plan." The mingled laughter of the four riders filled the car. Katherine was thankful to have Abigail with them during this trip and trial.

Standing in front of the Whitehall Hotel, Katherine's mouth dropped open—embarrassingly. Dread had transformed into excitement betraying the dire circumstances that brought them to the establishment. Lena giggled beside her, apparently the victim of fickle emotions as well. Situated on a corner, the three-level red brick building was lined with window after window, each adorned with curved white rod iron beneath it and graced with thin white curtains. Black shutters covered the lower part of each window, offering privacy for the occupants.

Katherine sensed Abigail come up behind her then felt a hand on her back, nudging her forward. Mason was parking his auto in a gated lot. Despite the brisk air, Katherine's palm felt sweaty as she gripped the handle of her small luggage piece. Beside her, she saw Lena switch her suitcase from one hand to other, then wipe her palm on her dress. She smiled at their similarities.

While the Forders handled details and their luggage at the hotel counter, Katherine took Lena by the arm and sauntered through the lobby. Rich red carpets lay atop white tile floors. Large velvet covered chairs with high backs formed sitting areas around heavy cherry wood tables. Two chandeliers hung from the ceiling between the four suspended fans that whirled. Two large fireplaces graced the lobby at either end, each offering warm heat from a popping fire. Wooden staircases led to the top two levels.

Soon, Mason walked over and handed Lena a key. "You two will be next door to us in Room 204. You have a private bath." A grin spread across his mouth. Katherine's face followed suit. "Ladies, we'll all freshen up, then eat. We have a little over an hour before we have to be in court, which is one block away."

"Thank you, Mr. Forder." Lena's voice was clear and confident, but Katherine was certain that Mason, like her, saw the tears well up in the young woman's eyes.

"Be back down in ten minutes." Abigail winked at the two sisters, then tugged on Mason's arm to pull him toward the stairs.

Katherine ascended the stairs slowly with Lena. Her sister spoke but kept her eyes on the sights around her.

"If we weren't here for such a bad reason, I'd be more excited about our adventure. It's nice to travel outside of Layton, don't you think?"

"No. You've had a spirit of adventure all your life. I'm more of a homebody."

They looked at one another and giggled.

While Lena washed her face in the small porcelain sink in the room, Katherine stood before the mirror attached to the wall. She spread her hands over the cotton of her best Sunday outfit. The cream, long sleeved dress had pale blue stripes from shoulder to hem. Three slightly ruffled layers graced the bottom of the dress. She tightened her low, loose bun, then placed her small straw hat atop her russet locks. She would give up her tight bun, wanting to appear more confident and less rigid in demeanor, yet not fully understanding why she felt that way. She stared at the navy ribbon on her hat. It complimented her hair and the pale stripes of her dress. *Nice.* She gathered up her gloves from the suitcase and folded them into her small, cream clutch. Her navy shoes threatened blisters if worn too long, but they would have to do. Lena had brought her best dress as well, and the deep green color helped brighten her pale features. Their packed wardrobes consisted of one more church dress and their best house dress. Grabbing their overcoats, the women headed downstairs and joined the Forders for nourishment in the dining room.

The women's heels clacked rhythmically on the tile floor, echoing their arrival to the courtroom. Mason seated them on a bench and excused himself to speak with the attorney who was seated at a table on the other side of the wooden half wall. Katherine noticed a smattering of unfamiliar people seat themselves nearby. One young woman was weeping quietly; a man who appeared about the same age was comforting her with his arm gripped snugly across her shoulder. Katherine took hold of Lena's hand. Abigail took hold of the other. Lena was strong, full of conviction, and level-headed, but Katherine wondered how she, or anyone, would hold up replaying the humiliating acts done against her, and knowing that the person she was condemning was her kin. *Dear God, help Lena to say whatever she needs to say.*

Concern for Lena was met head on with sadness over the loss of a brotherly relationship—or what it once had been. Her thoughts led her to Ben. She'd loved Joe, maybe she still did, but she'd inherited him. He'd betrayed her blood. She'd chosen Ben and offered herself to him entirely. He'd betrayed her being, but she still loved him.

Mason stepped into their row and crouched before Lena; his eyes met Katherine's before he spoke. He cleared his throat. "Joe has another victim. A woman from Greenville." His head nodded backward, indicating the weeping female two rows ahead of them. Katherine's stomach knotted at the news. She heard Lena stifle a sob. Mason reached up and took Lena's hand in his. "They can most likely convict Joe with her testimony and her eye witnesses. Lena, you don't have to testify against him if you don't want to."

Katherine gasped awkwardly. *Eye witnesses?* She felt blood pumping frantically through her veins. Not only had that poor girl been humiliated and damaged by her brother, but others had been there to see it—thank God for witnesses. Abigail grasped her hand and she felt her squeeze it. Katherine looked over at Lena whose face appeared staunch and firm. The relief she expected to see on her sister's face was not there.

"Will my testimony help in any way?"

Mason seemed to pause and collect his thoughts. "There are no guarantees, but the attorney thinks your testimony might increase his sentence should he get convicted."

"I'll testify."

"Lena, you don't have to." Katherine turned in the bench and faced her sister head on.

"Yes. I do." Lena's brows furrowed. "I'm determined."

Mason stood. "Alright then, I'll let the attorney know." He patted Lena on the shoulder, nodded toward Katherine, and then squeezed his wife's hand. "She's a brave woman. She's doing the right thing, ladies." One name kept Katherine from trying to coax Lena into a different decision once she saw her determination. Perhaps that one name was part of the source behind her sister's decision. *Clara.*

Katherine felt Lena trembling. Commotion to her right caused Katherine to turn and look. She knew instantly why Lena trembled. The lunch she'd eaten in the dining room rose to her throat, and Katherine tugged on her ear.

Handcuffed and escorted by two uniformed policemen, Joe entered the courtroom. His head hung low, but just before being seated next to the attorney on the other side of the courtroom, he raised his eyes and looked directly at them. His chin quivered. Katherine stared. Cold, harsh, biting air was all that passed between the brother and his sisters.

Twelve jurors entered the courtroom and sat inside a partitioned area. Katherine gazed at them thinking that any one of them could easily have been her neighbors, as common looking as she and Lena. The judge entered the courtroom, and on command, all present rose. Katherine stood, not as a sister to the man on trial, but as the staunch matriarch of the family.

One hour into the trial, the woman from Greenville relayed the sickening tale of what Joe had done to her. He'd come upon her in her kitchen as she was washing dishes. When his proposition was resisted, he began to hit her, ignorantly unaware that her screams reached her husband, who was Joe's friend, and a neighbor who were together in the garage cleaning his auto. They sprang into the kitchen just as Joe's fist hit her face. He had her flat on the floor with her dress hiked to her waist. He was positioned over her in an immoral, invasive way. She stated that what they observed had not been his first strike nor his first action against her. The husband and neighbor both testified and verified her story.

Next on the stand was Lena.

Katherine sat in utter misery as Lena's words replayed the account she'd heard her tell more than once. The moments were surreal, as though neither Katherine nor Lena were physically in the courtroom. When Katherine found the grit to look at Joe, she saw his head was stooped low so as not to see his sister testify.

At one point, Katherine noticed that Lena's eyes widened. She paused for a second or two in her testimony, then sat up straighter and continued. What had crossed her sister's mind at that very moment? Neither the judge nor the attorney seemed to notice the odd transition. If Abigail or Mason had noticed, neither let on to Katherine that they had.

As Lena continued, Katherine's memory flashed back to their childhood when fourteen year old Joe swept in as the heroic knight and slew the angry dragon holding four year old princess Lena and her older sister captive. Although the scene was only child's play, Lena's affection toward her protector was not, for she had grabbed him around the legs proclaiming, "Joe the Knight is the bravest man in the kingdom! He won't let anything hurt us!" The irony made goose bumps crawl on Katherine's skin. The irony that her own daughter's childhood had been tainted by the once heroic Joe the Knight made her shudder.

Thoughts of Ben also invaded Katherine, and she felt ashamed that they drew her attention away from Lena's words. Over five years ago, her husband had spared Faye Forder from a fate similar to the testimonies she was hearing. Yet, at the time, Katherine hadn't viewed his act as heroic because it had led to a kiss driven by emotions. Katherine had embraced his heroism too late.

Lena left the witness stand and stoically returned to her chair. Katherine wrapped her in her arms and sat in silence. The court would adjourn until tomorrow, so Joe was escorted from the courtroom without a look back at his sisters. As Joe exited, Mason explained that's Joe's state assigned lawyer would try to create doubt in the minds of the jury, so they wouldn't convict him. The small party stood to leave the courtroom. Katherine wondered how in the world a jury could begin to doubt what they had heard today.

With few words between them, Katherine and party walked back to the hotel. It was late afternoon. Since Lena asked to be excused for a nap and Mason needed to tend to paperwork in his room, Abigail insisted, Katherine join her for a stroll on the sidewalk, to meander in and out of the stores. Abigail spied a small rose brooch in a window. "It's not real, but it's beautiful," she said as she selected it and took it to the cashier. "A gift of love for our brave Lena." Katherine recognized that Abigail showed love by sharing not only her time, but also her resources. The gracious act warmed Katherine's heart.

After a light dinner at the hotel, Lena, who had eaten little and remained understandably quiet during the meal, excused herself again to prepare for bed.

Katherine kept her promise and phoned Clara, who deemed it necessary to holler her words so Katherine could hear them far away. *"Yes, Clara, I can hear you."* Evening had become night and ushered in sleep, then morning woke bright and clear, as though it were promising an end to the abhorrent events on trial.

Knowing how Lena struggled with shame, Katherine was stunned at the fortitude Lena and the other victim and witnesses showed in answering the questions the opposing lawyer had worded with twisted truth as he presented an opposing side of the story. When the testimonies were complete, the lawyers each addressed the jury. It had been a three-hour-day before lunch and a two-hour-day since. As mid-afternoon ticked on the clock, the jury was dismissed to make their decision. Katherine exhaled deeply. She would painfully hope the day's end revealed a just future of Joe McGinn. Katherine heard the door behind them open and shut as attendees exited for fresh air, water, and to stretch their legs, she presumed. Indeed, she needed refreshment herself.

Mason waited to speak with the attorney, making their party the last to leave. Eventually he escorted them to a private room and had sandwiches and colas delivered while they waited. In less than two hours, the attorney entered the room and announced that a verdict had been reached.

Bound and led, Joe entered the courtroom. Katherine noted that his cold stare at them transformed into one of anger when his eyes looked beyond them to his right. It was a fleeting look, but it made the hair on her arms stand up. Protocol tamed her curiosity, and Katherine wouldn't crane her neck to see what had distracted Joe moments before his life could drastically change. His lawyer pulled out Joe's chair and motioned him to sit. The jury settled, then the judge entered the courtroom.

The setting seemed to shrink and envelope her. Katherine's breathing felt rapid and shallow. Her senses were heightened. Lena wheezed. Mason sat tall, like the sentry that he was to her and Lena. sounds around her. Abigail's knuckled wrapped around Lena's hand were white. The Greenville victim wept. A man behind them cleared his throat. A juror sneezed. The lawyer's shoe clicked as his leg shook up and down. Joe shifted his position and the chair creaked.

Upon command, Joe and his lawyer stood. The judge silently read the verdict handed to him, then addressed the jury to state their decision. The verdict was uttered, and life was altered. Joe the Knight would spend the next eight years in prison. Lena moaned, and her head fell against Katherine's shoulder. The weight of Joe's actions coupled with the burdens she'd borne the last five years invaded Katherine and she wept quietly.

Joe was escorted away, without a glance at his sisters. Katherine ceased weeping, slowly exhaled, then uttered jumbled words of gratitude to God that Lena and Clara were safe.

She gathered her sister in her arms and let Lena sob against her chest. Abigail rubbed their backs. Mason excused himself, stating he needed to speak to someone before he got away. At his declaration, Katherine felt Lena turn her face toward the courtroom door. Lena's cheek rose against Katherine's bosom. Was her sister smiling? Surely not. Momentarily, Mason returned and caught up to the attorney. Words of gratitude were expressed, then the weary Layton party left the courtroom. Lena's arm was hooked inside Katherine's as they walked behind the Forders to exit the building, remaining a few paces behind the couple.

"I thought I'd feel nothing but relief, Katherine, but I'm so sad."

"Over Joe?"

"Over loss. So many things that should have been good and enjoyable vanished from our family."

"You and Clara—you're goodness—to me."

Lena smiled, and Katherine thought it half-hearted and obligatory.

"I have to trust that God is up to good somehow." Lena blew out a breath.

"It's not easy to take the bad with the good."

The irony of her own statement knotted Katherine's insides. She certainly hadn't done that with Ben.

"Nope, it's not. That's where faith comes in."

Katherine felt Lena take her hand and squeeze it.

"Katherine, I went through an awful experience, but I don't know why that other girl was raped, and not just beat like me. I feel so sad about that. What keeps me from going crazy and giving in to my shame is the hope that God will use it for good."

"You're brave."

"For now. I could cower at any moment—depending on which emotion I give in to."

"Do you remember telling me that you forgave Joe?"

"Yes."

"Do you still forgive him after testifying?"

"Katherine, I'm never going to forget, and I may have to forgive many times over, but I don't want to be a slave to anger or fear or bitterness—or even shame. Wouldn't Joe enjoy knowing I was pushover? So, as hard as it might be, I'm not gonna let him ruin me, even though my emotions may be at war with me for a lifetime."

Tears were rolling down Katherine's cheeks, and she wiped them with her left hand—where her wedding band should be displayed. She was growing weary of crying.

"Lena, I admire you. I reckon I don't know what to say."

"When my emotions teeter-totter on me, and I lose heart or try to run, you may not admire me."

"I'll be there for you when that happens."

Katherine noticed that they had reached the hotel. Abigail pulled her hand from Mason's arm and turned toward the sisters.

"Mason has determined it is too late to drive home, so we suggest the evening be filled with street browsing, dining, and phone calls to those we love in Layton. If you two are up to it."

Katherine looked at her sister. "Lena?"

"I'm starving! And I'm up for a little adventure. Time to think of happier things."

Three hours later, weary in body and soul, they began the walk back to the hotel. Katherine was grateful for the laughter she'd heard from Lena that evening. However, now Lena sighed heavily and blew out a breath. "So much for my happily ever after. No man will want me after what Joe tried to do."

She's teetering.

"Lena, don't give in to the dark—the shame. Joe didn't touch your heart and soul. Some man will come along who is honorable enough to see your goodness and even your weakness and love you for both."

Lena clasped Katherine's hand. "He was there. In the courtroom."

"Who?" *The man who would love her? That made no sense.*

"Ben."

Katherine felt her body go clammy.

"Impossible."

But she immediately knew it wasn't. She knew he lived in nearby Commerce and worked for Mason. Katherine didn't doubt that Mason had kept him informed.

"I thought I recognized him yesterday when I was on the witness stand. Then today, he acknowledged me with a nod of his head. I knew for certain it was him when Mr. Forder shook his hand. He limped out of the courtroom."

"I'm sure you're mistaken." *The Forders knew he was there? I feel like a fool.* Katherine suppressed the deep anguish that began to rise in her.

"I'm sure I'm *not* mistaken."

Katherine's pride wanted the conversation to end, but her curiosity wouldn't allow that. Her insides shook as anguish over being dismissed by him was evolving into anger.

"You said he limped?" *What had Ben gone through?*

"Yes."

"What else did you notice?"

"I noticed that he cared."

"How could you notice a feeling?"

"He sat forward, made eye contact, as though he were telling me to keep up my courage."

Katherine no longer suppressed her anger. Lena didn't know that Ben had made his choice years ago to not come home.

"You make him seem heroic, like all this is a scene in one of your novels. Real heroes return to those they love."

"Believe me, Katherine, I know this is no scene in a novel." Lena's voice rose. "What happened to me and what I had to do these last two days was very real and something no woman should ever have to endure. I was able to testify simply because God helped me."

Her sister began to wheeze.

"We need to sit so you can catch your breath."

"No. Keep walking. Anyway, what do you mean heroes return to the ones they love?

"Nothing!"

Katherine swallowed her bile.

"I'm ashamed of talking to you this way, Lena, after all you've been through."

"I know I may sound silly to you, but I drew strength from seeing Ben there."

"I would have too."

"Katherine, you're talking like a crazy person."

Tell her.

"Lena, years ago I wrote Ben and asked him to come home. He didn't. Instead, he wrote and told me if I filed for divorce, he would sign the papers."

Lena gasped. Her wheezing increased.

"Oh, Katherine. I'm so sorry. Why? Why didn't you tell me?"

"Because I was hurt, embarrassed, and ashamed. You're the only person who knows."

"That's why he only sends letters to Clara?"

"I guess. I've never read one of them."

"I've misjudged you."

"Your judgement came from your limited knowledge."

From the day she'd met Ben, Katherine had always felt safe in his presence until the moment she told him to leave and not return. It baffled her that she had not sensed his presence in the courtroom the last two days.

"Lena, why didn't I feel him there in the courtroom?"

"Katherine, I don't know. Goodness, I thought I knew you through and through, but I realize I don't."

"I didn't know Joe was bothering you."

Katherine felt Lena's grasp on her hand tighten.

"I reckon, we both withheld something from each other. That saddens me."

"And I'm sorry we did, Lena."

"I'm ready to be home and see Clara."

"Me too."

Lena's wheezing had lessened when she stopped Katherine and took both her hands. An auto beeped, and a family passed them by.

Abigail Forder called out from her place ahead of them on the sidewalk, "You ladies okay back there?"

"Yes. We'll catch up." Katherine responded without making eye contact.

"What is it Lena? You stopped me."

Silence. She heard Lena take a deep breath and let it out.

"Katherine, like us, Ben needs to go home to Layton. It's where he belongs."

Home. The longing for Ben to be there was fervent, but what did Lena expect her to do about it?

Chapter 24

1925 | Commerce, Texas

He hadn't prepared himself for the encounter. Ben shook his head back and forth and rubbed his palms over his face. Watching Joe shuffle into the courtroom handcuffed had felt like a boulder hit his chest. The man he'd once called friend, then brother, was now labeled enemy. Hearing Lena bare the details of her humiliation had made Ben's stomach lurch and his anger pulsate throughout his body. But the sight of Katherine—that had caused his breath to still. His entire being ached, and the intangible pain was far worse than anything fire had inflicted on him. His love for her drew nourishment from her presence. The sensation was deeply intense, and he wondered how she could not have felt it.

Despite her rejection of him, Ben longed to go to her, hold her, comfort her, and kiss her. After all, they were still married. She'd never sent him divorce papers. Although Mason had urged him if he didn't go home, to at least make himself known to Katherine at the courthouse. Ben had argued in his mind that the circumstances of a trial were not the place to make amends with his wife. How easily the mind can deceive itself. Even when Mason noticed him there and came to shake his hand, Ben was staunch against the man's urgings to go to her at that very moment.

In vain, he tried to absorb the feel of his daughter through the nearness of Katherine. Who was caring for their child? The irony of his question made his head ache. *He* should be the one caring for their child.

Whether she realized it or not, Lena had spotted him the first day from her view on the witness stand. He'd seen her expression change briefly to raised brows and a slight tilt of her head when she glanced his direction. He had slipped out before she left the stand, not willing to risk her bringing Katherine over to him when court adjourned. But today, her smile at him as she lay against her sister was a picture he would treasure in his mind's eye. He had gladly captured the moment before he left the courtroom under a load of shame for not speaking to his wife.

Hastening to be out of sight before Katherine emerged from the courthouse, he limped to the bus stop across the street. A modest town compared to St.

Louis or Dallas, and a metropolis compared to Layton, the city of Collin was filled with beeping horns, crowded sidewalks, grocers, the smells of restaurants, and at last the sound of a bus braking for the stop. At the edge of town, Ben exited to wait at the motor lodge where he'd spent the night.

"Headed home?" The clerk handed Ben his luggage from behind the small counter.

"Yes. Mind if I wait here in the lobby?"

"Make yourself comfortable."

Ben sat on the only chair in the lobby and tried to avoid the loose spring protruding under the fabric of the cushion. His luggage rested on the floor beside him, and he draped his coat over it. A small table covered in a layer of dust rested next to the chair and hosted a magazine dated two years back. He swatted a fly from his face.

Henry was due to arrive in a half hour to drive him home in his auto. As he waited, Ben allowed his thoughts to return to Katherine. Having seen her, he doubted he could continue to survive on memories of her and written longings to his daughter. He would need to move home or give them up completely. He could no longer live in this veiled relationship. Katherine's physical presence had jolted him to understand that his daughter existed in flesh and blood. He'd slowly grown accustomed to Clara being an image in his mind and a longing in his heart. The realization shamed him.

At the sound of Henry's beeping horn, Ben stirred from his musings, grabbed his overcoat and luggage, and situated himself in Henry's passenger seat as the auto engine rumbled.

"You ready to head back, or do you need to eat?"

"I could grab a sandwich. You hungry?'

Henry laughed. "I'm always hungry. I passed a small diner about a block over. Besides I could use some coffee."

Henry's pride and joy on wheels had them at the curb in front of the diner in no time. Settled into a booth, Ben contemplated the menu. He knew Henry well enough to know he would order tuna on white bread. A middle-aged woman with graying hair made her way to the table with a pencil and pad in her hand.

"I'll have a pimento cheese sandwich on rye. And a pickle. With a cola."

Ben smirked and kicked Henry under the table. "And this growing boy will have tuna on white bread, french fries, a piece of apple pie, and hot coffee." He was amused when the waitress looked directly at Henry and raised her eyebrows. Henry laughed. "I'll take what my old man ordered for me." The waitress rolled her eyes at both of them and huffed away apparently unamused.

"So, is the trial over?" Henry cleared his throat before inquiring.

"Joe was convicted on two counts of assault, one count of attempted rape, and one count of rape. He'll be in jail for the next eight years. Hearing the testimonies set me to thinking about my Mama and all my Pa put her through. To think that Joe did that to Lena made anger well up inside me."

He heard Henry blow out a breath. "How was your sister-in-law?"

"She's a strong woman. Mason came to me afterward and spoke briefly. He had told her she didn't have to testify, but she wanted to anyway."

"Sounds like an honorable woman. Testifying could not have been easy on her."

"I could see the pain on her face."

"And your wife…was she there?" Henry fidgeted with the salt shaker.

"Yes."

"Did you speak?"

"No, she never saw me, but I couldn't take my eyes off her." Ben lightly hit his fist on the table. He focused his gaze out the window.

The waitress brought the drinks.

"Thank you, ma'am," Henry uttered as he stilled the shaker in his hand.

"Are you alright, Ben?"

"If I were indifferent, I would be. But, I still love her, and I want my child, so no, I'm not alright."

"For as long as I've known you, Ben, you've never been indifferent."

Ben turned his head and looked Henry in the eye.

"I'm a shameful Papa. How could I have faith, but be such a weak husband and father? I'm no better than my own Pa. He used strength to hurt his family. I'm using weakness."

Ben became uncomfortable under Henry's gaze. His friend took a deep breath and let it out.

"Go home, Ben. Go, and may God help you."

Ben had no argument against Henry. The young man knew exactly what he needed to do. Ben nodded his head in acknowledgement of that truth. He saw a grin spread on Henry's face.

"I've about had enough of you here in Commerce."

The tension was broken just as the waitress arrived with the food.

An hour later, the men entered their boarding house in Commerce. The phonograph was playing while some residents lingered in the front room over books, cards, or checkers. Mr. Cramer rose to meet them. Seeing the man wince as he rubbed his knuckles, Ben wondered when someone else would have to take over his job. His work and his wife's cooking were their room and board, and seeing that they were related to the owner, Ben hoped the Cramers would be allowed to keep their home here once they had to retire from their duties. Mr. Cramer was dressed in suspenders with a beige shirt beneath them; the clothing didn't hide his protruding belly.

"Welcome back. Mrs. Cramer gave me strict orders to bring y'all to the kitchen when you got here. She's got coffee and oatmeal cookies, and an ear for knowing what happened."

Ben looked at Henry, who smiled, then replied, "Good! I'm hungry."

The kitchen was warm from the oven and smelled of coffee, fried chicken, and cinnamon. Ben chuckled quietly. Cinnamon and furniture polish had always been the scent of Mrs. Cramer.

"I've got two plates covered with a dishrag over there if you men hadn't ate." Mrs. Cramer wiped her brow with her apron as she spoke.

"Henry said he's hungry." Mr. Cramer pulled a chair out from under the table and pointed to Henry.

Ben laughed out loud. "Mrs. Cramer, truth is, we had a sandwich at the diner about an hour ago, but I could use some coffee, and I can't pass up your good cookies." Ben looked at Henry whose face seemed hot and red.

"Is it fried chicken?"

"Yes, Henry, and green beans, and tomatoes." Mrs. Cramer lifted the rag off one of the plates.

"I'll take a plate, some coffee, and some cookies."

"I like a hearty eater," Mr. Cramer explained as he patted his protruding mid-section.

Mrs. Cramer handed the plate to Henry, "You're gonna eat me out of house and home. You best be finding a wife to do your cooking."

"Ah, Mrs. Cramer, you know you'd miss me if I got hitched."

"There's that fine young woman at church," Mr. Cramer interjected, "widow Caroline."

Henry coughed. Ben suppressed a laugh.

"Well, sir if I get a hankering for a woman with four wild, ornery youngins', I'll be sure and handcuff myself to widow Caroline."

"Them youngins'? They just need a Pa."

Ben heard Henry's tone turn serious. "Yessir, you're right, but I don't believe it's supposed to be me. God knows my heart."

Truth can be painful. Mr. Cramer's innocent words felt like a knife plunged into Ben's own heart. His little girl needed her Papa.

As they ate, Ben filled the Cramers in on the trial and what seeing Katherine had done to his insides.

"Mrs. Cramer, I tell you. Henry and me talked about this riding home. I can't survive being away from my child any longer. If I can't live with the woman and child I love, I'll live near them."

"Ben," Mrs. Cramer took his hand, "it seems to me you got no choice about your wife and child who's in heaven, but since you got one of each still here on earth, there ain't never been a reason good enough to choose being away from them. You best choose Layton over Commerce."

"But…"

"But, nothing. You know from your boss that there ain't nobody else in her life. And besides, you'll always have a place here to come visit. You and Henry, y'all like younger brothers to me. Well, Henry, I suppose, he's like a son." She reached over and pinched his cheek. Henry laughed. "So, I plan to always be in your business." Her finger was pointed directly at Ben. "You ain't disappearing like you did before. But, I'm telling you, have the courage to be rejected in person. Go to Layton. That nice Mr. Forder—he can find someone else to do your job."

Ben lay in his bed later that night with thoughts, questions, and planning keeping him wide awake. When the alarm clock in his room passed midnight, Ben rose from the bed, dressed, and walked gently into the parlor and sat on the couch. He'd want to do right by Mason Forder both as an employee and friend by giving a lengthy notice. Ben grunted as he thought about obtaining another job. The railroad wouldn't be an option, since Layton was still a flag stop town with no rail yard to offer a job located in Layton. Riding the rails would take him away from home, and if he were going to make this move, then he certainly didn't want to be traveling once he arrived. He couldn't go without a job for very long. He had very little money set aside since he deposited most of it in the account for Katherine. He huffed a breath. Was he risking their provisions if he left his job and moved? He shook off that question. Maybe Mason would have a job for him at the lumber mill or cotton gin in Layton. He'd ask him.

Doubt invaded his thoughts. Getting a job was one matter to see to but finding a place to live was another. Unlike Commerce or any of the other towns he'd lived in, Layton had no boarding house or apartments. "You're a fool, Ben Williams." His agitation brought him to his feet, and he paced the floor. "No, you're a coward." He rubbed the back of his neck. A headache was forming down the middle of his head. In response, he dropped to his knees. "Lord, I reckon I've lived with loneliness and remorse too long. I've been angry at Katherine for rejecting me. I convinced myself my daughter would be better off not knowing me. I've been wrong about all of it. I know you've been telling me that in my heart. Forgive me for ignoring your prompting. Forgive me for my pride. I want to go to Layton. I want to be with Katherine and Clara. I got my plans on how to make it happen, but I sure could use your plans instead."

Once he'd prayed, Ben slipped back to his bedroom. Sleep began to take over. The time was three o'clock in the morning. It was a good thing tomorrow was Saturday, so he didn't have to report to the mill at six. He'd made a mess of resting.

Slightly embarrassed, Ben made his way to the kitchen the next morning after nine o'clock. Grabbing coffee and a couple of biscuits Mrs. Cramer had covered on the table, he made his way to the back yard of the house. The air was cold, and his breath blew smoke. He pulled his coat tightly around him, thankful for the coffee mug to warm his hands. He'd heard commotion and hoped to find Mrs. Cramer out there. He owed her an apology for missing breakfast unannounced. Instead, he found Henry and Mr. Cramer sawing a large piece of wood.

"Morning." Ben raised his coffee cup with both hands secured around it.

"Rough night?" Henry looked up, then blew on his hands.

Ben's mind went instantly to the night five years ago when he'd wept unashamedly in the St. Louis house and came to the table the next morning after everyone else had arrived, unable to suppress his despair at having learned he had a daughter. He wondered if Henry's mind had wandered there as well.

"I was up a while, thinking."

He saw Henry nod his head as though he understood why and agreed with the reason.

"What are you two doing?"

Henry picked the saw back up. "We're replacing the third step off the side kitchen door. It's rotten."

"Need help?"

"Nah. But, thanks. I'm just taking time to learn from the expert before I head out this afternoon." Henry winked.

Ben understood his silent communication. With his arthritis Mr. Cramer was unable to do the work alone. Ben's stepping in would risk offending the man, who had not quite come to terms with his physical struggles.

The weekend rolled past him, and by the time Monday came, Ben had contemplated his plans thoroughly enough to give notice to Mason Forder.

"Ben, as your friend, I am glad you are making this decision to go home. It's what I wanted you to do all along. As your employer, I can't guarantee anything at the mill or cotton gin in Layton other than regular labor. Your pay would decrease."

"I'll take it, Mason."

"Good. Count on it—you'll be the first one I come to if an office position opens up."

"So, I'm officially giving you my one month notice."

"Alright. We're in agreement."

A feeling swept through Ben causing his heart to leap and his lips smile. He hadn't had the sensation in years, but he recognized it as his long lost joy.

Chapter 25

1925 | Layton, Texas

"Thank you, Gabriel." Standing on her front porch, Katherine ran her fingers over her chapped cheeks. The weather outside was below freezing. "Want some coffee before you leave? It's mighty cold outside."

"No, thank you, Miss Katherine. I need to get back home. I reckon your ceiling's as good as new now." The awkward man with the cleft pallet blew on his hands to warm them, then turned and walked down the front steps. His horse was covered in a large blanket and stood attached to his wagon that rested near the tree line. The bare branches of the trees cast a gloominess over Katherine. Like Clara, she looked forward to the warm weather when the butterflies would flitter, or dance, as Clara declared, in the air.

Gabriel waved as his cart turned onto the dirt road. "I'll be back to check on you next Friday." Katherine acknowledged him with a similar wave, then sighed. Gabriel seemed to have recovered somewhat from the grief over his mother's loss that had recently transformed him into a recluse. He'd always taken care of their animals when they were sick, but Gabriel's ability to do odd repair jobs was a recent discovery. She couldn't deny that his help had become more valuable than at any other time in her life. Joe had occasionally been around to make repairs and cut firewood for the sisters. With his absence, and of course Ben's absence, the two women found themselves needing help far more often than Katherine wanted to admit.

Wendell had come and cut firewood for them last week. Carl Justice had repaired the water pump when it froze two days ago. Somehow Gabriel had gotten into the habit of coming by every Friday to check on them. Katherine hadn't asked for the arrangement with him nor agreed to it, but neither did she reject his kindness. Need can alter one's pride, she supposed. Today Gabriel had patched the kitchen ceiling where rain had leaked through.

Katherine stepped back into the house and closed the door behind her, then glanced at the grandfather clock mounted on the wall. It would chime one o'clock in fifteen minutes. The fire was warm, popping, and enticing. With a hint of self-indulgence, Katherine decided that before she started sewing together the front and back of the green dress she was making for

Clara, she would sit by the fire and enjoy a cup of coffee. Lena was due home from the diner at three o'clock, giving her plenty of time to relax, sew the dress side seams, then heat the meatloaf from the icebox. On her way to the kitchen, she paused in Joe's room.

"One day, we'll have to pack up this stuff." The words made her shutter. How did one go about putting a man's life into a trunk? A knot formed in her stomach. She knew exactly how to go about doing that. She'd done it before with Ben. Her chest tightened.

Expecting to hear Clara playing in her room, but sensing only silence, Katherine detoured into their bedroom area. Clara lay face down on her bed with her teddy bear clasped in her right hand. Her breathing was heavy. "Clara?' When her daughter didn't acknowledge her, Katherine stepped next to the bed and bent to see if Clara's head felt hot. Realizing she didn't, she leaned down and kissed her hair then chuckled.

Clara had napped yesterday as well, and Katherine attributed that to the restless night her daughter had the night before. She had finally crawled into bed with Katherine and fallen asleep. This morning her little girl must have worn herself out. She'd pretended to be Lena at the diner and had cooked imaginary meals as Gabriel worked in the kitchen and Katherine sat at the table sewing and eating more than her share of imaginary food.

Alone in the quiet front room, Katherine no longer fought her mind from dwelling on Ben. Ever since Lena had told her he had been in the courtroom, Katherine had agonized over being so close to him, but so separated by a huge emotional cavern that she didn't realize his presence. She reckoned he saw her at the front of the courtroom from his seat in the back. The fact that he didn't acknowledge her, much less ask about Clara, testified to her that he no longer cared for her at all.

"I'm a conflicted soul." In the most vulnerable part of her being, Katherine knew that she had still not forgiven herself for the death of Sammy. She felt responsible since he had been in her care at the time he died of the snake bites and held a grudge against herself. Far worse than her feelings about herself were her emotions about Ben. She tried to forgive him over being weak in a tempting moment, but she carried anger for his rejection of her and Clara, and that anger kept bringing the kiss to the surface.

The creak of the rocker filled the air. She tugged on her ear, then sat the coffee cup on the cold wood floor as her mind wondered to a scripture Pastor Wendell had read Sunday. *Forgiving one another just as God forgave you.* Immediately she understood the truth of the verse. God forgave. Her grudge and her pride were sins against God first, then against Ben.

Weary in both heart and soul, Katherine relinquished her fight, surrendering five years to one moment.

"God, I confess my grudge and pride. I ignored you in my heart all this time when you told me to release myself from responsibility for Sammy. I am so sorry Sammy died, and I know it will always be a sad memory, but I leave my burden of his death with you." She let the shame sink in and felt it in every fiber of her being, then released it. She wiped her face with her apron. She felt the freedom from self-condemnation, but she had more emotions to relinquish.

Katherine pushed aside her anger at Ben and let her mind dwell on the kiss between he and Faye. She dwelt on his refusal to return home. She absorbed the betrayal, jealousy, and hurt, letting them saturate her heart. She embraced the sorrow. Her body moaned, and she sensed a momentary death under the weight of it. "Dear God, forgive my bitterness. Take it from me. Restore my heart with you. Restore my marriage. Give Clara what she has lost in Ben's absence." Then willingly she forgave him. With a repentant heart she released the sorrow and bitterness and embraced the love she had for Ben Williams. She sucked in a breath, recognizing that she'd been dead inside for five years and hadn't even known it. Katherine rested in the relief forgiveness offered.

Tonight she would write Ben another letter. She knew Carl or Mason could give her an address. Wait. Perhaps she'd send a telegram. She giggled at herself. Whatever mode she used, tomorrow she would again beseech Ben Williams to come home.

The clock chimed half past three and pulled Katherine into the world around her. She heard Lena come through the back door.

"I'm home." Lena's wheezing preceded her into the front room. "I'm not sure who is colder. Me or Gitter. I've got him settled in the shed."

Katherine would keep the personal encounter to herself for a bit until she determined how best to contact Ben. However, she was certain the joy would shine through and reveal her secret. She stepped into the moment.

"It's been too cold for you to ride the cart home these days, Lena. You can't take shifts from now on unless Mr. Justice can drive you back and forth."

"We can't always depend on our friends, Katherine and risk wearing out the relationship. We got to learn to make our own way."

"I worry about your breathing. That's all." Lena bent down, and Katherine felt her warm breath, as her sister hugged her shoulders. Katherine rose from the rocker. "Here, sit. I'll get you some coffee."

Lena sat. "Did Gabriel stop by today?"

"Yep. Our ceiling is all fixed."

Just as Katherine turned to head through Joe's room and back into the kitchen, she saw Clara coming through the other side.

"Momma. I took a nap."

"I know you did. You took a very long nap. All that pretend cooking must have made you tired."

"I just wanted to rest, and then I woked up when Aunt Lena slammed the door. She made my head hurt."

Lena called out from the rocker. "I didn't slam the door, Sweetie. But, I'm sorry your head hurts. Come sit with me."

Katherine hugged Clara and noted that her forehead was frighteningly hot. She observed her daughter crawl into Lena's lap and begin to tell of her cooking adventures. Katherine caught the fear in Lena's eyes, and they stared at one another. She watched Lena run a hand along Clara's cheek. Katherine nodded a yes. "I'll also bring Clara some hot tea."

Katherine heard the retching before she heard Lena cry out. Somehow cognizant to turn off the stove so the kettle wouldn't overheat, Katherine ran into the front room in a state of panic. Lena was covered in vomit, clutching the limp body of Clara. The teddy bear lay on the floor.

"Get a cold cloth, Katherine!"

"Clara! You can't die. Not my baby. Not my baby." *Ben, our baby.* Katherine wept hysterically.

"Katherine! She's breathing! Get a cold rag to rouse her." The crazed mother moved to the kitchen, pumped water onto a cloth lying nearby, and ran back into the front room.

Clara roused enough that the women carried her to Katherine's bed. Lena hauled in cold water from the outside pump and made a bath, but Clara's body was too sick to be moved, so Katherine pulled the clothing off her little girl and took the cold rag Lena had dipped into the tub. Together the two of them washed down Clara's lethargic body. Three hours brought no change in Clara's condition as her fever remained high and her vomiting continued.

"She needs the doctor." Katherine looked up at Lena and handed her the rag that was now warm. Her hand trembled.

"I'll run first thing in the morning when the store opens and ask Carl to go for him in his auto."

"I'm scared she may not be with us in the morning. Lena, I cannot live if she doesn't." *Ben. We need you.*

"Don't think that way right now. It's too early to panic. Let's just keep doctoring her and doing all we know to do." Katherine pulled strength from her sister who was bruised in body, but not in resilience.

They swapped buckets back and forth all through the night, letting one be washed and cleaned with Lysol while the other was being used to collect the fluids that Clara's small body released. Katherine loathed the smell of Lysol since the day it had been used to clean during the mayhem of Sammy's death.

Katherine never left Clara's side. Lena paced, prayed aloud, and kept cool cloths coming. Morning light came through the bedroom, and Katherine roused from her position draped over the bed with her arm resting across Clara. She made eye contact with Lena who came toward her.

"Katherine, I'll wash the clothes that we soaked in the bucket of Lysol, then I'll head out to the store as soon as it opens and contact the doctor. Right now, I'm making you some toast and tea. And tea for Clara, if she can keep it down."

As mid-morning slipped into lunchtime, the doctor ended his exam and gathered up his medical bag. He patted Clara on the head, then motioned for Katherine to follow him out of the bedroom.

"It's possible Clara has typhoid fever, or it could just be food poisoning." He cleared his throat.

Katherine gasped. Tears welled in her eyes.

"But, we bathe, and she washes her hands, and…"

"Katherine, I don't doubt you practice good hygiene. You will probably never know the source."

Katherine dropped her defensiveness. "Will she survive?" Hearing her own question made her weep.

"I believe she will. But, keep her indoors, bathed, drinking plenty of water, and keep the house quarantined until the symptoms have long passed. Boil all water before you use it."

"How long?"

"Three weeks." The doctor continued. "The fever and other symptoms can come and go. She'll likely get a rash if it is typhoid. I'll check on her a couple of times a week if I can get here that often. Katherine, remember she'll be very weak. Hide your fear. She doesn't need to see you frightened."

"But I am frightened."

"She's too weak to fight for herself. She needs you to fight for her. Trade that fear for courage."

On an ordinary Saturday afternoon, two days after Ben resigned with Mason, he received a phone call.

"Ben, this is Wendell Carlson."

The phone wobbled in his trembling hand.

"Wendell."

Ben swallowed against his emotion at the memories that flashed before him. A friendship, no a brotherhood of sorts, had been severed years ago, and the pain of it hit him full force when Wendell spoke.

"Wendell, I'm a little dumbstruck."

A mild humph came through the phone.

"After the trial, Mason had told me how to contact you. I hope you don't mind. He thought I might be able to talk sense into you some day. I should have called sooner."

Ben smiled.

"I find that I don't mind at all."

"He told me about the accident that happened years ago."

"Katherine, never told you?"

"No. I can't say she ever eluded to it at all. But, you could have told me. You just stopped writing."

"She never came to the hospital when I wrote and asked her to come. I was on my deathbed. So after that, I gave in and let her and Clara go."

"I am sorry for that, but why didn't you tell me all this yourself?"

"You were Katherine's pastor before you were mine."

"I was your friend. I been praying for you all these years. Ben, we'll talk about this more, but I called today for a specific reason.

"I reckon you did."

"You need to come back to Layton."

"I am. In a month. Not sure where I'll live when I get there."

"No, Mason told me about your quitting the job to move in a month. I'm not talking about that. Ben, you don't have a month to spare. You need to come home now."

Once again, Ben was dumbstruck as Wendell explained a dire situation.

God, indeed, had a plan of His own. Ben Williams was leaving Commerce in a matter of days and with a great sense of urgency.

Chapter 26

1925 | Layton, Texas

Katherine sipped on a cup of cold coffee, not remembering when Lena served it. Her sister was asleep sitting upright in a rocker, despite the sun shining beneath the outside door. The hours keeping watch over Clara had blended into each other and become the next day. Fever caused Clara to mumble for her Momma, Aunt Lena, Sammy, and her Papa. Her body continued to reject and expel fluids.

Katherine had no doubt that word of their situation had spread. Carl Justice dropped by with clean sets of sheets from the motor lodge. Louise had insisted the ladies would need them. Carl was dressed in a suit, causing Katherine to realize it was Sunday. "Ask the church to pray for my Clara. I'm afraid she's dying."

Carl took her by the shoulders. "Doc assured me when he came by the store yesterday after he left here that he's hopeful. Pastor Carlson was there getting his mail and heard what Doc said. If I know Pastor, he'll have us praying together." He turned and walked off the front porch and headed to his automobile. Katherine offered a weak wave to Mrs. Justice who was waiting for him.

After stoking the fire in the front room, weary Katherine lay down next to Clara on the bed and shut her eyes. Lena was lying nearby in Clara's small bedroom. Sleep was a risk Katherine was unwilling to take. Once Lena was rested and could take up her vigil, Katherine might finally allow herself to give in to the need.

Fear crept into the tomb-like room and taunted her, threatening to invite Death in for a visit. Worthlessness blew in to remind her that one child had already died under her care. She fought the mockers with the only weapon she had. Prayer.

"God, please don't let Clara die. She doesn't even know her Papa loves her or that I love her Papa."

A knock on the front door roused Katherine. Hesitantly she rose and tidied her hair bun before she made her way to the front room. The thought occurred to her that she probably reeked with the odor of sickness. Opening the door and peering through the screen, she saw Wendell sitting on one of the rockers as though he were keeping watch. A glance at the grandfather clock on the wall told her she'd fallen asleep for a few hours despite fighting against it.

"Pastor. Have you been here long?" She opened the screen door. Cold air seemed to swirl around her face. Wendell stepped inside so the door could be shut.

"Katherine." With the respect of a Pastor and the compassion of a friend, he touched her shoulder gently then glanced at his watch.

"I've been here a little more than an hour. Amy sent me here as soon as we finished lunch. I tapped a few times, but I didn't want to disturb you."

"You've been sitting that long?"

"I've been praying that long." He smiled, then removed his hand. "We prayed for Clara at church today too."

"Thank you. She's resting better, but still calling out in her sleep. She's so hot. Still can't keep down nothing. I'm scared."

"Is there anything Amy and I can do for you? Would anything help?"

Time held its breath waiting for Katherine to respond.

"Her Papa."

She watched Wendell tilt his head slightly.

"She needs her Papa."

Katherine felt hot tears stream down her cheeks, and amid troubles, her spirit stirred. Perhaps a five year burden would be removed. She watched tears pool in Wendell' eyes.

"Of course." The tears escaped his eyes. "Consider that taken care of."

"Wendell, he may not come."

"He'll come."

As though that request had been the only reason Wendell had kept vigil, he turned and hurried through the doorway. The cold air blew back on Katherine.

"Don't you want coffee before you go?"

Without turning around, he yelled back at her. "No, thanks." He trotted to his auto.

Tuesday morning, Clara sat up in bed and quickly grabbed Katherine's hand that was resting on the bed's edge. Both she and the bed were drenched. Katherine began to cry happy tears as she explained to Clara that her fever had broken. Within the hour, she and Lena had bathed Clara, changed the sheets, and prepared broth with toasted bread for the patient. An hour later, Lena danced around the room in exaggerated hideous motions because the food had stayed down.

"You're silly, Aunt Lena!" Clara laid her head back and laughed out loud.

Motivated by the sheer, visceral relief at Clara's improvement, even if it could be temporary, Katherine undid her bun and let her tresses fall below her shoulders, then she joined hands with Lena and danced around the room celebrating. Clara clapped and giggled. Lena's wheezing brought the silliness to an end.

"Go lie down and sleep, Lena."

Her sister didn't hesitate to enter her bedroom once she'd kissed Clara on the top of her head. Katherine sat on the edge of the bed and pulled Clara to her for a gentle hug.

"I have something to show you." Katherine's stomach knotted. Despite the apparent improvement in Clara's condition, she didn't want to risk her daughter passing without knowing of her Papa's love. The timing may not be perfect for telling her, but the urgency was.

Her daughter smiled, but her brows furrowed. Katherine rose from the bed and made her way to the little storage room. She shuttered. Cold air or faltering courage? Kneeling beside the dusty trunk that contained Ben's letters, she shuffled a shirt or two around, moved a bundle of letters belonging to her, spying the gold band still tied into the ribbon. She grabbed the letters addressed to Clara Williams. The paper was cold to the touch. She brought the tied bundle to her cheek and let the chill caress her.

For more than five years she had hidden the love of Ben Williams in this dusty, crowded room. She'd kneeled over this very trunk while bitterness, longing, guilt, love, deception, and disappointment tugged at her. The doubt she felt now was so tangible she sensed its breath. Would her daughter love her or despise her for the news she was ready to share? Her pulse quickened.

God, keep Clara from being bitter toward me. It's too much for her to carry. Mend what is already broken.

Katherine made her way to the bed with the letters hidden under her apron and crawled up to sit next to Clara. Sunken cheeks and dark circled eyes met Katherine as her daughter turned and stared at her. She could read the question and curiosity in Clara's eyes. The mother cleared her throat.

"Clara, I've told you that your Papa loves you, right?"

"Yessum."

"Well, it's true. It's also true that I need to tell you I'm sorry."

She held the letters out and pointed to the top ones. "See these words? They say Clara Williams."

Her daughter gasped. Katherine continued.

"All of these letters are for you. Your Papa mailed them to you."

She saw anger, then sorrow, then confusion cross the pale, sickly face. Katherine began to weep.

"But I was mad at your Papa because he hurt my feelings right after Sammy died, so I asked him to leave." Katherine wept.

"So he's bad?"

"No, honey. He made a mistake, and said he was sorry, but I stayed mad at him. I ended up making you sad because I didn't let you know he wrote you letters. He loves you."

Clara began to cry.

Oh, am I making a mistake telling her. Should I have waited until she felt better or was older?

"Clara, I told God I was sorry for being mad at your Papa. I want to tell you that I'm sorry too. Can you forgive me someday?"

Clara wiped her cheeks with her slender fingers. She looked her mother in the eyes.

"So he really didn't leave because I was ugly." Clara's finger touched her angel kiss. Sorrow coursed through Katherine. What an ugly lie Clara had dealt with because of her Momma and Papa.

"What's Papa's name?"

"Ben. Ben Williams"

Clara whispered the name with a reverent tone, then lay back on her pillow. Tears ran down her temples. Katherine felt her daughter's tiny, slender hand clasp her trembling one.

"Momma, I forgive you. But, I might feel a little mad too."

Katherine bit her tongue to hold back the chuckle at Clara's truthful response. She squeezed Clara's fingers.

"Of course you do. Maybe one day, you won't feel mad anymore. Clara, Momma is so, so sorry."

She unsealed the first letter. "Would you like me to read them to you?"

Clara sat up and covered her mouth. Katherine instinctively dropped the letters to grab the bucket, but instead of retching, she heard the wonderful sound of laughter from her girl. "Yes! Read!" Katherine did.

"*My sweet Baby Clara, I love my little girl…*"

"Momma, where's Papa's house?"

"He lives in a town called Texarkana" She pointed to the postmark on the envelope. "See it says that name right here." She remembered noticing the post mark change from St. Louis to Texarkana with the last letter he'd written her. Over the past years she'd pondered what had taken place in the three months between those two cities causing Ben's heart to turn from wanting to come home. Each time she posed the question, her heart whispered the same answer. *I happened*. From the core of her being, Katherine knew that she was the reason Ben had never returned.

Clara rubbed the postmark with her finger.

"Maybe he can live here."

"Maybe."

At this moment, Clara needn't know that Ben had refused to return home, nor that she had sent for him through Wendell.

Clara lay back and listened, clutching each letter after her mother read it.

"Dear Clara,

I miss my sweet baby. Though we have never met, you are not a stranger to my heart. I pray that I will not be a stranger to yours, but I worry I will be as you grow and come to understand my absence. I do hope you will come to understand that God is never absent.

I cannot believe that you are one year old. Did Momma and Aunt Lena sing to you? I pray that you are a happy child. Did you get your gifts from me? I hope you enjoy your teddy bear. How I would love to see you in your new dress…"

"Papa gave me my teddy bear." Clara's realization was voiced in a whisper.

"Yes." Katherine's next words were uttered in her heart. "And your tea set, and your clothes, and your coat, and so much more purchased with his money. I do not think your tiny soul can handle knowing that right now."

Letter after letter they read, then as Katherine placed the last one back in the envelope and handed it to Clara, the tiny child who'd felt ugly, unloved, and unwanted, lay on her pillow—no doubt, as Katherine could observe, exhausted and exuberant. She clasped the letters in her arms and began to drift off.

"Momma?"

"Yes?"

"When I wake up, I want Aunt Lena to draw a Papa butterfly in my book. You will tell me what he looks like and that will be the colors, and red, for love."

"That's a good idea. You rest, now. And Clara, I am sorry I hurt your heart."

"Momma, we can fix it. I'll send him a letter to come home. I'll say the words, and you write them."

The next morning Katherine sat up in bed feeling warmth against her back. Turning over and touching Clara, she knew her fever had returned. Katherine scrambled from the bed. As her feet slapped against the cold floor, she hollered. "Lena!" Within moments the sisters were cooling Clara's body with a wet rag.

Mid-morning a knock sounded at the front door. Hesitantly, Katherine rose from the rocker next to the bed and slogged to the front room. Lena was asleep in Clara's bed. Perhaps it was Doc who was knocking. Standing before her when she opened the door was the tall, dark-haired son of Pony James, the produce delivery man for the store. She could think of no reason for him to be on her front porch.

"Hello, Wallace."

"Hello ma'am."

"How can I help you, young man?"

"At the store, Pa heard about your little girl being sick. He's sending you some vegetables and fruit. Said that's what my Ma would want him to do."

Katherine smiled, warmed by the kindness of the merchant. She had no doubt he could not afford to give his food away. She watched the young man lean to his right and pick up a small box of produce.

"It's a might heavy ma'am. I'd be happy to set it someplace for you."

"How about the back porch." Katherine motioned toward the outside rear of the house. It was then she caught sight of Pony James seated on his cart, bundled against the cold. She waved. He returned the gesture.

"Wallace, let me give you some money for this."

"Oh, no ma'am. If I go back to that cart with money, my Pa is likely to tan my hide. It's a gift from our family."

Katherine lifted her hand to her heart. "Please thank your Pa and Ma for me."

The young man turned and walked down the front steps, holding the box against his chest.

"Yes ma'am, I will" He paused and turned back to face her. "And I hope your little girl, Clara, gets better real soon. We'll pray for her."

"Thank you."

Wallace turned and eventually disappeared around the corner of the house. Katherine closed the door, stoked the fire, then headed back to sit with Clara, and tried to nibble on the bread and cheese Lena had situated on the dresser. Less than an hour later, another knock sounded at the front door. Perhaps this would be the doctor. She certainly wanted it to be him.

Some moments brush by us unnoticed and unfelt; others arrive and cling to us for a lifetime, and we are no longer the same.

"Coming."

She hurried, then turned the cold metal knob and pulled the door toward her. Her entire being felt the transformation. She managed to whisper his name.

"Ben."

Chapter 27

1925 | LAYTON, TEXAS

Ben entered the town. Cold air bit at his cheeks and fingers. He pulled his gloves from his coat pocket to warm his hands and began the mile distance to the house, the place that was still home in his heart even after five years of separation. Though dear friends resided in Layton, the only people he was driven to see with urgency were Katherine and Clara.

He was grateful the train depot was empty, save the attendant, whom he didn't recognize. Not a soul appeared to be stirred by the train's whistle. Ben stood for seconds and let the sight of Layton comfort him. Mason Forder had relentlessly and shamelessly nudged him back here. *Thank you, Mason.*

Passing the Justice Store, he felt a pull to go inside, grab a cola, and greet Carl Justice, who had proven as faithful and dependable a friend a man could hope for, despite the lack of words and the miles that had been between them. Carl had been a father figure to Ben in the past, and he knew through his arrangement with Mason that Carl had been taking care of Katherine and Clara. Indeed, Reverend Lilley had been a gentle watchman, but a mere shadow of Carl Justice. Ben would never be able to repay Carl for watching over the money he'd sent to Katherine and Clara, but soon, he would try to express his gratitude in person.

The parking lot was empty, save one automobile and a cart. His eyes were drawn to the doorway. Was Lena inside working the diner or would he encounter her at the house? Surely she was at home with Katherine since Clara was so sick. The cart made him feel nostalgic. It had been a while since he'd depended on a cart for transportation. He smiled at the thought of the mule Gitter, and his mind flashed back to his streetcar rides in St. Louis. Such contrast! Ben shifted his luggage to his other hand and kept walking.

His thoughts turned to Pastor Wendell Carlson, and potent gratitude surged through Ben. The man had been a friend, a brother, and a pastor perfectly intertwined. Although he had summoned Ben to Layton, Wendell was unaware of his arrival time. Ben wondered if Katherine realized the pastor had contacted her. When he'd picked up the phone call that night at the boarding house and heard Wendell tell him the news of Clara's typhoid fever,

Ben felt his heart stop. He longed to see Wendell in person, and he would once he had his family gathered in whatever shelter his arms could provide.

Halfway between the store and home, Ben's eyes spotted weeping willow trees displaying their bare, spider-like branches. He'd noticed them years ago the first day he'd been in Layton. It was under those trees that he had shared with Katherine the plans to enlarge the house. Their privacy had needed a place to dwell. It was under those trees months later that Katherine had shared the news of her pregnancy. Privacy had made itself at home in their bedroom. Even as the years of separation threatened all he held dear, Ben had never forgotten the sensation of his hand on Katherine's midsection where their child grew, kicked, and squirmed. He sniffed and wiped tears from his eyes. *Blast it, cold air!* He smirked at his own thought, knowing full well that memories had conjured the tears and the sniffling.

His maimed leg ached, yet he strove forward. *Will Clara or Katherine find my scars and limp repulsive?* Pulling his coat further up his neck and tighter around his body, Ben attempted to catch his breath. The cold air turned it into smoke, but chilling air was not the cause of his lungs labored effort. Arriving home was taking his breath away.

The house came into view causing adrenaline to course through his body. Those he treasured, those he needed were tucked within the walls of that structure. Five years had yielded its wear and tear on the house. Weathered wood was visible where paint had once been. The front porch appeared to have loose boards. The bushes on the side of the house nearly covered the windows. The shed leaned to one side. The crepe myrtles were…*Sammy*. His son's grave was nestled among the crepe myrtles. His heart tightened. "I miss you, Sammy." From his vantage point, he thought he saw the simple headstone. *Soon.* Ben would visit his son's grave, but for now he had a daughter he needed to meet and take care of. *Oh, God, please don't let Clara die.*

Ben placed one foot in front of the other and made his way to the porch. A sign on the door made him gasp. *Quarantined. Of course.* He rested his luggage near a familiar rocker. Memories from the porch swarmed him—star pictures in the sky, harmonica tunes, phonograph songs, Sammy's trains, a ring on Katherine's finger—and they dizzied him. Ben stood at the door trembling as he removed his gloves, formed a shaky fist, and knocked, timidly at first, then with demand. "Despite how Katherine may react, I have a daughter behind that closed door, and for all I know, she is a dying daughter." The wind blowing around him did not reply.

His ears picked up the sound of rustling inside the house, causing his gut to twist. As the door creaked open, fear of his reception grew. Would he be an unwelcome guest? Slender, disheveled, and appearing forlorn, beautiful Katherine stood before him.

"Ben."

Five years of silence nudged itself between them, but Ben shoved it aside. He drank in the sight of her, filling his parched spirit. His heart beat. His lungs breathed. The sensation seemed suddenly new and amazing. Had they not functioned since the day he'd left her?

"Hello, Katherine."

"You came."

"Clara?"

Katherine sobbed. Ben felt his stomach lurch. He pulled her through the doorway and onto the front porch, their breath creating a dreary fog around them. There was a question he had to ask. Emotion told him that as long as he didn't ask, his daughter would be alive in his heart and mind, yet he forced the question through his lips.

"Has she passed?" His body gave way. Then Katherine's arms reached and held him up. His reaction must have frightened her, for she seemed to gain her composure and take on the strength he'd lost.

"No, I feared she might, but the doctor is hopeful." Katherine released her hold, and he felt her slender hand clasp his.

"Come meet your daughter."

Relieved that his child was alive, Ben wept. Embarrassingly. Katherine stood shivering with him on the porch while he got control of his crying, then led by his wife, Ben stepped through the rooms of the house, detached from sights and sounds, save the picture his eyes settled upon briefly. Framed in a gold, filigreed frame sat an image of an infant wearing the delicate dress he'd bought her. *My Clara.* The brief glimpse made his heart leap.

With his hand still clasped by Katherine, he stood at the bedside where he'd long ago loved his wife and became a father. He was now a Papa seeing his child for the first time. His eyes gazed upon the slender figure covered in quilts, clasping a teddy bear. *My teddy bear?* Though tousled, her russet hair was pleasing to his sight. Ben's eyes fell upon her face, and his breath hitched when he saw the angel kiss that graced her cheek. His beautiful child. He felt Katherine squeeze his fingers. Ben removed his coat.

"Clara." His wife bent over the sleeping child and gently shook her shoulder with her free hand.

"Clara. Can you open your eyes?"

Nothing could have prepared Ben for the moment his daughter opened her eyes and beheld him. His blood pumped wildly through him. Curiosity, then awareness, seemed to move across her face. She reached a tiny hand toward him.

"Papa."

"Clara."

Salty tears fell on his lips as he spoke. He cradled her slender fingers within his hand. Clasping a hand of both his wife and daughter, Ben felt the sheer pleasure of relationship as tender as the Creator must have intended when he created human beings. He dropped to his knees at the bedside, pulling Katherine down with him.

With a glance at his wife and then at Clara, he was poised to pull his child into his arms.

"May I?"

Clara responded by pulling back the covers. Ben rose, slid his arms beneath her, and brought his daughter to his chest. Stepping backward, he seated himself in the bedside rocker and held his little girl tightly, running his hand over her russet locks. Her soft, slender arms were wrapped around him. His finger petted her angel kiss then wiped the tears from her eyes.

"My beautiful Clara. Papa loves you."

"You came."

"I should have come long ago. Forgive me."

He felt her head nod back and forth. Then his daughter slipped back into sleep.

Katherine had settled on the bed, and Ben heard her gently weeping. He placed Clara on the bed then sat next to Katherine. A moan escaped him when she rested a palm on each of his cheeks and patted him tenderly, sliding her fingertips over his cold skin. He gazed at the tears falling down her cheeks as she gently wept.

"I know you're here now for Clara." She snubbed as she cried. "But, I wanted you to come so long ago."

Her words made no sense. *Long ago?*

He moved in and placed his burly hands over her feminine ones.

"Long ago? When you refused to come to the hospital with Clara while I was dying, I gave up hope."

He watched her forehead wrinkle. Her head shook rapidly from side to side, and her fingers tightened against his cheeks.

"You nearly died? I don't know what you are talking about."

"Yes. I was in a terrible train accident. I wrote you a letter about it and asked you to come to me."

Katherine gasped.

"I never got it. Is that why you didn't answer my letter?"

Despite the cold air surrounding him, his body felt flushed.

"What letter?"

"The one that said, 'Come home.'"

"I never got it. I would have come and never written you about divorce"

He saw shock register on her face.

In slow motion he pulled her hands from his face, kissed them, held them tenderly, then rested them on his chest. The physical contact evoked longing to know her wholly, in body and soul. He needed more of her. She slid her hands up and enveloped his neck. He grasped her waist, leaned in, and touched his lips to hers. Their tender interaction was so much more than he had dared hope for. Their years of passion, agony, hurt, hope, love, and apparent misunderstanding collided while they clung to one another.

"I wanted you," she whispered against his lips.

He pulled away just enough to see her eyes. "I love you. Can you forgive me for not coming? For not speaking to you at the courthouse?"

He saw a smile spread across her lips. "I already have." Her grip tightened around his neck. "I love you, Ben. I never stopped. Can you forgive me for not coming to the hospital?"

"I already forgave, and now I know there was nothing to forgive after all. I thought you didn't want me. You thought I didn't want you. I'm bewildered. But, we'll sort through the confusion. We can put it behind us."

They held one another in silence letting their bodies and tears express what their words could not. The world was void of all other inhabitants in those brief moments. He kissed her moist lips, tasting the sweet and salty flavor of their hindered reunion. "My beautiful Butterfly."

Ben reached over and picked his daughter back up settling into the rocker once again. Sudden uncertainty of his standing with Katherine and Clara came over him and doubt shouted thoughts at him. Were these moments nothing but a surge of emotions? Would she trust their daughter with him? Was the love she claimed strong enough to restore their marriage? Would she be repulsed by his body if she did give herself to him emotionally and physically? Would Clara hate him? Would his child refuse him? Time would reveal both the frailty and the strength of their marriage and his family.

With his daughter in his arms, he determined not to dwell on these thoughts, and with his wife weeping next to him, Ben took her hand gently and rubbed his thumb over her knuckles.

"Thank you, for bringing up our daughter. You've carried a lot of responsibility on your shoulders. Katherine, all the hurt between us can be released if we want it to be. I do."

"I do too. I meant it when I said I love you."

Ben's heart beat against his chest at her words.

"I love you, too."

He leaned carefully over his daughter and placed a kiss on Katherine's cheek. She responded by pulling his left hand away from Clara and holding it in front of her.

"You're wearing your ring."

"Yes."

He watched tears pool in her eyes and felt pity for her when her cheeks turned pink. Yes, he had noticed that her left hand was bare. No, its absence had not surprised him. Yes, he would ask to place the band on her finger again, when time was in his favor. However, in this very moment, he simply wanted to relieve her of apparent embarrassment. He turned the conversation.

"Should I put her back in the bed?"

Katherine wiped her tears then smiled. "I think that she would stay in your lap forever, but if she gets sick, you will wish you weren't holding her." His wife nodded toward the bucket. "She's kept that pretty full." She released her hold on his hand.

The thought of his daughter being so sick sent a wave of sadness through him. He stood, gently placed her in the bed, covered her, then kissed her cheek. He pulled the rocker closer and motioned for Katherine to sit. She did. He took his daughter's hand and held it while he sat next to her on the bed.

"So, Wendell called you?"

"You knew he called?"

Katherine answered by shaking her head back and forth.

"He called Saturday." Ben spread a large grin across his face, "I was coming anyway. The telephone call just got me here sooner."

He watched Katherine's hands leap up to cover her mouth.

"I asked him to call you, but not until late Sunday afternoon."

Ben felt a smile spread across his face.

"Then, I reckon Wendell called on his own accord."

"So much to figure out." Katherine bit her lip as she spoke, "You were coming home anyway?"

"I'd already given my notice to Mason."

He cleared his throat.

"Did you know I was working for Mason in Commerce?"

"Yes." Her chin touched her chest.

"Katherine, with a little bit of time, I'll settle in. I can find my own place here in Layton again and be near you both." *Is that disappointment on her face?* "For now, may I stay in Joe's room until Clara is well?"

"Your place is here, in this house, with us. I want you here."

"Are you certain?"

She leaned forward and kissed him on the lips.

"Yes. I said that I love you and want you."

His body and soul responded to her.

"Ben, before Clara got sick, I was already going to send for you again. I got my heart right with God the other night. I'd been holding on to a lot of bad feelings. I finally dropped my guilt over Sammy. I released the pain of what happened with Faye, and I confessed my bitterness toward your not returning to me."

He kissed her in return.

"Katherine. I had a similar experience not long ago too. I'm still a man of faith." He patted his heart. "I asked forgiveness for neglecting my wife and daughter and for ignoring God every time He told me to go home. I determined to come here and be the father she needed, whether I lived with you both or not."

"When Clara got sick, I couldn't leave her. Could think of little else. I haven't left her side. So I hadn't sent you a telegram or a letter asking you for the second time to come home. That's why I asked Wendell to contact you."

Ben let out a sigh. "I understand, Katherine. Knowing you wanted me—our family—all these years eases the hurt, despite the confusion."

She chuckled. "Clara had declared she would tell me words to write you a letter. Of course, she had no idea I was already going to send for you."

He treasured her words, but they were pieces of a puzzle he needed to put together.

"So, she knew about me all along. You read her my letters?"

He saw Katherine's cheeks turn bright red.

"She came upon Sammy's grave a few months ago."

The words scraped his heart.

"I found myself explaining Sammy and his father, and she asked if Sammy's father was her papa too. I didn't deny it, but I didn't explain it either. She assumed you left her because she was ugly. When Lena was beat, I asked Clara if Joe had hurt her body. She said no, but that he had been telling her you left because she was ugly, and you didn't love her."

Ben's stomach knotted. At the thought of Clara living with a monster, he stood and paced, although he realized he was at fault. Katherine began to weep again, so he sat back down and held back the anger at himself and at her. Grace. He wanted to extend grace, but her words were difficult to hear. However, weren't her words the result of his not coming for his daughter despite thinking Katherine had refused him.

"Forgive me, Ben. Once she was old enough to wonder, I always assured Clara you loved her, but let her think you were sad over Sammy and left."

He watched Katherine shake her head back and forth, "I had never told her about your letters. Never even opened them until two days ago, waiting for her to be old enough to somehow understand. She had a relief from the fever, so I read each one to her, and she's kept them near her ever since. I told her that I had asked you to leave because you made me sad."

She leaned over him and Clara to lift the extra pillow on the bed. Ben's mouth fell open when he saw the envelopes addressed to Clara Williams.

"I asked her forgiveness. She was going to tell me words to write to you asking you to come home, but the fever took back over her senses."

Ben sensed awkwardness trying to settle in. He remained speechless, emotions warring with one another inside him. Katherine stood from the chair, went to her knees at his feet, and looked up at him.

"So much misunderstanding between us, Ben."

Before him lay an opportunity to reunite with his wife, to live with his daughter. Had he not needed and begged for grace and forgiveness himself? Hadn't she as well? Had he not hurt her as much, no more, than she had hurt him? He wanted grace between them. *God, help me.*

"Katherine, listen. We both agreed to let go of the hurt between us. God has forgiven us, and we've offered forgiveness to each other. I'm sure hurtful memories or revelations will continue to come our way, but we cannot dwell there."

"Our consciences can be clean?"

"Yes, Katherine. We both gave in to our hurt of rejection, and we shouldn't have. If for no other reason but Clara, we shouldn't have responded toward each other the way we did. We offer grace to one another—like God offered to us."

He pulled her from the floor and drew her into his lap.

"If you need to hear me say it again, I will. I love you. I want you."

She placed her arms around his waist. Ben enveloped her, resting his cheek on her head. Once again, their bodies said what words could not. He finally whispered one last nagging question.

"Did *you* read any of my letters?"

She looked at him.

"Every one of them. Time and time again."

He rubbed his thumb across her lips, then pulled her up and nodded toward the rocker. Once again she seated herself there.

"I wrote you many more letters after that awful one saying I would sign divorce papers."

"I never got them."

"I never sent them. I was stubborn and determined to leave you alone."

"What did you do with them?"

"I kept them."

"Can I see them?"

He touched her neck and slid his hand down her arm.

"Maybe later. The letters are filled with so much love, but also so much pain. There's been enough pain for now. Don't you think?"

"Yes."

Curiosity emerged from behind the other emotions he felt.

"Katherine, when did you mail the letter to me asking me to come home?"

"I remember like it was yesterday." Her eyes closed for a moment and she sighed. "It was after I got your letter about becoming a believer. And after the package that you sent to Clara—the one with the dress and teddy bear."

Ben hunched over and covered his face with his hands. He could feel the blood drain from his face. He spoke into his palms.

"I know why I never saw the letter."

"What did you say, Ben?"

He turned and looked Katherine in the eye.

"I know why I never saw the letter."

His wife's mouth gaped open.

"Why?"

"I mailed those a couple of days after July 4th on the morning I left for an extended railroad run. That's when the accident happened. I never returned to the boarding house in St. Louis."

He felt Katherine's hand grab his fingers and squeeze.

"The owner packed up my things and took them to the railroad office to be mailed to me, but I never received the package. I was told there were letters in it. I figured they were the ones I'd received from Wendell."

Ben pulled his hand free, then grasped both of Katherine's shoulders.

"I would have come. Oh, dear God, please help us. I would have come then."

Katherine wiped tears from her cheeks.

"What about the letter telling me of the accident? What happened?"

He slid his hands down her arms and intertwined their fingers.

"I don't know. I dictated it to a nurse while I was alert, then just as I finished, medication was taking over. She said she had an address on file, but I knew that was St. Louis, so I gave her your Layton one."

"Ben, maybe it went to St. Louis and got put in that same package. I'm so sorry."

"I should have written again. It was two months before I was fully alert from medication and realized you hadn't responded. I was angry and gave up."

He cleared his throat.

"Katherine, we have so much to talk through."

"Ben, what happened to you in the accident?"

"I was burned and thrown from the train."

She gasped.

"I'm scarred, Katherine, and…"

Ben's next thought was lost when Clara moaned loudly and stirred beside him. For the first time, the father witnessed what the sickness did to his daughter. A door opened behind him and a familiar female voice filled the air.

"Katherine, I'm awake…" He heard her gasp and turned to face her.

"Ben!"

"Lena."

The reunion was nothing more than a broad smile and a pat on Lena's shoulder as his attention returned to Clara, but his insides quivered with the joy of seeing Lena again.

Chapter 28

1925 | LAYTON, TEXAS

She felt his fingers brush hers as he reached for the bucket handle. He'd kissed his panicked daughter on the head and assured her he would return once he emptied its foul contents. Katherine had seen sadness move across Ben's face when Clara retched then dry heaved. While she and Lena pulled her daughter's cotton gown over her head, careful to keep the soil away from Clara's hair, she watched Ben walk out the back door of her—their—room to empty the bucket. His limp was pronounced. Katherine realized she knew nothing of the pain he'd suffered in an accident. Once again, he was more than words in dated letters. He was flesh and breath, and she felt sorrow that that he'd obviously suffered physical pain separated from his wife and daughter. How had it felt to give up hope that she would come to him? The question made her chest ache.

Her eyes fixed themselves on him, and despite the sickness in the room, Katherine's heart swelled with joy. She felt her cheeks heat. *I'm behaving like a school girl.* She loved Ben Williams. The last time he'd walked out that door, sorrow and despair had pressed upon her. Today, forgiveness made her feel giddy—except when the seconds of fear surged through her whispering "Don't trust the joy. It's too good to be true." Shaking that sense of doom each time it came, she focused on the hope in their expressed words. She focused on hope in God. He would sustain their marriage when human nature and calamities fought against their covenant.

Clara was too weak to sit in a bath, so together she and Ben washed Clara's body with cool rags, while Lena put a clean quilt on the bed. Katherine heard Ben hum as he slid the cloth along their daughter's arms. The sound of his deep voice soothed her, almost lulling her to sleep. She felt the extent of her weary muscles and heavy eyelids as she let his tune caress her.

"What are you humming?"

"I didn't realize I was." He chuckled lightly. "It's a tune called 'Content,' I reckon."

She watched him drop the damp rag in the water bowl then look directly in her eyes.

"Katherine, I can count on one hand the times I've hummed in the last five years." His eyes glanced at Clara. "Even though my—our—little girl is sick, I feel peace. I'm with my family where I belong. Taking care of them like I should."

His words brought Sammy to mind. Ben had looked at Sammy with same loving eyes he cast on Clara. What a good father he had been to Sammy. Having Clara made Katherine keenly aware of Ben's loss.

She felt his damp hand grasp her empty one. "Do you think we can start over—you and me?"

"We already have." She freed her hand and dipped her fingers in the water bowl, then ran the moisture over his palm and hers. "All clean."

Suddenly she heard Lena clear her throat. "Don't get me wrong. I like what I hear, but I reckon I'm not supposed to be hearing it. Tender ears and all..."

Katherine heard Ben laugh then watched him splash water toward her sister.

"We just kept you from eavesdropping!"

"Ben Williams! You calling me a busy body?" Katherine laughed as she slid a clean gown over Clara's head. How good it felt to hear them tease one another again. She felt Clara shift in her grasp, then heard giggles escaping the sick girl.

"Aunt Lena is a busy body, Papa!"

"Clara, did you say 'Ain't'Lena?"

"That's her name, Papa. She's not a bug like an ant." Clara laughed at her own joke

"It's true, Ben," Lena interjected. "She came to that logic when she was barely four. I was hanging clothes on the line, and she stood staring at an ant bed. That's how my name came to be."

Ben's laughter filled the room. Katherine stood and took her daughter into her arms, feeling as though she would explode with happiness in that very moment. She saw Ben stand then felt him envelope them in one arm, motioning for Lena to join them.

There they stood, in the middle of an unkempt bedroom with the scent of sickness and Lysol surrounding them, huddled together, four people needing one another desperately, each one of them fractured in some way, but coming together as a whole.

"Welcome home, Ben." Lena's voice was a soft whisper.

"Welcome home, Papa." Clara's voice was a loud declaration.

Tears filled Katherine's eyes when Ben reached over and kissed his daughter on the cheek.

"I love you, Clara." Ben's voice was the sound of contentment.

The party broke free from one another, and Katherine felt Clara lean toward Ben. "Hold me, Papa."

She released their daughter into his arms once he sat down in the rocker.

"Aunt Lena, draw me a Papa butterfly."

Regret trotted through Katherine at the question etched across Ben's face. He knew nothing of her butterfly book.

"That's a good idea, Clara. But first, why don't you show Papa your butterfly book. You can tell him all about it. If you feel like it."

"Momma, give it to me."

Katherine reached inside the dresser drawer and pulled out the brown, leather-covered booklet. Clara took it from her.

"Aunt Lena, can you tell Papa about my butterflies?"

Rather than feeling left out of the moment, Katherine felt herself smile. Of course, Lena should tell Ben about the book. It was a treasure shared between her sister and her daughter. She felt Lena's eyes upon her and looked to see her furrowed brow.

"Yes, she can." Katherine winked at her sister as she replied.

When Lena sat on the bed, Katherine moved to sit down beside her, but Ben's voice stopped her in motion.

"Katherine, let me sit with Clara and you go get some sleep. Once Lena's done here, she can do the same thing. Y'all have cared for her day and night. Let me do my share." His eyes seemed to plead with her while his smile seemed to assure her. She could trust her daughter to his care, if only she would. She did. Katherine leaned over and touched his shoulder.

"Thank you. Wake me if you need me. If she needs me."

She didn't want to depart from the child and husband, but the lull to sleep she'd felt moments earlier when he hummed seeped back into her.

Katherine walked through the doorway, through the kitchen, then collapsed onto the bed that had been Joe's. Her eyelids felt heavy, as her world stilled, and darkness relaxed her.

Katherine felt the bed give way to his weight and stirred just as Ben quietly called out her name. The nearness of his body sent goosebumps over her as she woke from her fog. His scent was familiar, as though she had woken up next to him every morning for the last five years. She suppressed a giggle when her senses hinted that he could use a bath. She supposed she could use one as well. A memory awakened. Lavender. Suddenly, she wanted to bathe in lavender. She opened her eyes, then had to squint against what seemed to be bright morning light.

"Good morning, Butterfly." Ben's smile spread across his face and the sight of it delighted her. Delight? Her daughter was deathly sick, but Katherine managed to feel delight. These contradictions of emotions puzzled her. She felt her cheeks heat. He'd called her his Butterfly.

"Morning? What time is it?"

"It's six in the morning, Wednesday."

Katherine sat up in the bed.

"Wednesday? Lands, Ben, you let me sleep that long? You didn't wake me when the doctor came? Clara! How is Clara?"

Her husband laughed and patted her hand.

"Settle down, Katherine. Clara is fine. In fact, Clara seems lots better."

"Better? Did the doctor say so?"

"The doctor didn't come but sent word on the phone to Carl Justice that he would be here this morning. Carl delivered the message yesterday afternoon."

"Carl came."

"Yep, and you slept through it. Lena did too."

Realization set in and Katherine felt her eyes widen. She brought her hands to her mouth.

"You saw Carl."

She watched tears pool in Ben's eyes.

"Yes, I did." A grin spread across his face, showing his straight, healthy teeth. "No one knew I was here 'cause I came straight home from the depot. Then I found myself quarantined with my family and couldn't leave to see anyone. Didn't want to leave. Surprised us both when we stood facing each other in the doorway. We about shook one another's arms off, then gave up and hugged one another, patting each other on the back."

"That makes me happy for both of you. Ya know, Carl and Louise never let me forget that they thought we should be together. And, she kept your letters to Clara out of our box, so Joe wouldn't see them."

Ben's warm hand touched her cheek. "So I was told. Carl and I caught up a bit yesterday when he was here. Seems he didn't care about the quarantine when he walked in and sat in your rocker. Oh, he promised to send a telegram to my good friend Henry and the Cramers. 'Clara alive. Marriage alive.'"

Ben winked, sending heat through Katherine's body. She was certain her soul took a deep breath, inhaling the joy of that truth.

"I'd like to hear about this good friend, Henry. And of course, the Cramers too."

"I'll fill you in sometime." Her husband covered his yawn. "But now, Mrs. Williams, it's time for you to see your daughter."

Katherine's stomach growled. Ben smiled, then touched her middle, causing her heart to thump against her chest.

"Yesterday Lena heated some cold biscuits for our lunch and made eggs for supper. We agreed rest was better for you than food."

Katherine smirked. "My stomach seems to disagree, but I don't."

Ben chuckled. "I think there's a stale biscuit or two left over." His grin looked mischievous. "Lena slept through the night in Clara's room, and when she woke up, decided to bathe her, so I slipped out and made oatmeal and coffee before waking you. Eat up."

Her nose suddenly took in the aroma.

"And, once Clara is bathed, then you and Lena can have the room to yourself for your own baths. I'll take me a nap here on this bed."

Katherine longed to stay put and lay beside him in the bed, but she pushed back the covers and let him pull her to stand on the floor. He winked, then immediately moved to lie down.

She noted the wrinkles under his eyes. She noted his light beard. She noted the gray in his hair. His limp appeared more pronounced than when he'd arrived. Weary-looking Ben had aged beyond the five years they'd been separated. She supposed that heartbreak, loneliness, fire, and pain could do that to even the best of men. She also supposed that time had done the same thing to her. Katherine realized her hands were far from soft and, as Lena often reminded her, she wore her hair in a tight bun that made her facial features appear stark, accenting her pursed lips and jutted chin. *No more.*

"Good *night*, Ben." She smiled. "I'll wake you for supper if you're still sleeping." She wanted to bend down and kiss him, but he hadn't attempted that with her, so doubt crept in. *Blast it!* With a boldness that had been stifled by her taut bun, pursed lips, and jutted chin, she bent down and kissed the man on his lips. He responded by returning the kiss and clasping the back of her neck.

"Katherine."

Her name was spoken between a smile and a heavy sigh, just as she watched his eyes close. She stood up straight, stepped quietly from the room, and slid the doorway curtain closed, leaving her husband to sleep in the warmth her body had left in the bed.

Katherine tapped on the door to her bedroom and announced herself before pulling it completely open. The sight before her made her bounce up and down on her toes. Beautiful Clara was standing in front of the mirror in her flannel blue gown while Lena combed her russet hair. Her face was no longer pale. Her cheeks appeared rosy with health instead of with fever.

"Momma! I'm all better. See." Staying turned toward the mirror, Clara extended her arms out in display. Katherine made her way across the room with large strides, then leaned down and inhaled the scent of her little girl.

"You smell like honeysuckle."

"Aunt Lena got her special soap for me. We celebrated the special occasion."

"Those are big words for you."

"I'm kinda smart."

Katherine laughed and rolled her eyes at Lena, who was laughing as well. In a breath, all joy and color drained from Clara's reflection. Katherine's laughter ceased, and she turned her daughter toward her, suspecting she was ill again.

"Where's Papa? He can come in 'cause my bath is over. Did he leave?" Katherine heard her daughter begin to cry. She wondered if Clara had been asleep yesterday when Ben talked with Carl, because she seemed to panic anytime he left the room.

"No, Clara. Papa is asleep."

"Can I see him?"

Katherine glanced at Lena, needing reassurance that Clara's wounded heart would someday heal. Lena smiled at her.

"I'll get in the tub. Why don't you and Clara tip toe over to look at Ben. Then you can bathe when I'm done."

Katherine mouthed "thank you" and gathered Clara into her arms. She noted that her body was cool to the touch and no longer feverish. The child had always been tall and slender, but sickness had revised slender into thin. "Clara, you can see, but let's not wake up Papa. He needs some sleep."

"Yes ma'am." Katherine felt Clara lay her head against her shoulder.

"Clara," the mother whispered, "your Papa is here to stay."

Seeing Ben asleep in the bed, Katherine sensed that Clara felt more at ease and understood that although he may not be with her every moment, he was not leaving. Katherine understood that truth too. Her husband was here to stay. She smiled against Clara's russet curls as they returned to the bedroom.

When Katherine put Clara down, she moved to the kitchen to get them oatmeal. She sipped the good coffee her husband had made as she dished out the warm cereal.

Returning with filled bowls, she saw Clara open the dresser drawer and pull out her butterfly book.

"Momma, come look at my Papa butterfly."

"Are you hungry?"

"In a minute I will be."

Katherine chuckled, said a quick prayer, and managed three bites of oatmeal before Clara's pleading look to show her the butterfly made her set the bowl aside.

Katherine gathered Clara into her lap and sat in the rocker. She watched as her daughter's fingers turned each page gently until she found the one she wanted.

"This is my Papa butterfly," Clara pointed. "You like it?"

Katherine's heart pumped quickly. This butterfly was unlike any of the others Lena had drawn or brightly colored. The drawing was Lena's, but the uneven coloring, escaping the lines here and there, was not. She nodded her head back and forth.

"Lena drawed it, but I colored it. See, it's all red."

For love.

"It's beautiful."

"It's red because I love Papa so, so much."

"It's my favorite one, Clara."

Katherine leaned over and kissed her child's cheek. Then Clara turned to the beginning of the book, and for at least the hundredth time, Katherine listened as her daughter explained the colors of each butterfly and its name. Oh, how Katherine truly loved this book that displayed the heart and emotions of her little girl. When the ritual ended, Katherine set up a game of Jack's on the bed for them to play.

The door to Clara's room opened as Lena walked out. "Your turn." Katherine rose from the bed, and Lena took her place. Before heading into Clara's room where the tub was set up, Katherine made her way to the other small room that was storage. As she grabbed the door knob, Lena's voice called out.

"Katherine, what are you doing?"

Feeling embarrassed, Katherine froze in place.

"Just looking for something."

Lena laughed. "Uhm, the tub is in Clara's room."

"I know." Katherine groaned. "What I want is in here." She heard the bed squeak. "Stay put, Lena." She pulled open the door and gingerly made her way over the stored items to Ben's trunk. She got on her knees and opened the clasp.

"I can see you. You're opening Ben's trunk."

"Papa's trunk! Can I see?"

Katherine rolled her eyes. "No, Clara. Not now."

"But Momma…"

"Another time, Clara." She began to rummage through the contents.

"Katherine, are you going to take a bath or clean out storage?"

"Blast it. I'm gonna take a bath when I find what I'm looking for."

Katherine shifted Ben's shirts to one side of the trunk, pausing as she always did, to inhale his faint, lingering scent. She sighed with contentment. Soon his shirts would be saturated with his smell, once they had pulled out his trunk and returned the contents to their rightful owner. He appeared so thin she wondered with pity if the shirts and pants she'd kept hallowed in his absence would now hang from his body much like a child playing dress up.

Underneath the clothing lay his letters. She pulled the bundle to her heart. She loosened the ribbon that had kept the bundle intact while their marriage floundered and freed the small gold band that bragged on the fact that she had given herself to a man for a lifetime. Tears pooled from her eyes, and Katherine caught them with her right hand, then took the ring and slid it over her third left knuckle and let it settle around her finger like one settles in at home after a long day's work. Had Ben noticed that her hand had been bare? If so, how that must have made him doubt her words assuring him of her forgiveness and love. His hand was adorned by his band, and Katherine suspected it had never been removed, for she'd noticed it sat deeply grooved into his skin. How she wished now that her finger had been adorned with the wedding band when she opened the door to him—a testament of her fidelity at the very least.

Condemned to the bottom of the trunk lay a tin of lavender lotion. She had untied it long ago from the bundle of his letters to her. She wondered if the lavender scent would still linger after five long years of being sealed up. She opened the tin and the scent accosted her. Although the lotion was no longer a creamy white substance, the clear, gummy one carried the scent she was after.

Katherine put the clothing, letters, and other contents back into the trunk and with the tin in her banded hand, without an explanation, she made her way out of the small room, into the bedroom, then immediately into Clara's room where the tub awaited. As Katherine suspected, Lena would not be satisfied with silence.

"Katherine?"

"Lavender lotion, Lena. I wanted my lavender lotion." She closed the bedroom door, but not before hearing Lena giggle.

Two hours later a knock came to the front door. Clara was on the bed playing with her doll, while Katherine swept the bedroom floor, and Lena stood over the stove preparing vegetable soup.

"Maybe the doctor is here. I'll get it, Lena." Katherine set the broom aside and made her way to the room where Ben slept. She saw him stir.

"Katherine." He sat up and ran his fingers through his hair.

Lucky fingers.

"Did I hear a knock?"

"Yes, I hope Doc is here."

She watched Ben move to get out of bed.

"I'll join you in a minute, Katherine."

His voice was raspy, and it caused her to smile. She watched him trudge his way through the kitchen, then open the back porch door. She wondered if he'd grown used to indoor plumbing and how much of an adjustment trekking outside to a smelly outhouse would be.

Katherine made her way to the front door and opened it to greet the doctor. Relief as strong as the blowing, cold wind sweeping over her.

"Good afternoon, Katherine. Sorry to be so long getting back out here. How's our patient?"

Katherine clasped her hands under her chin.

"She seems so much better today. Maybe she's well. Is that possible?"

The doctor stepped inside, and Katherine closed the screen and door behind him. He handed her his bag and proceeded to pull off his coat.

"It's possible. I've seen typhoid last a week, and I've seen it last a month or more. Did she ever get a rash?"

"No. That's good, right?"

"Seems so."

She led him to the bedroom with Lena on her heels.

"Clara, the doctor is here." Clara was sitting up in the bed.

"I'm all better now, doctor."

Katherine watched his eyebrows raise and was sure she saw a small grin spread across his lips.

"Why you certainly look better, Clara. Mind if I look?"

"No sir."

Katherine turned toward Ben as he entered the room. His shoulder brushed hers when he came and stood beside her. His face looked moist from where'd he apparently wet it, and his hair lay smooth against his head, but she noticed water on the hair at the back of his head.

"Papa!" Their daughter began to rise from the bed.

"Hi there, honey. Stay put so Doc can check on you."

Honey.

Katherine's heart warmed.

"Doc." Her husband nodded and extended his hand toward the doctor and they shook. "It's good to reacquaint."

Katherine, Ben, and Lena stood side by side in silence as the doctor checked Clara for rashes, swelling, and fever. He pressed on her skin.

"Has she eaten?"

"Yes, sir. Aunt Lena gave me toast. Then I wanted oatmeal. And I ate it. And my tummy doesn't hurt. And I didn't get sick."

Katherine snickered as Clara flashed her toothy smile. "She's right—toast and oatmeal." Katherine chuckled.

"And, little lady, "the doctor tapped his chin with his finger as though he were thinking, "do you have a headache?"

"Oh, no sir. I forgot all about headaches. My head feels real good. And, I took a bath too."

"All that is good news." The doctor smiled.

Lena clapped.

Katherine sighed loudly. She felt Ben lace his fingers with hers and squeeze. Then, as though they were nestled next to one another, holding hands on a blanket, finding pictures in the stars, she felt his finger glide back and forth across her wedding band. The moment simply winked at her, then excused itself, so she and Ben could focus on Clara's wellbeing. The doctor turned toward them.

"Well, it certainly appears she's over the worst of it. In fact, she appears healthy. I think it is safe to say she didn't have typhoid fever. Perhaps a form of food poisoning not as severe." Katherine leaned into Ben. She felt him release her hand and then place his arm around her shoulders. "She may get tired real easily for another week or so. That's normal. If the fever comes back, call me, but I suspect it won't. Keep her on easy foods for a few more days while her body adjusts."

"What about the quarantine?" Katherine was relieved that Ben asked that question.

"I'm lifting the quarantine on the family, but I'd prefer Clara stay inside or sit on the porch for a few minutes if she wants fresh air until the temperature stays warmer than the thirties."

With that, the doctor let himself out, then the family of four hooped and hollered, hugged and kissed, and thanked God for the good news.

In the midst of the celebrating, Katherine felt Ben's lips against her ears. "You smell like lavender, Mrs. Williams, and you're wearing your ring." Her entire body warmed, and she squeezed the warmth into a smile. His grin nearly made her knees give way.

As late afternoon set in, Katherine found herself in the front room dusting. Ben was playing checkers with Clara at the kitchen table, and Lena had her nose in a book. Life felt good and normal. "Thank you, God, for healing Clara. For bringing Ben home, and that Lena is safe."

The sound of an automobile coming into the yard got her attention. Glancing out the window, Katherine stilled. By the time a knock sounded on the front door, Katherine was already standing over her husband at the kitchen table, her gilded left hand resting on his shoulder.

"This is a knock you need to answer, Ben."

He turned and looked at her, his eyebrows furrowed in a question.

She simply smiled and motioned toward the front door.

Chapter 29

1925 | Layton, Texas

Sometimes life offers up circumstances we'd just as soon change for the better, but we make the most of it anyway. Such would be his friendship with Wendell Carlson. Looking the man in the face, Ben felt the deep impact of his presence over memories more than five years old. A renewal did not have to be put into words.

Time, perhaps fatherhood, for Ben had learned of his children, appeared to have been generous to his friend. Wendell stood before him on the front porch looking kempt and confident in his overcoat that revealed a shirt and tie beneath it. Rather than forming wrinkles or graying his hair, Ben surmised that time had chiseled maturity into peaceful looking eyes, a smooth, broad smile, and a hairstyle that implied an age the mature could trust and the young could approach. He looked very much like the curves of his penmanship had suggested in the letters from years ago—wise, understanding, bold, and sincere. Lines from Wendell's letters ran through Ben's mind in the split moment between seeing and speaking.

"Wendell." The name pushed through the lump in Ben's throat. A grin invaded every inch of Ben's face, causing his eyes to squint and his cheekbones to brush his temples. His friend stepped through the doorway, took Ben by the shoulders, and with no restraint, pulled him into a hearty hug.

"When I heard you were here and that the quarantine was lifted, I dropped everything and came."

"Thank you, Wendell."

The men separated, but still needing the affirmation of each other's presence, they shook hands vigorously. Words gave way to laughter at their childlike excitement until Wendell collected himself and they released their grip.

"Clara is better?"

"It seems so."

"Thank God. And, how's Katherine?"

Ben realized they were standing just inside the doorway and cold air was blowing in. He chuckled.

"Here, come inside." Ben shut the screen and door. "She's good. We're off to a good start. Seems she made her peace with God and with me. I did the same. He felt one side of his mouth turn up. "We got a good bit of things to work through, but I reckon we're willing to face 'em."

"That's good to hear. Does my soul right well." A grin spread across Wendell's face. "I'll probably get me a big hug and kiss from Amy when I tell her the good news." Ben hoped so.

Pastor removed his outer coat, then Ben led him to the kitchen. Sammy had died in the kitchen, and the memory of Wendell caring for them while Sammy's dead body lay nearby chose this moment to invade Ben's thoughts. He shoved it aside. Now was a time of celebration. His wife and daughter sat at the kitchen table, staring at a checkerboard. Ben bit his lip to hold back a smile. Clara had clearly outplayed her Momma. Unless she had changed, Katherine had never been one for enjoying checkers. She'd simply occupied Clara and given Ben uninterrupted time with Wendell. He suspected she was eager to see their friend.

"Pastor! Can Maggie come play? See, I'm all better?"

Ben watched Katherine rise from her seat and move toward Wendell without pause or hesitation. She grabbed his arms. Pastor's response to Clara was apparently lost to the moment.

"Wendell. My baby girl is well. My husband is home. My heart is right. Thank you."

As his wife began to weep, Ben moved to touch her back as Wendell replied.

"Thank God, Katherine. Thank God. This is what I've been praying for, my friend. Amy will be beside herself." His friend glanced toward Clara. "And as for Maggie comin' over, I hear you need a little more time to rest, but maybe I can work out a quick visit for a hug."

Clara shared her toothy grin, causing her angel kiss to rise. Unable to resist the love and sheer joy he felt at the sight of her, Ben walked over and grabbed his daughter into a tight hug. He felt her thin arms come around his neck. A slender hand patted each shoulder. He eased his grip enough to lean in and press his lips to her angel kiss. Her scent filled his lungs, and her warmth seeped into his skin.

Wendell lingered for a half hour then left with the promise of bringing Amy and the children by for a quick greeting before Sunday.

Since a constant watch over his daughter wasn't needed anymore, Ben found himself at a loss to occupy his time when Clara lay down for a nap in Lena's front bedroom. The women folk flitted about the area where she had lain throughout her sickness, scrubbing the bedroom floor, airing out quilts, washing down the bed frame, wiping down the wallpaper, somehow, he supposed, trying to rid any threat of an illness returning. He hovered nearby.

It humored him that every few minutes, they'd bark out an order for him to assist with a task they could surely do themselves. At last, they must have tired at explaining what they needed done and just went about completing the work on their own. He decided to excuse himself and go find work better suited for him. Leaning over Katherine, who was stooped down scrubbing the floor of Clara's little side bedroom, he touched her shoulder. "Holler if you need me. I'm gonna see what trouble I can get myself into around this place."

He managed to chop wood despite his aching leg, then meandered over to Sammy's grave. The cold air bit at his neck and cheeks as he bent over the grave. It was well tended, but he recalled Katherine saying Clara had discovered it, which implied it hadn't always been visible. A mess of emotions welled up in him as "what ifs" invaded his thoughts. *A person shouldn't dwell on the "what ifs" of life, for regret can dry up a person's soul.* Ben knew the truth—Sammy's life would have been a difficult one the older he became. The world didn't make things easy for a deaf and crippled human being, no matter how broad his smile and how gentle his heart.

Ben reached inside his pocket and rubbed the rabbit foot Sammy had treasured. He refused to think that Sammy's passing was a good thing, but he could embrace that it was a gracious thing; after all, his boy's body was well and whole in heaven. "I love ya, boy, and miss your smile, Samuel Benson Williams." He felt tears roll down his cheeks and licked them away. He'd licked a lot of tears in the last couple of days. Funny thing—tears of sadness and tears of joy taste the same, distinguishable only by the heart.

Night time began to set in prompting Ben to return through the backdoor. As he entered the kitchen, the smell of fried pork chops filled his nostrils and made his stomach growl. Lena stood over a skillet on the stove, turning the browned meat from one side to the other with a fork. The grease sizzled and popped. Honestly, Ben couldn't recall tasting food as good as what came from Lena's kitchen. Another skillet sat on the next burner.

"Lena, you standing over that stove is a sight for sore eyes."

His sister-in-law turned toward him wearing a smirk and shook the fork in the air. "Get over here and earn your supper, Ben Williams. I got some fried taters that need turning, then put on a plate." Ben stood with his mouth gaping at the sight before him when Lena turned. She was wearing her "Aunt Lena" apron that had been a gift from Sammy. His four-year-old handprints were stitched on it just as Ben recalled, but beneath them was another set of small handprints that he reckoned belonged to his daughter. Lena must have realized his surprise, for she softened her teasing tone and pointed to the second set of handprints. "Clara insisted. I hope you don't mind. I'm quite fond of the apron."

"It's perfect."

Ben picked up the spatula lying next to the stove, licked the grease that dripped onto his wrist, and turned the potatoes. He inhaled the scent of onion filling the room. Ah! He loved fried taters and onions.

"Ben, seeing you in the courtroom… well, I can't rightly thank you enough or tell you how much it meant to me."

"Lena, I never stopped caring. I should have had the courage to come home. I'm ashamed." Ben smiled. "You are the bravest woman I've ever met. When I heard what Joe had done, I hated him. I had to work through that with God."

"Me too. The anger won't seem to die. Every day it wakes up when I do, ready for a full day of hard work on my heart. Only God can help me smother it, so I can live my life. I figure one day it will finally weaken enough to lose its fight."

"There's a part of me that understands…"

"I'm glad you're home. How did you fare all those years?"

"A simple question with a complicated answer. I reckon I was alive but had no real life away from my family."

"Ben, why? Why didn't you come when she asked you to?"

"You know about the letter?"

"Only for a few weeks. She never said, so I assumed, I reckon everyone assumed, that she never wanted you back."

Ben moaned. So much misunderstanding.

"I never got the letter, but she didn't know that."

Lena gasped.

"There's a lot we have to talk through, and that will be Katherine's story to share or not share with you."

"Ben, all those years. How lonely."

"Yep. For both of us. Katherine had you. I had a friend in the hospital chaplain until he moved. But, God gave me a younger brother of sorts in my friend, Henry. He's like family. I'm grateful for you all, but the fact is Katherine, Clara, and me never had each other like we should have."

Lena reached over and squeezed his hand. "You're right." She released her grip.

"Henry. Nice name."

Ben rubbed his chin and grinned at Lena's diversion.

"One day I want him to meet y'all."

He raised his eyebrows as he nodded toward the stovetop. "He likes to cook."

"I hope his food tastes better than yours as I recall it."

The two of them laughed.

"Did Katherine ever tell you about my comin' to be a believer?"

"Only that you had. She told me when she mentioned Pastor had stopped by."

"I'll tell you the story one day."

"I hold you to it. Now, get busy!"

Ben rubbed his palms together. "Taters…"

With the apron obviously not lost to Clara as she and Katherine entered the kitchen through Joe's room, most of the supper conversation centered around Clara asking questions about her brother. Ben supposed the furrowed brow on Katherine's forehead meant she was concerned that the conversation was painful for him. On the contrary, pride and delight danced inside Ben at the opportunity to talk about his son with his daughter.

"I got one of his trains. Momma said I could have it. Is that okay, Papa?"

"Yes! Maybe we can play with his trains sometimes, together."

Clara glanced at her mother, Ben noted, as though he'd suggested some forbidden act. A smile came across Katherine's face, then she nodded a yes. That toothy grin made another appearance on Clara's face.

"Tonight, Papa?"

Ben laughed. "How about tomorrow?"

"Promise?"

"I promise we will plan on it."

Clara's wrinkled brow told Ben she didn't quite understand his meaning, but she apparently latched on to the word promise, for a smile boasting of victory eventually forced its way onto her lips.

Lena excused herself early so that she could get up and go to the store first thing in the morning and inquire about getting back to work. The diner opened at 7:00 A.M., an hour before the store took customers.

"I'll drive you there," Ben offered. "I need to pick up some supplies, contact Mason Forder about a job, and let you help me pick up whatever food stuff we need."

"Can you get me there by seven o'clock and pass the time 'til the store opens? I might get to work the breakfast shift if I'm there early."

"It's a deal. And, Katherine, I think I'll take that bath I've been needin'."

Ben slipped away to Katherine's bedroom. He wondered if he would ever think of it as *their* bedroom again. He supposed time would answer that question for him. Meanwhile, he'd attempt to practice weak patience and weaker restraint approaching his wife with physical intentions. As he soaked, his mind played back the conversation he and Carl had about Katherine's money.

"Best I could tell, she took care of Clara's needs and some wants with the money. I can also recall a couple of times or more her using the money for a repair around the house. Ben," his friend had carefully explained, "it looks to me you got a balance of three-years-worth of money in there. It's none of my business, but it seems you were paid well or else you lived like a beggar on your own." Carl grinned. "We can work with Mason to transfer that money and yours from the Dallas bank to where ever you prefer."

Dipping his head into the water, then wiping his face with his hands, Ben pondered his approach with Katherine. He had an idea to present and wanted to make sure his timing was respectful to her. The last thing he wanted to do was imply she had not kept up the place. Over his short time here, he'd noted brown spots on the ceiling, chipped paint on the house, and broken boards on the porch and steps. Anger rose up toward Joe, who had the skill and most likely the means to make repairs but didn't. What a scoundrel!

Approaching Katherine about repairs would be easier than sharing his other ideas about the house. He had a hankering, and it appeared, some financial resources to make life easier—perhaps an indoor bathroom, maybe electricity, perhaps a used auto. How about a telephone? Ben chuckled. Was he more of a city folk than he realized? No. He belonged with Katherine, even if that meant a cart and an outhouse.

Clara had fallen asleep in Ben's lap about an hour after his bath, and he made no move to transfer her to a bed. However, when bedtime came for him and Katherine, he sensed an awkwardness in his wife. He'd learned that for weeks the child had slept with her during the ordeal with Joe and on into the sickness. Could his wife be struggling with her assumption he expected to share a bed with her?

"Katherine, let me carry Clara to your bed, just in case she needs you in the middle of the night. As promised, I'll sleep in Joe's room."

He expected to read relief on her face, but on the contrary, couldn't decipher her odd expression. Again he suspected her disappointment. Dare he hope so?

He kissed his sleeping daughter on the forehead as he lay her on the mattress. He then turned to his wife who stood beside him, longing to pull her forcefully to him, feel her against him, and not let go. But, with restraint, he kissed her lightly on the lips.

"Good night, Katherine."

Once again, her look intrigued him. Her lips parted as though thoughts were trying to escape, but none did, other than a simple good night.

Unaware of the time, but eerily aware of a presence, Ben startled in his bed. His eyes focused and then his fears subsided. Clara stood beside his bed with rumpled hair, clasping her teddy bear. A glance at the clock showed him it was half past eleven at night. She spoke before he could.

"Papa?" The childish whisper was high and shaky. "Are you dead?"

Ben pulled a hand from under the quilt and touched her shoulder.

"No, honey. I'm alive. I was sleeping. Are you sick?"

"No. I was afraid you left, then I saw you, and I thought you died." She whimpered.

Ben pulled the quilt back from the side where she stood. "Here, sit next to me." Clara slid onto the mattress and rather than sitting, she lay next to him, her head against the side of his arm. He felt her shiver and pulled the cover over her.

"Papa, is it time to play trains?"

A slight chuckle.

"No, it's still sleeping time. Can you go back to sleep?"

"Maybe. Papa, will you be here when the butterflies dance? After it's warm, that's when they dance."

He assumed she meant fall when the monarchs migrated.

"Clara, I'm here to stay and live with you and your Momma. Even if I go to off to work, I will come back here when I am finished."

"And don't forget about Aunt Lena. You'll live with her too."

'Ain't' Lena. He'd have to adjust how he referred to her. He grinned.

"Yes, and 'Ain't' Lena. And yes, I'll be here when the butterflies dance."

"Yippee."

"Yippee?"

"That means I'm happy."

"Yippee—me too."

He heard and felt her giggle. How had he lived one single day without knowing her? The realization of what he'd given up in the misnomer of respect for Katherine caused his chest to ache.

"Does your Momma know you left the bed?"

"No, she was sleepin'."

"We best get you back, or she'll worry."

"In a minute."

And within two, his daughter was back, sound asleep. Ben lay there with her for another five minutes or so, then uncovered them, rose, put his pants over his long johns, and bent to pick up his child. He carried her into the bedroom, where she'd apparently left the door wide open, because he'd heard Katherine shut it as he was sliding into Joe's bed. Just as he bent to lay her in Katherine's bed, his wife's voice floated over to him.

"Put her in her bed." Ben asked no questions and did as she instructed. He left Clara's door half ajar, then whispered a good night to his wife as he headed back toward Joe's room.

"Come lay by me." Stunned, Ben stopped in his tracks, wary he may have mistaken her words. He turned his head toward her.

"Katherine, what did you say?"

Despite the darkness around them, his eyes had adjusted enough to detect her smile.

"Come, lay by me." Katherine rested on her side and turned back the covers.

Oh, how he yearned for her entire being, yet he would let her guide their physical nearness in the infancy of their renewed relationship. The kisses and touches since his return had been tender and sweet, but full of restrained passion for him. Would the hurt between them attempt to roar and threaten their desire when they did give themselves fully to one another again? Ben refused to embrace that worry. Besides, with Clara nearby, just recently awakened, and her door ajar, he sensed that tonight they would simply, but deeply, take pleasure in intimate companionship.

He walked to the main bedroom door and gently closed it. With his eyes on hers, he advanced to the bed, removed his pants from over his long johns, then slid into place beside her. The quilt, the mattress, and his pillow could have been made of thin glass, so gentle was his approach into the bed.

Katherine was beautiful. Her russet hair freed from clips and braids, cascaded over her shoulders. He pulled her to him and held her tightly for soft, quiet moments, then turned on his back and drew her to him. Her head rested on his shoulder. Her hand lay on his chest.

"Can I see your scars?"

Panic threatened his answer.

"Yes." He began to unbutton the top of his long johns, but her hand grasped his fingers.

"Let me." Button by button his wife subdued his fears. Ben sat up and pulled the underclothing free from his chest and arms, then lay back down.

Her hand slid over the scarred flesh of his torso. He felt her fingers glide over the ridges and indentations of uneven skin. She then took his arm and he breathed rapidly as she ran her fingers down the length of it, touching his unevenness.

"Are they painful?"

"Not now."

"I can't imagine the pain you went through. I would have come to you."

"We're together now."

Her hand stilled. She looked him in the eye.

"Scars are permanent."

"Only on my skin. Not inside us, Katherine. Do you agree?"

"Yes."

His restraint lessened, and he reached over and kissed her forehead, then brought his scarred arm around her, enveloping her, holding her to his bare chest, feeling her against him. Her palm rested on his scars. He dwelt on the sensation.

"My skin is blotchy, Katherine. Some pink, some white, some brown. It looks as bad as it feels. I'm blessed that I can hide my scars under my clothing."

"You never have to hide them from me." Her lips were warm against his cheek when she kissed him. "Tell me everything about you, Ben, from the moment I let you walk away. Then my turn."

He chuckled. "Do you have all night?"

"I do."

Like a pair of butterflies dancing a courtship ritual, he and Katherine moved back and forth sharing tales of their separation. His wife heard firsthand of street cars and baseball games, of wailing as he learned he had a daughter, forgiveness in a boarding house kitchen, of making money plans with Carl and Mason, of nurses and burn patients, of Leon Machette's stories, of Rev. Lilley and his own pain, of Henry, and of the renewed kinship with the Cramers. Along the way, his wife interjected her side of life and the rare moments that broke it's monotony, such as placing one-year-old Clara in the dress he'd bought for her and getting a picture made. She talked of friendship with Amy Carlson, Abigail Forder, and Louise Justice. She explained about her job and the time that Joe had spent making furniture and preying on his family. She assured him that his daughter was safe from the harm Joe had brought upon them. They apologized again for stubbornness and resigned to the unsolved mysteries that had kept them apart. They answered one another's questions and filled in the blanks of their stories the best they could.

And some time before the dawn broke, they discovered each other again as husband and wife.

Clara never stirred.

Lying next to his wife he'd loved only moments ago, Ben felt himself drifting to sleep. Would she want him here when Clara woke up? He turned to get out of bed.

"Stay."

"Clara?"

"She'll know you belong here."

He stayed.

And doors…the rest of the house needed inside doors. He smiled, then let sleep overtake him.

A reverberating clatter in the kitchen caused Ben to bolt up in bed. Katherine stirred, but didn't waken. His entire being felt the impact of seeing her lying next to him. His heart thudded against his chest. Had his own heart been the clatter awakening him? He grinned. No, something had sounded from the other room. A glance at the clock showed it was six in the morning. He grinned again. Why, he must have gotten at least a couple hours sleep. Rising from the bed then slipping his pants on, Ben tiptoed over to the door and pulled it open to glance in the kitchen. Standing at the sink with her back to him was his sister-in-law.

"Lena?"

He watched her jump.

"Ben! You scared me."

He closed the door behind him.

“I heard a loud noise.”

“I dropped the skillet. ‘Bout dropped it again when you scared me.”

“Let me slip outside for a minute, then I’ll come back and make coffee. I know we gotta get out the door.”

“I thought you just came through the front from outside. Joe’s bed was empty when I walked…”

Lena turned from the sink and stood with her hand covering her mouth. Her eyes glanced at the bedroom door where he lingered, then he watched her cheeks take on a deep, red glow.

Ben laughed at Lena’s pickle. Her hand dropped to her leg with a slap.

It seemed that embarrassment gave way to contentment. The blush faded, and a smile spread. “Good mornin’.”

Chapter 30

LATE WINTER 1925 | LAYTON, TEXAS

Katherine's mind wandered through a labyrinth of household scenes as she stood over the ironing board. She'd had been surprised when the next Friday that Gabriel was due after Ben had returned, he hadn't shown up with his usual offer to help around the house. She'd come to realize that he must have gotten word at the store of Ben's return and brought his handyman plans to a grinding halt. She was even more surprised last night, three weeks later, when Ben had announced that Gabriel would be coming by in the morning to help with some repairs.

"Gabriel?"

"Yes. Gabriel."

"When did you see Gabriel?"

"Ran into him at the store. I was gettin' the hinges for the doors on my way home this afternoon. Turns out he likes to hang doors."

Stoking the fire, Ben had laughed at his own teasing. Katherine had neither laughed nor spoken. She'd simply stared at her husband, puzzled.

"Unwrinkle that pretty forehead, Butterfly." Ben had put down the fire stoker, walked over and squeezed her hand as he spoke. "I could use the help, and Gabe's bringing something with him to make the work more tolerable. You know I'm a sorry excuse for a handyman."

"Well, I disagree. You're mighty handy to have around." She'd winked, and his hand had moved to linger on her cheek.

She took pride in the work Ben and Carl had done the last few days to measure and cut out the wooden doors and paint them. It had taken a couple of Saturday afternoons for the men to complete the task, and Katherine had enjoyed spending that time at the store working on accounts and chatting with Louise. Clara was getting her own big bedroom. Katherine thought it nothing short of luxury for her child, and Clara had talked of nothing else since Katherine and Ben had told her their plans. Lena would be getting a door to her bedroom as well.

To make room for Clara's clothes, she and Lena had cleaned out Joe's dresser and stuffed his clothing into a pillow case early this morning before

Clara awoke. Then they began to decorate Clara's room and put her items in the dresser drawer. Katherine swapped out their brother's old quilt for one of the spares. Clara helped by carefully arranged her tea set and butterfly book on a small table Lena had taken from her own room and given to her. The teddy bear and doll rested on the floral quilt.

Yesterday Ben had carried Clara's trunk into the room, along with a wooden box he'd dug from the storage. It would now hold Sammy's trains. He and Clara had painted the box together while Katherine had stood inside the kitchen and eavesdropped. The memory warmed Katherine's heart.

"Papa, can I paint it all by myself?"

"Sure. Just let me help you dip the brush in the paint."

"What song are you humming, Papa?"

"Am I humming?"

"Uh huh."

"I reckon it's called 'Sweet Clara.'"

"It sure sounds pretty."

"Just like you. Here, put your hand on mine when we dip the paint brush. Is that a good idea?"

"Sure is."

"You two are making a mess."

"Momma, it'll wash off. Don't worry. Won't it Papa?

Katherine rolled her eyes thinking of what Clara had said. For the last three weeks, she'd verified all of Katherine's and Lena's comments with her Papa. Katherine didn't view it as disrespect, but rather a sign of Clara's awe at having a father to learn from.

The only remaining task was moving Joe's dresser items out of the pillow case and into his trunk and storing it away. Katherine suspected it would take some rearranging of the items in the trunk to make room for Joe's clothes. She and Ben planned do that together after supper. Katherine blew out a breath. She was not looking forward to rummaging through Joe's personal items.

Focused back on the moment at hand, she set down the iron, then folded the warm, crisply ironed skirt and placed it on the kitchen table. She wiped sweat from the back of her neck and blew out a breath that fought its way out before her lips spread in a smile over the sound floating into the kitchen. Clara was humming in her new room. She had plopped on the bed as soon as she had done her kitchen sweeping, announcing that she would sit there while her papa "stuck her doors on." Katherine picked up a small yellow checked dress and began to slide the iron over the fabric. She sighed contentedly. *Luxury? Why, "Yes," she wanted to shout to the world, her girl deserved some luxury for all her innocent life had undergone.* Ben made his way through the backdoor on his first trip bringing in the doors from the shed. Gabriel was due to arrive any moment.

"Whew! It's cold outside. Come warm me up, wife."

"Watch it. I got an iron in my hand."

Katherine chuckled as Ben propped the door against the kitchen wall, then made his way to stand behind her. She felt his arms come around her waist and savored his warm breath and cold cheek on her neck.

"Papa, is that my door?"

Her husband didn't budge from his position against her.

"Yes, honey."

"I was just wondering. Papa, don't forget my other one."

Katherine felt a grin spread across Ben's face just before he released her from behind, then brought himself toward her with one arm around her waist.

"Your daughter is bossy." His whisper was accompanied by a wink.

Ben Williams had been home for a month. For Katherine, some of his return felt like the early days of marriage. The simple, delightful awareness each morning that he lay beside her. The sounds and motions of his presence. The giddiness provoked by his touch. The scent of him. The security of his strength. But much of it felt deeper. The offering of loving an imperfect man who loved her in return, despite her own imperfections. The faithfulness of a tried and proven person—scarred, but not damaged. The companionship of parenting. The wholeness of a spiritual bond. In truth, Katherine realized their marriage was the miracle of forgiveness and restoration by the hand of God.

A thud on the front door startled them both, and Katherine felt Ben pull away from her. She heard the springs of Clara's mattress give way as she apparently slid off the bed.

"I'll answer it, Papa," their daughter announced. Katherine saw Ben hustle through Clara's room to get the front door. "Wait. Let me answer it, honey."

Ben's response was hasty and hinted of urgency. Katherine's eyes followed him through the house until he was out of sight. He'd tweaked Clara's nose as he passed by her. Why the anxiousness and urgency? Was he nervous about having Gabriel under their roof?

A shrill bark filled the air. Katherine gasped. Surely not. Surely Gabriel was not going to entice Clara with a dog. Prompted by curiosity, Katherine set her iron on the kitchen counter, then headed toward the front door.

"Momma, something barked!" Clara was already in motion when Katherine passed her bed. They entered the front room together where Gabriel stood in the doorway. Ben was turning to face them. Katherine's mouth fell open as Clara bounded over to Ben whose arms were filled with a furry bundle.

"A doggy!"

"This here's Pistol," Ben declared. Her husband's lips lifted on one side. Katherine watched as Ben kept his eyes locked with hers and knelt so Clara could touch the dog. Her own lips formed a smile as she moved her glance to Gabriel standing with the look of a proud father-figure.

"Pistol? I've met Pistol." Katherine got a warm feeling over her skin.

"Me too! At the store. Remember Momma?" Clara's voice was high-pitched.

"I remember."

"His eye looks weird, Mr. Gabriel."

Gabe petted the dog as he explained. "Clara, that eye don't work right. He cain't see with it. But he's okay."

"Oh. Poor doggy. Momma, is he coming to stay today 'cause Gabe is helping Papa? I can carry him and take care of him since he can't see."

"You best ask Papa that question." Katherine raised her eyebrows at Ben whose grin encompassed his entire face.

"I met Pistol yesterday and heard from Gabriel how Clara was wanting a doggy. So, if Momma doesn't mind, I thought we could keep him."

Katherine smirked. "Keep him?"

"Pleeeeease!"

The mother part of her couldn't hide her amusement any longer as Ben and Clara simultaneously pleaded with her, their eyebrows raised in earnestness. The similarity between them did not go unnoticed, and Katherine delighted in the observation.

"Clara, you have to help take care of him every day."

"Me and Papa will, right Papa?"

Katherine hoisted a hand to her hip and repeated her daughter, "Right, Papa?"

She leaned in and touched the dog's soft fur. Did Ben realize this was Pirate?

"Right."

Her husband bent and handed the dog to Clara.

"Thank you, Papa! And everyone!"

"He'll have to stay on the back porch or outside most of the time, but why don't you take him in your new room while me and Gabriel work."

"Yes, Papa! Ca'mere, little doggy."

Gabriel's voice broke into the conversation. "He just did his business. He ain't got fleas. I checked him. Bathed him too. He's right ready to be a fine pet."

"That's a relief." Katherine laughed as she watched Clara cuddle the dog like a newborn baby while Pistol whined and wiggled to be free.

"He's a mighty fine dog, don't ya think, Katherine?"

"Yes, Ben, he's mighty fine, even with a bad eye."

"Let me get my tools." Gabriel excused himself. Katherine took the moment alone with Ben to tease him, standing before him and placing a hand on his shoulder.

"So, tell me, Mr. Williams, how did we come to be dog owners?" Ben's cheeks turned red.

"I saw him in Gabriel's wagon and thought for sure I was looking at Sammy's dog, Pirate, a pound or two bigger in size."

"Come to find out, you were."

"You know?"

"Sure do. I recognized him when Clara and I saw him at the store around her birthday. But I reckon you know that." She laughed.

"Heard the story from Gabe, 'cept for the part that you knew it was Pirate." A momentary pause came between them. "I should have asked you first, Katherine. I didn't mean any disrespect, and it didn't occur to me until right now that the dog might be a bad memory for you. I just fell for him the moment I laid eyes on him—again. And I reckon it's kinda like having a piece of Sammy around."

His kindness and the slight hesitation in his speech that hinted at nervousness touched her heart. In truth, the dog had meant so much to Sammy she couldn't bear keeping it after he died. With Ben back home and her family together, having Pirate with them delighting Clara felt right.

"I'm glad he's back."

"You are?"

"Yes. Surprised?'

"Yes."

"I might slip and call him 'Pirate.'"

"I got an idea about that."

His hand grabbed hers and pulled her into Clara's room. Katherine looked back at the sound of Gabe coming through the front door. She nodded for him to follow them. He did.

Pirate had settled onto Clara's lap and was letting her pet him.

"Rub his ears. He likes that." Gabriel spoke up from behind Katherine.

Clara did as he said, and Katherine smiled as the dog sighed and closed his eyes. Ben cleared his throat.

"Clara, since Pistol has a hurt eye, what about calling him Pirate? Lots of pirates have a bad eye and wear a patch on it."

Katherine sweetened the suggestion. "Sounds like a good story name. Pistol Pirate."

"Little doggy, your new name is Pistol Pirate, but I'm calling you Pirate." Clara hadn't hesitated in her decision. "Can we get him a patch?"

"Aargh!" Katherine bellowed.

Laughter filled the room.

When supper ended, Lena kept Clara occupied with the dog and a card game of Slap Jack. Katherine took Ben by the hand and led him to Clara's new room. Caution prompted her to close the door, lest she come across anything in Joe's belongings Clara should never see. She pointed to a pillow case bulging with Joe's personal belongings from the dresser.

"Thanks for helping me with this, Ben. When Lena and I cleaned out the dresser this morning, I couldn't get Joe's trunk open to store these in."

"It's all going in the storage room, right?"

"Yep, then no trace of Joe is left in Clara's new room."

"How heavy is that pillow case?"

"A might heavy." Katherine winked at her husband.

Ben grinned. Katherine sat beside him and watched as he knelt on the floor and worked on the trunk lock with a pocket knife that had been among Joe's things. He felt the lock loosen, and with a yank, was able to pull the lock apart. The lid squeaked as he opened it.

Katherine peered into the trunk. Postcards and letters addressed from Joe's friends in nearby towns lay scattered in disarray. Mixed among them were magazines and some pictures of an unsavory sort. Joe was not a good person.

"This is more of Joe than I want to see."

"I agree," Ben huffed as he stood. "Can you empty the pillow case things into the trunk while I make a spot for it in the storage room?"

"Yep."

She felt Ben pat her head before he left room, opening the new door to let himself through.

Katherine sneezed as she rummaged through the paper items, stacking them in some type of order to make room for Joe's clothes. She discovered her brother's Bible and examined it. The cover was stiff, and most of the pages were stuck together on the edges from lack of use. It had been a gift from their mother. A few empty liquor bottles were wrapped in newsprint. What was their significance among the many others his reputation afforded him? Katherine laughed when she read a chain letter that Joe had participated in, guaranteeing him that for the contribution of ten cents, he would receive $1500.00. No doubt, the letter was a fluke.

Tears sprang to her eyes when her hand found the old toy sword Joe had played with as a child. Joe the Knight—but not the hero. She shoved an old hat aside and found a wooden train piece. This she hadn't seen since childhood. Joe had shared his train pieces with Sammy, but for a reason she'd never know, he'd hung on to this one.

Her eyes caught a stack of papers banded together. Most other papers were strewn carelessly about, so the bundle peaked her curiosity. She undid the rubber band and sorted through varied items. Her hands glided across a brown memorandum book, and she thumbed through the pages seeing handwritten accounts of money Joe had spent on liquor, sundry items, and apparent gambling at card games. She huffed. The next item was an insurance benefit certificate from the Order of Woodsmen issued in 1911. She unfolded it to see that she and Lena were the benefactors should he die before age fifty. Katherine sat stunned at the revelation. She should check to see if he had kept up the payments. Lying beneath the certificate were Joe's railroad papers, his building permit, a loan document from the bank for the auto, a couple of report cards, and a sealed envelope.

Katherine turned the envelope over in her hand and felt a gorge rise from her stomach. She forced it back down. The paper wiggled between her trembling fingers.

"Katherine, I cleared a spot..."

Ben dropped down beside her.

"Butterfly, what's wrong? You're white as a ghost."

Katherine could form no words and was certain they would stick in her throat trying to escape. She simply handed the envelope to Ben.

Her husband gasped.

"This was in the trunk?"

She nodded a yes, then stared at the envelope addressed to Katherine Williams. The postmark read July 20th, 1920. A printed return address on the right hand side read *Pine Bluff Hospital.* Complete with the address. The envelope had been opened.

Ben's voice was raspy, "Katherine, this has to be the letter I had sent from there. The one asking you to come to me."

"I've never seen this in my life. Oh, Ben, I promise you, I've never laid eyes on this before."

She began to weep.

Ben pulled out the letter, unfolded it, and handed it to her. The lines were read in whispers.

Dear Wife and Baby,

They are sending me to the hospital in Texarkana. I was in an accident and am barely able to move. I am burned. The doctor said I might die.

Katherine reached over and touched his scarred arm.

So in case of my death, I will have money for you. Should I never see you again, Butterfly, I love you and my precious Baby and will see you in heaven. At least now I know I will go there. Please forgive and be happy. This could likely be my last letter. The nurse will give you the address. I beg you to come and bring our baby. I will love you as long as I live. If I die, then I will finally be free of my lonely love for you. For I do not think human love will follow me to my grave. You are my darling, beautiful russet Butterfly. Tell my baby Clara I love her. I am weary.

So, Goodbye.

Ben

P.S. Cottonline Hospital, Dudley Street, Texarkana, Texas Come see me here.

Katherine turned into Ben's shoulder and wept, letting the letter fall to the floor. She felt his own tears hit her cheeks

"How? Ben, how did Joe get this? The Justices always kept your letters out of our box."

"I don't know, Katherine. Dear God, help us. We had so much needless pain between us."

"I would have come, Ben. Me and Clara, we would have come."

Their lips found each other. The kiss was salty and hard, as though all the pain and confusion and guilt of the last five years was forcing its way out through their lips. She felt Ben pull away and look her in the eyes. Then just as quickly pull her back to him. This kiss was one of desperation for a life they had missed together. A third was filled with determination that nothing would come between them again.

At last, they pulled away from each other. Katherine's lips felt bruised as she gasped.

"Ben, this is dated July. Louise Justice used to always visit her ailing aunt in July before she passed away three years ago. Another person was probably working the post office."

A knock on the new door between the room where they sat and the front room drew their attention.

"Momma, can I come in my room now? Is the trunk gone?"

"Almost, Clara."

Katherine looked at Ben, who took the letter and envelope and slid them into his pocket. Then together they dumped the pillow case contents into the trunk, caring less if there was any order to what they did. Katherine walked to the door where Clara waited while Ben hoisted the trunk into his arms and headed out the other door. Only then did Katherine open the door. She wiped her face of tears.

"The room is all yours, Clara. Ta Da!"

Clara spun in a circle. "I'm so happy!"

The child caught her balance then looked up at her mother.

"How about you, Momma. Are you so happy?"

Katherine bent down and scooped Clara into her arms.

"Yes, I am."

"But, I think you've been crying."

"Sometimes, people cry when they are very happy."

"That's right, Clara." Ben's warm voice floated across the room. His arms were freed of the trunk.

"Are you happy too, Papa?"

"Yes."

"If anyone is interested to know, I'm kinda happy myself." Lena stood in the doorway with a fist propped on one of her hips. The teasing tilt of her head hinted at the Lena unscathed by the predator who'd lived within these bedroom walls.

Pirate barked.

The happy family broke out in laughter.

Part Three
Life Moves On

Chapter 31

March 1925 | Layton, Texas

As the middle of March taunted the town with both warm and cold weather, life for Katherine and Ben had settled into a comforting routine.

This particular day had Katherine longing to sit in the fresh, brisk air. She stuck her head inside Clara's doorway while balancing a bowl of apples and a knife. Tomorrow her family planned to eat supper at Pastor Wendell and Amy's house. Ever the challenged cook, Katherine had finally mastered making a delicious apple pie and would be bringing one for the occasion.

"Clara, get your coat. It's nice enough outside that you can sit on the porch for a spell."

"Can I bring my jacks?'

"Sure."

Katherine made her way from the kitchen and set the bowl and knife in her front room rocker, grabbing her sweater from the nail next to the front room fireplace. She and Clara would await Ben's return from the mill where Mr. Forder had graciously hired him two days after Clara had been declared well. Her daughter, covered with her brown coat and yellow knitted cap, skipped passed her and opened the door.

"Don't let the screen…"

Slam!

"Sorry, Momma."

Katherine shook her head from side to side. The child didn't know her own strength. The clock hanging on the wall between two rockers chimed on the half-hour just as Katherine noticed two letters on the fireplace mantle. Ben had left them there after reading them to her last night. She grabbed both envelopes and stuffed them into her apron pocket. The words had stirred him, making him pensive and sentimental, and it had moved her to see him so deeply connected to the men who had penned each letter. A desire to read the letters again whispered at her. She gathered the bowl and knife and pushed open the door and screen with her foot. She closed the door, just as a breeze whipped around the corner of the house. Slam! Katherine bit her lip and smiled at Clara.

"Oops. The wind surprised me."

"Oops!" Clara laughed.

"If the wind gets you to coughing even one time, we're heading back inside."

"Yes, Momma."

Clara jumped up and scurried to the window where her red Jacks ball had rolled.

"Momma, can I have a apple?"

"They're for the pie I'm taking to the Carlson's tomorrow, but you can have one slice when I cut the first apple."

"I can't wait to play with Maggie at her house. Are you gonna make the red skin come off the apple like one big ribbon?"

"I'm gonna try." Katherine patted Clara's head.

"Can I have that instead? Yummy."

"Sure."

Sheer joy warmed Katherine's insides as Clara went back to her game of Jack's, singing some original tune about playing princess with Maggie. God had seen fit to restore a marriage and family, despite what their frail, sinful humanity had thrown at it.

Katherine sat down in a rocker, cringing at the creak her movement caused when the porch gave way to the motion. Pirate had barked when the door slammed and bounded from the side of the house. He now rested at Katherine's feet. Placing the bowl and knife on the porch, she pulled the letters from her pocket. She heard Pirate sniff. "No apples for you, matey." Her mind wandered to the changes she'd noticed in her husband upon his return. Yes, his body had aged with the specks of gray in his hair and the wrinkled skin around his eyes. His look had matured handsomely, and she took pleasure in these changes from the moment he walked through the front door and back into their lives. *He left through the back door, and I let it close behind him. He returned to the front door, and I opened it widely for him.*

Of course, his burns had scarred his outside, but inside, Ben's scars of bitterness and self-sufficiency had healed. His laughter and humor once again filled her life with pleasure. His seriousness over spiritual matters was something fresh he brought to their renewed relationship. As much as his laughter brought her joy, his prayers brought her comfort.

As Ben dwelt among friends and family in Layton, no longer a lonely soul, she noticed an intentional gratefulness on his part for those moments—often spoken aloud to those he was around. If moments were tangible, she would collect them for him as a treasure and store them safely away.

However, she knew from Ben that loneliness had been his constant companion during their separation, but not his only companion. Katherine would never meet Reverend Lilley, yet she held tender feelings for him in her heart. From Ben's narrative recollections, Katherine heard how the man had been a savior of sorts for him at the hospital, no doubt sent by the Savior. She pulled the reverend's recent letter from its envelope. The words had burdened Ben. Thank goodness he now had a burden bearer both in God.—she smiled—and in her.

> *"...I cherish these years I've spent with my granddaughter. I know too well how fleeting time can be with those we love. Ben, your last letter saying you reunited with your wife and child made this old man sit up from his sick bed and hoot. Cherish your moments.*
>
> *The doctor doesn't have much good news any more. Says the best I can do is be comfortable in my last days of life. My body is ready to give up the fight against my bad kidneys. Don't fret for me though. I'm ready to see my wife, children, and Savior. I'll be leaving my precious grandchild in good hands with her other grandparents. I'm thankful to have known you, Ben Williams. You grab hold of what our Good Lord has for you and you hang on when it's not the best life has to offer."*

She slid the letter back into the envelope, careful not to tear the thin paper, and put it securely in her pocket, sliding the next letter out simultaneously and praying as she did so. "God, help the reverend pass on with little pain. Help his grandchild with her grief. Give peace to Ben."

Henry Jones. The man's penmanship was heavy enough that she could feel it when she slid her fingers over the envelope. She recalled the fondness in Ben's voice that first night he'd shared the history of he and Henry held. Her husband and Henry had written back and forth almost every week since

Ben had returned home from Commerce, and he had shared every letter with her and Lena, and most parts with Clara. Henry's humor made them laugh. His letters made him feel familiar, as though he'd walked through their front door to sit at their kitchen table for supper. The adventurous spirit presiding in both Lena and Clara had them declaring at the end of each reading that the family should take a ride to Commerce and visit *their* friend. Katherine skipped to the middle of the letter.

> *"...I had a stop-over in Texarkana recently, so I hoofed it to a drugstore for shave cream and ran smack-dab into nurse Coreen. (Mrs. Katherine, I reckon Ben told you she's the one that put up with him when he was all messed up.) She didn't recall me at first, but when I mentioned you, Ben, she fit the pieces together. Poor woman. Seems her husband was hit by an auto and killed last month. Something about coming home from a run to the bank. Left her with two youngins. She's supposing she'll move back in with her folks. I was sorry to see her so sad.*
>
> *Little did I know more sad news was waitin' on me. Got a telegram from my Pa saying my Mama had disappeared for three days. I fretted and prayed, wondering how far a sick woman could get on foot or worse, if she'd been snatched by someone. Her "walks" as she calls them are getting worse. Got another telegram a couple days later when I arrived in Pine Bluff, sayin' "Found. Dazed, but well." Course I had to wait for a letter to get more detail. Seems she took off and was found in a neighbor's barn two miles from home. I immediately planned to move back to Stillwater, but my father insisted no when I telegrammed him. All is back to normal, which isn't normal at all really. I reckon I'm staying put in Commerce. The Cramers haven't seen the end of me yet..."*

Henry's humor had returned from that point forward in the letter. Staring at the pages now, Katherine's body stiffened at the discomfort, perhaps shame, she felt in thinking of another woman caring for Ben. If humanity could reverse direction and undo the past, she would certainly undo the mix-ups with her and Ben's letters. She shook the feeling from her mind. After all, the way she, Ben, and Clara were able to tightly knit their lives together since his return confirmed that God was renewing their bond despite the past. The renewal was nothing short of a miracle.

Her thoughts moved to Henry's Mama. Ben had shared what the young man had divulged about his mother but had never given her condition a name. *Insanity?* Her suppositions made Katherine's hair stand up on her arms. Although Ben told her Henry had never been in the darkness, she couldn't help but wonder if that could change. *Poor Henry.*

She returned the letter to her pocket and began her task. Just as she started peeling the last apple, her hand slipped, and she nicked her left pointer finger. "Blast it," she said under her breath, out of Clara's ear shot. She was wrapping her finger in her handkerchief when the familiar sound of Gitter and the cart came from her left. Pirate jumped up and ran toward Gitter, barking playfully. The mule was either deaf or had enough determination to ignore the persistent dog.

"Pirate, get back here," Katherine commanded.

She watched Ben slip down from the cart right there in the front yard rather than pulling it back to the shed. He grabbed the dog.

"Come here, matey."

Clara was up and at Ben's feet before Katherine could tell her differently

"Papa!"

Pirate bent down and licked Clara's forehead. Katherine watched as Ben bent over and kissed their daughter on the cheek.

"How's my little Butterfly?

"Good."

She watched them approach her, hand in hand.

"And, how's my russet Butterfly?"

Katherine was glad to see him hand the dog to Clara. She was longing for him to grab her into a tight hug. She rose.

"Slightly injured." She held her finger up for him to see. He kissed it. It amused her that he didn't inquire about the cut. He'd finally realized she nicked herself quite frequently in the kitchen.

Ben sat in the rocker she'd vacated, and Katherine was delighted when he pulled her down into his lap and rested her against him. The creak of the rocker against the porch was hardly a nuisance this time as she focused on her husband. He smelled of lumber. She heard Clara giggle and turned to see her watching them.

"Momma, you're too big to sit in Papa's lap."

"Honey," Ben remarked, "There's always room for your Momma." She felt his cool lips brush her cheek.

Clara made a kissing sound and giggled again.

"I got good news today, Katherine."

She sat up with eagerness.

"Mason called. Next week, I'll become the manager of the mill.

Katherine gasped, but Ben kept talking.

"Seems Mr. Yost has decided to move in with his son and daughter-in-law in Wylie. Says he's too lonely here in Layton since his wife passed—what about a year ago?"

"Ben, that's real good news." She clasped her hands under her chin as excitement raced through her. Once again Ben would do a job that he enjoyed. Would his pay go back to what he'd had in Commerce? She hoped.

"Your pay will be more?" She bit her lip.

"Greedy Butterfly, aren't ya?"

Katherine giggled. Ben rubbed his hand on her cheek.

"Yes. I'll make what I made in Commerce. Which is surprisingly generous because the Layton mill is smaller."

She hugged his neck. "Mason is a good man."

Clara came and stood next to the rocker, letting Pirate go free to roam the yard.

"Papa, I visited Sammy today. Do you miss him?"

"I sure do, honey."

"Me too."

Katherine felt Ben's chest rise with a deep inhale before it relaxed again.

"He'd sure love his little sister."

Her husband reached down and pulled Clara onto her lap. Katherine shifted her weight then clasped her arms around her daughter who was wearing her favorite pair of worn overalls now speckled with white paint. Clara's curly hair tickled Katherine's chin.

"See, Clara. Room for both of us," Katherine whispered.

"Is Lena home yet," Ben asked. "I got some more good news to share."

"She was reading in her room."

"Well, I'll just have to let Clara tell her later. I'm about to pop with the news."

"Ben? Tell her what?" Katherine grinned.

"Papa, tell us." Clara's palms had grasped Ben's cheeks.

"Katherine, remember our talk two nights ago?" He spoke with lips scrunched between Clara's hands. Katherine noted the playfulness in his eyes.

Katherine scrunched her brow to focus then recollected the conversation. She yelped.

"Ben, did you buy an auto?"

She watched Clara's hands jump from Ben's cheeks to cover her own grin.

"Papa!"

"Well, I have one waiting for me if you approve. Mr. Yost is selling his, and I made him an offer, dependin' on our talking tonight."

"Yes." Katherine was taken aback by her own response. Not too long ago she'd thought Joe ridiculous for wasting money on one. Not too long after that she'd felt strange riding in an auto with the Forders. She bit her lip. A woman had a right to change her mind. Money was Ben's concern now, and she suspected their own auto would be far more common than what the Forders drove.

"Can I go tell Aunt Lena?"

Katherine released her daughter. "Go."

She looked her husband in the eyes. With a serious tone coming from a heart that might burst from love and appreciation, she spoke.

"You're a good man, Ben Williams. I love you."

"I love you too, Butterfly."

Katherine was sure she heard Lena hoot, but Katherine didn't give one. At the moment her husband was kissing her passionately.

Chapter 32

MID-SUMMER 1925 | LAYTON, TEXAS

"Thank you, Pony and Wallace. I'll give my family your regards." Ben wiped the summer sweat from his brow. As he pulled away in his auto, he waved to the father and son sitting on their fruit and vegetable delivery cart. They'd encountered one another inside the Justice Store when Ben had stopped to get the mail and drop Lena off for her Saturday shift at the diner.

"You like baseball, Wallace?" Ben noted the baseball in the young boy's hands.

"Yes sir, I do. I hear about it from talk at church or school."

"I'm a baseball fan myself."

"Who you root for?"

"The Cardinals." The memory of attending the game with Eddie Martin now seemed like a dream and an event he figured was far out of reach for Wallace and his father, Pony. He'd keep the memory to himself.

"Ben," Pony spoke up, "I got me some extra pints of blueberries on the cart. My wife says they's too sour to sell, but I forgot to take 'em from the cart. Seeing we got plenty at home, why don't you take some to Miss Lena. From what I hear about her cooking at the diner, I reckon she can make just about anything taste delicious."

"I reckon you're right. In fact, I know you are." Ben patted his stomach to validate his point.

"Mr. Williams, have you ever gone rabbit hunting?"

"Why, Wallace, I can't say that I have."

"Well, then," Pony interjected, "the next time me and Wallace plan to go, we'll get you to join us."

"There's nothing better than rabbit stew." Wallace rubbed his belly imitating Ben's recent gesture.

"It's a deal. How 'bout I bring my Pastor along? He's good at fishing, but I never heard him talk of rabbit hunting. He might like it."

"Bring him."

He liked Pony James and his son. Katherine had told him of their delivery to the house when Clara was so sick. He always enjoyed the brief, unplanned encounters they had at the store.

Black dirt created clouds behind Ben's second hand Ford auto. The beads of sweat traveled rapidly down his face and neck. The Texas summer was dry and hot. He'd driven Lena to the diner for her shift, and when she'd gotten out of the auto, he noticed the back of her dress was saturated with sweat from resting against the seat. His own back was no different.

Pulling into his yard, he was thrilled to see Clara come running from the back porch. The child's cheeks were red from the hot air. He pulled the emergency brake back, released the left peddle, turned the gas down, and got out of the auto just as she reached him.

"Papa!" Her impact as she grabbed his legs set him off balance. He inhaled and spread a grin over his face, favoring her childhood outdoor scent. His fingers ran through her moist hair.

"What did you get at the store?"

"A piece of taffy." He held out the small candy for her to grab. She did.

"Thanks, Papa." She undid the wrapper and slipped the candy into her mouth. "And, you got a letter. I see it in your pocket."

"Uh hum. From Henry."

"Did you drink a cola?"

"Sure did. I had me a Dr. Pepper this time. Brought one home for your Momma too."

Her nose wrinkled up. "Yuck."

Ben grinned. "Remember, it doesn't taste like pepper. You've had some before."

"But, I still don't like it 'cause I don't like pepper."

He hoisted her into his arms, then leaned over the auto door.

"And I got some blueberries from nice Mr. James and his son."

"I know Wallace. He's a kinda' old boy, but he's nice."

Ben laughed.

"Why don't you carry your Momma's cola bottle while I carry the blueberries."

He watched his daughter try to match his stride and shortened his steps to meet her own. He walked onto the back porch where the dog lay sleeping, and chuckled when Pirate barked obligingly then returned to his nap. Ben had to step over a bowl of beans. Clara addressed him proudly as she walked into the kitchen through the back door. He followed her.

"I'm snapping beans for Momma."

"Good job. Is Momma in the kitchen?'

"Yes sir."

"Yes, I am." His wife looked up at him from her place at the table as he entered through the screen door. She let the snap beans in her hands drop into a bowl. Ben set the berries on the table, pulled his handkerchief from his pants pocket, and wiped his face and brow.

"Momma, here's your cola. It's the pepper kind."

"Thank you."

Ben bent and kissed his wife on the cheek.

"Enjoy your pepper cola while I read our letter from Henry."

His wife chuckled before replying.

"Oh, good. I like hearing from Henry."

July 21st
Commerce, Texas

Dear Ben and Family,
I seat myself to write you with a cola beside me.

Ben and Katherine grinned at one another.

I reckon the sweat drops I already see on the paper will make the letter spotty when you read it. Lands, it's hot here in Commerce. I hope you all are faring better, but probably not. Makes me wish for the swimming pond near where I grew up in Stillwater.

"Where's Stillwater, Papa?"

"Oklahoma."

"Oh."

At five, his daughter was clueless about geography.

I've worked four weeks non-stop. Passengers on the trains aren't kind in the heat, waving their fans, demanding a cool drink. I wonder if they ever considered how hot these uniforms are we must wear?

Well, I'm home for four days and it's a good thing. When I got here, I found Mrs. Cramer laid up in the bed. Seems she was in the hospital with chest pains. They sent her home after a couple of days and told her to stay in bed. She's fussing about it, but she's not trying to get up.

Katherine gasped over the woman she'd never met. "Oh, bless her heart."

Mr. Cramer flat out told me he's worried about her. Ben, he's in a lot of pain with his joints. They stay swollen. Place is looking more shabby than I ever saw it. He can't tend to it.

The owner came to me last time I was home and said I could live here rent free if I would manage the place. She even said she'd consider selling the place to me if I was interested. Of course, I'm not made of money, so I won't be buying the place. But, I'd like to manage it and get free rent. So, day after tomorrow, I'm interviewing for a job at Commerce Henderson Hotel. I could work there and manage the boarding house too.

First thing I'd have to do is find someone to cook. Arlen's wife has been cooking, but they are fixin' to move out in two weeks. His ma is ill and they're gonna move in with her in Flaydada. I'd need to fill their room. Turns out a new renter is moving in to the fifth bedroom next week. The Cramers will stay put, and the owner says they could pay a small grocery fee. There's a lot to think about. On second thought, maybe I don't want to manage this place. Joking aside, by the time you read this letter, I might be the manager of a boarding house or a hotel employee or both. Or, I might be right back on the trains. Tell Clara that I put a frame around the green butterfly picture she drew for me. I was happy to get it in your last letter. It's on the table by my bed. Tell her green is my favorite color.

Clara clapped her hands.

Has Miss Katherine driven the auto yet? Might be safer than riding with you.

The three of them laughed together.

Maybe your sister-in-law can mail me a couple of good recipes in case I find myself in the kitchen here.

Good talking at you, Ben.

Your friend,
Henry Jones

Ben didn't hesitate to share the idea that came to mind as he read the letter. Henry's words about the Cramers laid heavy his heart. He cleared his throat.

"Clara, how about finishing those beans on the back porch."

"Yes sir."

When their daughter was out of ear shot, Ben posed his idea.

"What do you think about a trip to Commerce? The four of us. Y'all could meet Henry and the Cramers."

"I'd like to meet them. They're like family to you."

"Yep."

He saw her wrinkle her brow?

"In the auto?"

"No, Butterfly. I was thinking we could ride the train."

"What about the mill and the diner?"

"Maybe we could go for a weekend. I bet the diner could spare Lena for a Saturday. We could travel Friday evening. We'd travel back after church that Sunday if I could arrange a stop in Layton on the Lord's Day. If not, well, me and Lena could try to work something out. I'd want to arrange things around Henry's schedule, so he would be there."

His wife squeezed his hand.

"You wouldn't mind traveling?"

"Not with you."

"I'll send him a telegram Monday."

When Monday came, that was exactly what Ben did. On Tuesday, Lena arrived home from her shift and surprised him with a telegram at the supper table. He read it aloud.

"Come week from Saturday. Spare room."

Eleven days later, Ben escorted his family onto the train at the Layton Depot. Seated next to his wife, watching her gaze out the window, contentment surged through him. Clara sat across the aisle firing questions and observations at Lena in the next seat. A few months ago, when he'd left Commerce on this exact train, he was uncertain if he would meet his child before she died of typhoid and uncertain if his wife would continue their marriage.

The train slowed and pulled into the depot at Commerce where the sights were familiar and welcoming to Ben. He rose and pulled Katherine up from her seat, then assisted Lena and Clara. Taking his daughter by the hand, he guided his wife and Lena down the steps.

"You three wait here while I look for..."

His words were cut short by the greeting of his friend.

"Ben!"

He spotted Henry taking wide strides toward them. His blond hair blew in the hot, slight breeze as a broad smile was spread across his face. The dapper young man wore a tie and jacket—quite matured from the wet-haired young man with grease on his fingers that he'd met at the Martin's dining room table. Ben cleared the gap between them, embracing his friend with a quick hug, then he tugged Henry toward his family noting that he'd toned down the aftershave from his earlier days.

"Henry, this is my wife, Katherine." Ben felt proud of the lovely smile, slight blush, and twinkle he saw in his wife's expression.

"I'm very happy to meet you, Henry."

"Does my heart good to meet you."

Ben watched Henry glance to Katherine's left.

"And this is Lena."

"Happy to meet you."

Had Henry just blushed? The sight amused Ben.

His friend knelt and extended his hand toward Clara.

"So very nice to meet you, Clara."

"I made you another picture, Mr. Henry, but it's in our bag."

"I'm glad. And… I hope your Momma and Papa don't mind, but I've got a roll of Lifesavers for you."

Ben nodded yes when Henry glanced up at him for approval. Henry slid the striped roll from his pants pocket and handed it to Clara.

"Thank you."

"You're welcome. Boy, this is a good day."

Ben blew out a whistle. "Sure is."

"Sure is!" Clara echoed.

"I guess we better get your bags. My auto is over there behind the post office. Hope y'all don't mind piling in together."

Ben gathered their two bags. Henry joined him and took one of them.

"Clara—she looks just like you, Ben. Got her Momma's lovely hair though. You look the best I've ever seen you."

"God restored my family. Henry, I'm a happy man. How's Mrs. Cramer?"

"Excited to see y'all. But otherwise not good."

"How 'bout Mr. Cramer?"

"You can see for yourself in a minute."

The three ladies piled in the back of the auto. Ben slipped into the front seat after he and Henry secured the luggage onto the running board.

Ben entered the comforting, familiar front room of the boarding house where the scent of cinnamon and furniture polish welcomed him back. His family stood beside him. A glance at the female trio revealed that each of them was scanning the room with their eyes.

He snickered when Katherine gasped.

"Electricity."

He whispered in her ear, "Yes, Butterfly, and indoor plumbing."

Lena dismissed propriety. "I could live here."

Henry laughed.

Katherine giggled. "It's lovely." Ben felt her squeeze his arm.

"You'll meet most of the residents at lunch," Henry explained.

"Mr. Henry, Papa said he lived here two times. How many times did you live here?"

"Well, first of all, why don't you just call me Henry. And, I've only lived here one time."

"Momma, can I call him 'Henry'?"

Katherine turned toward Ben and shrugged her shoulders. Ben nodded a yes.

"Yes, you can."

Clara continued her conversation.

"Henry, do you know that Sammy, my brother, lived here too?"

"I sure do."

"Did you know him?"

"No, but I wish I did."

"Where was Sammy's room, Papa?"

"Well, we shared a room on this floor." Ben pointed down the hallway. "That door right there."

As he spoke, Mr. Cramer emerged from his own rooms, directly across from where Ben pointed.

"Well, who do we have here?" The large, jovial man winked at Ben.

Henry had not misled. Mr. Cramer's fingers were swollen, knotty, and curled. Ben hoped his daughter didn't point them out.

"Brought my family to meet you." Ben stepped up and patted the man earnestly on the back. "Mr. Cramer, meet Katherine, Lena, and Clara."

"Mighty fine family. Mighty fine. And how are you, little miss?" He had directed his eyes to Clara.

"I'm pretty good. Kinda tired from the train."

Henry was the first to laugh, but Ben and the others joined him.

"Would a cookie make you feel better?"

"Sure would. Momma, can I have one?"

"As soon as we settle."

"Henry," Ben motioned, "lead the way." His friend grabbed a suitcase and headed toward the hallway.

"Miss Lena and Clara, if you don't mind, you'll be staying here in my space." Ben noticed the blush again. He observed Henry bend down to address Clara. "It's your Papa and Sammy's old room."

"We don't want to put you out." Lena sounded sincere, yet Ben noticed a similar blush on her cheeks.

"Oh, I'll be staying in there with the Cramers. We got it all worked out." He pointed across the narrow hall.

"That's right, Miss. We got it all worked out." Mr. Cramer's voice carried from behind Ben.

"Is this your suitcase, Miss Lena?" Henry pointed to the bag he was holding.

"Yes, thank you, Henry."

Ben elbowed Katherine. She smiled. The repeated blushing must not have escaped her either. He watched Henry set the suitcase inside the door.

"Ben, you and Miss Katherine will be upstairs, in Arlen's old room. Follow me."

"Henry," Mr. Cramer spoke out, "I'll wait for you here. Best hurry. Mrs. Cramer might pull herself out of bed if I don't get you all in to meet her soon." The older man's laughter filled the downstairs.

"He's a dear man, isn't he, Ben," Katherine whispered with admiration in her voice as they headed to the stairs. Both Clara and Lena were close on their heels.

"One of the best men I know." Ben pushed a piece of loose hair from Katherine's cheek. "By the way, nice butterfly clip in your hair. I ordered it sitting in that very room downstairs." He was rewarded with a blush and a smile.

Once the couple's suitcase was deposited upstairs, the group made their way into the Cramers two rooms, and Mr. Cramer led them to his wife's bedside. Tears filled Ben's eyes at the sight of the once strong woman, now weak and pale. The scent of cinnamon he'd always noticed on her was replaced with a medicinal odor. He bent and kissed her cheek.

"Mrs. Cramer. I couldn't stay away any longer. I had to come see you. Brought my family."

"Ben Williams, you bend back down here and let me give you a hearty hug." He did. Then she did.

Ben took Katherine by the hand.

"Mrs. Cramer, meet my wife, Katherine."

"You're lovely, dear."

"Thank you. I'm so happy to finally meet you."

"And, this is my sister-in-law, Lena." He motioned with his hand.

"Beautiful green eyes. Heard you're a right good cook."

"Thank you. Your home is lovely."

Ben turned to find Clara standing against Henry in the doorway and rubbing a piece of hair between her fingers. Was his lively Clara suddenly struck with shyness?

"Clara, come meet Mrs. Cramer." His daughter obliged but grabbed his hand as she stood next to him at the bed.

"Mrs. Cramer, meet our daughter, Clara."

He noticed tears roll down the dear woman's cheeks.

"Why Ben, she's lovely. Got her Momma's pretty hair and slender build, but the rest of her looks just like you. Hello, Clara. I reckon it's strange seeing me in the bed."

"Are you sick?"

"A little bit. My doctor says I gotta rest."

"I was real sick one time, but I got better."

"I hope to get better too. My, my, my, sweet girl, you remind me of Sammy."

Ben thought his heart would beat out of his chest with pride. Clara's eyes widened, and her toothy grin made an appearance.

"I do? Papa, did you hear that?"

"I sure did!"

"Well," Henry cleared his throat, "I best get in the kitchen and work on lunch."

"I can help if you'd like."

"I need all the help I can get, Miss Lena. This is my second day to attempt cooking. The first day was a burnt mess. And I considered myself a good cook, imagine that."

Ben winked at Henry as the couple left the room.

"Well, little miss, how about we go to the kitchen too and get that cookie?"

Ben smiled at Mr. Cramer.

"Bye, Mrs. Cramer. I might draw you some flowers or maybe a butterfly."

"I'd like that. Bye, now."

His daughter skipped over to Mr. Cramer without hesitation. Ben knew instantly that she'd noticed his hands because he saw her eyes bulge.

"Do your hands hurt, Mr. Cramer?"

"Sure do."

Ben followed them out the doorway and stood nearby as they walked to the kitchen conversing.

"My Papa has a hurt arm. But it doesn't hurt."

His daughter giggled at her word blunder. Mr. Cramer laughed as though he were Santa.

"Sammy had hurt legs."

"Yep. I used to carry him."

"You sure are nice."

When they reached the kitchen, Ben immediately returned to find his wife seated in a chair by the bed. She was holding Mrs. Cramer's hand. Ben stayed put, unnoticed, in the doorway.

"You took care of Sammy after his Momma died." Ben observed Katherine pet the blemished hand of the only other woman whom she knew to be like a mother to Sammy.

"I did. Loved that boy like he was my own."

"Me too."

"He was happy as a lark when he left here knowing full well he was getting him a real Momma. That boy liked you."

"I miss him."

Ben slid a hand into this pant pocket and rubbed the rabbit's foot. He smiled. It seemed his wife felt safely vulnerable with Mrs. Cramer.

"I know you do, dear."

"It was my fault."

"No. It was an accident. Now you let go of faulting yourself. Listen to me. Those kind of thoughts are useless."

Ben grimaced at Katherine's words. How deep were the roots of her guilt?

He watched Katherine take a long breath and let it out. "You're right, Mrs. Cramer. I sent my guilt a running, but sometimes it returns, begging for a place to stay. I reckon I'll be slamming the door in guilt's face for a long time—with God's help."

"Guilt's an ornery thing."

"Yessum. Well, I thank you in person for the fine journal you gave me for our wedding. I treasure it to this day. The notes about Sammy, the recipes, well, all of it, was mighty thoughtful."

"You're welcome. Now then, tell me about your Clara."

Ben chose that moment to slip away. He didn't want to disrupt the scene before him. To speak so openly with Mrs. Cramer, Katherine must have thought he'd remained with the others. Their conversation stirred his soul, proving that kinship is not bound by longevity or brevity. They both are powerless over what hearts hold common.

Chapter 33

MID-SUMMER 1925 | COMMERCE, TEXAS

The scene in the Cramer kitchen rivaled the one Ben had just admired in the Cramer rooms. Once again he stood in the doorway observing and welcoming the joy he felt. Henry and Clara were standing side by side at the kitchen counter, each cutting vegetables. He noticed a pot of potatoes boiling on the stove. Henry laughed when Lena mocked his lopsided chunk of tomato then proceeded to demonstrate how to properly quarter the slippery item. Ben couldn't recall seeing Lena this lively from the time he'd returned. He pondered the two young adults before him, letting his mind delve into the "what if's" where he rarely allowed himself to go. If Henry did have a dark place hiding inside him, would it cling to Lena's and or could they become each other's light? *God, help them, please.*

Clara sat next to Mr. Cramer at the table. A checkerboard lay before them, and next to it, a pack of Wrigley's Double Mint Gum—Mr. Cramer's trademark. Clara had no doubt noticed it sticking from the front pocket of his overall bib. Ben smiled. Mr. Cramer was being kind and patiently allowing her to explain how to play checkers, even as she vigorously chewed her gum.

Clara paused in her explanation, sniffed, wrinkled her nose, and declared, "Something smells like potatoes."

Ben dissolved into laughter while walking through the doorway.

"Lands sake, Henry. You trying to kill those tomatoes with a knife?"

Ben heard Clara's chair squeak across the linoleum floor. "Let me see!" She stood on her tiptoes beside Henry. "Henry, it's easy. Just cut like Aunt Lena does, right Papa?"

Ben patted Henry on the shoulder. "Like Lena does."

Ben didn't get the humorous retort he expected. Instead, he watched Henry turn to Lena and offer up a childish grin before speaking. "Right. Like Lena does." His sister-in-law rewarded Henry with an eye roll.

Clara returned to the table. Ben opened his mouth to excuse himself and meander outside the house when Katherine walked into the room. The emotion hit him like a speeding train. With Katherine beside him in the room, somehow images of his first wife, Addie, filled his mind. As the cook, she'd flit about the kitchen and allow no one underfoot. The result was always a delicious meal that nearly rivaled Lena's.

"How can I help, Lena?"

"Me and Henry can handle the food, if you'd like to set the big table in the next room."

Ben saw Katherine blush slightly, as though she might be embarrassed, but when Lena turned around and wiggled her eyebrows, Katherine bit her lower lip then smiled. Like him, she must have understood an unspoken message. Lena wanted this time with Henry.

"Well, in that case," Ben interjected, "why don't you join me for a walk, Katherine? Then you can come set the table."

"Papa, I'll just keep teaching Mr. Cramer checkers." The man cackled.

"You do that."

Holding his wife's hand, Ben walked around the boarding house, noting his observations to Katherine. A rotted piece of wood on the back steps and a hole in the screen door on the side testified to Mr. Cramer's inability to make repairs without assistance.

"Mr. Cramer always took pride in his work. I betcha' it's hard on him to let things go. Then to be worried about his wife too." Ben let out a deep sigh.

"Good thing Henry will be here."

"Yep." He turned and winked at Katherine. "Reckon he just found himself a cook?"

"If you mean Lena, why there's no way she'd come here to work." Katherine's brows were crinkled.

"Oh, I can think of one way she might agree to move here."

"Ben Williams!"

"I know you've seen the looks between them, even in this short time we've been here."

"I have. She's never talked about a boy or young man before except in her old fairy tales or the stories she shares with Clara. I reckon she seems smitten. But moving away to marry someone? I don't see it."

"Maybe…my Butterfly, you just don't want to see it. Lena is more adventurous than you." He leaned over and kissed her cheek to soften his truth.

"I was adventurous when I married you."

This time he kissed her lips.

"Ben, uhm, it doesn't seem that Henry's like his mother."

"No, I've never seen him in a dark place, as he calls it. I reckon he's fine."

"Like Lena is fine? If she wanted to, she could get overcome with shame or feel unlovable."

"Yes, I reckon, like Lena. Would you worry if they fell in love?"

"No. I want Lena to have what I have, without throwing any of it away."

He felt the intensity of her words and her emotions.

Hand in hand, with few words, they walked the grounds, stopping only to pluck wild bluebells "for the table" Katherine had noted. The comfortable silence between them came to an end when he felt her pull at his arm just as they passed the vegetable garden.

"Ben, where is Addie buried?"

She tugged at her ear. He swallowed.

"About two blocks away, behind the Baptist church."

"Can I see her grave?"

A pregnant pause settled in him.

"I shouldn't have asked. I'm sorry, Ben."

He turned to her and could feel the intensity of his own look.

"Don't be sorry. I haven't been there in a long time. Since before I met you."

"Not when you came back to Commerce?"

"Neither time." He released his grip on her hand then ran his fingers over his jaws. "Being separated from you and Clara felt like all the pain I could bear. But, now… now I'd like to show you."

Standing beside the wife he loved, Ben found himself staring at the grave of the wife he'd once loved.

"Katherine, does seeing this grave bother you?"

He clasped his arm around her shoulder and squeezed. His wife's look was filled with peace, and it was beautiful to behold."

"No, it makes her a real person to me. It makes me understand even more how blessed I am to be loved by you. I'm reminded that God arranged for us to meet and fall in love."

He laid his head against her shoulder. “I wish I hadn’t messed with his plan.”

“We’re putting that behind us.”

Ben raised his head, then pulled her into the fold of the arm resting against her back. He couldn’t resist kissing his wife.

“Thank you for sharing more of yourself with me, Ben.”

Katherine’s whisper filled one tiny place in his soul he hadn’t realized was empty. Here in Commerce, Katherine had embraced who he was before he loved her. Perhaps one day, he would ask her to travel to Texarkana or St. Louis and embrace who he was while he loved her without ceasing.

After a hearty lunch, Henry suggested that Ben and his family join him for a ride and a walk down Main Street in Commerce. Mrs. Cramer needed to sleep. Mr. Cramer bowed out, saying he had accounts to look over.

“We’ll only be gone about an hour. Then, Ben and I will help you get some of your handyman chores done,” Henry explained.

“Now, Ben’s a guest, he don’t need to work while he’s a visitin’,” Mr. Cramer chided.

“That’s right, Henry, I’m a guest ‘round here now. I reckon you’ll be serving me some lemonade when we return before you tackle that chore list.” Ben patted his friend on the back in a heavy, exaggerated manner, but his motion stopped when he noticed Henry’s face turn red. *I’ve embarrassed him...in front of Lena.*

“Truth is, Mr. Cramer, I was hoping I could work with you two this afternoon—like we used to do.”

Ben felt Lena elbow his arm.

“Well, gentleman, times wastin’ and I got window shops to look at and stuff to hanker for but never buy.”

He turned and took Katherine by one hand and Clara by another. Henry opened the screen door, and Ben led his family out, with Lena behind them. When he heard the door close, Ben glanced back and found that Henry had already matched his stride to his sister-in-law’s step. He was also certain that a hint of after shave wafted through the air around them.

The evening came and with the meal behind them, the sisters made their way to Mrs. Cramer's bedside. Pride swept through Ben as he watched his wife and sister-in-law tap on Mrs. Cramer's door, juggling warm cinnamon-sugar cookies and magazines. "Us ladies need to gossip with Mrs. Cramer," Lena had informed both Ben and Henry. His sister-in-law's blush and glance at Henry when she spoke didn't escape Ben's notice. Her humor made him grin. He took pleasure in the camaraderie Katherine had eased into with the lady of the house. Of course, he'd expected no less, from Lena who seemed to never meet a stranger. Some of the other residents settled in the front room after Mr. Cramer turned on a record. Henry was seated in his favorite brown chair by the window looking at something in his hands. Clara was propped against the couch, on the floor, surrounded by colored pencils and some paper.

"Clara, whatcha' drawing?"

"Papa, I'm making Henry a picture like I promised. And, I'm gonna draw Mrs. Cramer one too."

"That's nice."

"And, I'm gonna ask Aunt Lena to draw me a butterfly."

It was then that Ben noticed the object of Henry's attention was Clara's butterfly book.

"Ok."

"It's a mighty nice book, Clara." Henry stood and attempted to hand Clara the book.

"Mr. Cramer gets to look next."

"Yessum."

Ben watched Henry hand the book to their friend, then turn to him.

"Let's head out to the porch. It's not too warm outside."

Ben thought it was very warm and bugs were a nuisance, but he conceded, and led the way to the front porch steps.

"You're a mighty fine host, Henry."

"Thanks. I got a lot to learn, but I think I'm gonna like overseeing this house. Wouldn't Mrs. Martin in St. Louis be surprised."

"You were very generous today. I was busy paying for colas and you were busy winning female hearts with your purchases."

Henry patted his own shoulder causing Ben to roll his eyes before he continued.

"Katherine's so practical, that she refuses to buy a magazine. I know my mouth hung open when she walked up to me with two in her hand. And that toy butterfly you bought Clara is already a treasure."

Henry chuckled. "I couldn't resist when she said, 'That red butterfly sure is pretty, but I know I cain't have it.' I snatched that toy up and told her, 'I've never seen such a pretty red butterfly, and I think you're the best person in Commerce to have it, seein' you got a butterfly book and all.'"

Ben shook his head side to side, grinning. "I reckon you saw the red butterfly in her book. The Papa butterfly."

"Yep. Kind of stirred my insides, seeing how she showed her love for her Papa."

"Speaking of love, Lena…"

"Lena what?" Henry's voice resembled that of a boy in puberty.

"Lena loves butterscotch. I'll never hear the end of it 'how kind Henry is, how nice of Henry to notice what I like…"

"Well, I don't have a problem with her saying that."

"I reckon you don't."

"I need to ask you something."

"Okay."

"You know me right well.—- all my fine qualities." A smile spread across Henry's face. "And my struggles. I was wonderin' if you or Mrs. Katherine, aren't too worried about the darkness coming over me, so to speak, if you'd allow me to write Lena and court her from a distance."

"You really like her?"

"She's mighty fine. Yea, I do. What I know so far, and I suspect all I might come to know if you and then her will allow me to."

"She's got her own darkness, so to speak."

"I reckon any woman would whose gone through what she has could struggle with feeling bad. But, she's got her faith too. Seems mighty strong."

"I think it is. I think she is too."

"So, what about it, Ben, can I write Lena?"

Ben's mind instantly flashed back to 1918 when he'd asked a similar question.

"Katherine, might I write to you? A man gets lonely on the rails and weary of talking with crude and brute males, and well, I'm on a new crew and don't know anyone and..."

"Yes."

He'd smiled and touched her arm.

"Should I beg your post number from your brother?"

She'd tugged at her ear. It had delighted him.

"Eighteen." She'd whispered, "Same as my age."

"Ben?"

He roused from his reminiscing.

"I suspect she'd like that very much. And I reckon Katherine thinks the same thing. So, yep, Henry, if you want my blessing, you got it."

He looked his friend directly in the eyes. Henry blew out a breath then let out a hoot under his breath. Ben laughed. He stood and pulled the younger man to his feet for a hearty handshake. Henry Jones may become his actual brother after all.

"You gonna soak those letters in after shave?"

Henry reared back his head and guffawed.

On Sunday afternoon Ben bid the Cramers and other residents good-bye then loaded his family into Henry's car to head to the station. Lifting Clara from her mother's lap then assisting Katherine out of the vehicle, Ben noted that Henry had left the driver's seat to assist Lena.

"Clara, Katherine, let's say our goodbyes and get you two settled on the train. I'll get the suitcases to the baggage clerk." He reckoned Henry wanted a more private good-bye with Lena.

His sister-in-law stood beside the auto door as Henry turned to face Ben and his family and stepped toward them. Katherine and Clara both hugged the young man.

"Thank you, Henry for having us here and for being a good friend to Ben," Katherine smiled, "and me."

"Thank you for coming—friend."

"Bye, Henry. I hope you like your new picture."

"I like it a lot, Clara. Thank you."

Ben reached to shake Henry's hand, and the two of them locked eyes. A wide grin slowly made its way across Henry's face, and his head nodded backward toward Lena.

"Come see us in Layton. Soon."

"I reckon I will. Soon."

The two men shook hands. Ben shooed his family toward the train then headed toward the baggage clerk. Returning to the passenger car, he found his seat next to Katherine who leaned on his arm. Her lavender scent teased him. She nudged his side and pointed toward Lena who was clasping an envelope in her hand. Clara was less discreet.

"Papa, Henry wrote Lena a letter. He's really nice."

"Nice indeed, Clara." He winked at Lena. Contentment rode the train home with them.

Chapter 34

September 1925 | Layton, Texas

"I can't wait to give this letter to Lena." Katherine waved an envelope in the air as she hurried through the front yard. Ben had picked her up after her work ended at the Justice Store. He was still sitting in the auto. She relished the wink that he gave her, knowing that he was just as happy about the correspondence as she was.

"Hurry on. I'll check on Gitter before I come in."

Katherine smiled and strode across the yard, crunching early autumn leaves beneath her feet. It was a refreshing Saturday afternoon. She took the steps one at a time, pulled on the screen, then pushed open the door. She made an immediate right inside the house and stood in Lena's doorway. Her sister was hemming the bottom of the new pale green dress she had sewn.

"I've lost count of the letters addressed to Lena McGinn and postmarked Commerce."

Katherine waved the envelope in the air, then sniffed it.

"Smells good. I wonder who it could be from."

Lena had dropped her sewing and sprung from the chair she'd been occupying. Her fingertips were clasped around the top of the envelope.

"Another letter! This makes the fourteenth one since we left Commerce."

She watched her sister sniff the envelope, clasp it to her chest, then fall backward onto the bed.

"Henry Jones, is the most romantic man in the world."

Katherine laughed.

"Is he your Prince Charming?"

"Yes." The answer arrived at Katherine's ears in a whisper.

"I love seeing you so happy, Lena."

"I am happy without any doubt."

"So, if Henry grows antsy with just writing letters and decides he, you know, wants a wife, would you…"

"Yes! I'd say yes. No doubt about it. Do you know something I don't?" Lena wiggled her eyebrows so high they were lost in her hairline

"Oh, goodness no. But if I did, I wouldn't tell you."

Katherine took on a serious tone.

"You're not worried?"

"About a man's touch? No, I don't think I am. I've searched my soul. When the time comes, I'm certain I'll feel no different than any jittery bride."

"Then, as a former jittery bride myself, I think you'll be fine." Katherine winked.

Lena covered her face with her hands and the letter.

"Katherine, you're standing in the doorway. Anybody could hear you speaking about such things."

Lena's hands dropped to her lap and spread a smile.

"Now scoot on, I got a letter to read."

Lena had put a vegetable soup together earlier in the day and let it simmer. Just as the sun set, Katherine called the family to table. The smell of cornbread permeated the kitchen from the plate piled high with warm servings. Glasses of sweet tea sat on the table next to bowls steaming with soup. Ben entered carrying Clara on his shoulders.

"Smells good." He kneeled and placed his daughter on the floor. "Lena is still in her room." Katherine tingled when the right side of his lip hitched upward.

"Let's start without her. Clara, hop on up to the table."

"Yessum. Momma, why isn't Aunt Lena coming?"

"I reckon she's writing a letter."

Clara put both her hands over her heart and wiggled her head back and forth. "Oh, Henry. I miss you so, so much. You're really nice. I want to marry you. Oh, and please send me some butterscotch."

A trio of laughter filled the kitchen.

"I reckon you better not say that to your Aunt Lena."

"Yessir." Clara smiled. "But I'm gonna be thinking it in my head all during supper."

Katherine reached over and tugged a piece of Clara's hair. "You silly girl."

When the Williams family had gotten a good ten minutes into the meal, Lena bounded into the kitchen.

"Sorry I made you wait."

Katherine rolled her eyes at Ben, whose reply was the same action.

"You didn't. We're already eating. See?" Clara pointed to her half-empty bowl of soup.

Katherine watched Lena's face turn beet red.

"Oh. Well good."

"Soooo, how's Henry?" Clara's words were stretched the length of a country mile.

"Henry's busy, but good."

Ben cleared his throat.

"Speaking of Henry. I have some news."

Three spoons hit the table at once. Katherine raised her eyebrows and stared at Ben. She noted that Lena and Clara had done the same.

Ben chuckled.

"What news?"

"Well, Lena, and my other two dear ladies, seems Henry has invited us back, and we're heading out Friday afternoon for Commerce."

Lena hooted. Clara stood and jumped up and down. Katherine reached over the table and took her husband's hand.

"Ben Williams, you are full of surprises."

"You up for another adventure, Butterfly?"

"Yes.

"Are you well enough to travel?" He winked at her as he mouthed the words.

She nodded yes. Their good news remained a secret between them for now, but certainly not much longer.

It was a sheer pleasure for Katherine as she watched Lena leave them behind to be the first one off the train. Her sister had spotted Henry the moment their rail car pulled into the depot. The truth is, Katherine preferred to watch their reunion from the window and drink in the sight of it. She felt Ben clasp her hand as he too glanced out the window. A broad smile stretched across his face. The young couple clasped hands immediately, and

Henry leaned down and kissed Lena's cheek in proper form that must have been a challenge to his passion. Katherine squeezed Ben's hand.

"Momma, can we get off now?"

Ben stood and pulled Katherine from her seat.

"Yes, let's go ladies."

His hand felt warm against her back as he guided her down the stairs. Clara had stepped off first.

"Henry!" Katherine watched as Clara ran and stood in front of the young man and clasped Lena's hand. He bent to meet her at eye level.

"Clara, I am so happy to see you again."

"Me too. Aunt Lena is the most happy prob'ly."

"A ha!"

Katherine noticed Henry wink at Lena as she and Ben approached.

"Mrs. Katherine, welcome back. I can't say how glad I am to have y'all here again. All of you." He smiled at her.

"I am happy to be back."

"Good to see you." Ben's grasp on Katherine's fingers was released as he shook Henry's hand.

"You too. Let's get the luggage and head on out."

Within moments the family once again piled into Henry's auto—this time Lena occupied the front seat. Katherine bit her lip and enjoyed the sight in front of her, but not near as much as she enjoyed the snug fit of her husband beside her.

Henry turned off the auto when they reached the boarding house. Katherine noticed that Ben only grabbed Lena and Clara's shared suitcase as the party headed to the front door. She suspected he was distracted by his excitement. Mr. Cramer greeted them, and the pain on his face as he moved about made Katherine's heart ache. Like before, they all said their hellos to Mrs. Cramer who was still bedridden. Out of the corner of her eye, Katherine saw Henry hand a key to Ben. Her husband eased up next to her at the bedside and took her hand.

"Well, Mrs. Cramer, it's time." Katherine saw him wink just as the ailing woman clapped her hands together and smiled. "Don't you worry about a thing around here. Have a good time."

Henry cleared his throat. "It just so happens that the county fair came into town yesterday. Miss Lena, Miss Clara, would you like to attend with me tomorrow?"

Even as she absorbed the unexpected news, Katherine laughed as Clara jumped up and down repeating "yes" many times over. Lena's reaction was just as humorous. She'd been standing next to Henry but turned and grabbed both his arms upon hearing the news. "Yes!" As quickly as she grabbed him, she let him go. Katherine noticed the young man's wide smile.

Before she could speak, Ben leaned over and whispered in her ear. "I have other plans for us, Butterfly."

To the group he announced, "Henry, I hope you don't mind, but we'll join you after lunch time. Katherine and I have some plans of our own."

"Of course." Henry winked.

"Papa, please come to the fair with me."

Led by his fingers laced with hers, Katherine moved toward Clara with Ben.

"Clara, I promise you that your Momma and I will come to the fair after lunch. But until then, I have a surprise for her. Can you stay here and let Aunt Lena, Henry, and the Cramers take care of you and not feel worried? It will be your own special adventure until we see you tomorrow."

A warmth surged through Katherine at his words. Clara's facial expression displayed fear, confusion, then understanding, and finally peace.

"Yessir. I can stay here just fine. Does Aunt Lena know the surprise?"

"Nope. Because it's a surprise." Clara laughed when Ben tweaked her nose.

With that, he instructed Katherine to kiss Clara goodbye, and he did the same. With a thank you to the fine people surrounding them and a shrug that said she didn't know what was happening, Katherine followed her husband out the door and to the auto where he got her situated.

"My russet Butterfly, time for our own little adventure."

The lobby of the Henderson Hotel in Commerce took Katherine's breath away as she stood next to Ben at the mahogany counter while registering. The surprise of an attendant taking the auto to park it for Ben had just settled down when she entered the welcoming area. It was twice the size of the lobby hotel in Collin where she and Lena had stayed with the Forders. Lush ferns in ceramic pots stood on tall, white pedestals strikingly situated on the blue and green tiled floors. Light blue chairs with gold-colored trim were arranged in seating areas around the lobby that show pieced a curved staircase adorned with brass handrails. A bellman spoke to Ben, then took their suitcase and headed to the stairs.

"Thank you, Mr. Williams. Your package arrived and is in your room waiting for you as will be your luggage. If you need anything, please let us know." *Package?*

Ben took her hand and she felt his warm lips against it. "This way, Butterfly." Speechless, she let him lead her up the stairs to the fourth level and first room on the right where he inserted the key into the latch, grasped the knob, and pushed the door open. An audible gasp escaped her lips, and she felt her cheeks heat up. Ben chuckled and motioned her inside.

"I've never seen anything like this."

Katherine twirled to view the entire room. The largest bed she'd ever seen was covered in a dark green velvet spread. Pillows inside silk white cases were propped against an ornate mahogany headboard. She squinted and realized that birds and flowers were carved into the wood. A fire was burning in the white marble—*marble?*—fireplace. Two light green velvet chairs and a small table sat in front of the fireplace. The scent of evergreen filled the air. Ben took her head and gently turned it to the left.

"Look there, Katherine."

Her eyes focused on a large room boasting white, shiny tile, a marble sink, a toilet with brass flush chain, and… a ceramic tub with gold fixtures. Why two people could sit in the tub at the same time. Once again her cheeks heated.

"Ben."

"I know, Butterfly. I've heard of places like this, but I've never been in one." She felt him pull her to the fireplace area, where she noticed a box wrapped in shiny pink paper adorned with a white ribbon.

"For you." His grin was lopsided. "Go head, open it." He handed the box to her.

Katherine untied the bow, soaking in the moment as the satin slid through her fingers. She laid it in the chair, then began to tear at the paper.

"I want to keep the paper. It's so pretty."

Ben chuckled.

She pulled the paper away and saw the name Fields and Taylor printed on the box. The words evoked a long sigh. Never in her days did she think she would hold a box from the finest store, so she'd heard, in Dallas. She turned to look at Ben.

My goodness, the man looked handsome with his rascal's grin. He kissed her cheek. "Open the lid."

She did. A memory rushed in. Ben had asked her once if there was anything she wanted. No one had asked her that question before, and his question had made her feel cherished. Now, here she stood holding a box that contained some of the most beautiful items she'd ever beheld. She set the box in the chair. One by one she lifted the treasures from the box. She pulled out a light cream silk dress adorned with pearl buttons, a pair of white heeled shoes, a white satin hat with clear rhinestones and a small feather, white stockings, and a bead-covered clutch purse.

"Ben, these are beautiful."

"I can't wait to see you in them for dinner tonight at Nicholson's Steak House."

"Ben, I don't know what to say. The clothes, the steakhouse …" A broad smile spread across her face. She reverently laid the items in the chair then tightened her arms around his neck and kissed him.

"How did you do this?"

"I had Abigail Forder order the clothes for you, so they should fit. Women know about that kind of stuff. She had the package delivered here. Mason and Henry helped me with the rest."

"I will feel like a princess."

"Lift the tissue at the bottom of the box."

She looked at him and raised her eyebrows before lifting the tissue paper. She bit her lip at the sight.

"Do you like it? I know I do." That rascal grin made another appearance.

Katherine lifted the lacy night gown from the box and held it before her.

"It's beautiful."

Heedless of the gown he was wrinkling, her husband pulled her to him and kissed her deeply. When he pulled away, he took the gown into his hands.

"Now, I order you to take a bath and then come out in your new clothes. I'll be waiting patiently. Dinner is at six this evening."

With that, she watched him lay the lacy gown on the bed, then took up her new gifts and turned toward the bathroom. Why, from her earlier view, she hadn't noticed the bottle of bubble bath sitting on the tub. She bent down to read the label. *Lavender.*

When Katherine did emerge from the bathroom, she stared at Ben who was dressed in a new blue suit and sitting in one of the velvet chairs. He'd turned the chair to see her entrance.

"You are the most beautiful woman I've ever laid eyes on, Katherine. Come. Sit next to me."

Careful to smooth her dress before she sat, Katherine took her seat and set the beaded bag on the small table. Ben moved to the floor and bent down before her on his knees and clasped her hands. His scent wafted toward her. Bayberry? Katherine could feel her heart pounding in her chest.

"Katherine, I broke two of the vows I made to you before God on our wedding day. My lips were unfaithful, and I did not cherish you as I should have by not returning home. I chose to be a coward."

Tears rolled down her cheeks. Ben reached into his pants pocket and pulled out a black velvet bag and rested it beside him on the floor.

"I Ben, take you, Katherine, again, to be my lawfully wedded wife. To have and to hold from this day forward. For better, for worse, for richer, for poorer, in sickness or in health, to love and to cherish until death do us part. I here to pledge you my faithfulness."

Without a pause, he took the velvet bag and handed it to her. She rubbed her finger over the fabric, then pulled it open to peer at the treasure. A ring with two small emeralds and six pearl chips graced the inside of the bag. Ben pulled the gold ring from the bag and slid it on her right ring finger.

"With this ring, I wed thee again. With my body, I thee worship, and with all my worldly goods, I thee endow."

He stood and pulled her to him. Katherine tingled and let out a soft moan as Ben kissed his bride.

Lena was mistaken. Ben Williams was the most romantic man in the world.

The mid October air blew Ben's hair as he made his way into the front yard and parked his auto. He felt the tension of a harried work day in his back and welcomed the thought of the weekend events. Henry was coming to Layton and was due within the hour.

Just as Ben closed the auto door, movement near the crepe myrtles caught his eye.

"Lands sake! The butterflies!"

Ben ran into the house. The smell of chicken and dumplings made his stomach growl instantly, but he didn't pause to appreciate the delicious aroma. Instead, he bounded through Clara's room and stood in the kitchen doorway.

"Clara!" His daughter looked up from the table where she was stirring cornbread batter.

"Come outside! The butterflies are dancing!"

Happy yelps sounded from all three females in the kitchen as Clara leapt into Ben's arms.

"Here, ride on my shoulders."

With his daughter situated, Ben ducked his way through the doorway and onto the front porch. Monarch butterflies migrating south filled the air around them. Ben dashed around the yard as Clara bounced on his shoulders, her laughter mingling with the cool breeze. Pirate's bark filled the air and the dog ran in circles. A quick glance showed him that his daughter's arms were extended in the air with her fingers spread wide.

"Aunt Lena, you're getting married when the butterflies dance."

"Yes, I am, Clara! Isn't it wonderful!"

Ben soaked in the sight as his russet-haired daughter walked before him strewing wildflowers down the aisle. Her green dress accented her russet curls. At the front of the church Wendell Carlson stood next to a beaming Henry, who was looking unusually dapper in his tweed suit. Earlier, Ben had helped the groom, whose hands shook, tie his tie and straighten his collar. Henry assured him it was eagerness that had him on edge.

Ben's russet Butterfly stood on the other side of the pastor. Like her daughter, the green in Katherine's dress made her face radiant. One hand held a bouquet of flowers while the other rested on the tiny bump of her belly. In five months, God willing, he would become a father for the third time. Clara had squealed when the news was shared with the family. Lena had winked and let on that she was surprised. The young woman knew her sister's demeanor well enough to anticipate the happy announcement.

The Justices and Forders, along with numerous other friends, filled the church pews. Seated on the front row across from Henry was Mr. Cramer. He'd ridden in with the groom. Ben would see him to the train station tomorrow. He knew the man was in physical pain, but Mrs. Cramer wouldn't hear of his missing the event and expected full details upon his return.

Lena would get another adventure. She and Henry would travel by train to Dallas, then Texarkana, Pine Bluff, then on to St. Louis where they would spend a night and day. Their journey would end in Stillwater, Oklahoma where Lena would meet Henry's family. None of them had traveled for the wedding. At the beginning of the next week, the couple would return to Layton, gather Lena's belongings, then head to their home at the boarding house in Commerce.

Ben would sure miss her cooking.

Amy Carlson touched the piano keys, and a sweet melody filled the church. Ben looked at his wife and smiled, then turned to Lena who was adorned in the same wedding dress his Katherine had worn. Her hand rested on the inside of his arm. He reckoned he needn't worry about the bride and groom's dark places; the two of them shone brightly together. After all, isn't darkness the absence of light?

"Time to get married, my dear, adorable Lena. Are you ready?"

"I am."

Epilogue

1927 | Two Years Later

"Clara, can you hold your little brother? I need to tend to your Momma."

Seven-year-old Clara sat on her bed and extended her arms toward her father. "Ca'mere, Jacob. Play with big sister. I've got a train."

The twenty-one-month old leaned forward from Ben's grasp and chortled as his sister wiggled the toy train car in front of him. Ben released the chubby-legged boy to his sister then headed toward his bedroom, rubbing his leg. Toting a toddler made the wounded appendage ache, but he didn't mind. Adjusting her apron while she emerged from the small bathroom installed off the kitchen, Katherine bumped into Ben.

"Sick again?" He moved loose hair from her cheek. Katherine was pale.

"Yes. I was never this sick with Clara or Jacob or for this long in the pregnancy."

"Need to rest?"

"No, I need to get done what I can while I'm feeling better. Where's Jacob?"

"Clara has him."

He put his hand around his wife's waist and guided her to the small storage room.

"Have you cleared out Joe's trunk yet—seein' it's been a year since he passed away from the pneumonia."

Ben and Wendell had visited Joe more than once at the prison, concerned about his soul. Joe had remained uninterested in both redemption and restoration. The visitors surmised that Joe's shame had hardened and transformed into bitterness. He had admitted to hiding Ben's letter about the accident, saying he'd been surprised to find it in the mail the day he'd brought the girl named Rosa into the store. He'd smirked and declared he'd hidden it to spite Ben. Katherine and Ben were the only attendees at the graveside service Wendell had led.

"Yes. I cleaned out the trunk. Finally." His wife displayed red cheeks and a sheepish grin. "I kept a few sentimental tokens, offered his clothes to needy bin at the church and discarded the rest for you to burn."

Ben chuckled. Katherine put her hands on her hip.

"What's funny?"

"I'm curious what you set aside for me to burn."

Katherine rolled her eyes.

"Lena can use the trunk for her baby's things."

"We could have four youngin's in the house." Ben whistled.

"For a little while, at least until Henry finds them a place of their own."

"Yeah, I reckon Henry won't wait long to do that."

After two years of marriage, Lena and Henry were moving to Layton. With both the Cramers passed and their own baby due in two months, Henry had determined Layton should be where he raised his family. He'd applied with Mason Forder and gotten a job running the diner and the small motor lodge. Katherine chattered daily about having her sister nearby again. Clara, too, assured her Papa that having Aunt Lena and Uncle Henry close by was almost as good as getting another brother or sister. Ben had to admit that he too wanted them in Layton. They were due to arrive any moment.

Surprisingly during the two-year period, the road in Layton had been paved and dubbed the scenic route to Dallas, causing local business to grow and expand. Mason Forder had lobbied long and hard for the improvement, stating the area could thrive with increased exposure and thus, more businesses. Ben for one, agreed with Mason and envisioned a town similar to Commerce. Most other Layton residents, his wife included, preferred for Layton to remain rural and quiet.

Wendell Carlson had obtained a reputation beyond the Layton borders as a caring pastor and a dynamic preacher of the Bible. The minister could easily handle a growing congregation as additional residents came to Layton. With automobiles becoming more common, many of Wendell's congregates already traveled from nearby towns. Ben was grateful to see God working through his friend.

Myers Garage had been built about a half mile beyond the Justice Store. Now a young teenager, Wallace James had begun to work there on the weekends. Unfortunately, due to his older model auto, Ben frequented the garage more than he preferred, giving him opportunity to know and respect the young man who proved to be hardworking and respectful.

Gabriel had found a woman from Copeville who loved him and agreed to marry him. The boy stuffed inside a man's body had finally grown to fit its size. With the confidence of being a loved husband with a wife on the home front, Gabe managed to run a thriving repair business as well as functioning as the local amateur veterinarian.

Ben continued to manage both the saw mill and the cotton gin in Layton. Mason Forder was a generous boss.

Standing in the doorway of the storage room, Ben eyed the cradle in the right-hand corner. A box labeled baby quilts sat in front of it; a small hole was chewed in the corner. Pesky mouse. Ben would set a trap. Another glance brought his attention to the worn leather bag that contained his important documents. The contents paraded through his mind. Certificates for both his marriages and the birth of his three children. His paperwork from the railroad hospital stay, bundled letters from Reverend Lilley, Henry, and those not sent to Katherine, his ticket stub from Sportsman Park, a certificate for his baptism, and other documents life would call upon from time to time.

Life.

"Ben, did you hear me?" Katherine's voice hinted at humor.

"Sorry. My mind wandered."

"Where to?"

"Right here." He pointed to his own heart. "I know life moves on, offering up its good and bad, but God's been gracious to me. I'm a blessed man."

She kissed his cheek and laced her fingers with his.

"Yes, you are. Now, speaking of life moving on, this household has two babies on the way that'll need this cradle. We better get to moving it."

"Yes, my russet Butterfly." He winked, released her hand, then bent to lift the cradle.

Outside, the crepe myrtles blew in the breeze and a single butterfly rested atop a small boy's well-attended grave.

An auto's horn beeped from the yard. Clara's voiced carried through the house.

"Aunt Lena! Uncle Henry!"

Author's Notes

Once again I am grateful to share glimpses of truth from my family history and letters discovered in family heirlooms. Thank you for reading the second novel in the Letters to Layton series. I am honored. Readers have been such a tremendous source of encouragement.

My deepest appreciation goes to my husband. Thank you for patiently helping me carve out time to write. As this book was being created, we faced some difficult challenges while also celebrating new careers, a marriage, and the birth of our first grandchild. God remains faithful in all situations.

Thank you to my beta readers, Lynn, Paul, Michelle, Patty, and Julie. I also extend thanks to my editor and to Mavi. I am indebted to each of you for helping beautify the story. I value your input and appreciate your time. You are some special folks.

The characters of Reverend Wendell Carlson and Amy, Reverend Lilley, and Mason and Abigail Forder all have traits of two pastors and their wives that God placed in my life. I am deeply grateful for my childhood pastor, Dr. Jimmy Lilley and his wife Bonnie. I am also grateful for Dr. Johnny Hunt and his wife Janet. He's been my pastor since 1987. Both pastors have proven to be lifelong friends to my family in more ways than I can enumerate. Like Mason Forder, Johnny Hunt is generous in spirit and action, and he is also a good boss, whom I've had the privilege to work for since 1991. Pastors, your impact on my life is immeasurable here on earth. Thank you for faithfully preaching God's Word and living it out day by day.

It was difficult to place Lena in a battered situation, especially suspecting that was a glimpse of reality from family history. If you find yourself in a similar situation, seek help. I extend respect and gratitude to my friend, Mary Francis Bowley, who began a ministry for mistreated and trafficked women. Over the years, God has used this organization to rescue woman after woman physically, emotionally, and spiritually. I thank her for being obedient, determined, and faithful in this role. On a lighter note, I enjoy sharing a grandson with her.

I offer a high five to my young friend, Brody Becker. It was his four-year-old voice and mannerisms in my head as I brought Clara to life.

I thank the Portiers for the knowledge of antique automobiles they shared with me.

To my Lord and Savior Jesus Christ, thank you for forgiving me. To my Heavenly Father, I praise you for being merciful, gracious, long suffering, and abounding in goodness and truth. I am guided and sustained by your Word.

If you like pictures, check out my *When the Butterflies Dance* page on Pinterest at *kimwilliams0903*. I'd love to hear from you at *kimwilliamsbook@gmail.com*. You can follow *Kim Williams Author* on Facebook, *kimwilliamsbook.wordpress.com*, and my author page on Goodreads. I welcome reader reviews. Thank you for reading my story.

Kim

Made in the USA
Lexington, KY
07 October 2018